You Belong With Me

Also by Mhairi McFarlane

You Belong With Me

A NOVEL

Mhairi McFarlane

AVON

An Imprint of HarperCollinsPublishers

HarperCollins books may be purchased for educational, business, or sales promotional use. For information, please email the Special Markets Department at SPsales@harpercollins.com.

Originally published as *You Belong with Me* in Great Britain in 2024 by HarperCollins Publishers.

FIRST U.S. EDITION

Interior text design by Diahann Sturge-Campbell

Library of Congress Cataloging-in-Publication Data has been applied for.

ISBN 978-0-06-341725-0

24 25 26 27 28 LBC 5 4 3 2 1

To Kay Miles

Prologue

"It's someone for you."

Edie frowned after Meg spoke. She took off the oven glove and placed it next to the pigs in blankets, crossing the room and weaving past her grinning, flushed sibling. Meg reflexively removed her paper hat as if a hearse rather than her elder sister was passing.

Edie knew exactly who was at the door, and yet she still didn't know, both at the same time. Perfect certainty and the precariousness of hope.

The Christmas Day cook's cava had her bumping along merrily as it was; now she face-planted down a log flume of it.

The caller at the end of the hall came into focus, his face partially obscured by a large, brown-paper-wrapped bunch of white roses. Fireworks went off inside Edie.

"Are roses kind of 'cheating husband' cheesy? I don't speak fluent 'flower,'" Elliot Owen said, lowering the roses and offering them to her.

He somehow looked better than she remembered.

He was in a grey winter coat, with a turned-up collar, that whispered *at least a grand, possibly even two*. His dark hair had been unusually short for a role but was now grown out a little and starting to curl.

Edie accepted the roses with a small exclamation of gratitude, momentarily unable to respond.

"You're not pissed off I've crashed your Christmas Day?" Elliot said, an anxious look she knew so well crossing his face.

"No . . . I'm merely stunned at seeing you," Edie said, inclining her head toward the flowers. "Thank you. Cheating husband."

"I haven't, obviously," Elliot said.

A few beats of creaky silence followed as the remark landed heavily: first the idea of marriage and then the notion that he could somehow cheat on her in their current circumstances.

Edie had absolutely no idea what to say, so they were left looking at each other with a *you go first* intensity and longing. She was glad she'd declined the "Santa's Chimney Legs" deely boppers.

"I didn't come round only to be a flashy shithouse with a bouquet," Elliot said eventually.

"I was going to say—I'm pretty sure delivery isn't that much extra if you'd wanted to pay for it," Edie said, trying to emulate a level of *savvy-comeback* composure she didn't feel.

She was incredibly touched and excited that he was here. She also didn't think microdosing Elliot Owen was ever going to work, so she had the roller-coaster sickness.

Call her a pessimist, but an inner voice was already scoffing: *yeah, lovely, he wants to call in and see you on Christmas Day, but imagine the emptiness next year when he doesn't. When he can't. When you know why he won't.*

This was precisely why she'd ended it. She wasn't going to perform the emotional equivalent of barefoot free-climbing the Burj Khalifa to prove it couldn't be done and confirm that falling the distance would break her. What they'd had was too perfect and good to end that way. She foresaw inevitable outcomes.

And yet, he was here. And suddenly nothing else mattered.

Elliot cleared his throat. "I wanted to say . . ."

Edie glanced over her shoulder as there was a scuffle behind them and a ceremonious closing of the dining-room door—as if a festive table full of people who'd been trying to listen in to catch the mood of the interaction had decided they probably shouldn't.

"The reasons you gave for dumping me—they were bullshit," Elliot said, breaking into a wide smile of nervous relief that he was finally risking saying the thing, and that Edie was at least smiling back.

"I've thought about nothing else but you since I last saw you," he said, as Edie tried to look intelligently neutral and not to fall forward into his arms. "You said you couldn't fit in with my career? And that I couldn't manage with your wanting to stay here."

"That was the size of it, yes," Edie said, leaning on the door jamb, supposedly casually but actually a little bit for support.

". . . Thing is, I want you more than I want the career. Why am I binning you off to make way for it? Shouldn't it be the other way around?"

Edie felt faint and hot in the misty December air. She was wholly unprepared for this and would need to hide in flippancy. "Is the plan for you to retrain as an electrician and plumber?"

"It's recession-proof work," Elliot said.

"Haha. You'd look like Derek Zoolander as a coal miner."

"Listen, I'm a twat who can't do anything else—I mostly enjoy acting. And I need to keep all my hot sluts in bunches of roses."

Edie properly laughed. She was a fool for him when he dropped posh actor Elliot and used his real accent.

"But I'm the only person in charge of my life. If I want the jobs I take to suit having a girlfriend in the East Midlands, they will. Simple as that."

A pause.

"Elliot . . ." Edie began. "It's amazing you'd offer." She adjusted her hands on the brown paper around the roses, felt her fingertips dappling it with sweat marks. "But I didn't give you up for trivial reasons. It was the hardest, most grown-up decision I've ever made, but I thought about it from every angle, and there wasn't any other way."

"You sound like my mum when she had our cat, Inspector Boursin, put down."

"Inspector Boursin?"

"Don't ask—Fraser named him. OK, look. Saying this next thing is more intimidating than when I auditioned for Christopher Nolan and he said nothing for thirty seconds and then kind of nodded . . ."

"Name-dropping, even now," Edie said with warmth, rolling her eyes.

"I'm gabbling because I'm so nervous," Elliot said, and whether he knew it or not, Edie was already in love with him harder than ever.

"The practicalities are pretty much irrelevant. You're not . . ." He paused and swallowed, hard. ". . . *replaceable*, Edie."

"Hah, well, *you* definitely aren't."

That was glaringly obvious. She wasn't easily going to settle for John Bloke after Elliot Owen. She felt like Lois Lane after a night sky flight with Superman.

"I don't mean in superficial ways. The time apart has proved it to me. I already knew it when you ended things—I just couldn't articulate it. It's all so clear to me now. From my perspective, anyway. I don't want to shake hands, leave you as some golden memory when I'm toothless watching quiz shows in a fireside chair, Edie. I don't want to try to fill the space where you should've been with other people, because we didn't even *try*. There isn't another you, for me. If you feel as much as I do, then we shouldn't be bothering with the 'if,' only the how."

Edie couldn't speak. Her throat had seized up, and she had a dull pain behind her ears. Comprehending that she'd been made a surprise offer of true love replicated a sinus condition.

It was more than this overwhelming confirmation of his feelings; it was discovering that she'd so efficiently minimized and denied hers.

Edie honestly thought she was done with living behind expertly constructed facades, and lying to herself. It seemed she wasn't, because Elliot had turned her case for their separating inside out.

He was right: the first principle was that they were, and remained, madly in love, not that his job involved a lot of travel. He had offered compromises—never demanded she leave her home—and she had still rejected them out of hand.

Why? All of Edie's objections really meant: *you're destined for bigger and better things (than me)*. She hadn't been able to bear attempting a relationship with him, not because it was truly impossible, but because she was so certain of failure. She'd used these two concepts interchangeably, when actually, they weren't the same at all. Acknowledging this put Edie's insistence they split up in a very different light.

She hadn't dumped Elliot. She had preemptively dumped herself.

". . . The only thing I don't know is if maybe you didn't feel quite enough for the huge hassle involved in being with me. If so, I get it," Elliot continued. "I'm sorry to put you on the spot. This definitely felt like a meeting not an email."

She could tell that while his voice stayed steady, inside, he was writhing. As soon as she found the words, she'd put him out of his misery.

Elliot's brow knitted. "Unless you're seeing anyone? I told Fraser not to tell me if he found out you were, but I'd hoped he

5

understood that meant he should still tell me, and then I could blame him for it when I lost my shit."

"No, I'm not." She paused. "I can't find a single flaw in your argument, to be fair. Never seeing you has felt a lot like bullshit. Also, if you think I've got the strength of character to say no to Elliot Owen *twice*, you're wrong."

"You'd be saying no to Elliot."

She understood his meaning. "Well, the answer to either of them is yes."

Elliot's eyes lit up, and hers shone with incipient tears she was definitely not going to cry, not when they weren't even at the trifle and cheeseboard course on the other side of that door. She owed him honesty about why she'd let him go, after his courage.

"The truth is . . . I'm scared," she said. Saying it out loud it actually felt cathartic, rather than stupid.

"So am I," Elliot said.

He stepped forward and kissed her, and it was exactly the right moment. It stopped them overthinking it. She'd forgot how his mouth on hers could make her feel, in that way you did when remembering was too potent and inconvenient.

Edie held the flowers over his shoulder, muttering: "Fuck, you're freezing" in self-consciousness as they disentangled, because the repressed passion in physical contact somehow managed to say more than anything in the last two minutes. If they'd started there, they could've saved time.

Elliot put a cold hand to her face and said quietly: "We're not making a mistake, you know. If you're right and what comes next is a massive mess that breaks both our hearts, then I'm afraid that's still what we've got to do. The only way out is through."

He glanced up and added at normal volume: "Oh, hi! Mr. Thompson!"

Edie turned to see her dad over her shoulder.

"Hello! *Huge* apologies for the interruption, but Megan's at the side dishes like a groundhog and wants to know if anyone has rights to second helps," her father said. "I quote her verbatim: 'Edith will go full Miss Trunchball if we finish the roasties, Dad—you know what she's like.'"

"Edie, you should've said you were having dinner—I'm so sorry!" Elliot said.

"I feel sure you're more of an attraction than the sprout and lemon stuffing, delightful as it is. Are you joining us, Elliot?" her dad asked.

Elliot looked to Edie. "Ehm . . . ?"

"Yes," Edie said, without hesitation. "Yes, he is."

She hung up his ridiculous coat in her hallway, alongside normal items of outerwear, like a nineteenth-century nobleman was time-travel visiting.

She found Elliot a chair, reintroduced him to Nick and Hannah, and made introductions with their plus ones, now that she had one of her own.

"Parsnips with maple syrup glaze, not honey, so no bees were exploited," her sister Meg said, as she heaped his plate. "Bee-keeping is like sending bees to war."

"Inglorious bee-sterds," Elliot said, and vegan ultra Meg actually *giggled*.

Edie watched, amazed.

Elliot was, in so many ways, a miracle.

1

Actually, Elliot Owen's presence was the headline miracle, what the newspaper trade called a *one-fact story*. (And thank God they weren't sniffing round this tiny Nottingham suburb with its solid Victorian housing stock and a large Lidl today.)

There was more than one unexpected marvel here, as far as Edie was concerned. Not least her formerly cantankerous if not quasi-estranged sister acting as her effusive cohost.

Meg, with her round face, blue eyes, and blonde hair in a dreadlocked ponytail, looked like a Cabbage Patch Kid after a week at Reading Festival. You would never know that she and dark, lampeyed, Clara Bow–esque Edie were related, and for a long time that had felt like a reflection of their relationship.

In this crowded room with steamed windows, the aroma of porcini mushroom gravy and a Bluetooth speaker pealing "Somethin' Stupid," Edie's world had taken a definitive, beautiful leap into a better future.

She'd never been the greatest fan of Christmas Day's suspended reality. Reality might've been a disappointing grind, but she could handle it. Suspending it left her adrift and exposed.

When she was living in London, Edie had dreaded navigating the politics of returning for the holiday, with her widowed, apologetic father and ornery little sister.

Her dad felt awful that it wasn't the celebration it would've been before their mum died, and Meg was constantly boiling, substantially correctly, with a sense that Edie didn't want to be there.

Edie felt painfully conscious their December twenty-fifth didn't look or feel like the spray-snow-encrusted vision of matching-pajamas and hot chocolate togetherness that it was supposed to.

There was a psychic deadlock of guilt, more guilt, and resentment that she couldn't spring them from. Not until Edie was forced back home in a social media shaming following the Jack Marshall Incident, their flamboyant elderly neighbor Margot died, and they collectively confronted the unresolved grief and regret about the loss of her mother.

The familial reconciliation and Edie reordering her life accordingly had ended up being more surprising than her falling in love with a famous actor who'd starred in a swords-wolves-and-tits fantasy saga.

So, despite there being a newly minted superhero here—Elliot's latest on-screen incarnation was *The Void*—it was already magical.

Edie was glad that she and what the tabloids termed her "superstar beau" had been sufficiently serious and/or relaxed enough about each other's status last time that he'd already met her dad, Meg, and her two best friends from sixth form, Hannah and Nick.

Hannah, a willowy and acerbic kidney doctor (*"nephrologist!"*) and Nick, a mod-dressing misanthrope and local DJ, had been lost to Edinburgh and an unhappy, controlling marriage respectively, and both were now back.

They beamed in warm recognition at the newcomer. Her old friends were plenty intuitive enough to interpret Edie's stunned, bashful glow and Elliot's hand shaking with everyone in turn. It wasn't a meal you just dropped in on as an ex.

Meanwhile, Hannah's girlfriend, Chloe, looked bedazzled in her first encounter, and Nick's girlfriend, Ros, sat nearest to them, completely neutral.

"Nice to meet you, Elliot. You're with Edie? How did you two meet?" Ros said, grinding pepper over her plate.

She had limpid, thoughtful eyes behind rectangular, amber-rimmed glasses. She was the sort of person to ask direct questions. *And how do you feel about that?*

Hannah and Chloe were each other's first same-sex relationship, in their thirties, and Ros had probed the intricacies with the unembarrassable, purposeful clarity of a first responder paramedic.

"I ghostwrote his autobiography," Edie said. "I do copywriting for my day job in advertising. As a special project, it kind of skill-mapped."

"Autobiography? You're very young to have an autobiography?" Ros said to Elliot, frowning in confusion. "Was it self-published?"

Edie stifled a laugh. She suspected that Nick had told Ros his friend had dated a celebrity, and Ros, New Agey and not much caring for conventional accolades, had forgotten. She was yet to put together that tale, with a photogenic man drinking red wine from a beaker.

"I'm *far* too young for one, Ros," Elliot said, with the practiced ease of someone who performed for a living. "I'm not sure I'm worth one full stop. But other ones were being written, and I was advised to do my own to counter theirs. It's not advice I'd take now, to be honest. Then again, if I hadn't, I'd not have met Edie."

"Did it sell well?" Ros said, clearly trying to ascertain Elliot's grip on sanity. *And are the other autobiographies in the room with us now?*

"It paid for my kitchen you like," Edie said, smiling.

She was delighted with her turquoise units, the shade of a Cadillac. After an adult lifetime of landlord magnolias and biscuits, she'd gone to town on color. Edie loved this bay-fronted, red-brick semi with its 1930s stained-glass door so much. *More than you per-*

11

haps should love things, she thought, but to Edie, it signified arrival, security, and belonging.

With her sister as lodger and her father a frequent guest, Edie was looking after them. And, whether they knew it or not, they were looking after her.

"Oh, did it now? You owe me a full English tomorrow, then," Elliot said. "A Meg-compliant full English."

He smiled a sly smile over his cup, having soft-launched the expectation that he was staying over.

Edie raised her eyebrows, though it had never really been in doubt.

"And you're a couple? I thought you said you were single, Edie?" Ros said, with more of her disarming frankness. She clearly wasn't going to squirm on worries like: *what if this is an on-off hookup without a label.*

". . . Yes, we're a couple?" Edie said, a statement with a question mark, looking at Elliot, her heart skipping a beat. They'd not ever used the word that she could remember, and Ros was bouncing them into agreeing formalities. It was the obvious conclusion of the doorstep chat, and yet it was all brand-new. Frank was singing "Fly Me to the Moon."

"We're a couple," Elliot said, answering her note of doubt with confidence.

They locked eyes in private wonder for a moment.

"As of today?" Ros said. Ros was a loss to Notts CID.

"We were seeing each other for a few weeks, four months ago. I guess it was a . . . fling?" Edie said, making an apologetic face at Elliot. "'Affair' makes it sound like there was infidelity involved."

"Wouldn't call it a *fling,*" Elliot said.

Nick offered Ros another glass of wine.

The chatter around them resumed, and they were relieved to be speaking one to one.

"Why not?" Edie said.

"A fling has built-in obsolescence," he said. "Did you ever think, *oh, here we are, having a fling?* I thought we felt serious from the start."

"We did." The introductions to each other's loved ones was proof they'd embarked on it in the style of it mattering. "I thought it was . . . I didn't know what it was, other than a very rewarding experience," Edie said.

Elliot laughed. "Like volunteering?"

"Exactly. Giving back to the high-profile thespian community."

"Very kind of you to extend a helping hand. Mucking in with the grunt work."

"Honestly, I think it gave me more satisfaction than the people I helped."

"I'll say."

Edie shook with laughter; Elliot grinned, and she had to stifle it before anyone tuned in to the intense flirting.

Elliot had sent Edie a postcard not so long ago, which was tucked into the vanity-table mirror in her bedroom. She could dart upstairs at some point to hide it. But what was cool—or indeed necessary—about pretending not to value it? It read: *I notice when you're not around.*

That he felt her absence enough to bother telling her about it had been incredibly touching to Edie. They'd cared about each other a lot, but his world contained so many distractions and opportunities that she thought he'd surprise himself by healing faster than he thought possible.

After all, wasn't acting about inhabiting another identity—intensely yet briefly—stepping back out of that skin, and moving on? What was temporary could be fully sincere.

Actors, their late neighbor Margot had once said, after lighting a Sobranie Black, *have vagabond souls.*

Yet he'd missed her sufficiently to come back. It was too huge a turn of events to be processed up front; Edie was still preoccupied with its enormity.

"What was it in your mind, back then? If never a fling?" Edie asked.

"The beginning," Elliot said, without hesitating.

2

Edie sat up in the pinkish bordello hue of her very *single-woman-taste* bedroom. She was wearing a T-shirt that read *The Horrors Persist Yet So Do I* with a picture of a gerbil in a fez, smoking—a gift from Meg which she wouldn't have worn in company if in her right mind.

At least the light was low. She'd inherited long voile curtains in a pillar-box red material that made a dramatic partner to her blush-pink Art Deco–style bed, chili fairy lights, and tasseled-pendant chinoiserie lampshade.

"Kind of Amsterdam window meets the feminist *Barbie*," Elliot had said last night. "There's gonna be big fights when we decorate together."

Edie had liked the assumption but pretend-objected to the description.

Elliot replied: "It's still my favorite room in my favorite house in the world, so keep it in context."

There didn't seem to be any amount of drinking that diminished his verbal dexterity.

Speaking of which . . . Edie noticed her phone on the nightstand, blinking with light. She pulled it out of the charger and inspected an unusually lengthy cascade of notifications.

WOW ❤️❤️
Go Edie! xx
Erm—what? AMAGING 🍆
OMFG is that who I think it is?! Is this NOW?

*This has blown me away NGL! Are you in the States? You can't be
here?? Do you want to get a drink soon? Ages since I've seen you xoxo
here's my number in case you don't have it . . .*
*Well, well, LOOK at what you found under your tree. Beats my fucking
Lakeland tea urn.*

Oh *fuck fuck fuck*—what HAD she done last night? On social
media, that was—the main thing she'd done was sleeping with
his face crushed into the left-hand pillow, out like a light due to
residual jet lag and their only going to sleep at about three a.m.

Edie clicked onto Instagram and, with a slow turn of her stomach, vaguely recalled being absolutely shitfaced on red wine and
high on love at midnight, when they were finally alone in the
sitting room.

She had taken a commemorative selfie of Elliot kissing her
face, her eyes squeezed shut in boozed-up, cartoon-stars-circling
delight. There wasn't loads of him in it, but there was enough,
given they'd been linked in the past. He didn't look much like
other people.

Edie had an out-of-character moment, the sort only ethanol
could supply: the heady sense you were freeing a part of your
nature you kept needlessly imprisoned. She'd captioned it with
one pink heart, and she recalled thinking it was definitely fine to
post it because they were so, so happy and looked so happy. How
could anything made of happiness be wrong?

SOBER REASONS, she now thought, furious with herself.
Like, *you've not told anyone beyond this property and its guests yet, and
a stupid pissed upload wasn't how you wanted to do it.*

Worse, her Instagram only had a modest 650 followers, but it
was set public.

She clicked on story views and scrolled through a long list of friends, relatives, colleagues, and cringed. She impulsively deleted the picture.

Just as the image digitally vaporized, Edie realized this, too, was an error. If it made its way beyond her profile and into the public domain, she'd removed the list of suspects. Plus, its disappearing stank of panic. It rather confirmed any suspicion that she'd been indiscreet. It flagged, *yes, that was a Story-story.*

Nor, on reflection, could she post a wheedling *throwback photo, guys, feeling nostalgic!* disclaimer, as when it came out that it was true down the line, people who knew her might be justifiably irritated at being bullshitted.

Oh my God, you absolute tit. You managed what, a grand total of six to eight hours of keeping this to yourself? Edie couldn't believe she'd gaily broadcasted it. Her boss Richard once told her she was her own worst enemy, and though the title of her worst enemy had been a keenly fought competition, he might be right.

She was near-tearful with hungover-dickhead remorse as Elliot stirred, turned over, and rubbed a puffy face worth a fortune. It had recently graced the cover of *Empire* magazine, tagline: *staring into The Void has never felt so good.*

He smiled at her. "Morning." His eyes settled on her expression. "Shit. What's wrong?"

3

"I posted a photo of us on my Instagram."

"I know."

"Do you?!" Edie's powers of recollection tuned in and out.

"Yeah, you were really proud of it. You were going to put a Taylor Swift song over it, but I think by that point you lacked the motor skills . . . 'Snow on the Beach,' was it? I'm not the expert on her you are. I hope it's not about a freak event ruining a nice holiday."

Edie wailed: "Why did you let me?!"

Elliot shrugged bare and gym-developed shoulders. ("Once I'm in the Void costume, it's only my lower jaw and upper chest left doing any acting.")

"Aside from the fact I'd had a skinful, too, why not? Are we hiding this?"

His nonchalance went some way to calming her. It had to be said, this was his area, not hers. If he wasn't bothered, should she be? Like when a plane had terrible turbulence and you were convinced it was The End, then you saw the cabin crew who do the route six times a day having a laugh.

"What if someone screen-grabbed it? I mean, they almost certainly will have for the purposes of WhatsApp chats. Then it ends up in the press."

Elliot shrugged again. "They'll write about me anyway, and last night you were very much of the attitude we should let them."

"Oh, for fuc— Drunk me should be shot."

Elliot smiled appraisingly. "Hey up. Not sure I ever spotted that drunk Edie is a chaos gremlin. Though to be fair, there have been signs."

He lifted the duvet that was bunched at his chest half an inch and gingerly peered under, as if inspecting damage, to embarrassed scoff noises from Edie.

Elliot hesitated. "If you can't remember posting that photo, can you not remember anything else after? That would be a shame."

"Weirdly, it's like I have an hour or so outage around the photo, and then I can remember again. I must've eased up on the Co-op merlot."

"Not weirdly. Some things are so incredible, even a hippocampus that's been holed below the waterline still insists on recording them."

"No way to refer to me," Edie said, and they both stupid-laughed, before Elliot held out his arms to her.

As before, Edie had discovered that having sex with someone who was held to be a symbol of sex was, in abstract, terrifying. In practice, it was just two people in bed who wanted to be there.

"There's something I failed to mention yesterday as I didn't want to spoil the vibe," he said, as she settled into his embrace.

"Oh, here it comes."

"I have to go back to America on the twenty-ninth. New York this time."

"For how long?"

"I'm not sure, probably at least a few weeks. I'll get back as soon as I can."

"What time are you leaving?"

"Er. Pickup at half five in the morning."

"Pfffft. *Take another chance on me, we can make it work and see loads of each other! Oh, wait, actually that was a one-night stand—there's my luxury sedan transfer to Heathrow. Toodle-oo, bitch, thanks for letting me rearrange your guts,"* Edie said, listening to the laughter vibrating in his ribs.

"You're gross. *Four*-night stand. My timing would be better if I'd planned to come round yesterday instead of having suddenly reached my absolute limit in missing you."

Edie was glowing again. She wouldn't have guessed it was spontaneous. Bloody actors.

"You did pretty well to find a florist's open on Christmas Day, then?"

"No comment. Some perks to being the sort of prick who has a personal assistant. I should go and see my family when I can get out of this bed and apologize for Brexiting their Christmas Day. Do you want to visit? I could suggest going out to dinner? There's not tons of privacy if you stay, but no different to here."

True that. Edie hoped what they'd imagined was stealthy quiet actually had been. Luckily, Meg slept like she'd been entombed. She'd be at work now, an early shift at the home that ended by lunchtime. Meg could be a salty customer, but she'd found her calling as a care worker, and Edie was very proud of her.

"I promised today I'd go on a walk round Wollaton Hall with my sister and Nick and Hannah, when Meg's shift ends. Feels a bit shabby saying *oh, I've got a better offer.*"

As was the way of life's complex psychosocial web over thirty, the walk wasn't simply a walk. It was keeping Nick busy on a day he couldn't see his young son, Max. It was something Hannah's mum could no longer do with her MS. It was brightening Meg having to work holidays.

"Do you want to come along? Then we can go to dinner at your parents' tomorrow night?" Edie said.

"Great. I'll head back and meet you there later."

"Sounds good, apart from the saying-goodbye-at-dawn-in-three-days bit," Edie said.

"The way I see it, the agony of parting was considerably worse when the idea was we'd never see each other again."

"I didn't say never—I said never say never."

For the first time since Elliot had been there, the temperature in the room fell by a few degrees.

After a moment, he said: "The only thing that spooks me about you is the way you were so matter-of-fact about ending it. It was, hands down, the most painful thing to ever happen to me, and I didn't see it coming. The memory of that conversation was the number one inhibitor to me trying again. The only way I could make sense of your steely certainty was that it *wasn't* as painful to you. I thought we were at least going to agonize about how to make it work. But no."

Edie gathered that *I've thought about nothing else but you since I last saw you* didn't mean all the thoughts were positive.

". . . I didn't come back because I thought I had a good chance," Elliot said. "I'd decided I'd take any chance."

After the dizziness and declarations of the previous day, she could see his point. He'd had to have enough optimism for both of them, both times.

Edie took a deep breath that gave her a sharp little pang. "I think you've confused my superficial coping mechanisms and capacity for emotional self-harm for a lack of giving a shit about a situation. Easily done. I fool myself, too."

"Really?"

"Yes. I wasn't blasé about ending it with you. Not at all. If it came across that way, it's because my control was for my self-respect and your benefit. I was trying to make it less difficult. My friends were put on notice that whenever paparazzi photos of you with your new girlfriend dropped, I'd need a whole weekend of palliative care. Deliveroo McDonald's nugs and six bottles of Whispering Angel. Ask them. It was called Operation Crankshaft."

"Why Crankshaft?"

"It was the military code name for bin Laden."

"Wow, thanks. Am I the terrorist?"

"The jihadist of my heart, and a mission I probably wouldn't survive."

Elliot laughed, but the mood was still clouded. Flattery about jealousy wasn't enough.

"My boss Richard once said I don't want good things to happen to me," Edie continued. "Subconsciously. He might be right."

"Why not?" Elliot said.

"I don't think I deserve it. Or I don't trust it."

"Why not?"

"I don't know."

"You want good things for other people you love, so why not yourself?"

"Maybe I don't *love myself*," Edie said, with necessary British-sarcastic intonation. "It's . . . it's that causing the bad thing to happen makes you feel in charge of what you believed was destined to happen anyway. Hope is opening yourself up to too much uncontrolled hurt. Self-sabotage is control."

"Hmm. I suppose I don't understand how someone so warm and generally . . . joyful can also be a complete catastrophist," Elliot said, making Edie smile.

"It could be because the first person who was meant to love me the most left me? Only a guess." That was a blurt. She hadn't expected to directly refer to her mother's suicide in this conversation. "I'm not saying that for some cheap point score sympathy vote," she said, as much a check on herself as him.

"If I thought you'd do that, I wouldn't know you at all. Or deserve to."

Elliot held her closer. Edie had forgotten his unique ability to pry things from her that she didn't intend to share.

If she was honest, Edie didn't always find his incisiveness, his eagerness to dissect the frog, comfortable. It spoke to a side of him that felt foreign: the L.A. world where you had expensive therapy, and a cavalier attitude to prescription medication. There was being seen, and there was being seen through.

4

After Elliot's robust indifference, Edie had started to hope her Instagram judgment fail had slipped past the censors and was a momentary lapse she could choose to learn from. Emphasis on the *choose*.

Yet her mobile shrilled with an incoming call from RICHARD within minutes of Elliot's taxi pulling away to his parents' house, so it was clearly nonsensical self-soothing.

Richard was her employer, proprietor of the ad agency Ad Hoc, and more intimidating than that, one of the human beings Edie most respected in all the world. He had a mind like a steel trap, the sanguine manner and good looks of Barack Obama at a podium, and suits so sharp it was like he fashion-directed *GQ*.

You did not fuck with Richard, and if you did, you'd most certainly find out.

She answered the call in a hot flush of trepidation.

"Ms. Thompson!" Richard said, vivacious and upbeat. "It's Boxing Day, and instead of enjoying a smorgasbord of cold cuts and my Uncle Stuart's tangy homemade pickle with a glass of midpriced champagne, I'm calling you. Can you imagine why that might be?"

"I have . . . one idea."

"*Do you?* I'm told there is a depiction of what the downmarket titles refer to as a 'steamy clinch'—you, with a highly significant other. It appeared on one of the devil's doodle-pads. Instagram, I believe?"

"Richard, I'm so, SO sorry—it won't happen again, I—"

"Let me stop you there. I'll tell you what I told my helpful source. Your private life is no business of mine, unless it impacts your work. Which to my knowledge, this time, it hasn't."

"Oh. Thank you."

Edie hadn't been quite sure what she was guilty of, she supposed, beyond *ongoing silliness in a public forum*. During her and Elliot's pre-courtship phase, they'd been papped arguing in the street. Richard had reasonably pointed out that this wasn't exactly the behavior he wanted the autobiography's publisher to see from the firm's supplied copywriter.

Yet, project over, project wreathed in bestselling glory, what *were* the rules on portraits with Elliot Owen?

"This isn't a telling off—it's to let you know that as well as a colleague feeling it was their heavy burden to notify me, I've also had a call from a silver-tongued gentleman at the *Mail*, wondering if I had any insights to offer."

Edie gulped. As she'd thought, it had escaped into the jungle. "Oh God. Why call you and not me?"

"Because the agency landline on the website defaults to my mobile, out of hours. If you've not been bothered, they haven't got your number, I assume."

Yet.

It was even more dispiriting to hear that Edie still had active adversaries within the Ad Hoc agency. It wasn't unexpected—her situationship disaster and ex-colleague Jack Marshall had been sacked, ditto his former bride, her ex-colleague Charlotte, and her frenemy and their foot soldier Louis. Yet the poison likely lingered in the system.

Being caught kissing a groom on his wedding day by the bride was the kind of infraction people tended to remember.

Several of those still present had signed a petition asking her to leave. Edie suspected there was a view that cheats had prospered, with her staying on the payroll and scoring remote working.

They were passably nice to her at the Christmas party, but then, people were to your face, and she had acquired a very famous ex-boyfriend since she last saw most of them. Guess they'd get even nicer now. To her face.

"Be on your guard that not everyone is behaving with honor about what you share online. I reminded Jessica that those who bully in my workplace, subtly or not, get their pink slips."

Oh, Jess. Edie had hoped Jess might've moved on. She was a comrade of Charlotte's and had been one of the first names on that petition. After Charlotte's departure, Jess had unofficially become a kind of leader of the office.

Her hostility especially stung Edie for a ridiculous reason: Jess, with her dirty laugh and line in sarcasm, masses of auburn hair in a topknot, peg trousers, and loafers, didn't present as any sort of sorority Mean Girl. She looked like someone Edie might've been friends with in the Before Times. To be disliked by her felt like a proper indictment: marked a traitor to the sisterhood by someone who'd not assign the status frivolously. Indeed, it made Edie the Mean Girl.

Of course, Jess and Charlotte would probably still be in contact, wherever Charlotte was now. It'd be Jess's duty to breadcrumb Edie disgraces, rumors, and talking points.

"What was Jessica's excuse for bringing it to you? Do they think I'm an embarrassment?" Edie asked, not really wanting to know.

"Oh, she harked back to the scrap in the street and some Ad Hoc clients grumbling at the time. It was a *thought you should know* before the media rang me, but I can spot a malicious stirring of the pot at my great age."

Edie mumbled thanks.

"So, is it all on and all in with the actor chap? Thought he was something akin to a harrowing ordeal to work with?" Richard said.

Edie understood the genuine paternal concern underneath the slight disbelief: Richard thought she might be picking Jack Marshall 2.0.

"Honestly, he wasn't—he's great. Absolutely nothing difficult about him at all. His critics were using *difficult* as useful shorthand for 'too smart to do what we want.' I went in with the same preconceptions because of his . . . status."

She felt like Elizabeth Bennet promising her dad that Mr. Darcy wasn't a proud dick after all and that the great estate at Pemberley wasn't a factor, promise.

"But you're not off to the Hollywood Hills?"

"We're trialing an arrangement where I visit him and we go to Nobu Malibu and eat snapper sashimi. And he visits me and we go to Bacon Derek's food truck at Sneinton Market for breakfast sandwiches."

"Splendid. Very on trend. It's what I believe is called the *high low*. In other news, I'd intended to leave this announcement until the New Year, but since I've got you now—how do you fancy running a Nottingham office for me? I've decided, with it having gone well for you since you moved up, it makes sense for you to helm the first official regional outpost of my empire."

"Seriously?! I'd love that."

Edie beamed in surprise and gratification: Richard praise was always earned.

"Great. I've earmarked premises in the Lace Market. Secondly, you're not a manager without someone to manage. I'm not going to lie to you, the response from the metropolitan elite here when I requested volunteers to relocate—on a generous package,

I might add—was quite something. I started compiling the greatest hits. 'Is it a market town?' to 'Is there a seaside?' 'Does anywhere make a serviceable *cacio e pepe*?' and my favorite—'Crouch End is northern enough.'"

Edie guffawed. Yeah, and she bet that many cast it as opting for a prison cell with Rose West.

"However, one brave soul not only stepped up but said he genuinely liked the idea—Declan Dunne. Do you remember him from the Christmas party? Tall. Irish, obviously. Sunny disposition. Strangely partial to exercise."

"I . . . don't, off the top of my head."

And new people don't really fraternize with the notorious wedding-wrecking tart who can even draw characters from fictional multiverses into the tractor beam pull radiating from her crotch.

"I think you'll really gel. He reminds me a lot of you, in some ways," Richard was saying. "Promising chap. I wouldn't ask you to spend all day together if I didn't think the chemistry was right."

"Understood," Edie said. "I trust your taste."

This was true, and yet, privately, she doubted. Declan might well have been infected by the sniping. Worst case, he was running reconnaissance. Pretty big commitment to being nosy, yes, but these days, Edie wouldn't rule out any far-fetched possibility.

"He's going to report to you at nine a.m. on the first Friday back. Thought it might be nice to start on a day where you can take him for a drink at lunchtime, and he's got the weekend to settle in."

"Typing 'get him wasted' into my Notes app as we speak, got it."

Richard laughed. "Not to pressurize you or make you dread Mr. Dunne's arrival—especially as it sounds like you're going to have a busy social life—but if you did fancy taking him under your wing and acting as local tour guide, it'd be hugely appreciated, I'm sure. He's the self-sufficient type who won't take much launching."

"I'll try my best. I can rank the pizza restaurants and save him from the fighting pubs, at least."

"One last thing, Edie. In case it wasn't clear, I will leave it to your discretion whether you want to confirm to your colleagues that you're stepping out with Marlon Nando's. Speak soon."

AFTER THEY RUNG off, Edie had a notion to check her Instagram followers to see if this guy had been curious about her. Yep, there he was: Declan Dunne, or @dunneonthewold. She hadn't recognized him to follow him back, and she remedied this now, thinking she had to be positive at the outset if they were soon going to be at close quarters.

She scrolled his profile. He was tall, attractive in an unkempt way, and good-natured to an extent that it transmitted through the lens. He looked like the result of DNA splicing Fred and Shaggy in *Scooby-Doo*. A mere four pictures ago, last Bonfire Night, was a photo of a grinning Declan proudly brandishing a sausage in tongs at a barbecue with her new nemesis Jessica wrapped round his waist, one of her hands making a peace sign. Edie twinged. *You like peace, do you? Not much of a peacenik as far as I'm concerned.*

The caption made it clear that Declan was a good enough friend to hang out at her house.

They were affectionate in the comments, too.

Aww. Love you, Dunny! King of the Cumberland Ring! 😂 *xxx*
Great to see you all! xx

Ye gads. Jessica had her husband still entirely Insta-visible within the last six months, so she doubted their bond was romantic, but the fact remained that Edie's Eden might have a snake problem.

No way had Jessica not warned Declan off working with Edie. If so, why didn't he heed it? It pretty much had to be a spying mission. Even if it wasn't intended as such, it might possibly turn into one.

She blocked Jess and set her Instagram to private. Gesture politics: there were still plenty who could pass her material if they wanted to, but Edie felt it necessary to make it clear to Jessica *she knew.*

It had been such brilliant news, and now this.

The high low.

5

They assembled at the gates of Wollaton Hall's majestic deer park in a subzero temperature, Hannah using the what3words app to share the precise location: *salt.metro.bounty.*

Last time Edie was here, she was being summoned by the director of Elliot's then-drama to explain why he'd gone briefly AWOL from the set. Said director was certain Elliot was busy between the sheets with his ghostwriter; in fact he'd gone into hiding after the news broke that he was adopted. At the time, Edie had thought the notion he'd be interested in her in that way was humiliatingly preposterous.

"I always thought that what3words app was for people who'd been abducted?" Nick said. "I wish someone would abduct me. Whose thoroughly dipshitted idea was this, anyway?"

He shuddered into the Liberty print scarf wound in the collar of his coat. Nick loved clothes far more than either of his female best friends did, so it was three-quarter-length wool with a houndstooth pattern. He looked clad for a first date somewhere smart, not trailing around a field.

It had taken Edie until now to replace her tatty tartan parka with something spendy in tailored navy with toggles.

"Mine. A Boxing Day walk has always been my family tradition!" Hannah said.

"Inherited generational trauma," Nick replied. "I notice both girlfriends made excuses." He looked to Elliot. "Idiot."

Elliot military saluted him. "Look, let's be real—I want to get laid."

"Jesus Christ." Nick pulled the vape pen from his mouth. "I thought we were going on a *walk.*"

Elliot had been there first when Edie arrived, his dark head bowed as he stared at his phone.

"Hey, the app actually calls the house Wayne Manor—playful," Elliot had said in greeting, looking from the handset to gesture behind him, up the hill at the Grade I Elizabethan stately home that had doubled as Batman's mansion.

Edie had a teenaged shiver of delight that he'd turned up: *ooh, that's my boyfriend* innocence that was Class A spiked with *that's literally Elliot Owen.*

You'd be saying yes to Elliot. His fame felt like a greater obstacle to her than to him. That was unexpected, but then he had been living with his double-identity imposter self for years and Edie for only months. He'd sought it; the spotlight had landed on her by chance.

Last time around, she'd perceived a shift in how she thought of him as familiarity grew: eventually he became someone she knew who was also famous, as opposed to a famous person she knew.

Their time apart had affected that a little. They were no longer in the bubble where he was making a show set in this city and they had regular work dates for her to transcribe key passages from his history. He'd been away and done freshly impressive things, and Edie needed to acclimatize again.

Meg joined them last, cheeks colored from having rushed, her blue scrubs covered by a brown teddy-bear coat that Edie had got her for Christmas.

"Sorry, sorry! I've never got that bus before—it took ages."

"It's OK, you didn't miss anything. The plan is doing more exercise," Nick said. His comedic grousing was an established habit, and everyone knew he was glad to be there, however well he hid it.

"Hi, Elliot, I didn't know you were coming!" Meg said.

"He explained why he was keen on coming in general, but you missed it—let's leave it that way," Nick said to Meg.

"Grateful for your restraint," Elliot said to Nick.

Another thing Edie appreciated about Elliot: he hadn't said *can't we be alone?* He was totally up for dossing around at Hannah's lovely flat in The Park after this, as he had been for Pictionary on Christmas Day.

Elliot told her it could work, but she realized he'd also thrown himself into showing her it could.

"I said the reward was pizzas and old-fashioneds at mine, Nick," Hannah said. "You accepted the terms gladly at the time."

"October Me hates December Me, I can tell you that much," Nick said.

"Excuse me. I'm sorry to intrude but I'm a big fan," said a well-spoken man with an intense gaze in a Carhartt insulated jacket. He looked about forty. "We never missed an episode of *Blood & Gold*, but it wasn't the same after you left."

"Oh, thank you," Elliot said smoothly, never startled, while the rest of them were visibly startled.

A stealth attack. It was Boxing Day! Fame didn't get public holidays—or rather, holidays from the public.

"Would it be OK to get a picture with my wife?"

They followed his pointing and saw that Carhartt man was an emissary from a group of seven wildly goggling people.

"Sure. Given there's more of you, shall I come to you?" Elliot said.

He walked over and shook gloved hands, submitted with charm to the rota of pleasantries and selfies.

"I would never ask that—way too shameful. Even if it was David Attenborough or something," Meg said, watching in bemused horror.

Edie thought this was true. Her sister had entirely her own rules of etiquette, and bothering notable personages was far too status-conscious lamestream.

"That was mad. I didn't even notice them noticing you!" Hannah hissed, once Elliot had been released from his duties and they'd stomped a short way into the park.

"Standing still for any period of time increases the risk," Elliot said.

"Like thrombosis," Nick offered.

"In the States, they're prepared to shout, 'Is it you?' but British people are scared of misidentification, so they like time to confer," Elliot said. "Like they're a quiz team."

Edie took Elliot's hand. She was aware, and wondered if he was, that she was instinctively doing it only once they were beyond any current onlooker sight lines.

It had a funny redolence of not wanting your peers at school to know, in case you got stared at and teased. She needed to feel ready, that was all. Edie wasn't quite ready.

"Shift go OK, Meg?" Hannah asked.

"Yes, it was quiet, and we had mince pies. After I helped John with the shower commode, I explained about the fecal plume."

"The fecal what?" Edie said.

"You don't know about the fecal plume, either?!" Meg said. "The dispersal of particles of waste matter when you flush the toilet! It's why you should always keep the lid down!"

"The fecal plume is one of the villains in my movie," Elliot said, and everyone laughed, Edie partly in relief.

She was lucky Elliot found Meg an offbeat pleasure.

Enjoy your soul-nourishing winter ramble; my sister's understanding of etiquette rules out asking for selfies and rules in discussing the arse aerosol.

"Oh look, a deer," said Hannah, not seeing a deer but obviously feeling as Edie did about pursuing this further.

Not long afterward, somewhere in their circuit of the park and across to the frozen mirror stillness of lake, they hit the moment of endorphin release when battling the elements started to feel hearty and life-affirming, instead of arduous. Even Nick became positive.

"Yesterday was magic, by the way, Edith," he said. "I thought we must do it next year, then fretted: what if any of us aren't available to do it next year? This is a curse of the human condition. I've discussed it with my counselor. Enjoy good times; don't become obsessed with prolonging and managing them. The only constant in life is change. *You cannot step twice into the same stream.*"

"I know you've switched to vaping, but are you smoking weed?" Hannah said.

"I'm making a valid observation about how life is in flux," Nick said.

"Why can't you step twice into the same stream?" Meg asked, fists balled for warmth in the front pockets of her coat.

"The water's moved?" Elliot said. "It's not the same water?"

"Five points to Owen—I think that's what the Greek philosopher meant," Nick said. "And in time, the water changes the rocks."

When the others had briefly strode on ahead, Elliot said to Edie: "My parents are looking forward to seeing you tomorrow. Fraz sends his apologies—he's off to his new girlfriend's in Suffolk."

"I'm looking forward to seeing them! Ah, Fraz. He and I still send each other links to idiot things every week. No words or explanation, only the raccoon getting chased by the police and so on."

"Sounds like my brother." Elliot paused. "You never sent them to me, though? Maybe I like felon raccoons?" He was smiling, making it clear this was merely curiosity.

"I wanted to message you all the time, but I knew I'd become quietly obsessed with it if we did. It'd turn into a drip feed of false hope. Then one day I'd see a story that would explain why you didn't reply as often anymore, and I couldn't face that—feeling like you'd betrayed me and our raccoon."

"I get it," Elliot said. "Or, I got it. All or nothing. I didn't want to be friends, either."

"Exactly."

Edie breathed in and out, a lungful of chill oxygen, and contemplated how lucky she was. Was that what she was frightened of, accepting good fortune? The way this walk was meant to go was Edie wondering if Elliot was only fifteen minutes' drive away, at his parents'—or zip-lining into a pool, somewhere exotic.

Instead, he was sharing the same what3words location with her: *i.love.you.*

They'd said it before and said it again, by the glow of the chili fairy lights.

That other version of her Boxing Day would've been a sort of agony, but there was safety in it—it contained no challenges for her, other than enduring it.

Edie thought about Nick's stoner wisdom. What part of not surrendering to happiness was fear of not staying that way?

When the good news and the bad news was: you could never achieve that certainty anyway. Let go and jump. Or rather, hold on.

6

Edie had stood outside the Owen family residence and rung the stiff brass doorbell many times, with various motives and turbulent misgivings, not so long ago.

She and Elliot had bickered at first, Edie certain he was a spoiled monstrosity. Then they'd become friends; then they'd fallen out over a misunderstanding where Elliot possessively warned his brother Fraser off Edie, as mutual feelings deepened. Then, amid the ambiguity, she'd shown up after Margot's funeral—full of perspective on carpe-ing the diem—and flat-out propositioned him. Fierce romantic entanglement ensued.

As a sort of muscle memory, Edie was almost irrationally apprehensive now. She had to remind herself that this evening she had no reason to worry, beyond wanting to continue to make a good impression on her sort-of in-laws. (Did they really think she was good enough, given their son could be dating an Oscar winner or Chanel muse? She might root him nearer home, she supposed.)

It was a short distance from her house to detached respectability in the affluent, Prius-owning suburbs, and yet it might as well have been Wollongong for her expectation of ever returning to this address. Immaculate Victorian redbrick chimney pots contrasted against a darkening winter sky.

When Elliot answered, he unexpectedly looked so preoccupied and downcast that she had a terror he'd had some sort of second thoughts. They'd parted earlier on warm terms, after a second night of trying to have silent sex at two a.m. while three sheets to the wind. It was slightly frustrating but mostly very funny.

He offered a lackluster "Hi."

OK, that was so not Elliot-like that it was clear something was up.

He took Edie's overnight bag from her and put it inside the door. "My parents are at a neighbor's cheese and wine thing. They'll be back by half six—we can walk over to the restaurant then," he said flatly, with tangible despondence.

"Is everything OK?" Edie asked.

"You've not seen the papers, then?"

Edie swallowed. So, in actual fact, he *wasn't* all right with the selfie mishap? Oh God, depending on how they'd angled it, she supposed . . . And she hadn't told him about the *Mail* calling her boss.

"No?" she said, untying the belt on her coat.

"Sorry, I shoulda said, but I've been nonstop on the phone to the usual crisis managers. Not that it's a crisis—it's merely bullshit."

"What is?" said Edie, now petrified.

Elliot held out a hand for her coat, and as he took it, he passed her his phone with his other hand.

Edie peered at a tabloid story on his handset. There was a grizzled-looking, gaunt, pensionable-age man sat in an armchair, staring into the camera bleakly, grey hair swept back and streaked with its original black. He looked like a survivor in a dystopia. In his hands was a framed photograph of an angelic, dark-haired toddler.

EXCLUSIVE: "MY SUPERSTAR SON IS ASHAMED OF ME." Elliot Owen's father gives first interview about his estrangement from the *Blood & Gold* hero and begs him to answer his calls.

"Fuck!" Edie exclaimed loudly. *"Answer his calls?"*

She skimmed down hurriedly, heart rate increasing as she did so.

"Wild, isn't it? Can't take calls he hasn't made," Elliot said. "Kind of works as a metaphor for everything untrue written about me. But they know I won't respond, so they're free to invent. I'm sure he was told what to say."

Edie read on:

"I messed up, horribly. I'd never say different," says the 62-year-old, in his spartan rented flat on the outskirts of Cardiff, a far cry from the luxury lifestyle of his 32-year-old son. Final notice bills are piled up on a side table, but David is adamant he doesn't want a penny from Owen, who's said to have netted £4 million from his latest action role. The widower is candid about his chronic alcoholism, which led to his fateful decision to get behind the wheel 29 years ago. His 27-year-old wife was killed instantly when he lost control of the vehicle in South Wales. Neither of them was wearing seat belts, and their infant son, then called Carl, was found miraculously unscathed in the footwell. David, who sustained only minor injuries, was jailed for manslaughter. His son was adopted by a barrister and his wife in Nottingham, who changed his name to Elliot.

Edie looked up. "The way he's 'David,' he's our pal, and you keep getting 'Owen,' like you're defending yourself in court!"
Elliot nodded.

"I lost the love of my life and 30 years of my life for that mistake, but losing my only child is too much," David says, finding it hard to speak with the emotion. "All I ask is that Elliot—he's still our little Carl to me—meets me, to hear my side of the story."

Edie looked up again. "You *did* hear his side of it? You saw him in prison?"

"Precisely," Elliot said. "He mentions that later on, but turns out it happened very differently to the way I remember. It's all blackmail—facilitated blackmail. Give me money or I'll keep saying you're a cold piece of shit and damaging your reputation."

Edie scrolled on.

David lost his job at a garage shortly before the accident and couldn't afford to buy his infant son Christmas presents. They were driving to see his parents in the town of Tonypandy when the accident happened. David intended to beg them for financial help. "There's no excuse for what I did that day, but I was a broken man, at rock bottom. I couldn't provide for my family. I wanted to escape my problems, so I hit the bottle. I couldn't have imagined that mistake would cost me everything."

Edie paused. "You kill your wife and you almost kill your son, and you're the victim?"

"Of course he is," Elliot said. "I was wondering why he didn't use the fact he'd no idea where I was or what I was called until that hack biographer told him I was a celebrity. Then I realized, it was because it'd show he didn't give a shit what happened to me until then."

Edie couldn't quite believe the extent of the scumbaggery.

. . . The only time that David cries during our conversation is when he says: "The thought of never meeting Carl's children, the only grandkids I'll ever have . . . that absolutely breaks my heart. When I go to sleep at night, I think about how I'm going to die, having never seen their faces."

"As if you'd ever let him anywhere near your kids after what he did to you," Edie muttered, then regretted speaking unguardedly in her rush of defensiveness.

Your kids. Their eyes met. It was a totally unbroached topic between them. Edie was thirty-six, and she knew they'd have to tackle it at some point reasonably soon. This very much didn't feel like the moment.

"Well, quite," Elliot said, after a pause.

There was only the soporific ticking of a large clock to soundtrack the tiny yet telling silence that ensued. Breaking eye contact to carry on reading was welcome.

. . . Owen gave an interview to the *Guardian* earlier this year, having become a patron of a charity for children in adoption and foster care. In it, he revealed he and David had no relationship by mutual agreement. "Not true," David says, shaking his head. "He met me once in prison after he got famous, to tell me not to embarrass him by talking to the newspapers."

Owen also told the *Guardian* that he considered his adoptive parents his "mother and father in every single meaningful sense."

"That cut like a knife, truth be told," David said, explaining he wasn't warned that Owen was going public about his background. "I know they're well-off and have provided for him, but blood is blood." He stumbles as he says this, aware of the heavy irony that Owen's beloved alter ego Prince Wulfroarer in the hit television series *Blood & Gold* was heroically loyal to his family crest. As David speaks, a man clearly laden with regret and not in good health, you can't help hoping that Elliot Owen finds some mercy for his real-life relations while there's still time.

"Haha, oh my God, this is such manipulative drivel," Edie said. "What the fuck has a character you've played got to do with it? The show also had killer bats who could survive fire—do they think that's eerily significant?"

"It's hinting: Elliot's a big fake, he's got all the power and not this poor old shattered abandoned guy who can't pay his gas bill," Elliot said. "None of it has to make sense—it builds a mood. Also, the reporter no doubt thinks what I do of my dad. But it's better copy to trash me as some ice-hearted VIP."

Edie scrolled further and reached an image of a striking young woman with shoulder-length brown hair, eyelashes spider-legged with mascara. It had the bleaching light and impassive expression of a passport booth photo. Edie put the parents' faces together and made Elliot: the hard angles and high cheekbones of his father's pinched scowl and the feminine, generous prettiness of his mum's features.

Owen's mother, Suzanne. The star was almost three years old when she was killed in the car smash that he miraculously survived.

Edie looked up at Elliot in concern, now saying nothing. She could see he knew exactly what part she was reacting to—he already knew the article by heart.

"I'd never seen her before," Elliot said, in a low voice.

"Never?" Edie said.

Elliot shook his head.

Finally, Edie fully understood the nature of this particular hurt. Elliot knew who his father was: he'd met him; he'd confronted that disappointment. And Elliot had been forewarned that some sort of tell-all was coming, even if he hoped his birth father wouldn't do it. His mother was an unknown quantity, and she'd always be that way.

"I don't think the adoption agency had much, if anything, to give my parents, bar a handful of Polaroids of me in a crib. When I found out the truth of this when I was eleven years old, I was very, very anti knowing any more. So she's only ever been a name to me. It hadn't occurred to me they'd use a picture, stupidly."

"I can't imagine how strange and . . . obscene this must feel," Edie said.

"Maybe I'm strange and obscene. Who avoids ever seeing a photo of their own mother?"

"You weren't given the choice!"

"There's a whole person I've disregarded. A person who gave birth to me. For all I know, she did what she did in getting into that car because she was scared of my father. Maybe she was drinking because he was? I mean, he's not telling the truth about me and him, is he?"

"No."

His phone started to vibrate and flash, and Edie looked down to see an international number.

She'd never known Elliot to drop a call before, but he took the phone, put it down on the hall table, and pulled Edie toward him.

"I wish I'd never done this job," he said, face buried in her shoulder, and she realized he was crying. "I fucking hate what they're able to do to me. All I do is put on masks and take them off again and avoid real life. In return, they get to say what they want about me. I've spent so much time being angry today that none of it's true, but maybe it is? Am I Carl or am I Elliot? Is Elliot a mask? I don't know who I am, Edie."

She held him tightly and said: "I do."

7

Sometimes, being with Elliot was like doubling as his security detail, making sure premises were safe for him to enter.

Instead of sweeping for explosive devices, they were scanning for excitable girls who were several proseccos deep, liable to shriek and produce phones, start collecting raw footage like amateur documentary makers. Or gangs of lads who behaved like trophy hunters, the selfie their scalp: *told you it was him.*

Usual British uptightness vanished: encountering a famous person was, in the twenty-first century, a combination of living totally in the moment and for many other moments, simultaneously. The embarrassment or pushiness didn't really matter as long as you came away with proof it had happened.

It wasn't that Elliot was in any physical danger—though Edie belatedly remembered stalkers were a thing, and he was at the level to acquire one. It was more the time-swallowing, overwhelming scrum that developed if someone recognized him in an enclosed space. Having said yes to one person, you had to say yes to everyone, and the ensuing fuss could obliterate the intended occasion.

"I have to remember that the twentieth person who asks for a picture isn't responsible for the nineteen other requests. You can't shortchange or blame anyone if you feel hassled and leave them with a bad memory," Elliot had said to her once. "It was implicit in the deal when I got the call to tell me I had the role."

Therefore, they'd come to a neighborhood Italian spot where the owners knew the Owen family of old and gave them the table furthest from other diners, and the staff knew not to ask for autographs. It still required that Elliot's parents and Edie go in ahead, secure their position, and only then, usher Elliot in.

While they were trying to catch the owner's eye, Elliot's dad, Bob, said: "If only we'd known letting him go to drama club when he was twelve would lead here, eh?"

Edie grinned.

"I do worry the latest escapade is going to make it worse," Elliot's mum said quietly. "*The Void*. I confess I'm not very interested in the jumping-off-buildings-in-a-tornado sort of films. Do you enjoy them, Edie?"

"Don't put her on the spot, Deborah!" Bob said.

"It isn't any spot—Edie's allowed her preferences, whatever our son has been up to."

"I think I'm Team Deborah on the building-jumping, though I did enjoy the *Bournes*," Edie said.

"Oh yes, was that the young man who couldn't remember who he was?" Bob said. "Some hair-raising driving in Paris in a hatchback? Very well made, I thought."

"That's him."

Edie knew Elliot's parents were bringing her into their confidence with this candor on purpose. It was signaling she was inner circle, and she appreciated it.

His parents were a vision of elegant sixty-something, middle-class solidity. They were so at ease with themselves and each other: Bob, white-haired, benign yet carrying authority; Deborah, serene and articulate with a sly sense of humor. She had a silver bob that ended in sloping points above a swan neck, and she was wearing a coat like a belted dressing gown, made of berry-colored cashmere.

As they maneuvered Elliot into the far corner of a table where he couldn't easily be identified or easily photographed, Edie thought on the irrevocability of fame, of all the unintended consequences.

She'd wondered if tonight might be strained, if the timing had been thrown off by David in Cardiff's fictions.

In fact, the exact opposite was the case; adversity made it shine brighter.

They didn't discuss Elliot's haloed career; instead, it was the urine that kept mysteriously appearing in an herb planter by the Owen front door.

"Fraz insisted the wee was from"—Elliot snapped a breadstick—"'either a passing tinker, a gentleman of the road'—I mean, it's not an area known for vagrancy—'kids in high spirits'—or, my favorite hypothesis—'a fox.' Why would a fox be having a slash in that? I mean, it's a wild animal? What's it neatly urinating in a piece of whimsical pottery for?!"

Edie started laughing.

"Then Fraz gets really creative and comes up with the theory that it's someone who knows it's my family home," Elliot said. "Cheeky little git. Anyway, long story short, Mum and Dad got Ring Video. Can you guess who the mystery boot filler has been identified as? In a M. Night Shyamalan–sized twist?"

Elliot's father shook his head in headmasterly disapproval, making it even funnier to Edie.

"Was it . . . Fraser?" she gasped out.

Elliot clapped. "Now, Edie got there straightaway. So why these two bought into the idea it was a targeted harassment campaign, I have NO IDEA . . . I know not all my work has been McKellen's *Lear* at Stratford standard, but suggesting I'd attract doorway pissers is a bit much."

They all died at this, Elliot rolled his eyes, and Edie felt such ease with them.

His parents politely asked after her family and her work, and she told them about her promotion running an office.

"You didn't mention that?" Elliot said, looking mildly perplexed amid the chorus of congratulations.

"I've not had a chance—it was only yesterday I got the call," she said.

"Well done," Elliot said, a little blankly.

Edie knew what he was thinking: it wouldn't suit skipping off for three weeks on the West Coast anytime soon. She was hardly going to look that gift horse in the mouth and say, *errrmmm, I've got a boyfriend?* like a Valley Girl.

She would've classed it a perfect evening until she went to the ladies' and a young woman in denim dress, hair up in a banana clip, loitered and pounced when she left the cubicle.

"Excuse me, is that Elliot Owen you're with?"

"Er. Yeah?" Edie didn't know what else to say.

"Could you ask your brother if I can have a picture with him?"

"He's having a quiet night tonight, but he might do one before he leaves—I'll ask."

Why did you assume I was his sister? WHY? circled round Edie's head like breaking news ticker tape as she washed her hands.

Edie had seen her general appeal as a person decimated on-line after the Jack Marshall Incident; no wonder she had paranoia about unworthiness. The words of her tormentors were tattooed on her brain forever. She'd imagined their greatest hits etched on her headstone: *Here Lies a Pig in a Ribbon. No One Did, Indeed, Ever Marry That.*

Edie had under one minute, while the girl washed her hands alongside her, to decide on a gamble. If Denim Dress's assumption was made for uncomplimentary reasons, it would be excruciating for both of them. If Edie didn't ask, it would live on rent-free in her head.

Before she hit the button on the hand dryer, Edie said: "Sorry. Can I ask—Elliot's not my brother. Why did you think he was my brother?"

The girl froze in surprise. "You've got the same color hair? You look like each other."

She said it easily enough and with a confused expression that told Edie it was the truth. She looked like she shared DNA with him?! Fortune favors the brave.

"Ahhh. *Thank you!*" Edie pushed her hands under the jet blast of the Dyson.

She organized a quick photo for Denim Dress before they left, Edie beaming and full of ravioli and goodwill.

8

On the walk home, Elliot's mother twitched Edie's sleeve, abruptly fascinated in how a house they passed had got a profusion of magenta bougainvillea to grow "in that lovely arched shape."

It was a few moments, and suggesting twine was involved, before Edie twigged that Deborah was inventing a pretext to hang back and put some distance between them and Elliot and his father.

"Edie, I'm sorry if this is overbearing or too much, too soon. My son's happiness matters to me too much not to risk grabbing this chance to speak to you."

"OK," Edie said, abruptly very worried. And things had been going so well. What was coming? *Now, I know a "pre-nup" seems unromantic . . .*

"Could we keep the fact we've spoken between us? Elliot's naturally very protective of you, and I don't know if he'd judge this outrageously overstepping."

Edie was now wondering what she needed protecting from. She didn't know if she objected until she knew what this was, but to say so felt combative.

"This sounds ominous . . ." she said more neutrally, trying not to make it clear her teeth were practically rattling.

"Oh, I hope it's not! I'm flapping. Bob and I are utterly thrilled you and Elliot have worked it out. You're remarkably good for him. There are so many girls who'd fall at his feet, and that's useless. I assume he told you what happened today? The story with his biological father?"

Edie nodded. "Yes, unfortunately."

"Elliot has this curse of appearing to cope when he's not coping. He makes sure everyone else is all right and ignores and denies his own needs. He was like that as a very little boy. You'd think coming from the chaos he had that he'd have been badly behaved or difficult, but he was like a tiny adult, checking I'd remembered my house keys. He had to be a grown-up, because the first grown-ups he knew weren't safe."

"I can see that," Edie said.

"When you had your time apart, Elliot talked about you a lot. I worried about him, how desolate he'd be if he heard you'd met someone else, and alone with his thoughts in some hotel room. His ever-tactful brother told him to cheer up because 'he has everything' and Elliot replied that none of it meant anything without you."

Edie flushed with pleasure. She wished she could enjoy his mother ratting him out like this, but the fact it was a preamble made her wary. Did she think they were unhealthily infatuated? Or that Edie had blown hot and cold?

". . . So, I hope you don't mind, he told me about your mother."

Oh. *Right.* Here we go. Edie steeled herself, hoping this wasn't a *go to counseling and don't bring any incipient mental illness into our family* speech. Edie had googled *is postnatal depression hereditary* herself. She'd be stiffly polite if it was, for Elliot's sake, even though it was a weaponization of a tragedy against her.

"I don't mind that he told you," Edie said honestly, thinking what she might mind would come next.

"It set me thinking. Aside from the obvious reasons you both get on so well, as bright young things . . ."

"Hah. Youngish."

"I don't know if this has occurred to you, but both you and Elliot have known profound loss and abandonment, at young

51

ages. I think there's a very deep level of understanding between you as a result."

"I hadn't thought of that," Edie said, rather startled that she hadn't. She'd thought their traumas were very different.

"I say 'abandonment'—I know your mother was very ill, and I am sure she didn't want to leave you."

"It's how it's felt at times, even if that wasn't what it was."

Deborah nodded. Edie saw now why she was keen to keep this exchange from Elliot. Heck of a pep talk. Twenty minutes ago, they were doing coffees and Ferrero Rocher.

". . . It's a very deep bond, as I say. I fear it could equally cause mistrust and push you apart, if you don't recognize it's there— especially with all the silly hoopla that surrounds my son."

"You mean we'd worry about . . . fidelity?" Edie said, too interested in what Deborah had to say to be embarrassed.

Edie realized at that moment, like being caught in a second's sun beam, a God ray on a chilly day, how she missed this kind of loving, knowledgeable maternal concern. There was no substitute.

"About fidelity, about careers, money. Anything, really," his mum said. "Don't let it, whatever it is, trigger the ongoing fear that, somehow, someone you love that much will leave."

Edie couldn't form a reply for a moment as she absorbed the weight of this.

Deborah glanced over. "Oh goodness, sorry! This has been such a lovely evening, and look at how I've ruined it! Bob always says I never really retired."

"What did you do?"

"I was a psychotherapist. I trained when the boys were little. It was to help Elliot, really. We didn't have the same understanding then about the body 'keeping score' and so on, but I knew he'd not been unaffected by his start in life. The attitude was that the first few years are 'pre-memory,' but of course now we know that nothing is."

Edie said: "Thank you for talking to me about this. *Really* thank you, not polite thank you."

"Oh gosh, I'm so relieved you're not offended. The stakes couldn't be higher for him where you're concerned, and . . . well . . . he's an extraordinary person, but vulnerable in ways only his close family understand. For years after he came to us, he was having nightmares so bad, the GP would've had us drugging him. I said absolutely not, of course."

"He was?" Edie said, freshly appalled.

"Oh yes. Some part of his psyche remembers his parents, re-members being put in danger. This is deathly private stuff, and I'd not say this to any girlfriend, Edie—I never have. But I trust you, and I trust his taste."

She squeezed Edie's arm, both in approval and to alert her to the fact that Elliot and his dad had stopped ahead of them and would soon be in hearing range.

Edie turned and hugged her. "Thank you, Deborah. I promise I won't repeat it, and I'm so glad he has you."

"WHAT WAS ALL that conspiring with my mum about?" Elliot said later in a half whisper in bed.

His parents were leaving at first light to visit Bob's sister in Cornwall, and she and Elliot had discreetly established between themselves that, given they'd have the house to themselves tomorrow, tonight could be respectfully chaste and involve pajamas.

Therefore, they were holding hands and talking like teens at a sleepover.

"She was thanking me for the charitable outreach of dating her undatable son."

"Funnily enough, I suspect she *was* saying something like that. She's been terrified my career prevents me having an in quotes 'normal relationship' with a nice person for ages. Now you're here, I'm sure she's taking no chances."

Edie adjusted her thinking, pondered that she'd shortchanged what she knew of Elliot's parents by wondering if they wanted him to bring home a glamorous Somebody. They wanted him to be happy. If it looked like she could achieve that, she was somebody. The values in this house resided in the right place.

"Edie," Elliot said, sotto voce. "Earlier you said 'your kids' to me. Sorry if I'm being paranoid, but I feel like assuming you're thinking the way I am has got me into trouble in the past . . ."

Edie held her breath. Uh-oh. That Big Conversation. She'd probably had enough of those today.

"Did you phrase it that way 'cos, option one, we've not talked about that yet and you didn't want to presume I'd have them with you? Or, option two, because you see our thing as a very intense rekindling that will quite possibly burn out, and if so, we'll go have kids with other people? Or, option three, you're letting me know you don't want them?"

"Emphatically, option one," Edie said. "Which are you?"

"Also one—that's a relief." Elliot paused. "I've not brought it up because whatever you want or don't want is fine by me."

"That's how I feel."

"OK. Thank God this was easy—I needed some easy," he said.

"We're being forced against our will to face up to our huge compatibility," Edie whispered.

She felt Elliot relax. She should try reassurance more often and was perhaps guilty of thinking he didn't need it.

"I'm so glad you're here," Elliot said. "Sorry everything was more fraught than intended earlier."

She could tell he was awkward about having broken down in front of her, and she didn't blame him. Edie recalled loathing her own public fainting and weeping fit on his set when being trolled online, what felt a lifetime ago.

"I very much want to be here for anything fraught or less fraught and all stories about your incontinent brother."

Elliot groaned and laughed, squeezing her in tacit gratitude.

As he went to sleep, Edie looked up at the slab of night sky in the window above them and thought that, while it was true they had compatibility, they didn't have stability. Today was yet another reminder that their village was built inside a volcano.

9

"Oh, I forgot to tell you, you got away with the Christmas Day selfie. The ruination of your maidenhood with me remains a dirty secret," Elliot said conversationally at the breakfast bar.

Edie leaned over the expanse of marble worktop separating them and kissed his two-day bestubbled cheek.

"What was that for?"

"Looking accidentally beautiful while eating a croissant."

"So do you. Though you've got some in your hair," Elliot said, brushing lightly above her ear.

Edie felt this was the likely outcome when she was trying to be accidentally beautiful plus pastry. The unexpected contact sent a tremor down her.

"How do you know I got away with it?"

"My publicist, Lillian, got a call from a bloke at the *Mail* and successfully convinced him that I was in America. And that it must be an old photo if it even was me, and that I was definitely single. It probably helped that she really believed what she was saying because obviously I'd yet to tell her any different."

"Oh, right," Edie said. She was relieved the unscheduled announcement wasn't being made. It was, however, a qualified relief, as the issue of how it *was* made remained. She was certainly glad Jessica didn't get to be town crier.

"Lillian wants a Zoom with you to say hi. Is the day after tomorrow OK? Is it all right if I pass your number on?"

Edie froze, mid-chewing, and frog-swallowed. "Say hi? To me? Why?"

Elliot started laughing and then couldn't stop.

"What?!" Edie wailed.

"Why do you always look like you've been caught wanking in a hedgerow by flashlight whenever anything comes up to do with this becoming public? Am I that big an embarrassment to you?!"

Edie reddened. "How dare you accuse me of hedge wanking!"

When Elliot had recovered, he said: "It's absolutely by the numbers stuff, dos and don'ts about calling her if a reporter's bothering you. I told her we were in a committed relationship—I hope that was allowed. Though I'm starting to wonder . . ." He grinned at Edie. "I will be arriving at Carrington in a bedsheet with spectacles over the top, and if anyone asks, I'm Chris Pine."

Edie snorted and muttered yes to Lillian, though she thought it was pretty weird to have a job interview about seeing someone. How had this happened? She could barely get a plausible match on Hinge for the rest of her thirties. From The Girl Nobody Chose (© Louis) to The Girl He Chose.

"Actually, I need to talk to you about something else work-related before I go," Elliot said.

"OK?"

They'd agreed Elliot's dawn departure wasn't a good fit with Edie staying over in a house with a high-tech burglar alarm system, so the plan was to part ways early evening. She was additionally dismayed they'd be having separate New Year's Eves, despite having investigated the feasibility of Edie going over there. The stubborn timing made it two days in the air to be ships that passed in the night.

No point complaining. It was what it was. He was who he was.

"It's about a role I might take."

"Right."

"That involves a sex scene."

"A what?" Edie said, adopting the stillness of a lizard. She remembered a howlingly discomfiting interview for the autobiography they'd done together when she'd asked Elliot about this subject. Then, it was agonizing as she wasn't meant to care. Now, it was agony because she did.

"Not like X-rated filth!" Elliot said, seeing she was mildly stunned.

But it was too late: Edie felt like an idiot potato.

She was continually thrown off-balance by him: one minute it was trattoria carbonara and *meet the folks*, and she was lulled into the illusion of a standard boyfriend. The next, she was being ambushed by Ridiculous Things That Never Happened. Who did you go to for advice on this?

That Elliot was going to kiss other women (or men) as pretend was, as he'd put it, always implicit in the deal. Amid all the logistics, such frivolities had been overlooked. Edie felt a crushing pressure to be a Cool Girl about it, and she didn't know if she was.

"I won't do it if you don't want me to do it. I mean it," Elliot was saying. "You matter more than any part. There won't be any bargaining or anything—if you aren't feeling all right, it's not worth it."

"I'm thinking if it needs this sort of buildup, it must be farmyard stuff," Edie said, interrupting to try to reclaim some ground.

Did she say no and sabotage his career? Or did she say yes and wreck her head?

"There's no nudity . . ." Elliot paused. "Or at least, *I'm* not nude."

"Elliot," Edie said abruptly, as yet again she'd not considered this possibility. (How? Denial, that was how.) "Don't wind me up. What exactly needs my permission?"

"The show is a dramedy called *Your Table Is Ready*, about this hectic restaurant in Manhattan in the 1990s that everyone who's anyone wants to go to."

"This is what you're going to New York for tomorrow?"

"Yup. I play front of house, maître d' guy Matteo, and he and Gaby, the head waitress, have this Bruce Willis, Cybill Shepherd in *Moonlighting* bickering, love-hate, sexual-tension dynamic. In the last episode of the first series, they're fighting after service and end up, y'know, grappling with each other."

"*Grappling?*"

"As in, the enemies-to-lovers thing abruptly explodes from the first to the second."

Edie's heart leaped at *explodes*, and she tried to banish mental imagery of spurting.

"You've already signed up for it?"

"I've said yes in principle, but contracts aren't signed yet. I can easily get my agent to haggle this scene. They won't lose me over it, I feel sure."

"Who plays Gaby?"

Elliot replied, with incredible insouciance as far as Edie was concerned: "Ines Herrera."

Edie stifled a *YOU FUCKIN' WHAT?!* and substituted it for a deliberately unimpressed: "Ah."

Ines Herrera, for God's sake. When she told Nick and Hannah, it would be what Nick called a "marmalade dropping" moment. Her name was synonymous with outrageously sexy.

Was there a Reddit thread to help Edie, here? *My Boyfriend Will Be Enthusiastically Simulating Coitus On-screen In Front of Millions With The Guatemalan Julia Roberts. Any Tips Or Hints On Retaining My Chill? PS It Will Probably Go Viral, Become A Cultural Touchstone For Frenzied Eroticism And A Meme Captioned With Things Like "Me Versus Jaffa Cakes" So I Am Ambushed With It Three Times A Week.*

10

"What does it involve?" Edie asked. "Apart from the obvious."

"Well . . ." Elliot got down from his seat, walked over to a bag slung on the kitchen table, and rummaged, producing a wad of A4 held by a bulldog clip.

"I was going to suggest you read the script. Then you know exactly what I know, and I can't misrepresent it in any way. This is episode eight at the end of the first season."

He handed it over.

"Why does it have your name across it in big letters on every page?" Edie said, leafing through.

"The watermark? If the pages get out, they know whose script it is and can collar whoever leaked it. Welcome to the showbiz jungle, baby. Nobody knows anything, and no one trusts anyone."

"I thought you were too senior for that."

"Oh, no one is. They'd shout at my agent first, though."

He gave her a winning smile. Edie smiled back and yet felt weak and sick. She wanted Elliot to herself; it was very early days to consider sharing like this.

She better understood why actors often dated other actors: it'd help if she had any reference points in her own career. She didn't have to French-kiss and fake-fondle the guys at the Vienna beef hot dog account.

"Got time now?" Elliot said. "Softer seat?"

They went through to the sitting room, with its two overstuffed sofas making a right angle.

Edie lay down on one, hooking her sixty-denier-stockinged

ankles over the arm, and began reading. Elliot lay out on the other, phone scrolling.

Her initial intention was to get the gist, as she was seven episodes behind, and then start skipping forward to find the rubbish. Very soon, Edie had forgotten that was why she was reading it.

Within ten pages, she was completely absorbed; after twenty pages, she realized that she straight-up loved it. She laughed. She caught her breath. She couldn't turn the pages fast enough to find out what happened next. Edie muttered one zinging Gaby line aloud to commit it to memory.

"Enjoying it?" Elliot said, and Edie nodded.

She felt like she knew these people, despite not being conversant with the fast-paced world of substance-fueled hospitality in the Big Apple, circa the Clinton administration.

And oh my God—she was, inconveniently, *achingly* desperate for fast-talking, charming-yet-damaged Matteo and whip-smart, insecure firecracker Gaby to shag. Even while she wanted Matteo to not be that man, right there. That said, imagining Elliot somewhat enhanced it, too. What a psychological mess this was.

When Edie got to The Scene, she didn't exhale for the four pages it took for them to spit insults, accuse the other of a crappy attitude, and deliver the mutual ultimatum that one of them was going to have to go—before they realized they didn't, in fact, only crave the other's absence.

As their fictional mouths met, Edie went warm and cold and physically felt things. *Neither of them can quite believe what they're doing, and yet neither of them can stop . . .*

Fade to credits.

Edie sat bolt upright and waved the script accusingly. "What was the word you used—*grappling*?!"

"Yeah," Elliot replied, also shifting to sit up and looking intimidated.

"More like you *devour each other* in a deranged level of desire. Your face makes contact with her chest quite explicitly."

Edie had to euphemize the nipple in mouth to cope.

"OK, look, I won't do it. I really want the role, but I am fairly sure they want me back, so I'll make it a condition they tone it down . . ."

"No!" Edie cried, startling Elliot even more. "It's so hot, and you have to do it! You can't pay off the mad buildup of Matteo and Gaby without this."

". . . OK," Elliot said, frowning. "Is this a trap?"

"No," Edie said, grinning at last. "I loved it so much. I even love that scene. I don't love you tearing away Ines Herrera's bra like a hungry wolf, but I'm still not going to ruin this piece of art. Just swear to me on your family's lives you don't fancy her."

"Oh my God! You loved it?! I loved it, too! The script I mean, not the wolf bra stuff."

"I'm going to need the promise."

"Ines? I swear. I've only met her on Zoom, and she seemed nice enough, but she gives her tiny dogs those hairdos with ribbons. I'm too busy fancying you. You honestly loved it?"

"Yes, I truly did," Edie said. "I can't believe how much. When The Cranberries' 'Linger' comes on the jukebox, in the half dark and they're alone! The way they stare at each other, and the whole mood twists and changes during the opening bars when they've ranted themselves to a standstill. And Gaby seizes him right on the words *it's just your attitude* . . . Massive swoon."

Edie sighed, with a degree of wistful lust.

Elliot put his phone aside. "Yeah, the script really conjures up an atmosphere, doesn't it? There's so much dialogue to learn, the way they talk at a mile a minute. I'm so pleased they brought it to me, because there'd be a long queue to play Matteo."

"It's going to be a huge hit."

As she said those words, Edie realized that this might in fact be the bittersweet part, not the topless snogging. Goodbye to Elliot moving back here for another five years, at least.

An inner voice, Margot's voice, whispered: *He never was going to, darling.*

"This response is beyond my wildest dreams," Elliot said. "*Not* to the sex. To be honest, I was half hoping you would object because I'm shitting myself about doing that justice. The rest of it."

"Only thing is, did you ever read the memoir by Robert Evans, the Hollywood producer? He said he deserved to lose Ali MacGraw because he left her on her own to make a film with Steve McQueen," Edie said. "As in: what was obviously going to happen?"

"Right . . ." Elliot said, smiling at her with starry eyes. She'd forgot how easy it was to impress even enlightened men by reading the books that they did.

"Am I freely and foolhardily letting you make *The Getaway* with Steve McQueen?"

Elliot gazed at her with a look of purest adoration that was as much reassurance as anything he was about to say. "I've got no interest in anyone I work with in that way—none. But the only thing that can really prove that to you is my word, plus time."

Edie nodded. She had unfortunately figured out that only by this becoming something she was used to would it ever not be intimidating.

"I'm so thrilled you like it, you know. Now I'm making this show for you," Elliot said.

He looked up at her under his brow, with dark eyes. He must be fully aware of his effect and unfair advantages in that moment.

"Is Fraser definitely not coming back today?" Edie asked.

"No . . . ?" Elliot said.

"I've got an idea."

She led him upstairs by the hand to the bedroom.

"OK, you can sit down there." She gestured at the bed.

Edie climbed onto Elliot, pushing him backward and pinning him down by the wrists.

"Tell me you *can't stand the disregard that I show to everyone, most of all, to me. No, actually, most of all, toward YOURSELF.*"

Elliot was both laughing and muttering "What the fuck?" under his breath.

"Say it! I want you to be FUMING."

"In a British accent or the American one?"

SOME TIME LATER, they lay side by side, staring up together at the skylight, in a sort of stoned haze.

"I mean," Elliot said, eventually, "there's taking it well, and then whatever that was."

11

Edie tapped her fingers as her apprehensiveness prickled. Elliot had passed on her number to his publicist, and here she was, him now Stateside, her still struggling to understand why this was necessary. Her laptop was on her old makeup table in her bedroom, and she was praying Meg didn't noisily slam the front door below when she came in from her Sunday shift shouting "MY MANAGER IS A FULL SHITEHAWK," midmeeting.

She'd reminded Meg, but Meg sometimes respected society's norms and other times decided society needed Megging up a bit.

Ping.

Elliot's publicist Lillian sprang into full-screen life. She was fifty-something, dark-haired, with shrewd eyes behind large black-framed glasses, and had the white shirt and minimal jewelry look of the tastefully wealthy.

She reminded Edie a little of the makeup artist Bobbi Brown, except she seemed more likely to read Edie her Miranda rights than recommend she contour her nose.

"Hi! Edie?" she boomed.

"Hi, yes! Nice to meet you. You're Lil—"

"Elliot tells me you're in a serious relationship."

Oof, OK.

"Yes."

"We're going to discuss how we manage this in the press."

65

"Right."

In this line of work, in sparkling offices in Manhattan (offices, on a Sunday? Maybe her home office?), you obviously didn't waste energy trying to ingratiate yourself without purpose. You're not in Kansas now, Dorothy.

"The difficulty we have in launching this relationship is that the images already in the public domain are negative," Lillian said. "We've seen a quarrel between you both in the street, and you making aggressive gestures."

Edie felt she was being told off. "That's the V-sign—it's popular here," Edie said, deciding that even if her humor went down badly, she was still going to use it.

"We can translate it into the American," Lillian said, and Edie couldn't tell if she was being dryly funny or merely literal.

"We weren't a couple then," Edie added redundantly, and Lillian regarded her coolly through her Prada eyewear, as if Edie had mistaken her for a relationship counselor.

"My advice in future is never lose your temper or argue—it makes the photos more valuable. If someone puts a camera in your face after a meal out and insults you to get a reaction, keep your head down. And hold his hand, so they can't use the pictures to claim you had a fight."

Edie nodded. She was going into witness protection.

"My suggestion to move the narrative forward from the fracas in *Noddingham*—we stage paparazzi photos, somewhere cute, maybe Central Park? Affectionate. Coffee cups. Woolens. Linking arms. Make it clear you've put that initial volatility behind you."

"*Stage* them?" Edie repeated. "Why would we do that? Elliot doesn't need to be more famous?"

Lillian removed her glasses, which Edie suspected she only did when addressing spectacular dipshits. "Do you want to go to restaurants, to cafés and bars, to parties with Elliot? Do you want to buy your own groceries and get your own flat whites, or send someone to get them?"

"Is this a trick question?"

Edie was starting to not like Lillian very much. She wasn't doing anything wrong.

"My point is: pictures will be taken anyway. We can control them, or not. We can write the story, or they will."

". . . The game is out there; it's either play or get played," Edie said. "That's Omar in *The Wire*."

Lillian flickered a smile. Breakthrough.

"Whenever new photos land, I'm going to give them an *unnamed source, close to you both* quote saying you're a healthy match for Elliot, not awed by his success—try to reframe those earlier images as a positive. Spunky British girl, heart in the right place. The whole kinda lovable Bridget Jones thing."

Lillian held her palms up and moved them in outward circles, like she was washing a window, and Edie feared she was gesturing at Edie's imaginary bum.

"Why don't you get his parents to say they like me? I'm fairly sure they do."

Lillian did a perceptible double take as she put her glasses back on. "Parents are quoted saying they like you when there's an engagement, not before."

"Oh," said Edie, as chastened as a primary schooler. She appreciated Lillian was allowing for Edie not being the Zoom-meeting girlfriend in six months' time, and maybe Edie should, too.

". . . But I don't really care what the press say about our relationship, if they have no real information?"

Lillian blanched. "You are a private citizen. Elliot is not. His career can be affected by the coverage of his private life. If it's mishandled, it becomes an image problem. Studios hire the whole package."

"Really? That's so . . . unfair."

"You think Ben Affleck got offered good roles by serious directors, twenty years ago, when he became a joke and a sideshow with Jennifer Lopez?"

Edie had never pondered the range of Ben Affleck's creative opportunities. "At least it worked out for them as a couple in the end."

"There are missing years on his résumé he'll never get back. Do you have any bitter exes likely to do stories?"

This was like a smear test for your lifestyle.

Lillian squinted at a note out of shot. "This Jack Marshall guy going to be a problem?"

Edie flinched at the thoroughness of her research and at that name. "Not an ex, and no."

"Are there any nudes or explicit videos of you? Anything where you're doing drugs?"

"Haha, what?" said Edie, guffawing, then remembering Lillian wasn't up for jokes. "Er, no, none. I'm old. And shy. And too broke for cocaine."

"None? At all?" Lillian said, in the same tone a GP disbelieved your alcohol units per week. "On your camera roll, even unsent?"

"Why would that matter?!"

"Because in an iCloud hack, they can get hold of those, too."

In that moment, Edie broke into a light sweat. She'd exited the world where images of her had little more currency than any other woman's. She had a bounty on her head and would be shot by hunters with Canon DSLRs.

Edie remembered the second time she'd met Elliot, an interview in a suburban pub, and in the few minutes where ripples of recognition erupted around them, it was like zombies sniffing a human in their midst.

Now her flesh was tasty, too. Fuck.

"No face recognition for unlocking your phone, or someone can wave it in front of you and open it. Passcode security only. I think that's everything for now," Lillian said, having destroyed Edie's peace of mind and struck fear into her very core.

"Thank God for that," Edie said, curt, smiling tightly.

"Listen," Lillian said, "take this thought away with you. I'm not your parent. I'm not interviewing you for a position. I'm not the neighborhood women you have wine with. You don't need to worry about being judged by me. I don't officially care what you've done unless it's illegal, and unofficially, I still won't care if it is. Disclosure is all I care about. If there's something you need to warn me about, the earlier you tell me, the better I can help you. Wait for me to find out on DeuxMoi along with everyone else, and we're playing catch-up."

"I'll bear that in mind," Edie said, now disturbed that she had no idea what a DeuxMoi was.

"Nice to have met you, Edie," Lillian said, before pressing *Leave Meeting* by way of farewell, and Edie thought: *was it, though?*

Edie flopped down on her bed and stared at the ceiling, as the enormity of what she had agreed to by kissing Elliot Owen on Christmas Day a few short days ago finally sank in. Faustian pacts had never looked fitter.

She had acquired huge bragging rights and lost her ones to privacy.

12

Edie was letting herself into the new office on the first floor of a converted lace factory. Its huge industrial metal pillars were painted a jaunty matte lilac, and the cavernous space was dotted with leggy, air-purifying plants left behind by the last inhabitants.

Two desks and a neon Ad Hoc wall logo had arrived, and some sweet-talking of the deliverymen saw the latter hung on the far wall.

Edie had firmly instructed herself to learn from the dramatic turnaround in her circumstances.

Not so long ago, every aspect of her existence had, not to overstate matters, sucked golf balls through a hosepipe.

Wrecked social life, knackered reputation, professional life in turmoil, tossed aside by a worthless man, reviled by many, loved by few, and exiled to the one place she didn't want to be, with a family she didn't know how to relate to.

Now look. *Just look.* She wasn't smug—it wasn't in her nature, and she was, as Elliot said, too much of a catastrophist.

But Edie knew to properly value this remarkable recovery, to back pocket the lesson for the future. Even when everything seems several hundred shades of shat-upon, you can come back from it. You might even benefit.

If Jack hadn't kissed her at that wedding, Richard might not have given her the project with Elliot, and they'd never have met. Unthinkable.

She daydreamed constantly since she last saw him. They'd not been able to put each other down when her cab arrived, and she'd shed a few tears at parting. Seeing her distress, Elliot had said:

"Sod it, I'll come with you and leave from yours at half five instead." En route, Meg had texted that she was going to kip at their dad's. Inevitably, when Elliot's airport ride pulled up, tailgate lights cutting through the fog like evil red eyes at that horrific hour, they'd not been to sleep.

Memories of shared confidences and intimacies by the glow of the chili fairy lights kept making Edie smile, feel shy, or shiver.

Once he'd left, she went back to bed and slept until midday, waking up to find a WhatsApp that she'd since reread seventy-eight times.

I've got a pint of black coffee with two sugars in the BA lounge, and I look like I've been exhumed by detectives who want to run toxicology tests to prove foul play. In a hailstorm. I wouldn't change a thing. Be mine forever? x

There weren't many commuters grinning like a lovesick clot in the first grey week back in January.

On the Friday morning that her sole team member, Declan, was due to start, Edie made sure she was in her seat, laptop open, at a frankly magnificent twenty past eight. She was a victim of her own excellence, as it was too early to get coffees and pastries without them going cold. Edie reckoned she'd trot out once she had settled Declan in.

They'd exchanged cordial messages confirming the location, in which it was impossible to gauge much about each other.

Edie had intended to use the extra time to check emails and be hyperefficient, but she ended up browsing gastropub menus in the Dales for tomorrow's trip with Nick and Hannah. The break hadn't fallen at an ideal time, leaving Declan on his own at the start of next week, but at least they had a day to get acquainted.

The clock ticked to nine, then ten past, then half past. No sign of Declan. Edie segued from surprise to judgment.

Not the greatest indicator, she thought. *If you can't be arsed to be punctual on day one, what else will you be sloppy about?* Pardon her for sounding like Margaret Thatcher, but it was an issue of respect to not roll up forty-five minutes after the fact.

He's never been here before. Maybe he's got lost, she chided herself. Then remembered, if so, he could call her. Mobile phones had ruined the middling excuse: nowadays, this sort of thing meant either huge crisis or flagrant etiquette misdemeanor.

Or, she could contact him?

Hi Declan, checking you're OK and can find the place? Let me know if I should come down and collect you! ☺

Two blue ticks, read instantly, yet minutes passed by and nothing back. *Wow, OK.*

Had Richard sent her a problem? Richard wouldn't have knowingly sent her a problem, so it'd have to be more sinister than that: someone who'd fooled Richard. Edie didn't think such an employee existed.

Oh God, unless this was the nefarious plan from day one? Jessica running interference? Disrupt the operation, tell a different story to Richard, besmirch Edie's capabilities. Choose someone he liked in Declan, who was what counterterrorism called a *cleanskin,* someone with no convictions who didn't fit the profile.

Admittedly, perhaps leaping straight to this sort of MI5 chat was paranoia.

Edie had always hated snitching, even before she became a prime snitch target. Yet by ten a.m., she wondered if she should just call Richard. *Bet you'd reply to contact made by him, huh.* If this was going to be warfare, keeping secrets for the other side wouldn't help her.

At five past ten, the door of the office banged open dramatically. A tall, lean, disarranged man of about thirty, holding a bike helmet, stepped unsteadily, glassy-eyed, over the threshold.

"Good morning, is it Edie? Hello! I'm so sorry I'm late—I've had a bit of a scrape," Declan said, in a strong Irish accent, which immediately made this information sound as if it was a charming gambit in a bucolic romantic comedy. "I think I was unconscious for a wee while. At least, I lost quarter to nine until about half past."

"Oh fuck! What happened?"

"A car knocked me off my bike. I woke up on a roundabout. I was zooming along like *I've got this Nottingham thing cracked*. Then crack."

"You're bleeding!" Edie said, pointing at the red mark that was flowering through his white shirt at waist height.

Declan looked down, swiping a luxuriant amount of his brown hair out of his eyes. "Aw, shit. So I am."

"You're really pale?"

He had that distinct quality of grey-green, about-to-boak clammy that couldn't be confused with his Celtic fairness.

"I am?" Declan put a hand to his glossily sweaty face.

"Declan, you shouldn't be here—you need to go to the hospital! Why did you come in?"

"I didn't want to make a bad impression."

There was a beat of silence, and they both laughed.

"Let me help you." Edie ran over to guide him to a chair, bearing his weight with some difficulty as he staggered. He was surely six foot two at least; if he fell onto her, it'd be like a skyscraper demolition.

She'd seen a first aid box in the corner and soon found gauze bandages inside.

"Uhm, do you want to . . . Or shall I . . . ?" she muttered,

73

realizing Declan was semi out of it and she was going to have to play nurse.

"Maybe if you pull your shirt up?" she said timidly, as he stood, unbuttoned it, and yanked it over his shoulders. *Ah, OK.* Edie did the obligatory teeth-sucking at the sight of blood: "That's quite a nasty graze."

Declan looked down and grimaced. The fact he was woozy made partial unclothedness and their physical contact less peculiar for him, Edie thought. Or certainly the lesser of his problems.

Meanwhile, Edie was fully sentient that she was winding a roll of cloth round a man's bare abdomen when she'd been expecting to ask him his Starbucks muffin order.

She kept up inane chatter to defuse any Indiana Jones and Marion energy flying around the room, but Declan swayed dangerously and caught hold of her to steady himself, so they were momentarily clasping each other. It jolted Edie. There was a definite jolt.

"Sorry, sorry, this is a bit much . . ." Declan said, and Edie said: "It's fine!" in her most chipper and very normal voice.

She got Declan some water and made some phone calls in the stairwell. They confirmed: 1. His being conscious and able-bodied enough to push his bike half a mile meant it was a taxi to A&E, not blue lights, and 2. Richard wanted her to lock up the office for as long as it took and keep him company.

When she came back in, Declan was looking angst-ridden, holding his phone.

"Now, I know the WebMD doomscroll is for suckers, but I've been researching head injuries and found out about this thing called the Talk and Die Syndrome."

He read from his handset: "*The person may appear fine initially and be quite talkative. They insist they're well because there isn't too much pressure on the brain yet. At some point, they worsen, lapse into a coma and brain death gradually occurs."*

"Sounds like exactly like any office job—you'll be fine," Edie said.

Declan burst out laughing, before wincing at the pressure on his wound.

"If this is my final *lucid interval* before the darkness takes me," Declan said, "I can already tell you're the right person to spend it with."

13

A wait with no end in sight was a baptism by fire for new acquaintances. Edie and Declan had hour upon hour of conversation to find after they arrived at A&E and no reference points for the other beyond sharing an employer.

Edie had kept to herself at Ad Hoc, with one dismal exception, and it had left her unprotected by a clique when scandal hit. She'd not expected to make friends since. She didn't have managed expectations so much as very low ones.

Yet she and Declan seemed to share a wavelength. If he was acting in bad faith, he was an even better actor than Edie's love interest.

Once they'd compared general notes on the agency's most colorful and trying clients, she learned he had vivacious twenty-five-year-old twin sisters on whom he clearly doted. He was evidently very close to his family in his Dublin suburb of Drumcondra. He had a thing for climbing mountains, shared Edie's love of Adam Buxton podcasts and *Twin Peaks*, and laughed easily and often.

Edie liked a generous laugh: her forays into online dating had taught her that men who could only assess and compete were absolute chores.

"Why did you accept the Nottingham gig?" Edie said, cracking the ring pull on a Diet Coke. "I heard it was a very tough sell to the Ad Hoccers."

"Ah well, I've never been here before, so I thought it'd be exploration." Declan sipped his 7UP. "A chance to discover a new realm."

"Hahaha. Like those Winter Wonderland experiences where the headline says *BLUNDERLAND*. The elves are all swearing and smoking, there's a dads' brawl in the Gingerbread House, and Rudolph is a depressed Alsatian in a tiara. Kidding, obviously— I'm very fond."

"Hahahaha. Santa's on the sex offender register. Nah, I'm not a London person," Declan said. "Been there two years and the experiment had concluded. I like fewer people and open spaces. Do you like being nearer your family?"

Declan had unwittingly passed a tiny yet matterful character test. He'd have been well within his rights to ask: *Why did you move back here?* and play innocent, despite the fact there was no way he didn't know. Nevertheless, he'd skipped the phishing attack in favor of something uncontroversial for Edie to answer.

"I live with my younger sister, so I must do! Yeah, it's been great, actually. It wasn't London's fault, but my life there didn't have much authentic goodness in it. It wasn't very real. I needed the factory settings reset."

Declan nodded.

Edie drank her drink and thought the elephant in the waiting room probably needed addressing.

"We should maybe get this out of the way—I know you'll have heard bad things about me, regarding weddings and ex-colleagues and a general dog's picnic. I'd say 'it's all true,' except, apart from there being a kiss, it isn't. I got turned into a conniving whore who plotted to steal a married man. In reality, it was a split-second moment of terrible judgment that cost me a lot. It was horrible for his wife, but she took pretty major revenge on me, not him."

"Yeah, Jessica told me of some uproar, and I said he was the one getting married and you're a nice-looking girl. Seemed obvious to me he was being audacious after too many black velvets. No one tries to kiss a groom on the off chance he's up for it, do they? It had to come from him."

"Thank you, exactly!" Edie said.

"I don't like gossip or judging people on one side of a story," Declan said, and Edie sensed him recalling things that had been said about her he'd rather not repeat. "I like to make up my own mind."

A far better analysis presented itself of the Declan decision to join her. They'd attempted to poison Declan, yet he hadn't drunk it. Declan was a long drink of antidote.

"I told Jess I don't know why you copped the flack you did," he concluded.

"I think blaming the succubus woman is too appealing to a mob," Edie said. "People like straightforward bad guys. Or rather gals. Not that I'm saying feminism should clear my name—it was still wrong."

"Yeah, I caught a big stench of sexism to the whole thing. I've seen plenty of that double-standard shite thanks to my sisters. Also, to be frank, did you not do this man's bride a fucked-up kind of favor? If he'd do that on his wedding day, imagine the hijinks by the golden anniversary. Probably find him cardigan off and dick loose with the whole bridge club."

Again, Declan's accent rendered this observation funnier, and Edie snorted.

Richard said they'd have an affinity, and Edie had doubted him. He was not only vindicated; she was flattered. If Declan was the male equivalent Edie, then that was fine by her.

Declan, for the fifth time, urged her to go home. "I'll be grand, honestly—this is such an imposition!"

"Hush," Edie said. "It's a Friday holiday."

Admittedly, the sentiment was promptly undercut by a very short man smelling of beer and damp cigarettes doing a moonwalk past them, singing "Smooth Criminal," punctuated by barking like a dog.

"Should've known my ex would turn up," Edie said, making a *such is life* face and offering Declan a Haribo Worm.

"Am I out of line in asking if the dragons series guy is your boyfriend?"

"I don't mind, and yes, he is," Edie said. This must be the first time she'd acknowledged it outside of her close circle. It felt really good.

"That's incredibly cool," Declan said, taking it in. It obviously had the status of quasi myth at Ad Hoc, and he'd not expected a straightforward confirmation. "I loved that show. *For the blades of my brothers!*"

Edie laughed. She allowed herself to enjoy it. In the captive tedium of an antiseptic-smelling room with plastic chairs, it was a talking point—and why not? There was only the looming risk of it becoming the most interesting thing about her.

"I may be speaking out of turn . . ." Edie said.

"We're into hour three—I want nothing but speaking out of turn," Declan said.

"I don't think your pal Jessica's the biggest fan of my relationship. She called Richard on Boxing Day to tell him about a picture with Elliot on my Instagram."

Edie didn't want to force Declan to take or change sides, but she didn't think it would hurt to make it abundantly clear there *were* sides.

"Really?" Declan said. "Wait, I saw the photo, I think? Did it have a Taylor Swift song playing? My little sister loves her and loves him, so I showed her."

"Oh God, the song *was* on it." Edie put a palm over her eyes and groaned. "I am SUCH an indiscreet twat."

"I wish my twattish moments involved me looking super glam

with some famous lad. I mean, maybe not a lad. You take my meaning."

"You've not left anyone in London? A significant other, as they say?"

"Oh, nah. Was with my first girlfriend back home a long time, school sweetheart thing. Fell to pieces at the end of our twenties, really messy split."

"I can't imagine you as a bad breaker-upper," Edie said, knowing she was being overly familiar and also thinking, needs must. They could be here ages.

"Messy in that it devastated both of us. She wanted me to move home and settle down, have kids. I knew I wasn't ready. Sometimes it's not that you love someone any less than they love you, but you can't give them what they want, you know? You'd make yourself unhappy trying to do it and that means you'd make them unhappy. But *I don't want what you want* only ever sounds to the other person like *I don't love you enough to try*. Or *I'm looking for a reason to justify leaving you*."

"Yes," Edie said. "Know what you mean." That summary hit hard.

"Declan Dunne!" came the call from the desk, and Edie patted him on the arm and wished him luck as he was shepherded away.

She blandly checked her phone for the umpteenth time and saw: *@elliotowenofficial has requested to follow you on Instagram.*

Edie clicked to a blue-ticked account and thought with surprise that it must be real. The profile picture was a black-and-white one from the *Guardian* that she could imagine Elliot signing off, and it had already collected hundreds of followers, the count whirling upward every time she refreshed the page. She accepted him, followed back, and WhatsApped Elliot.

Edie

Are my eyes deceiving me, or are you, the ultimate refusenik of social media, on Insta?

Elliot

Ugh, I know. Been persuaded it's a useful platform/counterweight to the made-up things. Bonus: I get to stalk you. ☺

Edie

Maybe now I'll stop getting @elliotowenswife in my suggested accounts. ☹

Elliot

Please don't follow my wife. It really wouldn't be comfortable for any of us.

A BASHFUL-LOOKING DECLAN was back in front of her in no time, a youthful blonde nurse in blue scrubs accompanying him.

"Hi, is it Edie?" she said. She had the 1990s Meg Ryan hairdo where you tucked it behind your ears and it immediately sprang free again. "I've come to speak to you myself because I don't trust this one."

"Oh?" Edie said, pushing her phone into her bag and standing up.

"No broken bones, some bruising. But he can't be on his own for twenty-four hours after a concussion."

"Sure I'll be fine . . ." Declan said, clearly one of many similar exhortations he had made.

The nurse held a silencing hand up. "Would you be willing to stay with him? Or vice versa. He needs rest, no caffeine or alcohol, and someone able to call us if his symptoms get worse."

"Of course!" Edie said reflexively, amid Declan's continuing protestations. "It's no trouble. I'm not leaving for my trip to Derbyshire until early afternoon tomorrow. You can crash at mine? I have nothing planned and a spare room."

Not only did she have one, but it was well furnished, nicely decorated, and devoid of lingerie on clotheshorses, sensitive teen-age diaries, or dildos. Edie had promised herself she'd always run a respectable room for her dad.

"As the lady says!" said the nurse, who seemed to have taken a shine to Declan, an arm around him as she propelled him toward the prescription bay.

As they walked out into the parking lot to their taxi, Edie thought, Declan was very welcome, but all in all it was bloody lucky they'd hit it off.

14

Edie messaged Meg to warn her she was bringing an unexpected visitor home. However, Meg was a fair-weather mobile phone user and sporadic bill payer, and it didn't show as read. Inevitably, when she and Declan got through the door, Meg was dancing to Rage Against the Machine in the kitchen, wearing T-shirt, knickers, and socks, smacking a spatula as a drumstick on the counter.

Meg screamed and grabbed a tea towel bearing the words *VISIT SKEGNESS: IT'S SO BRACING* to improvise a pelmet skirt.

"Who are you?!" she screeched at Declan, over the din of *NOW YOU DO WHAT THEY TOLD YA*. Would be nice if Meg did, Edie thought.

Edie located the speaker to turn off the music while Declan retreated back down the hallway, making fulsome apologies.

"Meg, this is my colleague, Declan. Declan, this is my sister. Meg, I did WhatsApp you."

Edie pledged a large Chinese takeaway with plentiful vegan options to ameliorate the situation, parking Declan with a herbal tea in the front room and leaving Meg to go upstairs and find trousers.

Bonhomie returned faster than she expected, which Edie attributed in part to her soothing front room, complete with vast cage for her birds, Meryl and Beryl. She'd gone hard on cozy: pillar candles in storm lanterns and a faux-fur rug that Meg objected to as it "encourages a lust for fur."

Edie once sweetly asked if fake meat gives you a lust for meat, and Meg said she only had Quorn pieces, which were not meat mimicry, and Edie liked getting on better with Meg too well to mention the Quorn ham slices.

"They're beautiful," Declan said, indicating the vivid plumage of the gray-and-yellow budgies.

"They belonged to my dad's characterful and glamorous late neighbor Margot," Edie said.

"Bit of a fascist," Meg advised. "But then so is my sister. She could really bake a cake, though."

"She left them to you in her will?" Declan said.

"Her estranged son and his nuclear-wintery wife turned up to do house clearance and were going to turf the birds out on their arses, so I intervened," Edie said. "Not thinking what I'd spend on Trill."

Declan gazed at her, visibly impressed, possibly imagining Edie some variant of Manic Pixie Dream Girl.

She checked her delivery app. "Our noodles are on Alfreton Road!"

The three of them ate on their laps, forked down platefuls of mapo tofu, mushroom chow mein, and spring rolls, companionably channel surfing.

Declan made a considerable effort with Meg, and Meg seemed surprised and then gratified that one of Edie's wanky ad exec associates from fancy London was, in fact, great.

"You work in a care home, which is one of the best things you can do for society," Declan told her. "I try to flog you things you don't need, for capitalism. One of the worst."

"To be fair, I love my gadget that mashes potatoes—it's amazing. I forget what it's called. Mashy, I think. Do you like mashed potatoes?"

"I'm Irish. My blood is part potato."

"You have to come back for dinner another time and try it," Meg said. "Right, Edie?"

Declan shot Edie a discomfited look: it contained an ongoing apology for abruptly inserting himself into her existence to this extent.

It provoked Edie to reply: "One hundred percent he does. I won't even need a hospital to insist, next time. And you can have wine on that visit."

She could see his body language easing.

"Then thank you very much. You're the only people I know in Nottingham, and you're a great start."

"You came here not knowing *anyone*?" Meg said with awe.

Edie privately congratulated herself on subtly challenging Meg's assumptions. Meg's identity was very home-city-forever, and she had an unexamined attitude that those who left were quitters and pseuds, no doubt based on feeling abandoned by Edie. Now, she could see it also involved bravery.

"I like a voyage of discovery."

"We'll look after you," Meg said, patting his knee.

There was something very solid about Declan: both in his broad shoulders but also his manner. He knew who he was, and Edie detected a sort of . . . center of moral gravity that she liked. She realized it made her feel—a funny word to apply, really—safe.

The reason Team Jessica loved Declan wasn't because he was one of them; it was because he was one of those people everyone loved, who became hotly contested territory.

Edie hadn't had a single qualm about him seeing her home, and that was an acid test of trust, she always thought. Someone like Jess would be hoping to find mold on her shower curtain. He mentioned his sisters a lot, partly to thoughtfully draw connections with Meg. He'd make a lovely dad, one day.

And he was well-traveled but wore it lightly: only a few years younger than Edie but he'd had many adventures, often solo. That sort of self-reliance was cool.

Edie suspected Ad Hoc and Nottingham wouldn't keep him long—she was unsurprised it ended with the girl back home—and was glad they got him passing through, before he settled down in Brisbane or Knock.

When Declan insisted honestly, he wasn't lying, the in-house band on a ferry crossing to Bilbao was genuinely called Smooth Passage, Edie near-prolapsed in laughter.

Declan looked back at her, warm appraisal of her written on his face, and she knew that his being clipped by a Toyota Avensis had fast-tracked a firm friendship.

EDIE WAS DRIFTING off around one a.m. when she heard an ungodly, primal howl from below her room that she recognized as emitting from Meg's lungs. She was out of bed and skittering down the stairs in seconds flat, adrenaline sufficient to lift a lorry from a child. Intruders were scary, but no one, absolutely no one, threatened her younger sibling without awakening lioness instincts in Edie.

The light was on in the kitchen, and Edie turned the corner and shrieked.

On one side of the room, there was Meg in her nightwear leggings and T-shirt, a serrated bread knife held threateningly aloft.

On the other was a fully naked Declan, staring impassively at the shelving on the far wall. To call it a dark, surreal tableau was to undersell it. David Lynch himself would decline to direct it.

"OK. What the fuck?" Edie said, heart blocking her throat, hands out and palms up, as if she needed to balance.

A few seconds ticked by where Edie tried to form her own interpretation and completely failed.

"I was down here making myself a midnight snack, and he walked in behind me with his penis PROUDLY ON SHOW . . ." Meg said, pointing the tip of the knife down at the offending genitals, as if Edie might not know where they were otherwise. *That's the schlong, officer!* "Scaring the shit out of me . . . And now he's not speaking, trying to freak me out even more!" Meg said.

"Declan," Edie said, trying to keep her breathing steady and her gaze locked on his face. Who or what had she allowed into her home? Declan was a huge man—it turned out, in more than one sense—and she felt the horror of putting Meg at risk. And herself. "It's a bit of a house rule that we don't walk around with our penises out."

"I'll fucking amputate it, flasher fucker! See how you enjoy your sick kicks then," Meg said, raising her arm higher, and Edie shushed her desperately. Meg committing bodily harm wasn't likely to improve things.

A small element of pathos: Declan had a bandage in the same place that Edie had wound her makeshift effort round him. She remembered blushing at being so close to a strange male torso. Well. If only she'd known she was very much on the beginner slopes yesterday.

Edie looked back up at Declan's impassive expression, trying to work out what was going on and why the friendly man of earlier had turned into this statue. Why wasn't he looking at either of them? Was this an effect of the concussion?

Hang on . . .

"*Megan*," Edie said, in an effortfully calm, low voice and using her sister's full name to get her full attention. ". . . I think he's sleepwalking?"

Meg lowered the knife. "Is he?"

"I think so. That's why he seems to be in a trance?" She turned toward him. "Declan. Hi? Hello?" Edie said, waving her hand, and Declan merely swayed gently, still staring beyond them at the shelving.

Edie had never encountered a sleepwalker before, and her introduction was a six-foot-two nude man hung like a donkey.

It was spookily like someone doing a youth theater exercise impression of a sleepwalker. A rather basic impersonation. It seemed like, if she made a loud noise, he'd be tricked into snapping out of it and laugh.

But if he wasn't sleepwalking, he was deliberately staging an impromptu full frontal with his new line manager and her sister to no discernible purpose. And not flinching when the latter was wielding means of violently cleaving member from body.

"What do we do? You're not meant to wake a sleepwalker?" Edie said uncertainly.

"You're not meant to make me look at your willy and balls when I want an almond butter crumpet, either," Meg said.

"I think you're meant to guide them gently back to bed?" Edie said.

"You first—I'm not touching him."

Edie had to admit, it was a worrying notion. "Where's the Skegness tea towel?" she said, with serious urgency, and at this point she and Meg simultaneously broke and started sniggering.

Suddenly, with the vacant yet deliberate lurch of Frankenstein's monster, Declan approached the swing-top bin.

He positioned his penis over it in such a way that strongly suggested Dream Architect had told him it was the toilet.

Whatever the correct protocols for managing somnambulism, before a stream of urine could appear, Edie involuntary cried: "Declan, no!"

He stopped what he was doing and woke with a start, his head jerking backward and then his face changing from the absent stare to one of greater comprehension.

"Where am I?" he asked, not unreasonably. New city, concussion, new colleague, hospital, strange house, and now he'd teleported sans clothes into a kitchen in the small hours. Like the man who fell to Earth.

"My house, remember? I'm Edie? This is my sister, Meg. You hit your head when you came off your bike. I think you've been sleepwalking."

Declan looked as if understanding was dawning, and then right behind the geography of where he was and the history of how he arrived here was biology: an awareness of nakedness.

"Uhm . . . Am I . . . Why . . . ?" He glanced down and almost started at confirmation of the sight of himself, an anxiety fantasy finally made real.

Edie gritted her teeth.

"Oh my Lord . . ." Declan said and put his hands over his crotch. Edie had never seen someone sweat like that before: his face became damp in a split second. Declan backed away, bumping into a worktop. "I hope I'm still dreaming."

"If you are, you're in my nightmare," Meg said. "Maybe don't go bare-arsed in bed if you're a guest."

This was the first time Edie had ever heard Meg chiding someone about modesty and etiquette.

"Meg, shhh."

"I wasn't—I had joggers on. I must have taken them off," Declan said, the full misery of his situation descending upon him. "I've not done any sleepwalking since I was nine or ten."

"Probably giving your head a bump shook it loose," Edie said.

"Were you nude then, too?" Meg asked, unable to let go of her indignance this fast.

Edie shushed her.

"I think I was, but . . ."

The unfinished sentence was that there had been less of him to go on tour.

"We'll leave you to get to bed," Edie said, hurriedly motioning at Meg to set the knife down and follow her—fleeing the scene before Declan had to despondently trudge back up the stairs, realizing he didn't need to cup his junk without his onlookers. Edie was not a physically confident person herself, and every time she put herself in Declan's nonexistent shoes, she flinched.

As she lay with her duvet up to her neck, she felt like she could hear his thoughts. It was as if they were psychically communicating.

There was the sound of something being pulled across carpet, and she realized he was putting a chest of drawers in front of the door to stop himself repeating the expedition.

Edie tried to think what she'd say in the morning to make this better. Her job was *choosing words designed to elicit a certain response or feeling*, after all.

The trouble with humor here was: it was too close to ridiculing the person's body. She could try for perspective?

Look, it's not a consultant telling you whether it's treatable, it's not charged with three counts of murder, it's not messing up your slot at the Super Bowl. It's just a colleague having more information about your anatomy than you intended. Information that she'll have forgotten in a week's time.

Yeah, that was straight-up untrue.

15

Edie went downstairs the next morning to find Declan gone. They'd bonded so brilliantly in A&E. What a development. Even though Edie hadn't done the exposing thing, she felt almost as embarrassed as he did.

Her phone had received his farewell.

MORNING. WELL THEN. Oh fuck. Infinity oh fuck. So, Edie, I thought I'd make myself scarce this morning, because holy fucking SHIT. Right now it's 8 a.m. and I don't know whether to open a bottle or a vein, tbh. You take care of me, let me stay at your house, and that was your reward. I am dying here. I can't apologize enough. I keep thinking what you and your sister must've thought I was up to, and dying all over again. D

Edie sent a lengthy, supportive, and carefully worded reply, insisting he had absolutely nothing to apologize for and she only hoped he was all right. She knew that however emphatic her words: 1. Declan would probably need months if not years to get over the horror, and 2. Their next greeting would redefine *uncomfortable*.

She was inordinately grateful for the mini-break to take her mind off it.

January was the most depressing of months, and with Nick and Hannah, Edie made a plan to cheer it up with a long weekend in the countryside: renting a cottage with a wood-burning stove, doing long walks, reading books in nooks, cooking hearty things that required oven-braising while the chefs got gradually less coherent imbibing red wine.

"Also, let's not be those people who get partners and start doing everything in pairs," Hannah had said on their WhatsApp group, Muffin Wallopers.

"You weren't really like that when you were with Pete, to be fair," Edie said, once they were en route, with Hannah at the wheel. "You were just in Edinburgh."

Hannah had spent a long time with dependable, solid, nice Pete, before realizing she was utterly miserable, having a one-night stand with Chloe, her now-girlfriend, and leaving him. Practically and logistically, the upheaval was over. Edie could tell that emotionally and psychologically, it was a work in progress. Hannah was dry as a bone and sharp as a scalpel; it would be possible to miss that she felt things deeply and was waterlogged with guilt.

"I *was* like that with Alice," said Nick, of his maligned ex-wife. "I think Hannah means now we are all actually happy."

She told them of Declan's nude walkabout: she felt unkind, using him for material, and did so without mockery or sensationalism.

Both Nick and Hannah shrieked and groaned and hissed through their teeth and agreed it was a mentally scarring experience for everyone but principally for Declan.

"Fair play to the bloke if he turns up at work next week. I think I'd ask the Home Office for a new identity," Nick said. "Unless I had the body of a Greek God and boasted one like a pipe of Pringles with a bull's heart atop it. Did he?"

"Can neither confirm nor deny," Edie said, squirming a little. She wasn't blind: that was a reasonably spectacular body, if you liked that sort of thing. Her interests were engaged elsewhere, and any dwelling upon it made her a voyeur.

"Oh my God!" Nick said. "He DOES! Are we sure he isn't a pajama-shunning braggart? *Oh, you caught me, with my tremendous hosepipe accidentally on show, what a devastating misfortune.*"

"That means either he does, or he doesn't!"

"It means he does," Nick said. "Everyone knows neither confirm nor deny means yes. Hannah, back me up."

Hannah waited until she'd completed a right-hand turn and said: "It's a coded yes usually, but I'm sure Edie only meant it as a no comment."

"Why not simply say *yes, the man's packing serious Nellie-the-elephant trunk*, if he is? It's hardly shameful," Nick said.

"Because he didn't choose to put it on display for discussion, no matter its impressive nature! Or . . . not," Edie finished, awkwardly.

"Aha, you fell right into my trap. Confirmed colossal."

Nick mimed holding something proudly with two hands, as if posing with a prize-winning zucchini, and Edie gave in and collapsed into mirth.

"Nick, if you want Declan's number, just ask for it," Hannah said.

After they arrived at the Airbnb in Hannah's Volvo e-car, Nick said: "Cottagecore, I love it!" taking in the view of the valley.

"It's an actual cottage," Edie said, heaving her luggage case over shingle with some difficulty. "What do you do to earn the core?"

"It's an aesthetic. *We* are the aesthetic. We must bake bread and raise backyard chickens." Nick threw his arms wide at the hillside, *The Sound of Music*–style. It was nice to see him happier.

His controlling ex-wife, Alice, had made contact with his young son, Max, fraught. Nick seeing the delightful if direct and unconventional Ros was a healthy step forward.

"You can raise them from the bags on the doorstep, anyway," Hannah said, checking the time on her phone. "Ocado's due in an hour."

They passed a very pleasant wintery day, allocating the bedrooms, walking two miles to explore the nearest village, and cooking coq au vin.

After dinner, Hannah was diving through the fridge. They'd broadly agreed on the online order and left Nick to hammer out the details and press *send*. Belatedly, Edie was remembering that when it came to food, Hannah and Nick represented the high and the low, respectively.

"Nick, where is the cheeseboard cheese?"

"There!"

"This?" Hannah said in disgust. "It's a massive lump of Cathedral City Extra Mature. The posh stuff?"

"There," Nick said. "Fruity one."

"Oh my God, is this Wensleydale with apricots?! Literally everyone in civilized society knows cheeseboard cheese means *nice piece of stichelton*. Or, if we're slumming it, camembert in a wooden box."

"Don't worry, my dear, there's a sausage of smoked rubbery deliciousness and a wheel of Dairylea triangles." Nick made a chef's kiss gesture.

Hannah stopped rifling. "Oh my Christ, I'm raging. What are we scooping it up with? Let me guess . . . Quavers?!"

"Oh, I suppose you'd want radicchio leaves and those incinerated-looking things made of fire grate ash. I got Ritz crackers and red grapes."

"Edith, Nick's waged class warfare on our cheeseboard," Hannah said. "He's gone fucking Arthur Seaton on my aged gouda."

"I do not pretend to understand the negroni-quaffing elite," Nick said. "You tofu wokerati. Cheese is cheese."

They unpacked Nick's provocative offerings onto chopping boards, refilled glasses.

"When are you seeing the prince?" Hannah asked Edie, once seated back at the cottage's table.

"Not until next month. Meeting him in London for a Friday night date, and we're coming back to Nottingham for the rest of the weekend. I'll let you know if we're around for a pint?"

"For sure," Hannah said. "I didn't expect to find Elliot so easy to talk to. He's so . . . approachable and un-precious, isn't he? And so clearly smitten with you. God, it's a real-life fairy tale!"

"Mmm," Edie said uneasily. "Isn't it. Which . . . don't exist."

"Do I, with my highly sensitive antennae, detect some pessimism?" Hannah said, hacking a piece of Cathedral City.

Edie adjusted herself in her seat. "Thing is, it's so . . . ambitious and unlikely, isn't it? I worry everyone thinks I can't see that, but I do. He's who he is—*fuckin' wow*—and I'm who I am—*lol*—and we somehow make the mismatch work? I know they're together by the end of *Notting Hill*, but Hugh Grant was at least posh and lived in London."

"And it was a film," Nick said.

"And it was a film. I think . . ." Edie was aware of the two glasses of wine powering her on to dare voice this: "I might be a phase he has to work through. The earthy-girl-from-home phase. To accept that this is the type of life he's left behind. I'm not a destination; I'm a stop on the way. I'm not Manchester; I'm Stalybridge."

She paused. "If that's the case, then he'll emerge from the experiment still this amazing prospect, and I might be a forty-something who's fit for no one else after being spun around and set down by Hurricane Elliot."

A short silence ensued while everyone absorbed the plausibility of what she'd said.

"The trouble is I'm not sure there are any safe prospects when you fall in love," Hannah said. "Look at me and Pete—solid as concrete until we weren't, and my leaving, and now being with a woman after lifelong straightness, properly did a number on him. We've had long conversations about whether I was 'pretending' when I was with him. Which I wasn't, but he can't get his head round it. From his perspective, my next choice of partner invalidated our entire relationship." Hannah broke a Ritz cracker contemplatively. "But no one would've told him not to ask the quiet, serious med student out, would they?" Hannah concluded.

"Yeah. Mine and Alice's first encounter was so romantic you'd have wept. Like that *Before Sunset* film, we spent a whole night walking around Prague. In the end, I did think about it and cry. If my flight hadn't been overbooked, I'd never have met her. I'd not have had Max if I had, though, so. Your beginnings are not the defining thing."

"Good point," Edie said.

"For what it's worth, Edie, at Christmas I thought how incredibly well suited you are," Hannah said. "There's no mismatch when you're in a room together, more like eerie similarity—right down to the way you joke. You are so at ease with each other."

Edie glowed.

"This is true," Nick said. "You're very same vibey. No one who knows both of you thinks it's unlikely at all, Thompson."

Edie leaned across the table and gripped Nick's hand, because this was kind of both of them, so *old friends*, and much needed.

"Elliot's chosen a big life." Hannah gestured at the dark garden beyond the casement window. "He couldn't un-choose it for you now, even if he wanted to. He was famous before you met him. You're a private person who never shouts about herself. He's the story, and you're the ghostwriter. The tug-of-war between these two things is inevitable. If you want it to work, you'll need to build a life together that's the right size for both of you and defend it above all else. I have confidence you will, because there is a total sincerity of intention with you two."

Edie knew Hannah was astute. Yet here she was casually offering some absolutely shining wisdom, while carving a Dairylea triangle onto a cracker like a plasterer with a palette knife.

16

They were examining the Airbnb stack of tattered Monopoly and Connect Four boxes after dinner when Edie's phone rattled in her pocket and she pulled it out to see:

Elliot
Edie, can I call you? It's quite time sensitive so now, if you've got a minute? X

She excused herself, found her big-knit cardigan, and stepped out into the frigid nighttime air, for privacy and better reception. Elliot rang within seconds of her pulling the door closed behind her.

"There's a stupid story about me I need to warn you about. I don't know if it's up yet, but it will be soon, I think."

Edie went cold-hot. "OK . . ."

"They asked Lillian for a quote, and she told them it was all bollocks, so naturally they're running it anyway with the denial."

"What is it?" Edie said, not really appreciating Elliot burying the lede.

"We went out for dinner in New York the other night as a cast get-to-know-each-other thing. We didn't realize we could be seen through the window. Lillian thinks they've cropped the photos so it looks as if it's only me and Ines there. There were about nine of us."

"Right," Edie said dully. She wondered if it was worth this agitated and detailed primer; it might be worse than Elliot was advertising, though *group dinner* didn't sound too dire.

"I'm so sorry. I hate that people close to me have to pay this shitty tax for my choice of career."

"It's not your fault," Edie said stoically. "I remember they did this with your costar Greta back during *Gun City*. Par for the course."

It was far from Edie's first rodeo when it came to witnessing that things in print didn't correspond with Elliot Owen's lived reality.

"Yeah, but it wasn't personally insulting to you then. If we went public somehow, then they'd do fewer of these. But it also brings trouble to your door, and all past jokes aside, I know why you're not keen. I don't want people taking photos of you going to Caffè Nero on the way to work."

"True, thank you," Edie said, though there was an honorable futility to this sentiment. They'd do it at some point.

She thanked Elliot for the heads-up and tried to sound mature and unbothered. They were on a one-bar phone signal that kept cutting out, which eventually made them politely agree to give up.

Edie sat at the picnic table, wishing she smoked, and hit refresh on the relevant website. Nothing and nothing and nothing. After ten minutes that felt like an era, teeth chattering, she was thinking she'd have to go back inside and pretend to concentrate on the board game. Edie could check again in an hour. She didn't want to see it for the first time with company.

Then with a jolt, on a final check, there it was on the right-hand side:

New Couple Alert: Elliot Owen and costar Ines Herrera pack on the PDA at a candlelit intimate date in NYC

It was one thing to know it was imminent and be reassured it was false. It was another to see this statement glowing black and white back at her as a clickbait announcement. *New couple.*

Edie steeled herself. *Right, deep breath: it's not true. You can read this and be just fine, maybe even laugh, because you have superior insight and know it's not true.*

As she opened it, she thought: *hang on—pack on the what, now? Have they got on-set photos already?* Elliot had told her they were a way off filming?

She scanned. Her stomach lurched. This story wasn't about words; it was told in pictures.

There were six of them total, the story padded out with photos of Elliot and Ines on-screen and one of their leaving the venue, some trendy-looking place in the West Village.

In the first image, Ines had her hand on the back of Elliot's head, proprietorially ruffling his hair as he leaned forward, speaking to someone unseen. It was a casual ownership gesture—one of the type that, in Edie's experience, only people who were very physically knowledgeable about each other otherwise would ever make.

In the second, Ines rested her head on his chest as Elliot laughed at someone or something out of frame. Again, it said: *we are a unit, a team of two.* With more than a hint of: *and we are boffing up an absolute storm.*

In the third, Ines had her arms looped round him protectively. In the fourth, she was whispering in his ear, a palm cupped to her face, as he leaned toward her to hear, with a look of concentration.

In the fifth, someone out of shot was taking a photograph of them, Ines leaning up to pose-kiss Elliot's cheekbone.

And in the sixth, which made Edie audibly and sharply suck in air with a yelp, Elliot's hand was on the table, Ines's over it.

She stared and stared. It was clearly reciprocal. Holding hands. At dinner. Which platonic coworkers sat there holding hands, after dinner? Let alone two people this superlative looking, who everyone would be looking at?

Ines was wearing large gold hoop earrings, a black silk top, and dark brick-red lipstick, hair gathered onto her head in a bun. She looked, with her almond eyes and pointed chin, like the flesh incarnation of a Disney princess.

This was the woman he'd be fake falling in love with all day, every day, for months? This was them at the *start*? It was nothing less than the photo set a private detective would bring you to definitively prove your spouse was playing away.

She had a light-headed moment of trying to recall a single time where they'd in so many words agreed: *we don't sleep with other people when we're on different continents, right?* Was covert flexibility A Thing, something she should've known about, in the endless sexual options of a famous person existence? He's not *faithful*-faithful, obviously. Don't ask, don't tell. He's still *Elliot Owen*—what did you expect, for God's sake?

If that was the case, they were over before they'd begun. She stared into the nocturnal middle distance.

Edie had recently seen Ines on the cover of a magazine, over-flowing from a satin basque, tagline: *INEScapable. Your Next Obsession.*

She was INEScapable all right. *What if I'm Stalybridge, not Manchester?* had a major revision: *what if I'm Stalybridge, and she's Las Vegas?*

She returned to her phone, stabbing at the keypad to bring the article back up on her screen. She didn't know she was crying until a large tear rolled down her cheek. Reading the text felt like driving a penknife into the flesh of her palm.

Elliot Owen and Ines Herrera appear to have confirmed rumors of a romance after a VERY touchy-feely display in New York last night.

The pair are set to star in the new HBO show *Your Table Is Ready* as sparring front of house love interests, and it looks like they may have one-upped their fictional counterparts.

They held hands, whispered, kissed, and cuddled over a candlelit meal at West Village hot spot Padrona—and they didn't care who saw.

Yeah, we'll come back to that fact, Edie thought, a molten lava of rage surging up inside her, to match the ragged pain.

"She was practically on his lap," said another diner. "They didn't seem very interested in the food . . . or in anyone else."

The dragon-slaying *Blood & Gold* heartthrob hasn't been linked to anyone since separating last year from model-actress Heather Lily, who publicly begged Owen to reconcile. Herrera, 28, has been single since splitting from her American football player ex last spring.

"They make a stunning couple, and everyone involved in the production is buzzing about the immediate connection between them," said a perfectly placed source. "Their characters are always at each other's throats and have a sizzling chemistry—they won't have to do much acting to portray it."

Reps for Owen denied they were involved when we contacted them for a comment, saying: "Their relationship is purely professional."

Somehow, the worst word in it was "immediate"—perhaps as it was the only one that offered an explanation for the complete cognitive dissonance of the man recently in her bed being the man in these images.

Edie read the story again, from the top, opened her mouth, and said: "Fuck you all," through a sob.

Fuck the tabloids who tormented people with these inventions; fuck the paparazzi who were enriched by long-lens shots through windows, and the picture editors who cropped the image to misinform. Fuck the television networks who got free publicity for their shows; fuck actresses who didn't care if they were manhandling another woman's boyfriend. Most of all, fuck the man who had made her heartfelt promises, who'd whispered sweet nothings and typed "be mine forever" and then went off to another country to LARP being someone else's, with the world watching.

17

Edie's phone buzzed, and she couldn't have ever anticipated a time she'd feel revulsion at that magical name appearing. But she did. Raw, ungoverned fury, the woman-scorned stuff there was classic literature and crown court cases about. If he'd been there in front of her, she might have slapped him.

Elliot
Have you seen it, and can I call you?

She replied with shaking hands. The anger, the disorientation, the jealousy, the betrayal, the fear of whatever was going on at Padrona she didn't understand. Edie had been kidnapped by the level of emotion and wasn't herself.

Edie
You left out the part where you and Ines are getting off with each other in every photo? Weird! And no, you can't.
Elliot
FUCK she's really OTT tactile like that with EVERYONE and you don't want to say STOP TOUCHING ME, but obviously it made for worse photos. I am SO so sorry—this is phenomenally grim and unfair, and I hate you going through it.
Edie
Er, if it's all her, why are you holding her hand?
Elliot
I wasn't. I put my hand down, and she put her hand over mine for about 30 seconds.

Edie

*THAT'S HOW HOLDING HANDS WORKS. You're gaslighting me—it's
not nothing when a newspaper can use it as proof you're sleeping
together, is it? Sorry if I'm being thick here, but are you?*

Her phone flashed with his call, and she pressed to end it. She
didn't trust herself not to shriek.

Elliot

*Of course not—it's absolute bullshit! Edie, I was a bottle of wine deep
and what you're seeing is a few minutes inattention with someone
being inappropriately overfamiliar. I really want to talk to you.*

Edie

*No, I'm not in private, I don't have good enough reception, and I don't want
your "this is how it goes down in the big city, little country girl" excuses.
People who are as famous as you and who don't want it to look like they're
shagging someone don't end up in photos like that. Have I misunderstood?
Is the issue that I've found out something about our deal earlier than I was
meant to? Because if so, I don't want any part of this deal at all.*

Elliot's reply this time stalled for a minute, and Edie took sav-
age, bitter pleasure in having shocked him into hesitating.

Elliot

*WOAH. I know my space on the moral high ground is very limited here,
but we know each other better than this. I was completely fucking
stupid to make pictures like this possible, but can we at least establish
that it doesn't represent anything unfaithful? Absolutely nothing of any
sort is going on with Ines. Zero.*

Edie's level of torture felt like her villain origin story. And as a
result, she was catching up in the rules of this game.

Edie

Lillian warned you how bad the photos were, didn't she? That's why you called to get me onside? But you were playing for time to see just how bad they were before you admitted to it? Were there other things that they didn't get a photo of?

Elliot

She said the reporter said we looked "cozy" and that it was a "strong story" from their point of view. She also told me, if I didn't want them to write a story like that, I'd not been very smart.

Edie

Why not pass that on? Why leave me to see it without that warning?

Elliot

Because I thought it was sadistically winding you up before either of us had seen it. Reporters say all kinds of things to goad you into admissions, plus add the fact I'd been drinking and could only vaguely recall she had her arm round me at one point. She was exactly the same with the director, but because he's 60, they didn't make anything of that.

Edie

Let's be grown-ups and call it what it was, shall we? You were flirting. Hard flirting with the woman you'd got a pass from me to have make-believe sex with. And you got caught. Now you want me to react by instantly agreeing you can't possibly be a cheater. Go to hell, Elliot.

Elliot

I swear I wasn't doing anything as proactive as flirting. I was being unassertive in not shrugging her off. I was drunk and tired, and actresses (and actors) are often quite mad—it's easier to go along with it when you've got to work with someone in long days.

Edie had no more to say. She wasn't fully sure what she thought or what she believed. After a few minutes of consideration, she turned her phone off completely. Elliot might notice his messages weren't getting ticked as received. Let him sweat.

It wasn't only about punishment and revenge; she didn't want to say things she'd regret.

Edie walked back indoors and through to the sitting room, where Hannah and Nick were shaking dice for Yahtzee.

"I need to get totally obliterated fucking drunk," Edie said.

HOURS LATER AND once in bed, knowing she was in no fit state to absorb its revelations but unable to resist, Edie held her phone power button until the Apple icon appeared and the handset rippled back to life.

Within seconds, Elliot's name sprang to the center of the screen—along with a horde of Instagram nosy inquiries, linking to the article, many no doubt awash with schadenfreude that she'd had a taste of her own medicine.

He'd said the Christmas night photo was fine, and it had led here. *Thanks for the humiliation.*

She expected to find multiple messages from Elliot, and possibly mounting frustration or even criticism at realizing she'd cut him dead, but there was only one.

Edie, I cannot fucking bear having hurt you like this, and I absolutely despise myself for my stupidity. If you want me to walk away from this job, I will. All I care about is you. I haven't been unfaithful—I wouldn't so much as think about it. There's no room left in me for anyone except you. I know that's just words right now, and I can't make it better. I love you. X

He was good at forceful declarations, and it had an effect on her. Yet he was right: it didn't mend it. Edie went to sleep in tears, pissed tears of complicated remorse.

She didn't, these hours later and having calmed down, think they were involved. It was too fast, and it wasn't the person she knew.

But she couldn't set it all aside as irrelevant, either.

Edie kept thinking about how remarkable Elliot and Ines looked together, how *right*. How much everyone would desperately root for them to be in love for real. She felt like she was defying the forces of gravity by trying to build something lasting with him.

18

Nick and Hannah quickly closed the clacky cover on the iPad, sipped coffee, and performatively discussed the weather when Edie entered the dining room. She was hot-showered and carefully pieced back together, full makeup. She was glad that she wasn't home alone and had to be presentable. Wallowing wouldn't help her self-esteem.

"I know what you're reading, you shits," Edie said cheerfully.

"How are you feeling?" Hannah asked.

"A bit numb and stupid and hungover and like last night was a bad dream," Edie said honestly. She'd replied to Elliot, and curiously, her message hadn't registered as delivered, making her think he had turned his phone off, too.

Morning. Sorry I had to stop then because I wasn't in a good state or capable of saying things that I'd want to stand by. I appreciate you saying sorry, and I don't think you've cheated, but I remain pretty hurt. I will let you know when I feel up to talking. E x

"It's a bloody bizarre thing, and you're allowed to react any way you want," Nick said.

"Thank you. I don't get why actors perv on each other when eating spaghetti on an office night out. I have never been for tapas with the agency and ended up licking Richard's face."

"OK, so if it helps," Nick said, "we've analyzed the data thoroughly and have some key findings."

Edie, pouring herself a coffee, said: "Haha, I KNEW it. Tell me your findings. I'm at a loss. I'm too biased, and I've had my mind mangled by tabloid spin."

"You're sure you're all right to discuss it? It can wait," Hannah said. She had been the one to hold Edie last night as she incoherently sobbed about her inadequacy versus: "*Inner Hurrah*—she's twenty-fucking-EIGHT, for fuck's sake."

"I would genuinely appreciate it," Edie said now. "If those photos aren't what they look like, then I don't know what those photos *are*. Which makes working out what I blame him for tricky. What is the penalty for a 'touchy-feely display'?"

"Court's in session," Nick said, pulling his chair up next to Hannah. "Crucially, in the material we studied, we see nothing that shows Elliot initiating the physical contact. That would've been the smoking gun. And counterintuitively, I think you can be fairly reassured there was no such moment, because the press would've definitely used it."

Oh God, that was true. If they'd had Elliot nuzzling Ines, it would've been right at the top. He'd not have got away with it. It was strange that he was exonerated by the same scrutiny that incriminated him.

"So, Hannah, what did we conclude?"

Edie's heart swelled with gratitude. They'd correctly intuited that Edie needed this mocking, to defuse its power over her.

"The most damning image is the hand-holding," Hannah said. "But was it holding? Here is my hand." Hannah laid it on the table. "I am Elliot."

"And I am Ines," Nick said. "People do often say we look alike."

"Now, note my hand is inert," Hannah said. "It is, at this juncture, an innocent hand."

Nick placed his hand on Hannah's and pushed his fingers over the top of hers.

"Obviously not perfect reconstruction, as she'd need to have been drinking and not expect my approach," Nick said, "making it potentially even more effective. But we have established that it is perfectly possible to do this clasping and it look like mutual hand-holding."

Nick opened the iPad, found the relevant image, and held it up. "No finger intertwining. Her hand over his, as he said. This has gone quite: *if the glove doesn't fit, you must acquit.*"

"So . . . he was preyed upon?" Edie said. "Hmm."

"Sort of. What we've concluded, Edith, is that it is clearly flirting," Hannah said. "She was flirting with him, and he didn't discourage her. We see no evidence he was ever flirt instigator. His role is passive, yet still a participant by default. Some would say that is flirting."

Edie had an uncomfortable moment, thinking: *have there not been times in your life where a small truth, taken out of context, became a big lie?*

She was even holding Nick's hand last night, and it wasn't as if that meant anything remotely lascivious. But she didn't have long-lens cameras pointed at her, in pursuit of standing up fraudulent editorial directions. Or not so far.

"In summary, we think Elliot's specific crime is flirting toleration, when spoken for," Nick said. "You need some sort of tracking device. I'd recommend slipping an AirTag into his Mc-Chicken next time you see him."

"So this, my safe space, is in fact the Justice for Elliot Owen headquarters?" Edie said. "Why do you two fancy him so much?!"

There was collective delight at her response, and she realized Nick and Hannah hadn't known what state she'd be in today, with some justification.

"We like him, true, *and* we think you're owed a big apology," Hannah said. "I also think stunning women who take the liberty of pawing men won't often get told not to. I think his claim of mad actress behavior might have some merit. It's not a normal profession. My friend once saw Miriam Margolyes swipe someone's cornet from their hand like a human seagull."

"Herrera can keep her hands off my Flake 99," Edie replied, and Nick said: "That's the spirit!"

What had Elliot's mum called this fuss? *Silly hoopla.*

". . . It's like joining the circus," Edie said. "All right, your findings are noted."

After milky tea, she was feeling almost human again when her phone buzzed.

Elliot
Would the time for talking possibly be in about half an hour? Can I come & see you?
Edie
You're not in New York?
Elliot
I've flown back. I've only got a couple of hours max before I have to turn around again. I don't want to intrude/fuck up your break any more than I already have, though, so don't worry if it isn't OK. It's not like I ran this past you.

Edie's heart was racing. She noticed he was too circumspect and/or gentlemanly to point out that you couldn't run plans past someone who'd turned their phone off.

She confirmed the address, in a state of mild shock. He'd traveled from the East Coast, for a couple of hours?

"Erm, so Elliot's coming over. At midday," Edie said blankly, to jaw drops from Nick and Hannah.

"Coming over, from where?! The Upper East Side?" Hannah said.

"Pretty much, yes. He must've got a flight after we finished scrapping last night."

As she said it, Edie realized that it sounded like Cleopatra summoning Mark Antony.

"Fuuuuuuck," Nick said.

"Is he joining the holiday?" Hannah asked, and Edie could tell she must really like Elliot, as this was said in excited anticipation, without the smallest, gritted teeth hint of *oh, thanks for turning our jolly into Kabul.*

"No, he's only here an hour or so—he's got to go back straight away."

"Wait, WAIT," Hannah said. "A man has come long-haul round trip just to say sorry to your FACE?"

"Yes."

"Jesus Christ, Edie?! He is besotted!"

"That's what he WANTS you to think!" Edie said.

"Handsome boy has got me fooled," Nick said.

"Stop taking his side!" Edie wailed, in humor and panic, to further amusement from Nick and Hannah.

"This is some Richard-Gere-in-*Pretty-Woman* shit," Nick said. ". . . Not that I am saying Edie sells sex. But if she did, Elliot would pay an absolute fortune for it."

"That was nearly tasteless, but you pulled it back round," Edie said.

"Thanks, it's a gift of mine."

Hannah checked her watch. "Nick, get your walking boots out. You and I are going to explore the Dales and leave them to it."

As they pulled on their outerwear in the hallway, Nick whispered: "It's all the drama, Mick—I just love it!" and Edie shouted: "I HEARD THAT."

19

Do NOT be impressed because he is beautiful, important, and he flew across an ocean for two hours with you, Edie told herself. *That is not what matters here.*

As soon as a black Range Rover pulled up across the road and Elliot, chin angled down and hands thrust in pockets of a double-breasted navy peacoat, ran across the road toward the house, inside Edie was screaming *HE IS SO BEAUTIFUL AND IMPORTANT, AND HE CAME ALL THIS WAY, FOR YOU!* FFS. Pathetic. Not the freedom that suffragettes died for.

Edie opened the door. They gazed at each other for a heavy, unsmiling moment, and Edie said: "Hello."

Elliot was evidently assessing how hostile she was, and Edie was wondering how he could bear no trace of a seven-hour flight. Genetics and first class, she guessed.

"Hi. Can I come in?"

She stepped aside. They walked through to the kitchen and into a silence you could slice with a knife from its oak knife block.

"I've had a lot of time to work on something better than 'sorry,' and I've not achieved much," Elliot said. "Edie, to be absolutely clear about our 'deal'—because I felt sick that you needed to ask that—what I'm offering, and what I want, is old-fashioned monogamy, not some creepy variant with loopholes. There's no small print to the exclusivity. I'm not operating on any *what happens on tour* sleazebag rules. I thought that was our understanding, and I think I'd said as much in, erm, *passion*, but probably the

113

weirdness of my situation—our situation—is that I really need to say it in so many words."

He was using his practiced actor poise for this nerve-racking speech, in cold light of day and after an ugly fight. Edie did not have that facility herself and felt her face grow warm and her palms slick in self-consciousness.

She knew exactly which conversation he was referring to, because it was in her internal inventory of treasured moments that she held secretly dear and that she'd never disclose to anyone, including, amusingly, him. It was a bit crass really, because he'd told her he didn't like talk of famousness in the bedroom. ("It feels like putting a distance with me when we're at our closest.") Nevertheless, she'd had her hands on him and breathed in wonder: "I can't believe so many people want you, and I'm the one who gets to have you," and he'd said: "The only one." *Nnnggg.*

The first rule of being-obsessed-with-each-other club is you don't do post-match analysis of the moments of heat. You conjure them up in memory on slow days at work, uncross and recross your legs, and pretend to be concentrating on the greenwashing in the budget airline campaign while remembering that Elliot Owen told you he'd never known desire like this.

"I hate that I forced you to doubt that. What happened was . . . completely disrespectful." He drew a breath. "Because so much of what's written about me is horseshit, somewhere along the line I became arrogant and lost sight of my own responsibilities. I thought because I knew I'd not committed any infidelity, all I had to do was reassure you it was trivial. Now I see that it isn't, not once it's out in the public domain and traumatizing someone I love. All I can do is say sorry, from the bottom of my heart, and that it won't happen again."

"Not sure I like you enough to call it *traumatizing*," Edie joked, now worrying she'd seemed crazy, but Elliot looked pained at this.

She'd said some pretty salty things when possessed by the green-eyed monster, she supposed. *Go to hell, Elliot* was very 1940s weepie.

Edie folded her arms. Anger had evaporated, even if the injury remained, and all she wanted to do was grab hold of him.

She couldn't make it that easy. She'd test the Hannah and Nick hypothesis.

"She was flirting with you."

"Yes," Elliot said, clearly having figured out that only total honesty was going to be sufficient. "She's one of those people who flirts like other people breathe, I think. Not that it's an excuse for me."

"You were flirting back?"

"I was letting her do it because it was easier and because I didn't want to get off on the wrong foot by slapping the behavior down."

"And it was flattering?"

"No, it was low-key stressful. You're trying to figure a new person out, and they're at second base before the plates have been cleared. When it comes to Ines, I just want to be friendly and not snipe at each other when we've got an early call and flambéed crêpes need setting up for eighteen takes. If we don't get on, given the amount of scenes we have together, this job will be pure anguish."

This landed as truthful.

"You don't have 'sizzling chemistry'?" Edie said, with quote marks.

"I hope we mimic that for the show, but no, not otherwise in real life. And I know exactly what that feels like."

Edie was unwinding and would have to concentrate on her last question. "Would you have told me what she was like with you if the photos hadn't come out?"

Elliot paused. "I wouldn't, because it would've upset you and there'd be no need to. I'd have made sure I didn't sit next to her at dinner again. That's sensible while we're long-distance, I think—neither of us need stupid things put in our heads."

Edie had discovered herself unexpectedly reluctant to tell Elliot the Naked Rambler story about Declan, even though it meant nothing and wasn't her fault. It started with a man staying over and ended with him stark bollock, and it just felt . . . tricky. She accepted the justice of what he was saying.

She hadn't planned her side of this conversation and had to take a second or two to work out what she needed to say.

". . . I think I should admit I'm not a Cool Girl, capital C capital G. I totally accept your work is going to involve getting off with other people—I deal with it by sort of . . . dissociating. I emotionally cut out. There will be a day soon when you kiss a stranger for hours on end and remove her clothing, and honestly, I'm not sure I cope with it. I just try not to think about it, which isn't the same thing. I know I wanted you to take this job, and I trust you. But there are limits to what I can handle. When I saw that story, I felt like someone who had agreed that her relationship involved breaking her own heart. In fact, when I saw that story, I wondered if I understood what I'd agreed to at all."

"It was hardly an oversensitive reaction," Elliot said gently, sounding more Nottingham than actor. "Anyone wired up in the normal way would hate it if it was their other half. I bloody would."

That was it: they were fixed. Edie felt understood. It turned out *being taken seriously* was the charm.

20

"I know I'm a big ask and this is a big ask," Elliot said, "but I've realized it's worse than that. I'm asking you to accept things I couldn't tolerate if the situations were reversed. I don't know what it's like to date me, but I don't think I could. Make that make sense."

"Really?"

"Yeah. If you'd said, *mind if I get off with some dude and put my mouth on his parts, it's to make a living?* I'd say *absolutely not and 'art' could get fucked.* Great to know that, on top of being an idiot, I'm a raging hypocrite."

"Did you say this to your ex? Heather?" Edie said. She wasn't trying to set up a competition, more seeking illumination of his nature.

"Ehm . . . I'm not trying to crawl for popularity, but it's never come up because it's never mattered to me like it would matter now. And I selfishly see you as safely outside of the nonsense I dwell in, so I'd not asked myself anything about equivalence. This is quite a learning curve for me."

"You haven't dated a Normal before?" Edie said, smiling.

"Not since I was one, too, though I reject your Normal/Abnormal binaries," Elliot said, smiling back. He paused. "I didn't manage good speech-writing on the flight, but I did try proper thinking."

"Apology accepted," Edie said.

"Can I hug you now?"

"If you must," Edie said, with a small smile.

Once he was holding her, Edie was faintly horrified to find she involuntarily started sobbing into his navy wool shoulder. *Relief, that's why,* she thought. *You saw their hand-holding, and for a split second, you really thought that newspaper might be giving you news.*

"Ah fuck, I'm so incredibly sorry, sweetheart," Elliot said. He'd never used that endearment before, and the tenderness briefly made Edie worse.

"S'OK, I'm exhausted more than upset, really," she said blearily, trying to pull herself together and absorb the moisture by wiping at her face with her sleeve. "Nick mixes strong margaritas, and they helped until they didn't. Plus, you actually being here is pretty trippy. How the fuck are you here?!"

Now that they were repaired, Edie was free to be a heady mixture of incredulous and elated.

"I honestly thought you might be finishing with me," Elliot said. "Fastest decision I ever made. Apologies to the planet."

"It's very movie star."

"Yeah, well, I wanted to make the size of effort that showed I understood the size of the offense."

Edie leaned up and kissed him, and Elliot responded like someone who'd been waiting for the chance and wasn't going to waste the opportunity. He was very good at kissing that was gentle and romantic at the outset and built to something more carnally intentional.

"Have you really got to go straight back?"

Edie was abruptly and specifically wishing it was at least a three-hour layover.

"Yup. I had to plead family emergency to get away this long." He brushed her hair over her ear. "But then again, it was an emergency, and you are my family."

Edie put her face in his coat and breathed him in, and he stroked her hair, and they spent a brief comfortable silence together, simply appreciating proximity.

Elliot glanced around. "Nice here, isn't it?"

"When you're not puking in the garden after reading scurrilous stories."

"You're not serious? Are you?"

He looked so afflicted that Edie quickly added: "If I liked diamonds, I could make you buy me a guilt gift, couldn't I? Is that a terrible gendered thing? Like a 'push present.' Rat tax. A bastardy sparkler."

"A diamond ring?"

Edie hadn't thought of that implication, and her scalp was suddenly hot with the force of cringe. She pulled away. "Oh God, no! Like . . . a necklace, I don't know. I don't know anything about diamonds. I was kidding."

Elliot gave her an unreadable look and said: "Where are Nick and Hannah?"

"Oh, they went on a tactical hike when they heard you were descending."

"They must be properly disgusted with me," Elliot said, grimacing.

"Annoyingly, no. They made your case."

"Oh. Now I wish I'd brought them something from duty-free."

It was barely worth Elliot taking his coat off, but he did anyway, and they spent a foolish yet rewarding half hour entwined on the sofa, trying and failing to concentrate on a conversation.

"Making out in someone else's front room. This feels like teenage babysitting," Edie said.

"Right, I knew leaving you this soon would utterly suck, but I best head back," Elliot said, checking a fancy watch.

"This is the craziest thing anyone has ever done for me," Edie said.

"I dunno, kissing you on a wedding day when you weren't the bride was probably crazier."

Edie put her palm over her eyes.

"Seriously. All I care about is that you're OK," Elliot said. "And that we're OK. Also, I should've remembered from that fight in the street we had what a terrifying adversary you are. Apart from anything else, I'm too scared to fuck around and find out, I promise you."

Edie fake-smiled because, on both occasions, the belief she was being rejected by him had turned her near-feral. Did he not understand the ferocity was in direct proportion to the fear?

They walked to the door and up to the end of path, holding hands.

"Oh—warning, Fraser called me when I was at JFK, so I had to tell him where I was going and why. He knows not to tell our parents and worry them. I also told him not to contact you even if he thinks he's being helpful, which means he's nailed on to contact you and make it worse."

Elliot hugged her tightly one last time and whispered in her ear, words about how much he cared that made her blush.

Spun around and set back down by Hurricane Elliot.

As the Range Rover drove away and pulled Edie's heart behind it like newlywed-car tin cans, she saw she had a WhatsApp from Fraser.

PLEASE PLEASE DON'T DUMP MY BROTHER HE WILL BE FUCKING UNBEARABLE AND WILL GET HIS GUITAR OUT AND TRY TO PLAY "LOVE WILL TEAR US APART" AGAIN, AND HE CANNOT DO THE INTRO PART *AT ALL*. PLEASE PLEASE I BEG I WILL PAY YOU TO KEEP ON BEING HIS GIRLFRIEND, GIVE ME YOUR SALARY SCALE AND I WILL MATCH IT 🙏

Edie snort-laughed and couldn't resist typing back: *too late x*. Only after she pressed *send* did she realize the polite kiss turned a two-word joke into a potentially serious statement, in the strange way that smartphone interactions operated on miniscule margins. Like when *OK!* was friendly and *OK* was sullen.

Fraser

Shit, please tell me you're joking? I was kidding, but seriously, I don't think he's looked at another woman since he met you. Those photos in New York are how he acts when one of my friends is all over him and he's texting me EXTRACTION PLEASE under the table. He's got really used to staying calm when people go weird around him.

Edie tried to reassure Fraser, but she couldn't get the Wi-Fi to hold steady for long enough. While she was pressing *send* in vain, another message arrived.

Fraser

I am only doing this because it might be necessary and NEVER tell him, because he'd kill me and it breaks bro code. But he's not going to bother lying to me, is he?

Attached was a screenshot of their WhatsApp chat:

Fraser

Purely theoretically, are you in there with Ines then? Was all the "PDA" an invitation to bang? It did LOOK like she's keen on you.

Elliot

Yes, thanks, that was very much the problem. I'd prefer it if she isn't. I don't need the drama, and I only hope she's not destroyed my life with the person I do want to sleep with. FFS you nearly had me typing "bang" there.

Fraser

Ines needs a very stern talking to about being too erotic a creature. I should visit you and deliver it. I'd go so far as to call what I am planning "a proper dressing down."

Elliot

What would I do without your wisdom and sagacious counsel.

Fraser

What's a sagacious council?

Edie laughed out loud. She trusted Elliot; she really did. She realized some part of her had been holding out on that, waiting until it was tested. Now it had been.

The strangest thing was, trusting him felt barely less frightening than not trusting him.

21

Edie

Declan, can I get you a Caffe Nero and breakfast on the way in today?
Please be quite bold: I intend to run a workspace that prioritizes ongoing
open dialogue, easy reach solutions, and a front-footed treats policy. E x

Declan

Thanks, I will have a large Americano, pain au raisin, and a scrubbing of
my temporal lobe of all memories of end of last week. D x

Edie

Coming right up. I will organize a Toyota Avensis drive-by: a second
concussion should do it. x

Declan

AAAAAAAARGH X

Auto-kisses with a male colleague off the bat wasn't the way Edie
would usually do business, but these were special circumstances.
If the man wasn't going to shrivel in ignominy and request a hu-
manitarian transfer back to London within a month, they needed
to be comrades. Before the streaking, they were well on their
way. They'd have to treat trauma as glue.

Edie marched in with line manager authority at just gone nine
a.m. and was glad of fussing with setting down his drink, pulling
the pastry out of her pocket, risking a quick glance and a chirpy
"Morning!"

Declan looked up at her with haunted eyes as she set her own
coffee down on her desk. Edie wanted to break the ominous

gap where casual chatter should be but couldn't think of a thing to say.

"Sorry, Edie," Declan said. "I keep having Vietnam flashbacks, and as soon as I do, I think how much worse it must have been for you and your sister . . . It was such an *untoward* thing to put you through."

He looked not sheepish but actually quite broken.

"Hey!" Edie said. "Stop this. You have *nothing* to apologize for. May I remind you that the person here who's made an absolutely horrendous arse of herself in front of ALL her coworkers isn't you? You're blameless."

Declan grimaced and nodded in a silent gratitude, and it occurred to her that he was more upset than she had realized. Perhaps unfairly, she'd thought some fallback of laddish bravado might have helped, but no.

"You know, every minute since I've managed to think about something else, BAM, it rears back up at me," Declan said. "A fresh wave of self-hatred. Like, how long was I there for? I don't even know."

"Hardly any time at all," Edie said, though as she said it, she thought Nude Seconds were an hour in clothed world. "Not to be insensitive, but this is a dynamite pub story at some point, you know. It will alchemize. My worst embarrassments are my best anecdotes."

"Comedy is tragedy plus time," Declan said. "Sorry for forcing you to witness the tragic sight of me on its way to becoming comical."

"You weren't a tragic sight," Edie blurted, and then almost imploded with self-reproach. There it was—*top fuckin' marks, Edith,* she thought: *the one thing you knew you shouldn't say, so you made sure to say it.*

She and Declan met each other's eyes in a second of wordless, blank tension.

"If it distracts, I had quite the shit explosion on my holiday," she gabbled. "A tabloid decided Elliot going for dinner with his costar was proof of boning, and I had to read about their being a 'new couple.' I felt like I'd been forced into public polyamory."

"Ah, really?"

Declan was not a natural liar, and Edie interpreted from his tone that this was not news to him. He didn't seem like he'd read gossipy tittle-tattle about hot actors . . . ?

Oh.

". . . Wait. Jessica's been crowing with delight that I've been cuckolded, hasn't she?"

Declan mumbled indistinctly, and Edie said: "It's all right—don't feel put in the middle. None of it was true, and Elliot and I are still together. I know you're going to be treated as conduit to That Slag Edie."

She was going to seal the deal and incautiously brag *and Elliot came to Derbyshire* then thought, you want that pumped into the bloodstream? Declan—Jessica—*Daily Mail*? Not only that—mercy-dashing over to see her would be taken as confirmation of the story.

"I'm pleased for you," Declan said. "I don't know why Jess and co can't let it go. Well, I do. They're jealous."

"Is that it? Edie did a shit thing so she shouldn't have good things happen to her?"

"Yeah, I think so. That and they all fancy your bloke."

"Not them, too. He has too many people fancying him. It's not good for a man. I made a point of not fancying him when I met him, as a political decision. Look how that's going."

Declan laughed. "You remind me of this girl back home, at sixth form. She won a place at Cambridge and completely aced every exam, and people got really chippy about *who does she think she is*, and she'd not done anything. I worked out that what pissed them off is that she didn't show off or lord it over them, so they had nothing to criticize. Getting a lot of that energy from their disapproval of you. Your crime is being happy with a guy and never showing off about it."

"Apart from one-off drunk Instagrams. Thank you," Edie said. "You're welcome to pass on to Team Jessica that we're still together. If they're going to ignobly glory in my romance going down in flames, it can at least be when it actually has."

"Understood. By the way, I don't know if"—Declan cleared his throat—"you told anyone at work about what happened on Friday? No worries if you did. I'm just girding my loins for the blowback. The GIFs of Michael Fassbender in *Shame*. Or something less flattering."

"Of course not!" Edie said, startled he'd even suspect it. "And I won't—you have my word. You don't deserve them being divs about it. Decent citizens don't stir things like that up for each other—I should know that better than anyone."

"If this isn't too much for the first day we're working together, can I tell you something, Edie Thompson?" Declan said, in his charming brogue. "I think you're a really lovely person."

"Thank you!" Edie said. "The feeling's mutual."

A moment passed.

"Do you know what, if you'd told me last year in the worst of it that I'd ever be sat with someone from Ad Hoc telling me I was a lovely person, I'd have called it science fiction," she said.

Declan paused eating his pain au raisin to chortle at this. "Life has a way of surprising you," he said. "Sometimes I'd like it to surprise me a bit less. I'm sure you'd like my life to have surprised you a bit less, too."

Edie laughed, and they shared a look, the "Smooth Passage" ferry look, when you acknowledge you've made a connection.

22

Edie had yet to return the favor and fly across water to visit Elliot, and yet seeing him in the capital was enough to make her feel out of place, a gauche tourist in a foreign land. His London wasn't her London as she remembered it: it was a parallel version, the playground of the rootless and very rich.

When they were confirming plans for the weekend, Elliot said, with throwaway grandeur that made Edie squirm: "Tell me what time you're getting in—I'll send a car to St Pancras for you."

He did a good job of impersonating a grounded, regular individual most of the time, but on basic analysis, he wasn't one and hadn't been for some time. Edie tried not to flinch at reminders: all relationships were a process of discovery about the other, right?

Elliot wasn't to be deterred by Edie's blushing protestations about swaglording, however.

("Right, then, let me phrase this differently: let me save us an hour and a half.")

The original plan of dinner and drinks had been revised by Fraser. He prevailed on Elliot to introduce Edie to his new girlfriend, Molly. They were throwing a party at a hotel out west, celebrating Fraser's promotion. He was in financial services, and Molly was a fashion buyer, and Edie didn't fully understand what these things entailed. Several friends from home were visiting, too, including Fraz's best friend, the apparently legendary, disreputable Iggy, and the pull was too great to resist.

Elliot had made extensive apologies to Edie, but Edie wasn't at all fussed, as long as they were together.

They'd thrashed this out on WhatsApps in different time zones. Elliot was back in L.A.; the *Void* film had wrapped, but he was needed for something called pickup shots. He was on set in sun-bleached studios in Burbank, wearing black contact lenses and a suit of dark green neoprene, his face drawn on with felt-tip markers for the CGI, as revealed by the scowling selfies he'd sent.

Edie was being suffocated by a cloud of mango e-cigarette and enduring someone blaring *Family Guy* in a queue for the No.58, as not revealed by selfies she didn't send.

Elliot

Being completely honest with you, I'm not sure about Molly. Bit . . . superficial, maybe? She posts Instagram stories where she's kissing Aperol Spritzes to Drake songs. Her family were all over me in an odd way when we met at Fraser's birthday, too. But Fraser's gone all in. So. Fail He May, Sail We Must.

Edie

Hah. I'd love to meet her. And I always enjoy Fraser's company. PS odd how?

Elliot

Yeah, it's the company that's the problem—Fraser's mates are a brace of wags. You know how ginger cats are silly? Prepare yourself for the human equivalent a lot of "orange behavior."
PS explain later. The short version is, I think they like high society.

So it was that on Friday evening, Edie rolled up in a black Mercedes outside a quietly flashy-looking hotel address with logo-ed awnings, downlighters, and a row of wooden box planters delineating premises from pavement.

She pressed *send* on her greeting—*Here! X*—as the driver heaved her no-brand trolley case from the trunk.

Inside, there was a scroll-like sweep of gold reception desk, and Edie felt conspicuously unsuited to the Daliesque luxe gorgeousness.

The women behind it gave practiced smiles of hospitality welcome, and Edie said: "Hi. Uhm, I'm with . . ."

Erk. Elliot usually used false names for hotels, like he was Bono. She'd not asked him what it was.

Both the women suddenly broke into looks of rapture and familiarity at someone over her shoulder.

Edie turned and saw Elliot, phone clamped to face, mid-conversation. He was pointing at Edie and pointing at himself, and then back down again at their check-in screens.

They nodded and beamed with a newfound degree of acceptance toward Edie, started tapping at buttons. A key with a tasseled fob was pushed across the desk and her luggage case was spirited away.

Elliot was wearing black jeans and a dark-blue T-shirt with sunglasses hooked over the neckline, his usual peacocky-actor-boy-off-duty uniform. It was February, but Edie had learned that Rich World was seasonless.

". . . Yeah, I know, but I think we're in danger of seeing Jesus's face in the tea leaves, if you know what I mean?" Elliot was saying. "I don't want to become scared of my shadow . . . yep. I mean, I take your point—you're the expert. It simply didn't register as alarming to me. You keep an eye on it. I will. Thanks. OK." He made the internationally understood circling-finger gesture for *I have to finish this, sorry* to Edie, who nodded.

Edie had grown accustomed to the never-ending phone call, as if Elliot were a stocks-and-bonds trader in the yuppie 1980s. She'd learned not to take it personally. She'd taken it personally in their very first encounter and got it out of the way.

Once done, he'd put his phone on silent, and *missed call* notifications and messages would rain like confetti across the lock screen. It would vibrate and push itself around the table like a resentful wasp.

While the verbal admin continued, he pulled her to his side and kissed the top of her head.

She slid her arms round his middle and linked her hands. As she did so, Edie noticed a row of people sat on a chaise longue nearby observing them both with wide eyes, as if the sofa were a Jeep that had pulled alongside a pride of lions on a safari. Phones were discreetly yet threateningly weighed in several palms. She could hear their thoughts.

Definitely NOT his sister or a P.A. Is it too close-range-obvious to get a picture? As this angle, I could pretend to be checking my texts?

She turned her face away from them.

Edie had raised Lillian's suggestion of a hard launch of their coupledom via staged paparazzi photos to a huge "YUCK" from Elliot.

("She knows my implacable aversion to anything like that, and I don't appreciate her using my girlfriend to try to get round it," Elliot had said. Edie had adolescent-thrilled to the casual use of the G-word. His name in glitter ink on her pencil case.)

"Who was that?" she said, as Elliot rang off.

"Lillian," Elliot said, beaming at her. "It's so good—"

"There she is! Edie Thompson!" came a possibly alcohol-amplified voice from across the lobby. "Soon to be Edie Owen! Or Owen-Thompson? Oh my God, I've got your Brangelina name. EDIOT. Hahahaha."

Elliot closed his eyes and pinched the bridge of his nose.

They were assailed by the hulking form of Fraser Owen, clad in a sky-blue cord suit, salmon-pink shirt, and white trilby hat, skidding toward Edie. He put his arms around her, swung her around in a bear hug, then took her hand and twirled her on the spot.

Fraser's Monster Energy drink behavior was sometimes awful-adjacent, but Fraser was impossible to dislike. Boisterous and silly, but kind. Undeniable shades of witless tomfoolery, no malice. The fact the two brothers were so different, Edie had observed, somehow made them even closer.

Fraser turned to address the sofa audience, who were now sitting very upright, in front-row seats at the Actual Gossip show.

"Just kidding, guys. They're not engaged. Do NOT tweet the *Sun* news desk—thanks for your cooperation."

"Jesus Christ our redeemer, Fraz," Elliot muttered, while Edie laughed helplessly in surprise-horror.

"We're all up on the roof by the pool—come say hi!"

"Not unless you take that hat off," Elliot said. "Why are you dressed like you're in a novelty skiffle band?"

"I'm taking no fashion lessons from disco tits Morrissey here."

"There's a pool?" Edie said. "Amazing."

"I'll show you . . ." Fraser said, bowing, extending his hand.

"Give Edie a chance to drop her coat and we'll join you," Elliot said, gently lowering Fraser's arm and ushering Edie toward the lift.

"Literally drop the coat, Edie, not anything else. Don't be taking her hostage for your dark purposes. No evil cradling!" Fraser said, as Elliot grimaced.

"Fraser, please take it down by at least seventy-eight percent if not a hundred."

His brother ignored him, checking his watch and pointing two fingers at his own eyes, then two fingers back at Elliot's, with a meaningful boggling stare, before departing.

Inside the lift, which had other occupants, Elliot said quietly to Edie with heavy sigh: "Every so often, I remember my parents saying: thank God Fraser doesn't do my job, because it would be like a coked-up raccoon hijacking a 747."

"He'd get 'Sex on Fire' on the sound system and fly it straight to Tahiti."

"And it'd crash into a mountain range while he was chatting up one of the bound-and-gagged air hostesses," Elliot said. "*Heeeeyyyy, so do you want to grab a drink when we land?*"

Edie glimpsed her starstruck, happy little face in the elevator mirror.

"It's so good to see you," Elliot mouthed, and Edie wilted at the thought of being alone together.

23

"Right, cursed object phone is on silent until tomorrow," Elliot said, putting it in his pocket.

He locked the door, revealing his intentions, taking his sunglasses off and throwing them on the bed, in such a way that Edie suspected she'd be the next thing thrown on the bed.

"My case is here already!" she said, thinking she sounded like an easily impressed provincial. The room was standard Elliot Owen: modish frame-only four-poster, multiple zones to the living quarters, and vast marble bathroom stretching onward toward the north of England in the distance.

"More importantly, you are here," Elliot said, focusing on her. "I've missed you so much."

"How much?" Edie said.

"I'll show you," Elliot said, and Edie felt all willpower dissolve as he moved in to kiss her.

"*Elliot* . . . we don't want to arrive an hour late, looking pointedly disheveled?" she said, as they gathered a particular momentum.

"Don't you? I do," Elliot said, untying the belt on her coat and starting to unbutton it. "I want to turn up looking like we were rescued from the Outback in a heat wave, after a fortnight of drinking our piss."

"Dammit, you know how to get a woman in the mood."

They paused getting off to laugh foolishly, and Edie thought it was their real superpower. The one that might outlast the scrabbling-to-get-each-other's-clothes-off era. That said, ever feeling indifferent about that seemed impossible. Elliot was a lavish gift unwrapped on Christmas Day, and she could barely believe she got to keep him.

They were interrupted by an artificial sound, which Edie realized was Elliot's phone making the iPhone tin can rattle ring tone.

"Not on silent?" she said disapprovingly.

"Fucking Fraser on fucking bypass . . ." Elliot said, digging it back out of his jeans pocket. "You, my parents, and him are all on a setting so *silent* doesn't apply."

"Oh."

Edie could hardly still disapprove.

Elliot scanned, hung his head, and read aloud in a psychopath monotone, as if the text were a letter from the Zodiac: "*Seriously, I can SENSE IT IS UNDERWAY. GET YOUR HANDS OFF HER. I know your room number. I will come and play 'Galway Girl' outside your door until you lose wood. FIVE MINUTES to the tin whistle if your tin whistle is outside your Levi's.*"

Edie shrieked.

Elliot shook his head. "I hate him."

"You can't negotiate with terrorists," Edie said, putting her coat on a chair.

She'd worked out the turnaround time between arrival and needing to be presentable was nonexistent—though not as nonexistent as Elliot would've made it—and had traveled party-ready.

"Do I look good enough for this place?" Edie said nervously, smoothing her dress and putting her hands on her waist.

(She was doing the *what, this old thing?* routine, although her low-cut velvet maxi dress with flutter sleeves, tight on the hips, had been selected only after three hefty online deliveries and a front room fashion show for her disapproving sister, who'd have attended in denim shorts. Meg had declared: "Andrea Dworkin said 'women's fashion' is a euphemism for men's fashion created for women. You are trussing yourself, in discomfort, for their gaze. Your power is illusory and heavily boundaried, like an Imperial concubine."

"And if I was oppressing myself for the benefit of their patriarchal gaze, which one would do the job best?"

"The long midnight-blue one."

"*Thank you.*")

Elliot looked her up and down now and said: "I don't think this place looks good enough for you. You have no idea how much I'm regretting saying yes to my brother's plans right now."

Edie smiled and stepped toward him to kiss him on the cheek.

Elliot jumped away. "*Don't* or I'll choose the threesome with Ed Sheeran."

ODDLY ENOUGH, HAVING threatened aural contraceptive guerrilla attacks, Fraser and Molly were nowhere to be seen when Elliot and Edie made it to the rooftop, the nocturnal London vista stretching out beyond its glass walls.

Elliot waved at familiar faces, but instead of approaching, he parked them at a cabana at the opposite end of the pool, away from the throng. They were unable to be overheard and could see anyone approaching, thus could have an express form of date before the rowdiness across the water enveloped them. Naturally, a waiter appeared immediately; it was that kind of place.

"What was the Lillian call about? Seeing Jesus in the tea leaves?" Edie asked, as she decorously moved the glacé cherry stalk to sip a Manhattan.

"Oh no, was that super indiscreet of me? It actually wasn't a conversation to be having in public, but I couldn't wait to see you," Elliot said.

"No, not at all, stayed very one-sided and gnomic. Hence you've intrigued me."

"You know I hated *The Void*, right?"

Edie nodded. One of their catch-ups after their hiatus had been about how much Elliot loathed being the lead in a super-hero big budget "tentpole" movie. He'd found it both stultifying in process and overwhelming in terms of responsibility.

("I thought of what George Clooney said: everyone told him he had to do *Batman* because it was such a smart career choice—it bombed, and he found out everyone's making it up as they go along. I've decided to do what appeals and sod what I'm being told to do for 'profile.'"

"Imagine Clooney being your career adviser," Edie had said. "Mine was Mr. Rumble, who told me to get shorthand and a shorter skirt.")

"OK, well," Elliot said now, "the plan for the publicity campaign, given I won't sign for another, is to vague it out. Not commit to a sequel but kind of bland-positive 'never say never.'" Elliot paused, beer bottle to lips. "You know, that thing you say when it's a no but you want to provide fake hope, instead of hard honesty and closure."

It took a second for Edie to realize she'd been the victim of a British stabbing.

24

Elliot smiled a small smile, but the resentment wasn't feigned. Edie had still not grasped the extent of the hurt she'd caused him. She asked herself: if he'd said the same when detaching from her, would she have tried again? Hard no. But he was who he was. He was the chooser.

"Wow," Edie said. "*Fake hope*. Yeah, no hope at all, none." She gestured at herself, the surroundings. "Welcome to Dumpsville. Population, not you."

"Only because I begged you. *Twice*," Elliot said.

"Is it possible you're not used to doing the running?"

"Ah, there it is. If in doubt, call Elliot a conceited, prima donna wankboy."

He grinned as his eyes slid toward her, and Edie tried to get a measure of this. It was definitely flirty play-fighting, but that didn't mean he was using dummy bullets as ammunition.

"No, a compliment. When so many people want you, rejection must hit all the harder as unusual."

"Hmm. You know, when you were asking me things for the book, and I said fame was, to my surprise, not a fix for a lot of things you subconsciously assume it will be? That's one of them."

"What is?"

"Lots of people wanting you isn't a cure for the one person you want not wanting you."

"If you mean me, luckily, I did, and I do. To a quite debilitating extent." Edie checked they were still speaking in relative isolation. "You can't accept it was terror of failure, not *not wanting this enough*, can you?"

"I'm trying, but if I'm honest, not really."

"Why not?"

"Because I was worried we'd crash and burn, too, but it wasn't nearly enough to outweigh the wanting."

He shrugged his shoulders, smiled apologetically, and drank his drink.

Edie sensed this had gone slightly further than Elliot intended. Also, it was a grossly unfair that he looked sensational when sulking.

His expression reminded her of his turn in a soft rock music video where he drove around the Mojave Desert being sexily furious a model had cheated on him, during which she implausibly needed to hitch a ride from him at an isolated gas station. Edie very much felt like the treacherous skank in denim hot pants having to plead for his passenger seat.

"Maybe the ratio of wanting isn't the differential. Maybe it's the relative levels of worry. As in, you're braver than me," Edie offered. She leaned over and kissed him on his silly mouth.

"Do not exploit my attraction to you as a conflict resolution tool, please. It will work pathetically well," Elliot said, and Edie recognized it as return peacemaking.

"*The Void*? Jesus? Tea leaves?" Edie prompted. "Bashing fainthearted Edie was a detour?"

"Oh yeah. Lillian's decided someone's leaking. I don't know if you've seen any stories, but the unnamed source quotes have said I'm 'disenchanted' with the role, and that I 'didn't get into this job to act to tennis balls dangling in front of green screens.'"

"Isn't that accurate?"

"It's entirely accurate—that's the problem. The screen thing I don't recall saying word for word, but it's 'disenchanted.' Lillian said, 'That's a you word.' Something I would say. Something I *have* said. Lillian said: 'You have a distinctive way of phrasing things, and it leaped out at me.' Ergo, Lillian thinks whoever briefed the *Hollywood Reporter* has spoken directly with me. There have been a few similar things, and now she's gone full Miss Marple."

"Shit."

"The only people I'm that candid with are you, my parents, Fraser, my two best mates back home, Al and Dan, and my musician friend, Cameron, who's in L.A. and got his own concerns and no love of the muckrakers. If Al and Dan are talking to the *Hollywood Reporter* after the school run in West Bridgford, I'm Shirley Bassey. It's genuinely comical to imagine it."

Edie frowned. "Not a long list, then? Could it be a third-party person, trusted by one of us?"

Elliot inclined his head toward the people nearby. "Who's the new factor?" he said very quietly.

"*Molly*?" Edie said in hoarse whisper.

"It's crossed my mind. No way am I blowing up my relationship with my brother, or his girlfriend, by insinuating it. That's a pickle, huh."

"Is Lillian pushing you to speak to Fraser?"

"Uhm . . ." Elliot looked uncomfortable, and Edie couldn't figure out why. "Lillian said it didn't start on the Molly timeline. It began around the time we began seeing each other again. I responded with considerable vigor to that suggestion, obviously."

"Fucking hell, what? You don't think . . . ?"

"Whoa, whoa. *I* don't think it, nor did I tolerate it being speculated." Elliot grabbed for her free hand across the table. "There's no world, no alt verse, in which you'd sell stories on me. I said to Lillian: 'I don't think Edie is incapable of this because I'm in love with her; I'm in love with her because of who she is—which is a person who isn't capable of such a thing. End of discussion.'"

"Well. Thank you," Edie said, grateful for his loyalty but also stung and recalculating regarding Lillian. She knew she'd not won her respect or affection by proxy, but treating Edie as a potential threat was something else.

In fact, now she thought about that Zoom meeting, it occurred to her that this was the underlying theme throughout: how might she do damage to Elliot, and how it might be mitigated.

"Musician Cameron in L.A. . . ." Edie said. "Not . . . Cameron McAllister?"

Edie felt foolish saying it, even though it wasn't, in this context, foolish. He'd had about six number one hits and currently had a Vegas residency. His Radio Two–friendly balladeering wasn't to Edie's taste, but his success was phenomenal: no aisle walk, signing of the register, or wedding reception was safe from him. The press loved the story: from Kilmarnock barman to the Scottish Sinatra, residing in Beverly Hills.

"Yeah."

"Oh my God, *Cameron McAllister* is one of your best mates! That's insane. Isn't he . . . a bit of a twat?"

Edie was being mildly provocative because she felt a minor quease, strangely akin to when a woman tried it on with Elliot. There was so much she didn't know about him. He wasn't only hers; he was many other things to many other people.

"A twat how?"

"An arrogant womanizer who leaves a trail of female devastation in his wake."

"He has a lot of casual flings, yeah, but no shortage of offers, so I'm not sure it's a vice, per se, just a lifestyle. He won't play the PR game when something has run its course, so the press always brands him a cad. The truth is he is got dumped by his first big forever love at twenty and it destroyed him, and every woman since is him trying to find her tribute act. Or hoping his ex will notice."

"Ahhh, the old sad shagger alibi. *I'm only doing it because of the hole in my soul, honey. Now pop your thong off.* Hahaha."

"You slag my friend off for things you've seen in gossip magazines, and I give you necessary, painful personal context, and you have even *more* of a go at him?"

"Kidding."

"Didn't you say I was a total loser who looked like a 'trainee barista' before you knew me?"

"Hahaha. I changed my mind. You can draw all the hearts in my lattes."

"Yeah, eaten *and* drunk your words there, eh? Now pleading with me for an extra shot in your macchiato."

Elliot gave her a knowing look at his emphasis on *pleading*, and Edie flushed: he was breaking the things-that-never-get-discussed-after-the-fact rule.

"Stop there, please."

"Hmm, as I recall at the time it was *please don't stop, Elliot . . .*" He smiled at her scowl. "Anyway . . . Cam's one of those hard-core heartbreak cases where he says he wishes she'd hurry up and get married and have kids so his hope could be definitively snuffed out, not wafting around still single but not choosing him. Every song is about her."

"Even the one about the girl who sleeps with his best friend and he forgives her, and she leaves him for the friend in the end anyway?"

The women at Ad Hoc had been known to well up over it on the radio. Call her a cynic, but Edie thought treating shagging your best mate as a verbal warning not an instant dismissal was destined for doom. DFD, as Elliot had once called it.

"Especially that one."

"Oof."

"He's written a song about us actually, you know. It's probably going to be a single."

Edie felt faint. "No way! You're winding me up . . . Oh my God, really?"

"We were having a heart-to-heart, and I said I had to go and see you, because I didn't know if every day that passed was the one where you'd meet the next person and I'd lose you. I didn't know which day was the last time I had any chance. He goes, 'Oh hell, that's a song,' and next thing I know, he's playing me 'Last Time.'" Elliot put his head on one side. "Not all of his stuff is my thing, but it is quite good, to be fair."

"Speechless," Edie said. "Can't wait for the women at Ad Hoc who hate me to wave lighters to it at the O2."

"They still hate you for the wedding thing?"

"The wedding thing and, I'm told by my colleague Declan, the Elliot Owen thing."

"Ack. Sorry."

"Not your fault."

"I have a lot to thank Cam for. He made me realize that the grueling prospect of standing on your doorstep and telling you I'd do anything to make this work wasn't hard, compared to not doing it."

"Elliot," Edie began, not sure what she was going to say but absolutely sure it needed saying.

"Oh, holy fucking fuck," Elliot hissed, looking into the distance, and Edie followed his line of sight.

A banner, along with the couple of the moment, had appeared behind the melee.

Congratulations, Fraser & Molly!

25

"Where's my brother?" Fraser called, and Elliot was out of his seat, hand held out for Edie, in a split second, weaving down the side of the underlit pool.

As they drew closer, Edie saw Molly was leaning on Fraser and extending the fingers on one hand for inspection by the women near her in an unmistakable way. Edie had an unwelcome flashback to Charlotte in the same pose at Ad Hoc—another lifetime ago, for everyone involved.

"We've done a bit of a bait and switch on you tonight, guys!" Fraser said. "This is actually our *engagement party*. Molly proposed to me this week—that's right, we're very modern, guys—and I said *yes*." He let the whooping and hollering subside before adding: "Molly's folks have very generously said they'll put a marquee up in the garden for the big day. We've called in a favor at their local church—my in-laws-to-be are tight with the vicar—so . . ."

Fraser waited until a hush had descended. Elliot hard-squeezed Edie's hand, and she recognized it as a contained panic signal.

". . . Wedding is in April! GET HAT SHOPPING!"

Cue cheering and whistling.

"April next year, right?" Elliot said to Edie, looking stunned.

"I feel like: *the wedding will be in a year and two months* is less of a thing you'd shout, before spraying Veuve Clicquot?" Edie said under her breath, looking back at Fraser now doing a Formula 1. He had a sidekick: a cherubic, ginger, curly-haired lad who Edie guessed was the notorious Iggy. All Owen family stories that noted Iggy's presence tended to be of the colorful variety.

"*Iggy*," they said, shaking heads, in the same way you'd intone *crack pipe*.

Fraser's powder-blue suit, his five-foot-nothing bride in a cerulean dress—the level of fuss did seem more consistent with that sapphire bauble on her left hand than with Fraser moving up to greater managerial responsibilities. But how could Edie have foreseen it? This was how she thought the Owens always rolled.

"No way . . ." Elliot said. She'd never seen him lost for words before. "He can't be for real."

Fraser and his diminutive bride-to-be were mobbed by eager well-wishers, and Edie and Elliot were edged out of the inner circle, waiting their turn in the scrum.

Edie thought this was no bad thing if it gave Elliot time to get his face straight. The indecent haste seemed to have floored him.

"Can I be your date for the wedding?" Edie asked, grasping for a nice thing to say.

"Sure. You won't need to get changed—we'll taxi from here," Elliot said, and Edie grit-smiled back at him.

"*ELLLLIIOOOOTTT!* You're going to be my brother," squealed Molly, bowling into his arms.

Elliot said: "Congratulations! Can I introduce you to my girlfriend?"

"Oh! Edie! I've heard so much about you."

Molly turned, face aglow. She was alive with the exhilaration of the occasion but strikingly pretty anyway: wide, round eyes; small, upturned nose; and wide, toothy smile. Her light brown hair was back in a loose plait. She was woodland-cartoon-animal cute, and after a second's consideration, Edie thought she should've predicted this would be Fraser's type. One thing Fraser always managed to be was wholesome. You could stick Molly on a *This Morning* presenting segment, no problem.

Both she and Edie made polite noises of enthusiastic greeting and did the little mutual back-pat party hug, though it was tricky for Molly to have much spare bandwidth for making new acquaintances given the circumstances.

An overclocking Fraser joined them. "See—this is why I had to whip you to be here on time!" he said to Elliot, grabbing him round the shoulders. "You and Iggy are my best men, of course."

"Congratulations, Fraz. You've told Mum and Dad?" Elliot asked evenly, and Edie knew exactly what he was thinking and feeling underneath the smooth surface.

"FaceTimed them this afternoon, and I've asked Molly's dad for permission. All sorted."

"They're excited, then?" Elliot said.

Fraser and Molly were vibrating at a frequency where Elliot's concern wasn't registering, which was just as well.

"Yeah, they love Molly . . ." Fraser held her hand as she twisted round and spoke to others near them, like a parent keeping hold of a willful child in a toy shop. "They were a bit shocked they've got less than two months to prepare, haha!"

"*Were they?* What's the thinking there, then?"

"Why wait?" Fraser said, shrugging, as Molly peeled off entirely to show another gaggle of girls her ring. "We watched *When Harry Met Sally*, and it clicked. When you know you want to spend the rest of your life with someone, you want the rest of your lives to start straightaway. *No, Iggy, YOU put that down, come the fuck on . . . !*"

Fraser's attention was captured by some other point of interest, and he capered off again. With bombshell dropped, his already divided attention span was fractured into a hundred pieces. He was full Imp Mode.

Elliot held a placeholder smile for onlookers as he said, in a low voice: "*What-the-fuck-just-happened-Edie?* They've known each other less time than we have. Nora Ephron films are not a You-Tube tutorial."

"It's . . . a lot," Edie whispered. "Also, being picky . . . hadn't Harry and Sally known each other about a decade? The whole point is it takes them years to realize?"

Elliot squeezed her hand again. "You're the voice of sanity I need. I also need another one of those," Elliot said, looking at a tray of beers. "I might need twenty. I'll go to the loo—get you another of those red things on the way back?"

Edie nodded, knowing a Diet Coke would be wiser. She'd consumed one skewer total of some spicy chicken business.

Edie saw Elliot seized by a guest on his way, so his return would not be instantaneous. She was going to have to do the dreaded mingling. Did anyone look approachable?

They were intimidatingly loud, confident, *Made in Chelsea*–ish: salon-blown hair, tanned legs jutting through splits in dresses, quilted bags on chains with logos, the men all bone structure and signet rings. They were what Hannah called "Upspeaking Yahs."

Edie had a pang for Nick and Hannah. Followed by a harder pang that these weren't her people and never would be, and that sharing taste in human beings mattered.

26

Edie surveyed the tables of food and the endlessly replenished drinks, no card machines in sight, and idly wondered: who paid? Was it Elliot, or was it Fraser, or both? Or neither? In Elliot's world, you never saw a bill, or the transaction.

There were many who'd revel in the rampant prosperity, and Edie felt guilty even analyzing it, both ungrateful and disloyal. They'd done the kids chat, not the money one.

Except one late-night confessional when she'd mentioned worrying about her dad's slightly threadbare existence and Elliot had said: "If you ever needed anything, you'd tell me, wouldn't you? You know I would fix anything you asked me to?"

Edie had said: "Yes, thank you," while thinking: *God no, but thank you.*

They said no more, as it was surprisingly sensitive. Your boyfriend buying dinner—lovely. Your boyfriend paying off mortgages—you're off the Normal map.

But it wasn't as if a broke partner was easy. If Edie considered Elliot's tax bracket a problem, it was the most champagne one imaginable. More than champagne, it was a *my private jet has the wrong color carpet* problem.

What was it that bothered her, if she drilled down? It was the inequality. Irresolvable inequality. If she and Elliot ever moved in together, it'd be to his house, not their house, because the idea she could meaningfully contribute would be farcical.

Edie thought of what Hannah said: *Build a life together that's the right size for both of you.* On basic floor plan terms, she could make her life bigger for him through his largesse and her compliance. He couldn't, realistically, make his life much smaller for her. It was a fairy tale all right: millionaire accepts life on Skid Row, for love.

Except it wasn't Skid Row: she cherished Carrington and her house, and she liked being in charge of her life.

This existential angsting wasn't helping, and she shook it off.

Edie decided her opener would be: *How do you know Fraser?*—preferable to striding into conversations and saying: *Hi, Edie Thompson, ad exec.*

"Hi, I'm Edie," she said to the nearest person, doing her most winsome smile. "I'm trying to meet people. How do you know Fraser?"

"Anto," the man said, extending his non-Peroni-holding hand to shake Edie's. He was a wolfish sort of handsome: very underfed facial contours softened by a beard, slim-fit jacket fastened with one button.

"Anto, that's a cool name—is it Italian?"

Anto nearly spat his beer. "*Anthony.* I like that, though. I might start telling people I am. I come from the Latin quarter of Stevenage."

"Hahaha."

"I work with Fraser. How do you know him?"

"Through Elliot."

"Ah, we know to hang back from Elliot's people. We don't know the correct protocol."

"Really?"

"Yeah, it's a thing with the brothers. Fraser's a pretty strict gatekeeper . . ."

He cast a glance at him that Edie followed. Fraser was doing Bez-style monkey dancing to Happy Mondays' "Hallelujah" and seemed highly unlikely to be a strict anything.

"*Fraser* is?"

"Yeah. Fraser is of Elliot. Elliot is of his friends and his girl-friends. There's layers of security to get past."

His girlfriends. Edie hoped the lightning bolt of jealousy that hit her out of the blue wasn't evident. She never wanted to think of herself on a roster.

"Hang on, are you here with Elliot, or are you *with* Elliot?"

Edie's stomach tensed. "*With*-with."

"He's not still seeing the Swedish girl from the end of last year?"

What? "Uhm, I hope not."

"Thank God for that—she was a law unto herself. Ungovernable. Always dragging him away by the scruff at intervals to broom cupboards. Seemed exhausting and eventful. Did you come far today?"

"From Nottingham," said Edie, clenched in misery, despising a faceless, nameless, libidinous Nordic rival.

Also, Elliot had been seeing someone while they were apart? He had no case to answer if so; Edie had openly said they were single and free. Yet it hurt. Badly. So much for *I've thought about nothing else but you.*

"Oh, my brother went to uni there! I used to visit him," Anto said.

There followed a discussion of which bars and clubs were still standing, during which Edie pictured a blonde kneeling in front of her boyfriend.

"I saw you earlier, actually, if I'm honest," Anto said. "I thought, who's that girl? Why is someone who looks like a Blythe doll not at the center of things? Makes more sense now I know you're with the Owen mafia. An Owen goomah."

"I don't know what a Blythe doll is but thanks, I think."

Anto swiped his phone open and showed her. Edie read: *Blythe is a fashion doll with an oversized head and large eyes that change color with the pull of a string.*

Edie paused. "Aren't Mafia goomahs mistresses?"

"Hahaha, oh sorry, yeah. Not implying anything—I just like the word. I'm a *Sopranos* ultra."

Edie fretted on the fact Elliot had lied to her regarding the Swedish girl. Unforced untruths were lies.

"Me too," Edie said, absently. "I rewatch 'Pine Barrens' at least once a year. It had me calling people at work 'rat cocksuckahs' way too much, though."

"Oh, I like you," Anto said. "I really like you."

Edie decided he went to an expensive school, as he had exactly that kind of edges-sanded-off patrician sexism. *I like you, you crazy little potty-mouthed thing.* Acceptance was his to bestow upon her.

"Want to meet some more people?" Anto asked, as if she'd passed a test.

Edie acquiesced with a smile and, his hand lightly on her lower back, Anto did the rounds.

"This is Edie, she's from Nottingham," Anto said, to bland indifference and flickering assessment. He weighted the pause with the skill of a practiced showman, adding: ". . . She's Elliot's girlfriend."

The air pressure changed, and suddenly everyone was aflutter, full attention, *hiiiiii nice to meet you what did you say your name was.*

Edie hated it. Not because she didn't get a small thrill at being his or being envied or admired for it—she had to admit that she did. But because it was so wholly conditional. If Elliot finished with her, he might as well have pushed her off the rooftop in terms of their correspondingly plummeting levels of interest. It wasn't possible to feel good about that. Edie knew exactly how empty those calories were.

She answered questions politely and asked questions politely, planning her escape throughout. Eventually, Edie thought: *hang on, where IS Elliot and my ill-advised cocktail?*

She excused herself and found him, besieged, because alcohol levels were high and inhibitions were lower. Even at London rooftop parties full of wannabe Gatsbys and Daisys, celebrity was celebrity.

She sussed that meekly waiting for people to disperse wasn't going to work.

"Elliot, can I borrow you for a minute?" Edie said, at an assertive pitch.

Eyes trailed her resentfully as she took him by the hand and pulled him out of the group and back up the side of the pool.

"Apologies, that became intense, and I don't want to offend Fraser's friends," Elliot said.

"I want to go back to our old table, but it feels like that looks too pointed now? Like we're not making the effort," Edie said.

"See what you mean." Elliot looked over her shoulder. "You know, if you kissed me, that would probably deter approaches. Just a thought."

"In spy films, the man always suggests they kiss so people *don't* notice them."

"Either works for me."

Edie's reticence to be linked with Elliot had only ever been about avoiding the deluge of attention, and meanwhile, she'd forgotten to value the part where he was always happy to go public with her.

Nick had said in the Dales: "Don't spend so much time looking for red and beige flags that you start taking the green for granted," to which Edie had replied: "Wise," and social media allergic Hannah said: "Jesus Christ, you understood that shite?!"

27

Some time—and a proper reunion, featuring no "Galway Girl"—later, Elliot and Edie lay awake against starched square pillows, room illuminated by pools of honeyed light from chintzy lamps, picking over the evening's events.

Edie wasn't surprised to discover that Elliot was a stern critic of the imminent nuptials.

"I'm going to have to talk to Fraser ASAP, and I'm absolutely dreading it. I rate my chances of getting through to him very low and my chances of making myself persona non grata very high. I know the nice brotherly thing would be cheering it on. But he has friends to do that. Unlike them, I can see where it ends. He'll take being a thirty-year-old divorcé very hard, however he may come across."

"You definitely think it'll fall apart?"

"Marrying his girlfriend this quick? After six months together? I mean, it'll be a miracle if it pans out, won't it? My parents are no doubt chagrined but won't be as direct as I'm going to be. Fuck's sake, I know he can be hyperactive, but this latest clownery is stretching credulity even for him. *Shotgun weddings.*"

"You don't think . . . ?"

"Oh, nah. Speaking figuratively. She was hard on the champagne."

Edie shook her head: "I guess . . . if they're happy . . . ?"

"They are, though whether there's anything like enough between them to get married is another thing." He paused. "Please don't repeat this next part, because I won't go anywhere near it with Fraz, but I think I may be a factor."

"You?"

"Yep . . . I hate talking about it, because there's no way I can without it coming across as self-obsessed, *world revolves round me* shit. This is why it's good to know Cam—he and I can privately compare notes on the insanity with no one calling us ego-ridden megalomaniacs."

"Allow me," Edie said.

Elliot laughed. "There's nothing I can't share with you. A thing Cam said to me early on was: 'getting famous is like winning the lottery.' All good when they're handing the big check over, but it affects everyone around you. You can't foresee the impacts. This is absolutely confidential, but Cam bought a large house outright for his sister. Her deadbeat, dodgy ex-boyfriend, who they hoped had gone for good, came straight back and proposed. Nothing Cam could do—it's her life. Not like you can revoke a gift like that, based on choice of spouse. He'd accidentally honey-trapped an absolute wastrel. Your success is a butterfly wing flap effect. More of an eagle wing flap."

"Fuck!"

"Yeah, so you see why being nice doesn't always cover it. No danger of that here, in as much as Molly's family are well-off, a little dynasty in their bit of Suffolk, I think. But I got the distinct feeling they've gone wild on Fraser as a son-in-law prospect because he's a package deal with me. Fraz is immensely good-natured, and that's the kind of thing he misses. I'm far more cynical and alert to it. They bombarded me with inappropriate questions when I met them. Molly's dad took me on a tour of his wine cellar. They'd volunteered to host Fraser's birthday—which seemed a lot—then specifically asked he bring me. Fraser saw it all as the generosity of their welcome and to me it felt more like the hospitality you get as veiled corporate aggression. 'We're in charge here. We've ordered for you.'"

"Maybe they were a bit overwhelmed by your status, and mishandled it?"

"I know. I allow for that. I know the difference between natural curiosity and how it feels to be sized up as a valuable acquisition. My instincts said, fame groupie social climbers who want the connection. I know that sounds awful. And in what world do you say: *they're using you to get to me*, and not expect your brother to hate you?"

"You don't think Molly is?"

The fact Elliot hesitated, Edie thought, said a lot.

"I don't know. I sincerely hope not. Fraser's never struggled for female attention, irrespective of anything I've been doing. If you'd asked me before today, I'd have said no, but now she's pushing to be Mrs. Fraser practically overnight . . . I'm not sure I can completely subtract it. Fraser's had to fend off her attempts to put me on her Instagram many, many times."

"I got away with it."

"That's different. I have to beg you to be seen with me."

Edie laughed. "I completely see the wisdom of what you're saying, and you absolutely have Fraz's back. I feel protective of you wading into this, though, because I'm not sure telling anyone not to marry anyone else ever goes well. I hope he realizes you're doing it because you love him."

"To be clear, I'm not telling him not to marry her. I'm telling him not to do it this fast."

Edie doubted Fraser would make that distinction and said nothing.

Elliot sighed. "When we were kids, he would climb trees so high the fire service had to get him down. He hitchhiked to Glastonbury with no credit card, kept all his cash in a Converse sneaker. He called it Bank of Boot. Of course, it got stolen, and my dad had to drive down and get him. When he was twenty-two, he went to Thailand with his best mate, Iggy—who, as you may have gleaned, is a complete mongoose. They had no jabs, flew out with no insurance. A tuk-tuk driver nicked their passports, and he had Dad at the embassy for hours with photocopies of his birth certificate, to get them home . . . You get the idea. This is absolutely consistent with Fraser's relentless pursuit of calamity."

"In light of this, can I be annoyingly logical?"

"You're the smartest person I know, so all and any confrontational opinions are welcome."

"If this is classic Fraser, then Molly's family might be an incidental factor?"

"Yeah, fair point. I suspect the full picture is petrol has met matches. Flammable has met accelerant. Anyway, enough of my whining. I hope you had a good enough time tonight."

Edie hesitated. Wanting to be a Cool Girl was at war with need for reassurance.

"I always enjoy seeing Fraser, it's . . . just . . ." Edie felt the booze, the emotion, and the environmental dislocation come together suddenly, like three lanes of traffic all green lit at once, moving forward and honking at each other.

"What?"

"I don't fit in with your crowd, do I? I thought the fact there'd be a Nottingham lot meant I'd be OK, but I'm still a sore-thumb outsider in her ASOS dress. And when it's not private schoolers with YSL handbags, apparently it's Cameron McAllister. I know you've made an effort with my friends, and I want to reciprocate. But if tonight's any test, prepare yourself for ongoing confusion about why you're with me."

Elliot blinked at her, and she felt like a dick.

"Sorry. That was a lot of words for *I felt stupidly lonely when you left my side. I need to be a grown-up.*"

There was a silence, and Edie pondered that drinking on no dinner was never wise.

"You know I said you're a catastrophist? I think it might be a full-on doom boner. Nothing gets you going like the chance to foretell disaster," Elliot said.

"Doom boner?!" Edie said, laughing in relief.

"One parody *Wolf of Wall Street* do thrown by my brother is not a litmus test of anything."

"Well, to make it worse . . ." Was she going to say this? It seemed she was. Elliot might not have done anything wrong, but she wanted him to account for the discrepancy, at least. "When I tried to socialize, I met some guy who told me you were seeing a very, er, volatile Swedish girl during our break? It intimidated the fuck out of me. I don't want to know about your exes, and he didn't need to tell me that, did he? It was the first day at school, I tried to make friends in the playground, and he promptly stuffed snow down the back of my coat."

"I was seeing someone who was what, now?"

"He said you had a fling with a very randy Swedish girl."

Edie waited for Elliot to look shifty. He only looked nonplussed. "I have no such ex. Genuinely. After we split up?"

"Yes."

"I didn't see anyone when we were apart—I told you that. I had no interest, after that karate chop to the windpipe you dealt me. Also, I'd have karmically felt I was giving you permission in return, and screw that. No way was I handing you a hall pass."

He smiled at her. Edie exhaled in gratitude at having normality as she currently understood it being fully restored. He could

gibe at her fickleness all he wanted now. It was almost worth being wound up about fictional Swede to vanquish her.

She pushed her arms round him and reminded herself that she
alone got to do this.

"Who told you that?" Elliot said.

"Uhm . . . Anto! Full name Anthony of Stevenage."

"Edie, I have no idea who this guy was, but he was probably
hitting on you."

"Hitting on me?"

"That's the only reason I can think he'd be lying to you? De-
stabilize your prey with undermining bullshit and then go in with
the feelings repair kit. Let me guess, you got compliments, too?"

Edie opened her mouth and closed it and said: "Hitting on me,
when I'm here with you, though?"

"*The audacity of hope.*"

Edie was at a loss to understand why anyone would do this,
which was no doubt what Anto relied on.

". . . That is so casually monstrous."

Edie had been briefly in the company of a supervillain and had
no idea. That was sociopathic straight after a "hello?" He knew
who she was from the start. He'd pulled a string, and her eyes had
changed color.

"My friends will love you. I hope it's very clear from that—
those weren't my friends. Could you eat? I say we get room service."

Edie beamed.

"Oh God, I could murder a burger and chips, actually. Is that
possible, when it's this late?"

As the words left her mouth, Edie thought: *you're probably in a
£1.5k-a-night suite.*

Elliot paused, and she could see him calculate this wasn't the
time to ridicule her naiveté. "Reckon it is."

• • •

THEY PULLED NIGHTCLOTHES on and ordered a decadent amount of food, putting it on the bed and eating it sat cross-legged.

"About your feeling out of place," Elliot said, in a different register to his joking, as he brushed his hands of chip salt, "the secret truth of my life, one that I've never told a living soul, is that I'm homesick as a permanent way of being. I've been homesick so long now I've almost forgotten how it feels to not be homesick. Worst of all, I don't even know what I'm homesick *for*."

"*Saudade*," Edie said, a Portuguese word she'd introduced Elliot to when they were falling for each other. ". . . *A profound longing for something or someone absent, that may never return.*"

"Exactly that. The only time I don't feel that way is when I'm with you. Before you came along, it was as if I was shut in a room no one else could get into. You came in and sat beside me. Not asking for anything, not with any agenda. Nobody had ever done that, and it was such a powerful feeling, not being alone. You do belong here, Edie, because you belong with me. And I belong with you."

He looked up, and tears were running down Edie's face, tears that she didn't wipe away.

28

Edie awoke to the minor confusion of blackout curtains plunging the room into a permanent midnight, and no one else in the bed. She sat up. No sounds of a shower running?

The mystery of Elliot's whereabouts lasted under a minute before he reappeared through the door, fully dressed, brandishing the ubiquitous phone, and looking like he'd had a day of meetings already.

"Morning. Brace yourself," Elliot said, seeing she was awake and switching a lamp on. "Someone sold pictures of us last night, and they're running already."

"Fuck! What?! Who did that?"

"No idea. My galaxy-brained brother failed to tell us that, though it looked it like a private party, it wasn't. I quote: 'We'd maxed the limit for how many people allowed up there with our guest list, so I thought that'd do it.' They were doing one in, one out, so there were members of Joe Public present throughout. Or we could be tidy and blame it on Anto of Stevenage."

"Oh . . . shit . . ."

"The other Chuckle Brother here had his phone on silent, so no one could get hold of me. I'd already told Lillian that, if she was asked to confirm we were together, she should say yes. She went with that. She used it as barter to stop them putting a 'Do you know Edie?' number to call at the end of it, too. I hope that's all right. I didn't see the mileage in lying?"

"Sure, yes."

Oh God, the hotline tip: she'd been through that mill. It felt like she was on Morrisons CCTV with a frozen chicken up her rain poncho and had made Crimestoppers.

A quietness fell as Edie digested the news that she was, at this present moment, naked in a four-poster bed and simultaneously exposed in unknown ways on another platform.

"Are you working up to being angry and freaked out? It's understandable if so. I put you in this situation, in more than one way, and it's not fun."

"No . . ." Edie said. "Unless I look like a root vegetable?"

"Derp. You look gorgeous because you are. Want to see the write-up? I personally think it's not too bad, but I'm a grizzled veteran of this shit, obviously. Plus, I know you weren't keen on the limelight."

"I knew it had to happen—it just made me anxious." She tucked the covers more tightly under her armpits and took a shaky breath. "Yes, bring it on."

"Here, stop you squinting at a phone screen."

Elliot picked up a laptop from the table at his side, opened it, and brought up a tabloid page.

He placed it on the duvet in front of her.

**EXCLUSIVE: Elliot Owen and the girl next door.
Star's new girlfriend is ad exec from Nottingham.**

Edie gulped and could feel a pulse in her neck.

It was deeply disconcerting to view photos of yourself you'd not seen before, or even realized were being taken, at the same time as a newspaper's website with huge international eyeball traffic.

Try the sensation of having been tagged in a Facebook album when in your cups, multiply it by many magnitudes, and take LSD.

Edie could see the pictures were all from a certain phase of the evening, after the engagement announcement, when Elliot and Edie had put a distance with the crowd, and he'd suggested they kiss.

George Michael's "A Different Corner" had come on, and conversation had rapidly disintegrated into meaningful looks, whispering secrets, and a watery-eyed certainty that every other lyric was uniquely pertinent to them.

She skimmed, heart thudding, over the half-dozen surprisingly sharp images for a sly amateur papping—thanks, iPhones—though it blurred her a little, flatteringly. The quality was a version of a filter.

As she scrolled up and down and up again, she marveled that they were actually . . . nice? Even very nice. You could risk "quite delightful."

They effectively captured the pretty intense adoration between them, Edie's face angled up to Elliot's like a sunflower to the sun, his arm wound proprietorially round her middle. There was one where they were kissing, which was pleasingly filmic and classy, not *heavy petting erection section hour at Mavericks Nightclub in Huddersfield.*

In the final one, Elliot's face was buried in her neck, a hand on her behind, an unequivocal statement that the paparazzi of the West Village would've loved.

"I didn't think we were *this* handsy obnoxious!" Edie said. "Are we this handsy obnoxious?!"

"Cameras lie," Elliot said, smiling. "They turn split seconds into major events."

They shared a look that said neither of them wanted to relitigate Ines Herrera.

Edie returned to the screen. Against all odds, she didn't hate the exposure. Maybe it was the power of a good dress or that she wasn't ashamed of her relationship—quite the opposite. If this was their official debut as a duo, it was legitimately charming. It accurately depicted two people in love.

The only thing Edie minded about these pictures was not knowing who took them.

It occurred to her that it was a true rite of passage moment for her: not your name in a headline but the mistrust of those around you. You had become a commodity of value and were forced to face the fact that you might know thieves.

Her eyes moved to the text.

He recently set tongues wagging with a loved-up display with costar Ines Herrera in New York . . . but it seems Elliot Owen's heart has been won by someone closer to home.

The *Blood & Gold* actor was snapped at a party in London this week with his girlfriend, Edie Thompson, 36, who he met when she was ghostwriter on his autobiography.

And as our pictures show, they made it VERY clear how they feel about each other.

They were first seen together in summer last year having a public argument in their home city, outside a local nightspot. Whatever the altercation was about, they've since clearly ironed out their differences, kissed, and made up.

"They didn't let go of each other all evening," said our witness. "He was the perfect gentleman, fetching her drinks and introducing her to everyone. They were kissing and cuddling in full view of all the partygoers and definitely weren't hiding the fact they're an item."

Thompson, who works at the Nottingham office of London-based ad agency Ad Hoc, lives in a city suburb in a modest £350k semidetached house, a far cry from the lifestyle of her new beau.

She remains an account manager and copywriter, according to the Ad Hoc agency's website. Meanwhile, Owen's star is on the rise since he won an army of female fans in the acclaimed fantasy saga. The 32-year-old heartthrob has landed roles as superhero The Void in the forthcoming Warner Bros blockbuster and has signed up as romantic lead in HBO's new series about a Manhattan restaurant, *Your Table Is Ready*.

Another source close to both said: "He loves the fact she's not impressed by his fame and treats him like any other person. Edie's very down-to-earth and opted out of the starry lifestyle of red carpets. It's clear she likes him for himself. Everyone is amazed by how hard and fast Elliot has fallen, but it's obvious she's very good for him."

Reps for Owen confirmed the relationship when we contacted them, saying: "It's early days, but they're very happy."

"My God," Edie said, looking up.

"What?"

"I think every word of this story might be true."

"Hahaha."

"Except my house was £370k."

She looked at her phone charging on the bedside table and scrolled through a waterfall of notifications so long, it'd take minute after minute to get to the end. The most recent was Richard. She unlocked and opened it.

Not one but two mentions of the agency? I'd like to shag Elliot Owen myself. R x

29

It was all very well thinking she didn't hate the exposé, but Edie realized soon after that she needed to warn innocent bystanders. It was a crash course in Being Elliot Owen. *Sorry I have unleashed this pack of hounds and grisly scrutiny upon you, purely because you happen to know me. It is not my fault, and yet it is, at the same time, my fault.*

You could be technically blameless and feel completely responsible at the same time, it turned out.

She called her dad first, hoping he was less likely to get grief now she wasn't under his roof. He was blessedly unconcerned. Having no social media, no streaming services, an old mobile phone that he treated as a walkie-talkie, going to the cinema once a year and taking only a hard-copy broadsheet, Edie wasn't sure he even grasped how famous Elliot was. Which she liked, as long as it didn't leave him unprotected.

"No fear, darling daughter, I will treat any members of the fourth estate as I do the callers who are convinced I need to switch broadband providers. Are you having a nice time in London? Oh good. Give my fond regards to Elliot, won't you? Sorry, got to go—the Tesco delivery van's just pulled up. Thank God I have some milk again—I've been stuck with your sister's nut juice. Now I am out from under her yoke of oppression, I have snuck in some orange biscuits, too. It's like Caligula's Rome here."

Meg was trickier.

"I think there was a man outside in a car with a camera, but he's gone now. You're coming back to Nottingham today? But not the house?" she said nervily, and Edie felt awful admitting she was at a hotel until Monday.

"We can stay at the house if you'd feel safer?" she said, to vigorous nodding from Elliot.

"Hmm, no thanks. You and Elliot grunting and rubbing on each other every time I leave the front room."

"I'm sure Elliot and I could observe a no grunting and no rubbing rule, if need be."

Vigorous head shaking from Elliot.

Meg said it was fine and being around their ardor would be worse than paparazzi. Edie recognized this concession as her sister's gruff version of consideration.

Edie reassured Meg that any pests would only be interested in photos of the actual girlfriend, hoping that was true. She was also aware that Meg had the capacity to give paparazzi serious trouble.

"Even if she hits them with an umbrella, your sister kicking off doesn't really feed any narrative they want to tell," Elliot said, once Edie was off the phone. "It'd play too much as *here we are, harassing her family.* And our being prepared to confirm we're together means Lillian can do deals with them, so try not to worry too much. I know it's easier said than done."

"Are you used to this?" Edie said. "Does it ever feel usual?"

"Erm . . . I wouldn't say it ever feels usual, but it starts to follow patterns and vague rules. When you can predict it, it's slightly less overwhelming. Remember that writer bothered my gran though? They always retain the capacity to disgust you."

Edie had a flood of follow requests on Instagram, shoals of unknowns trying to add her on Facebook, and her mobile flashing constantly with unknown numbers.

"This is the worst of it," Elliot said, squeezing her hand, as their people carrier wove its way into central London traffic. Fancy five-star places had fancy car parks, which meant you didn't need to leave by the front door. "You can't be the new girlfriend forever."

"Oh, good luck to the next one."

"That's not what I meant, and you know it! What do you want to do tonight? Free choice, completely up to you. I'm at your service," Elliot said. "I more than owe you."

"Hmm." Edie sat back against her leather, heated seat. At her service sounded promising.

"I'd like pints in an ordinary pub, a curry, and back to the room to watch *RoboCop*, which starts at ten p.m.," Edie said, much to Elliot's delight.

"I mean, Cameron says I can use his private jet if I want, but OK, sure. Wife beater, Nottingham's finest Ruby Murray, and a film that came out thirty-five years ago."

"It's a classic—maybe you've not heard of those, Void boy."

"Nice attitude. How about some respect for the way I pay for your shrimp curry?"

Edie was free to be irreverent, because Elliot, who always remained fairly pragmatic about work, had told her "some sort of rare magic" might be going on with *Your Table*. ("The script is incredible, as you know. I've seen the rushes, and everyone was slightly delirious afterward. Edie, for the first time, I think I might be making something that people are still rewatching and namechecking as a true great in twenty years, you know? I've never been part of that before.")

"Oh, Fraser and Molly are continuing the Indecent Haste Tour by following us up north and seeing my shell-shocked parents," Elliot said now. "Don't worry—I've made it clear we'll be on our own this evening. If I try to find time to see Fraser this afternoon for The Talk, is that all right, though? It looks like my only opportunity, and once they book caterers, that's that."

Edie said: "Of course."

To facilitate this, Edie made herself scarce when Fraser was heading over. ("He wants to discuss the stag do with me. Apart from the fact there's no time for that now, my urge to spend a weekend in Dubrovnik with his zoo of lowlifes versus using that time to see you is zero." Edie insisted Fraz's stag was a one-off and he had to do it. "Let's hope it's a once in a lifetime?" Elliot said, rolling his eyes.)

She'd never walked down the hill into the city center from the vantage point of a boutique hotel on its outskirts before, while her perfectly good home for which she paid a mortgage sat half-vacant nearby. Even when Elliot was doing Normal for her sake, it was Normal tilted off its axis a little. Bundled against the cold, she breathed into the red-and-blue woolen scarf she had wrapped round her face and grinned to herself: *I hope no one thinks I am doing this to go incognito.* She didn't think Elliot's fame had conferred any upon her.

Edie enjoyed an aimless mooch around the shops, phone scrolling over a coffee stop. She had time to skim endless brazen attempts at vague acquaintances trying to reacquaint themselves on her social media.

How did Elliot trust anyone in this environment? No wonder he'd largely sworn off it. Even secondhand, she felt as if she'd opened a door to every false flag and scammer in her orbit, a tsunami of snaky pretenders.

Speaking of which, who should be skulking in Message Requests on Facebook but last year's Groom of the Year, accompanied by a wildly hopeful friend request for good measure.

Jack Marshall
Little ET! Well, goodness, I kept meaning to check in and ask how you're doing, and then bugger me if I find out on the Sidebar of Shame! (Do they even still call it that? We're so old ☺) Glad it's apparently

going great guns with the actor. I've not seen his show, but I hear it's very popular, dragons and such? I don't know if you consort with the unfamous these days, but if you ever fancied mending some charred bridges, I'd love to share laughs like we used to again. I know you've got your grievances—you made that very clear ☺—I don't blame you whatsoever, but life's too short. Ping me for a pint anytime, same number. We certainly have a lot to laugh about, huh ☺
ALSO, there's something in particular that's come up in my inbox . . .
I want your views on it, and you have a right to give your input.
And finally . . . Charlotte's engaged again, don't know if you've heard.
I'm really happy for her. She deserves someone who wants what she wants. Sod it, I'll put it in three honest words instead of all this verbiage. I miss you. xx

Edie reread it in wonder.

ALSO, there's something in particular that's come up in my inbox . . . I want your views on it, and you have a right to give your input.

Did he think her too dim to spot a lump of cartoon cheese in a figurative mouse trap?

Charlotte's engaged again, don't know if you've heard. I'm really happy for her. She deserves someone who wants what she wants.

Hahaha. Only Jack would try to win a Goodwill Ambassador Award from his greatest disgrace. Collecting his award onstage: *I'd like to thank all the trusting women and the casual instant messaging formats that made this possible.*

Raising Charlotte at all—a topic Edie assumed he'd go no-where near—reminded her of Jack's brand of stealth: normalizing what should stay not normal.

Three honest words: well, honest-ish, Edie amended. *You miss having power over me. Having a tiny Edie figure to play with, in your little romantic diorama you've built. That's what you love, not any woman.*

Edie grinned as she reread his crawling. It was desperate. It positively reeked of his struggle to accept he'd been bested and binned. She didn't miss him, and she reveled in his total absence from her thoughts. Excellent.

She left Jack's message as *seen.*

30

Edie had respectably given Elliot and Fraser a clear two hours. Nevertheless, approaching the hotel room door (penthouse suite, of course), Edie stalled. She could hear the conversation on the other side of it, as clear as a bell. It was of interest.

"Who is Anto, exactly? Anthony?" Elliot was saying.

"Anto? Oh, from work?" came Fraser's voice.

"If he's ever within ten paces of my girlfriend again, I'm going to punch him. Or better yet, get some brick-shithouse-sized bodyguard to do it on my behalf and pay them a bonus for it. So, no more Anto at any events with me unless you want that scene, please. I'm not kidding."

Edie was embarrassed to hesitate. Somehow, she couldn't instantly bring herself to either depart or interrupt by knocking. She took a guilty step backward, which had no effect on her ability to follow what was being said. She'd make a call on whether to stay or go in a second or two; she was definitely about to walk away. She had some rights to curiosity regarding Anto.

"Shit, what happened?"

"He made up some bullshit to Edie about how I was seeing someone oversexed after we broke up last year. He properly upset her. Seemed capable of Mickey Finning her, to be honest. He was trying for a psychological Mickey Finn as it was."

Edie breathed out and thought: eavesdropping was improper, yet all she was gaining was reassurance.

"Fuck! What a weird thing to do. Didn't he think she'd ask you? What if you'd challenged him?"

"I suppose then he'd have been confusing me with someone else, whoops-a-daisy."

"I'll take him off the stag do list."

Edie raised her hand to knock.

"About the wedding," Elliot said.

What? They'd not done this yet? She put her hand down in confusion. She might lose Elliot's moment for this confrontation entirely. *Walk away,* she instructed herself. *If Fraser yanks the door open in a sudden fit of emotion, and you're stood there, it'll look awful.*

"Yeah?"

"You know all I care about is you being happy? And anything I say is with that aim in mind, not throwing my weight around for the sake of it?"

"Aww fuck, Lell. You only ever do the *you're a bright lad, so why draw cocks on your exercise books?* kindly teacher voice when you're about to lecture the shit out of me."

"It's great that you're both so keen on each other, but getting married this spring is nuts. Life is not the sort of Hallmark movie you watch on a tablet when you're poorly."

"If you know you want to do it, why wait?"

"To be sure of each other. To be sure it works. You need to have been through some downs as well as ups."

OK, Edie thought, *this is private.* Elliot would no doubt give her chapter and verse anyway. She turned to go.

"How long did it take you to be sure of Edie?" Fraser said.

Edie stopped, back to the door. This was why she should've exited before now. Her name had been raised again, and she absolutely shouldn't be privy to this, yet her feet might as well be nailed to the spot.

"What's that got to do with it?" Elliot said.

"Did I ever say *calm down, you've only known her five minutes* when you were spinning out about her?"

"Edie and I aren't engaged."

"Would it be too soon if you were?"

"Yes, that's why we're not engaged. Well, one of the reasons. I mentioned diamond rings once, and she looked like she was going to puke, so I don't know if marriage is her thing or not."

Edie flinched. Those wires were crossed. She didn't want him to think she was Bridget Jones. She didn't want him to think she was trying to tie him down, as a catch.

"There you go. You're not sure of how Edie feels. Molly and I are sure of each other."

"Bloody hell, Fraz, this isn't *Bridgerton*. We don't have to be deciding who we are or aren't going to offer our hands in marriage to after seeing them for six months."

"The fact we don't have to do it is how you know Molly and I are doing it for the right reasons. We want to. You don't want to be married, and that's fine, too."

"What's the drawback of waiting a year?"

"What's the point?"

"Like I said: so you've stress-tested what you have."

"Don't need to. We have complete trust we'll be OK whatever gets thrown at us. This is it for me. Forever. When you know, you know," Fraser said stoutly. "All I hope is she doesn't choose one of those dresses that look like she ballsed up a poached egg."

"I know you're a blind optimist, and that can be a positive, but it's not great when it comes to anticipating consequences. Don't put this kind of pressure on your relationship this early."

"See, you're calling it pressure, but commitment isn't pressure."

"Promising you'll spend the rest of your lives together after knowing each other months is pressure. You can have your own worldview, but I think that's close to having your own dictionary."

"Don't Elliot me with your clever arguments! So if Edie said, 'Please marry me right now—I'm totally sure you're the one for me. Also no one's ever given me pleasure like you have, take me now on the floor to the worst Radiohead album you own,' you'd say no?"

"Correct, I'd say no. To the wedding part."

Edie's breathing was heavy, she hoped not audibly.

"Why? You're mental about her."

"You've answered your own question. Falling head over heels in love is a temporary insanity. It's a flood of mind-altering brain chemicals to make you want to propagate the species. It's not any promise that you'll feel the same in a year's time. You have to let things settle down before you start making longer-term plans."

Temporary insanity. Edie felt like she'd had a particularly brutal netball tackle. He'd pretty much nutshelled her worst-case scenario for what was happening between them.

Be mine forever? That had meant everything to Edie when she read it, but a literal and practical nothing? She had that distinct flavor of nausea at hearing someone you thought you knew very well sounding unfamiliar. Discovering you'd mistaken your version of a person for the whole person.

"I dunno—I wanted to propagate the species with women I didn't love . . . it's no use, I know what you're projecting," Fraser was saying. "You know all the big words, but I know you too well. Things are very uncertain with Edie. Seeing two people hold hands and jump is making you think about your own problems."

"They're not uncertain?"

"You told me that the day after you and Edie got back together, she accepted a promotion at work without discussing it with you. You said it would keep her at home, and you didn't know what it meant."

What? That bothered him, but he hadn't said? They could've talked about that.

"You do know what it means—you're with someone who isn't

going to move to America for you," Fraser said. "As you say, she probably won't even come back to London. I get why you don't think it will last."

Edie's heart pounded in her chest.

". . . But I'm sure Molly and I will, so I'm marrying her. You're not confident about you and Edie, so you're not. I love you, and I know you're saying this 'cos you love me, but the call is coming from inside the house."

Elliot sighed. "This is extremely energetic deflection."

"That's what *you* are doing."

Edie finally found the will to walk away, far too late. She'd been paid her karmic dues as instant balance transfer.

All done with Fraser? she messaged Elliot, lame and culpable, fragile, having gone quickly back down to the lobby and done a circuit of the block.

Shit, sorry, darling, meant to say, he was stupidly late, but done now. He wouldn't hear a word of it, so there we are.

Edie sympathized, while wishing she hadn't, either.

31

"Hat or no hat?" Elliot said, proffering the sort of knitted beanie he'd been in the first time Edie interviewed him, when she'd inwardly scoffed at his self-importance.

She laughed in recognition. "Remember when . . ."

"Remember when you called me a big-headed twat, made me remove it, and we got mobbed? Yes. Expect to hear that tale in a speech someday."

This was pure Elliot: his flirting often hinted at a shared future. Edie tried in vain to fit together the casual adoration, this risk-taking with her expectations, with what Fraser had said. The exact opposite. His brother had prefaced his WhatsApps about Ines to Edie with: *He's not going to bother lying to me, is he?* How those words had turned from comfort to poison.

"No hat," Edie said, ruffling his shiny dark hair affectionately, as he stuffed it in his coat pocket. "I think it might draw attention indoors at night."

Approximately fifteen minutes later, she bitterly regretted both the no-hat policy and her inability to learn from the past.

"How fast can you drink?" Edie whispered, knocking back a quarter of a white wine in one go.

They were in a reasonably lively bar near the hotel, and Edie could feel pennies dropping. It was odd how you developed a sixth sense for it.

The trouble was, Edie thought, Elliot was pleasant to look at. It happened in stages. First, they walked in and existing customers scanned the newcomers merely reflexively. Then eyes settled on the fact that Edie's male companion was not only handsome but wore that special, indefinable aura of a polished-up, loaded person from another realm.

It wasn't that Elliot was showy, if you set aside coats that cost four figures. He was just a bit too chiseled and pore-less to be a standard sight in a regional boozer on a Saturday night.

Once he was being inspected for his intrinsic aesthetic appeal, there came the dawning realization. Didn't he have dragon-green eyes, at some other time? Wasn't he in armor? Was his hair a bit longer? Did he possibly wield swords in the direction of computer-generated, fire-breathing magical creatures? Clunk. *It's that guy. You know, the guy from that thing. What? It can't be. I'm telling you, it is. Look. Isn't he from round here?*

"We been made?" Elliot said, managing a deep swig of Estrella.

"We are in the process of being made, I think," Edie said.

Elliot looked over her shoulder at the crowded room beyond. "Given the size of the place and the level of pissedness, it might be an idea to cut our losses."

"Yeah." Edie sighed, having figured as much.

They downed another gulp each and communicated wordlessly: straight to the door.

Edie glanced back as they escaped and could see a group of half a dozen or so by the bar staring in wonder at them, mercifully not waving phones.

They were seconds away from figuring out that the couple leaving their round undrunk was confirmation of their suspicions.

Outside, Elliot pulled his hat on. "Is there somewhere quieter?"

"It's Saturday night," Edie said. "Nowhere is, really."

"I'm so sorry," Elliot said.

"Don't be. It's nice you tried."

She remembered when they were working on the book and

Elliot said something like: *people refuse to treat you normally then accuse you of not being normal enough.* Right now, she could see why known faces opted for nosebleed expensive private members' clubs and restaurants with doormen.

"OK, I may have a plan B," Edie said, putting her arm through Elliot's, as they winced against the chill. "It's crazy but it might just work. It's the best bad idea I've got."

She chaperoned him to a slightly out-of-the-way pub that no one would choose as a destination. It was a stopgap chain place, one for divorced men to stare listlessly over pints of mild and play the fruities. Its dreariness surely offered a high degree of safety.

Edie's mistake with the last venue was to choose one with the demographic of clientele to watch fantasy sagas and have Instagram accounts.

As they arrived, Elliot pulled his phone out. "Missed call from Lillian. And she messaged me saying she needs to talk ASAP. I'll tell her I'll pick it up when I get in? It's only afternoon, her time."

"Want to take it now?" Edie said. "I don't mind."

Edie got the round in, and Elliot paced the pavement outside, conducting what looked to be a very involved conversation. She worried in case he was recognized, but the combination of hat, frowning with handset on face, and the fact temperatures were too low for loitering seemed to be protection enough.

She twiddled the stem of her glass and mentally replayed the Fraser quotes for the hundredth time. Why would Elliot tell his brother they wouldn't last and freely hint at cohabitation and marriage on the horizon to her? *Eavesdroppers never hear any good of themselves.* Turned out clichés were clichés for good reason.

Elliot eventually swept back in, pulling the hat off as a statement of *fuck it.* He picked up his pint with gusto. "I need that."

"Is everything OK?"

Elliot swallowed and fixed her with a look. "A gossip site in the US is running the story that I flew back overnight to see you about the Ines story."

Edie's mouth fell open. "What? *How?* No one knew about that?!"

"Yeah. I'm now like *does my phone have spyware on it?* level of cold-sweat spooked," Elliot said. "I should've taken Lillian seriously earlier."

"The only people who knew about that were me, you, Fraser, Nick, and Hannah?"

"And my agent, because he had to know why I was pissing everyone off by pushing a table read back by a day. He told no one in the production the details, only *family emergency*. So yeah. Six people that I can identify."

"Is it worth me stressing again that I'd never do that to you?" Edie said.

Elliot leaned over and held her face. "Soft arse. Of course you fuckin' wouldn't."

"Never mind doing it to you, this isn't a story I want shared, either," Edie said sorrowfully, and Elliot dipped his gaze and murmured: "Sorry."

". . . Anyway, Lillian has moved to a war footing and completely rejects any tech interference speculation from me. 'Elliot, I believe in Occam's razor, and it does not tell me end-to-end encryption on WhatsApp has been hacked. We're not looking for Julian Assange. This is human fallibility, and it's someone close to you, with fewer scruples than you thought. We've opened the jar labeled *hard pills to swallow*.'"

"That's a very good impression."

"Thanks, I'm an actor."

He smiled, and Edie felt fluttery. Even in minor crisis, it was nice to notice they were still very much on a date.

"She pointed out the faster I figure it out, the better for everyone. But, how?"

"I'll check with Nick and Hannah about who they told, but they're so unlikely to have passed it on to anyone, let alone to someone who'd do this."

"You didn't tell anyone else?" Elliot asked. "I'm not saying you couldn't. As Lillian says, these conversations are being forced on us now."

"No one," Edie said, recalling her seconds-long madness nearly disclosing it to Declan, deeply grateful she'd thought better of it. "Not even my sister, given her interest level in my love life can be summed up as 'barf.'"

Elliot sipped his pint and shook his head. "I'm going to say it, because otherwise it hangs there as A Big Unsaid. Fraser's always been completely military drill on not telling people what I'm up to. He's beyond reproach. What's changed is that he's madly in love with Molly, about to make her part of the family. Naturally, he's telling his fiancée absolutely everything. She's got to be involved somehow. It's the only explanation I can think of. I'm going to have to cut Fraser out of the loop for a while and see if that fixes it, but I hate doing it. What a horrible fucking bind."

"Yeah," Edie said. "It's awful. Fraser's devoted to you. You don't know that it's Molly."

Edie's vanishingly brief encounter with Molly told her she was sweet and guileless. Yet Edie had missed the nature of Jack Marshall, not so long ago. Also, Molly might be—even unwittingly—doing the bidding of another, if her family were mercenary about Elliot.

"Lillian had a worse idea that I don't currently have the stomach for."

"What's that?"

179

"Telling Fraser alone something untrue and seeing if it filters through."

"Fuuuuuuck," Edie said, eyes wide. "Like Coleen Rooney with Rebekah Vardy."

"Well, *exactly*. I'm not treating my brother as an enemy combatant. I'm not testing him. Imagine if he found out I'd done that? Imagine the betrayal?"

Edie shook her head and put her hand on his arm.

"It gets worse when you reason it out," Elliot said. "If through this news blackout I have some sort of evidence his fiancée is likely selling me out, where will that leave me and Fraz? Molly will carry on denying it, because of course you would. Journalists won't reveal their sources. So I'd be asking Fraser to choose who he believed and that very quickly becomes choosing between us, full stop. What would I do if he came to me and said, 'Edie has done this terrible thing, here's reasonable standard proof. It's me or her,' yet you denied it?"

Edie nodded, hoping this was rhetorical.

"I know what I'd do. I'd choose you."

Elliot said this in a throwaway manner, as if it wasn't one of the most profound statements he'd made since they met. If this was a temporary insanity, fueled by oxytocin, he was writing some large checks off the back of it. They were sufficiently leveraged to be heading for the 2008 crash.

Edie gulped. "Really?"

"Yes," Elliot said. "Except if the bad thing was raging infidelity, then you'd have some ground to make up, little lady." He sighed. "How can I expect Fraser to be any different?"

Edie absorbed the seismic nature of that declaration. The pub's music system thundered with INXS's "Never Tear Us Apart," and Edie felt completely bewitched. Bewitched and bewildered.

You don't think it will last.

32

Things are back on track with Elliot Owen and his British secretary GF. But sources tell us that his closeness with costar Ines Herrera rocked their fledgling romance. The *Blood & Gold* alum had some explaining to do when snaps of him cozying up to the stunning actress in NYC dropped. We hear he jumped on the first plane home to placate his furious significant other that they were "just friends." It put HBO production *Your Table Is Ready* on hold, leaving execs majorly pissed. Looks like it did the trick, though: Owen and his civilian love Edie Thompson were all over each other at a London party last night. Maybe she needs to confiscate his passport.

"British secretary?!" Edie said. "Civilian love?! Fuck me."

"Hahahaha. It makes you sound like my wartime bride. Thinking about it, you'd look great in that style. Fancy role-play? I could be a soldier. Have you had some of the chickpea thing? It's really good."

They spoke in low voices, in low light. Having found a pub where Elliot could go unnoticed, Edie was emboldened that this unassuming Indian restaurant could work, too. Elliot kept his head down when being seated, and a clientele moved about less during dinner than drinks.

Edie had decided the details of the exposé could wait, but she finally broke and asked to see it during their meal. It was a two-part Instagram story on an account with two million followers. Edie felt as if someone had run onstage and yanked her trousers down.

"Why isn't it a full story in a newspaper, like the party?" Edie said, putting her phone away.

"No pictures, no proof. They can get away with it as a piece of trivia, but the way they got this is so clearly an invasion of privacy that they'd not want that much scrutiny, I bet."

"What if the party photos were a total stranger and nothing to do with this?"

"My take on the party story, on reflection, is that it couldn't have been a random chancer. To provide the material and have it run that fast means it was someone with a relationship with the press already. They had a contact, and they probably intended to get pictures of us beforehand, once they knew we were invited. The turnaround wasn't an average drunk person thinking, *hmm, I wonder how I earn from these sly shots on my camera roll.* They knew a journalist who'd pay them for it."

Edie absorbed this with a small shiver. "So, whoever sold those photos is the same person leaking about your Dales trip?"

"I don't know. I honestly don't know. It feels likely, but my feelings are now running hot."

Edie glanced around the room. "You know—about Fraser. What you could do is simply trust him. Tell him what's going on, and that you know it's not him. Ask for his help."

"Hmm, yeah," Elliot said. "Except it would be a delicate balancing act of making it clear I don't think it's him, without him quickly figuring out who I might like for it. I've already shown my hand on doubting the wedding. If he twigs I want him to investigate Molly, it could tip him over the edge. Don't forget"— Elliot dropped his volume further—"I have had to apologize for keeping something very important from him recently."

Of course: Elliot's adopted status had been known by all three of the immediate family, yet not by Fraser until it was about to make the news. Elliot had worried, when he found out from poking around documents in the loft aged eleven, that his brother would reject him if he knew that Elliot was adopted, Fraser was their biological son. Then, twenty years on, he was forced into telling Fraser the truth before the tabloids did instead—far scarier. Luckily, Fraser was astonished, emotional, but not angry. He wasn't the ragey type.

Edie nodded. "Consider that if it gets back to Molly that you're on to her, she might stop anyway. Problem solved," she said, tearing a piece of naan bread in a decorous fashion and dunking it in the chickpea thing. It *was* good.

"Except, if I know it's Molly and he doesn't, why would I sit back and celebrate Fraser signing up for a lifetime of her and her clan? That sort of behavior is a big character note. Other vices would follow. To say nothing of how little I'd want to be around her. Trust is like virginity and all that—you can't lose it twice."

Edie thought about what Elliot's mum said: *he was like a tiny adult, checking I'd remembered my house keys.* His conscientiousness was making it hard to let go. Edie felt loyalty to Fraser—loyalty he deserved.

"I know it's tough, but whether or not it is her and whether you catch her, I think you have to step back on the whole Molly-not-being-your-taste issue. You want to protect him and guide him, but Fraser's a grown-up making his own decisions. If he trusts her and it turns out it was misplaced, that's a matter for him. She's his choice. Fraser could've said: *oh, don't bother with Edie, she's not from your world, I want an intro to Margot Robbie.* I must've been a bit of a curveball, but he accepted me completely. You have to do the same with Molly. I think you owe Fraser that."

Edie pushed away again the thought of what Elliot had said about falling in love.

"You know, you're clever, and you're kind. It's a very good combination," Elliot said, gazing at her.

Edie tried to banish doubt and accept the compliment. She sensed their drawing a line under the hunt for the mole, for the time being.

"You're serious about *RoboCop*?" Elliot said, as Edie took her shoes off and jumped onto the bed. "I wondered if that was a cute joke."

"I'm not a Cute Girl." She patted the space next to her.

Elliot took his shoes off and joined her, and Edie settled in under his arm.

"Does being in films make you like films more or less?" she said, during the title sequence.

"Ones I'm not in are pretty much as they always were to me. Sometimes I find myself wondering what the director's instructions were or how they got a certain camera shot."

They watched the steady escalation of violence in a peaceable silence, Edie putting an arm over Elliot's stomach. This was so nice.

"This bit where they shoot all his limbs off disturbed the hell out of me when I saw it aged fourteen, even though you know they'll turn him into crime-fighter Metal Mickey," she said.

"I should think it did, it's an eighteen certificate. Fourteen? What kind of two-bit peep show in Rio de Janeiro was your dad operating?"

"Dad would never have let me see it—I was watching it round Joel Winship's!"

"Who was Joel Winship?"

"The contraband DVD dealer in my class. I used to go his

disturbing film parties." Edie interpreted Elliot's disapproving frown. "He wasn't a boyfriend—a gang of us were there."

"My mistake, you were committing other underage crimes. The BBFC is just a joke to people like you, I suppose?"

Edie started giggling helplessly, and Elliot used the moment of weakness to lean in and start kissing her. It had been a bit ambitious to think they could be entwined on a bed without getting distracted. Soon zips were being pulled down, and it was a game of mentally tracking where his hands were roaming. Edie accepted they weren't going to see the middle, let alone the end, of *RoboCop*.

Falling in love is a temporary insanity.

"You know, it won't always be like this," Edie said, drawing away from him, aware as she did so that breathing had become shallow. "I hope we're all right when it's not like this."

Lager was her sodium pentothal—lager, and the stupidity of listening at doors to things you shouldn't.

Elliot pulled back and started laughing, practically wheezing. "Fucking HELL, Edie. You can't be for real."

"What?!"

"This is your best yet. We're going to fail because we have jobs. We're going to fail because my brother knows some dicks. Now we're going to fall apart because we're too attracted to each other."

"I didn't mean that!"

Was he going to work out the connection? How to paraphrase him without him realizing he was being paraphrased?

". . . I meant, I know the beginning is super intense, and I don't want to think it's significant if it calms down a little. That's all."

Elliot propped himself up on his elbow and surveyed her with curiosity. "Are you subconsciously willing our demise so you can quit the ultra-high-maintenance, traveling-salesman boyfriend who's never here?"

His question was forthright, but his tone wasn't combative.

"I'm willing the exact opposite by trying to swerve any bumps in the road. Also, I like the way you're away a lot. It's restful and gives me time to recuperate from your brutal physical pummelings. I didn't do superhero body training in the gym."

"Here I am trying to work out how offended I am at you effectively saying *I won't always want to jump you, you know*, and then you're even more outrageous while I'm catching my breath from the first insult."

"Before you twist this any further, I'm not saying that. And I love how it is."

"Then why the coitus interruptus gloom-mongering?"

"Because I know the early days are a bit of a . . . fugue state, and I wanted to be honest about that. If there's a stage after, when it's less like this—I already know that I want that, too. I want grouchy Wednesdays as well as Saturday nights."

Elliot said nothing for a moment. "What have I done to make you think I don't?"

Well, this is awkward.

Edie felt sure that disclosing that she heard this would ruin the night. Elliot was taking her mysterious flash of insecurity with good humor. But confronting him—armed with a weapon she'd stolen—would very likely turn play-fight into fight.

"Nothing. I'm being nervy."

A beat of silence passed.

"Tonight, I told you that in a hypothetical it's-me-or-her war with my brother, who I've known all my life and love beyond all words, I'd pick you. I don't know how to embarrass myself by being more explicit than I already am with you, Edie. I spend quite a lot of time thinking, *did I scare her off by being too much? Stop being so tragically needy with her.* Then you bark *I KNOW THIS IS UNSUS-*

TAINABLE while I'm trying to undo your bra. It's quite a ride, you and me, eh?"

Elliot gave her a penetrating look, lit by the flickering bluish glow of crime-ridden science-fiction Detroit.

"I have no complaints about the way you are with me, Elliot Owen. None," Edie said.

"If you look for problems all the time, you'll start to create them. I'm wondering why you do."

Edie opened her mouth to reply.

"How do you even know the frantic lust will wear off, anyway?" Elliot said, returning to a lighter tone. "It's not following that pattern. I want you even more now than I did the first time. And I wanted you the first time an indecent and, frankly, creepily obsessive amount."

Edie's face grew hot. "Same here. On both points. You've turned me into a deviant."

"Oh really?"

"Yes," Edie said.

"Not seeing much evidence of that tonight. Seem more interested in Peter Weller, to be honest," Elliot said.

Edie laughed and took the clear cue to lunge.

33

If Cameron McAllister wanted to write songs about them, Edie thought, then this was fast becoming the keynote scene: Elliot saying goodbye to a sleep-fogged Edie in a darkened room, pre-dawn, him disappearing off to the airport. Put that groggy misery in your soaring chorus.

"I've done the checkout, so leave whenever you want, OK?" Elliot said, in nighttime hush, kissing her on the head and brushing her hair from her face. "We'll find another break in the schedule as soon as possible. You could come to New York, maybe? When this filming's not going to make me too scarce."

"It's about time I did the air miles for you," she croaked.

Edie put her hand over his and tried to pretend she wanted to say goodbye when she was still half in the dream she'd woken from.

They'd had an idyllic Sunday pub lunch the day before, walking distance from her family home, with her dad, Meg, Nick, Ros, Hannah, and Chloe.

They decided if Elliot got recognized, they were a large enough group to deal with it, yet no one looked twice. Edie buzzed from Elliot joining her life with such ease, and in turn he seemed to relax in the warmth of company that wanted nothing other from him but his in return. The therapeutic ordinariness.

Afterward, Hannah had texted her:

He's simply very GOOD at being famous, isn't he? If someone asks him what Brad Pitt is like, he'll tell them, with no showing off. Otherwise, he chats about your dad's new hash-brownie-loving neighbors. It's stunningly charming.

(Edie was glad she was equally keen on Chloe: she had a smile with many teeth, was always clad in a plaid shirt, and had a way of undercutting Hannah with affection that demonstrated they were equals).

"Hannah loves you," Edie had informed Elliot. "Hannah is so droll and hard to impress—I can't tell you what a coup this is."

She could've added that Hannah had never liked a boyfriend of hers before, except she and Elliot were observing a respectful omertà on exes—she only knew of silly Heather, he of the icky Jack—and Edie liked it.

"Brilliant. If you've got the best friend onside, it pays dividends down the years. A great investment. If I'm caught in a Miami strip club, smoking cigars with Kanye, she'll say don't throw what you have away over one silly mistake."

There he went again, rashly scribbling another zero on the check.

Edie lay awake in the grey early light and tried not to deflate with sadness at the emptiness of the other half of the rumpled bed, his coat no longer over the chair. She'd see him soon enough. This was the deal. And she needed to stop wistfully checking Flightradar24. Edie went back to sleep.

When she stirred at eight a.m., she had a WhatsApp from Fraser.

Hello, Thompson! 🖤 *My brother says you've got the morning off work today. Fancy a coffee in town, if you can be arsed? Mol's getting her hair done, and it takes AGES. Wouldn't blame you if you're at Owen Brother overload, however. Elliot won't leave you alone, will he? You need to carry a taser, tbqhwy. xx*

She smiled at the usual Labrador puppy ebullience of Fraser and arranged a date at the independent place near her office, where baristas with goatees and septum piercings took the apparatus and beverages very seriously, Wilco played, chairs were uncomfortable, and no names were written on cups.

Fraser breezed in ten minutes late, bending his tall form to crush Edie into a hug. He was in a burgundy Puffa with some fancy brand logo prominent, canary-blond hair artfully mussed, spicy cologne in the air. Edie sensed a few heads turning. Fraser had what the kids called *rizz*. The Owen brothers might not share genetics, but they certainly shared presence. They *gleamed*. How did Edie, who used to make new outfits for her childhood Barbie from cutting up old socks, infiltrate such a clan?

Hot drink acquired, Fraser and Edie made small talk about the stag do. Fraser pledged to keep Elliot safe from the fandom in Croatia.

"Molly says you're welcome to go on her hen in Palma, by the way . . ." (Palma, Edie thought. At no notice. Not quite her milieu.) ". . . But she totally gets you'd not know anyone, so maybe better doing dinner for four when we all get back?"

"Absolutely, sounds great. Please thank her for the invite."

Fraser squeezed Edie's free hand. "I want you two to hit it off so much, you know?"

Fraser followed this with the trademark glance around the room to assess who was present and if they could be overheard.

"Do you think Elliot's all right at the moment? Apart from being overjoyed to be back with you, obvs. I think that story his father did knocked him for six. Shit, feels so weird saying 'his father' and not meaning our dad."

"I bet." Edie thought Fraser had dealt with that blow magnificently well, from what she could tell. "He was upset at the vitriol at first, but equally, I don't think his dad had much ability left to disappoint him."

"The thing about Elliot is, he does that thing . . . what's the word for thinking? The thinking that men on horses do? In those shows where the women are in long dresses and it's all about proposing in gardens and having tea at each other's houses? In gloves?"

"Period dramas? A word for thinking?"

"Yeah, by men who are like this . . ." Fraser affected a haughty curl of the lip.

"Err . . . brooding?"

"Brooding! That's it. Elliot does a lot of brooding and over-thinking. I know I underthink everything. But he gets anxious worrying about all kinds of random, *out there* shit. He's always planning three chess moves ahead and too smart for his own good, you know? He doesn't have a cruise control setting."

Edie nodded and smiled in agreement, while wondering if this was leading to a request. Her brain, on the Owens subject, already had too many tabs open.

"You're so good for him, though. You can keep up with him and calm him down. I've never seen anyone who can do both before."

Edie beamed.

"Do you think someone he trusts might be selling stories on him?" Fraser said casually, and Edie's whole body went tense.

34

"Why do you say that?" she said.

With almost anyone other than Fraser Owen, Edie might smell a gambit. However, Fraser would never do that. He was devoid of machinations, low cunning, and deceit, and Edie knew the esteem he held her in was genuine. Even having overheard him being frank with Elliot about their shaky foundations, she never thought any different. Truthfully, it was Elliot betraying her there.

"There was the one about you and him at our engagement party. That was probably my fault, and I'm really sorry. People get wankered, and phones get waggled." Fraser gave a *what you gonna do?* shrug. "But it's not the only sneaky thing. Don't tell Elliot this—I'd feel strange about him knowing—but after the adoption came out, I set up a Google Alert on mentions of him. You know I generally stay away from that bullshit, but I didn't want any surprises for a while. As a result, I've caught a few things that made me go *hmm*."

Oh God. Neither of the brothers was telling the other about the leaking mole? The Leaking Mole sounded like a tavern in a fantasy novel.

"Too accurate?" Edie said, sipping her drink.

"Yeah, like it's been briefed by someone who knows a lot? Quoting Elliot's Elliot-isms? As you say, they're getting too much right, which is certainly a massive change. Then at the weekend, Molly shook the shit out of me by pointing out some American account she follows on Instagram had the story he came to see you in Derbyshire. I mean, how in the fuck? That knowledge was super locked down, he said? I only found out 'cos I happened to call him and could hear he was at an airport."

"Yes, Elliot's publicist told him about that one. I was pretty embarrassed—it made me sound like a banshee. Mind you, I was."

Wait, *Molly* told Fraser? Molly—she wouldn't actively alert him to her own misdeed, would she? Hope flourished that it wasn't Molly. Fraser could prove it if he'd not told Molly about Elliot's mad transatlantic dash beforehand, but he very likely had. Edie's purpose would be far too obvious if she asked.

"But who can it be? We'd not do it—his friends wouldn't do it. Your parents wouldn't do it," Edie said.

"Exactly. Super sinister. I best get to the bottom of it, because if it carries on, he'll think it's Molly, and there's no way it's Mol. No way. Don't tell him this, but she thinks Elliot's a bit distant with her as it is. She doesn't need this hanging over her."

Edie held her breath in case Fraser asked her if Elliot suspected his fiancée, but he didn't. She intuited it was due to Fraser not imagining his brother's thinking could be that far along rather than sparing Edie being put in the middle.

She and Fraser parted outside, a typically effusive farewell that involved her being enveloped in Puffa jacket to point of suffocation.

"C'mere! I'm so loving having you as a sister! Dunno what the whining soy boy did to deserve you, but I'm glad he did."

Edie WhatsApped Elliot as she walked to Ad Hoc.

Edie

Brace for news: I saw Fraser. He knows about the insider info stories—he'd noticed himself. Crucially, he said in passing *Molly* pointed out this weekend's one about you coming to home for an hour to see me. I don't think therefore it can be her? xx

PS I think I've fallen in love with your family, too, now, FFS. Can I keep access to them in the event of any separation?
Elliot
Interesting . . . Equally, pointing to something, exactly as you describe, establishes your innocence? Sorry, I know you'll think I'm an icy bastard, but this world forces you to become one. I really don't want it to be her. I'll bear it in mind, and thanks for the heads-up, though. If Fraz knows it's happening, that means I should speak to him. xx
PS Nope, scorched earth! The stakes are really going up for you, huh?
♥

As EDIE ARRIVED at work, Declan bounded out the doorway of their building, an unexpected look of concern on his face. "Edie!"

His desk on their first floor didn't overlook the street; he must've been peering out the window to know she was approaching.

"Everything all right?" she said.

"Behind you!"

Edie turned to see a man with a camera, kneeling on the pavement across the road, camera with large flash held aloft.

"Oh . . . Ugh," she said. It was both troubling and oddly anti-climactic at the same time. She realized she'd been so fearful of this prospect, and now it had arrived, and it was some middle-aged guy in a fleece with a piece of equipment you could buy from Currys.

Declan shrugged his jacket off his shoulders and held it in front of Edie, like a matador with a cape.

She started laughing.

"We can at least ruin the wanker's shots."

35

"Who's the white whale client for us?" Declan asked, Manic Street Preachers his soundtrack.

Edie feared this work environment would spoil her for all others. They'd introduced the rituals of Wednesday pizza and Friday afternoon cake break and were still performing well enough to get warm words of encouragement from Richard. ("Yet he still won't let me have *The Face That Lunched a Thousand Shits* as my email boilerplate," Declan said.)

"White whale?" Edie said absently. It hadn't been a morning designed to encourage her concentration.

"Yeah, like Don Draper with Coca-Cola. Who do we really want and can't get? I feel like a challenge. I feel like you and me could be the dynamos of regional ad agencies. I want awards. I want Richard hanging oil paintings of us as his king and queen. I want this office teeming with fresh hires to bully . . ." He swept an arm at the great space.

"Do you? Colleagues are a complication, in my experience." She gave an eye roll, and Declan smiled. "Present company excepted. Uhm, white whale . . . for me, Pepsi. Just their social media. Use the whole *Is Pepsi OK?* joke about that being their full name, and run with it. I love finding a weakness and making it a strength. Never got round to doing a proposal and putting it in front of Richard. My hubris is tempered by my laziness."

"Fuck, yes!" Declan's eyes lit up. "Can I start on that? You add to it, we take it to Rich as a joint project?"

"For sure. I do think fewer people around is giving our brains more space to breathe."

Edie relished the solitude, the two of them in a room that could comfortably fit twenty.

"This is possibly my cue to tell you something," Declan said, looking tense. "It's total crap, but I don't want you to hear it any other way, in case it gets mangled. I left the work WhatsApp group with Jess and the others. Jess and I aren't currently on the best terms."

"Shit! Because of me? . . . It was the story about me and Elliot at the party, wasn't it?" Edie said.

She was starting to understand Elliot's permanent homesickness. Before that cataclysm of a wedding in Harrogate—as rubbish as her life was, and as Elliot-less—she'd had tedious anonymity, and boy, she missed it.

"Yeah. She got snarky about it, and I defended you. She had a go at me for being 'a simp'"—Edie could see Declan judiciously editing himself as he spoke—"I said, you know what, I'm resigning from this discourse. Left the chat."

"I hate that I'm causing you trouble and losing you friends. Weren't you and Jess quite close?"

Aww. Love you, Dunny! xxx. A penny dropped quietly somewhere for Edie: Declan was a good-looking, personable man, and Edie had Jess bracketed under "married." However, she thought back to the jubilant look on Jess's face in that picture.

"Yeah, we were. I don't get it. I know she's tight with the fella's ex-wife, and pain was caused. But everyone's moved on. Why can't they call it blood under the bridge?"

"Maybe it's Jess being married. She can understandably empathize only with the horror had her wedding day being similarly detonated, not with one of the detonators. Which is fair enough."

"Jess and Wes have split up, actually. You didn't know?"

"Ah. No. They'd not tell me."

She got up to inspect whether a plant needed watering and peered out of the window as an afterthought.

"He's still there!"

"Lenny the Lens, you mean?"

"Yep. Must be waiting until I go home now, I guess?" Edie said.

Declan chewed his pen. "I dunno how you deal with it—it's so strange."

"I've never dealt with it before. This is the first time."

"Really?" Declan said.

"Fuck it," Edie said. "I'm going down there to talk to him."

"Is that wise?"

"What's the worst he can do? Take a photo?"

Declan grinned. "Have at it. You have what they call *moxie*."

Edie bounded down the stairs, out the door, and strode toward the man. He was having a cigarette and couldn't pick his camera up in time even if he wanted to.

"Edie," she said, extending her hand.

He wiped his free palm on his fleece and took it. "Alan."

"Where are you from?"

"I'm a freelancer. Sent by a picture agency." He paused. "Because you're the girlfriend of that actor," he added, as if Edie might otherwise think it was her work on the hummus-flavored crisps account.

"Then you sell the pictures to anyone who'll have them?"

"Pretty much."

"Are you waiting for me to leave work now? Didn't you get photos before?"

"Nah, they're a bit crap. Only took a few from behind, and your pal up there ruined the rest."

"If you get a decent one, you can go? Better for both of us?"

"Definitely." He dropped the cigarette and screwed it underfoot.

Edie checked her watch. "It's five to three—how about if I get a coffee at three and you get a picture then?"

"That'd be great. Will you be carrying it back?"

"The coffee? I can do, I guess? Does that matter?"

"If you've got the drink in your hand and maybe your pal with you, it'll look more natural."

"I see. I'll ask him. See you in a minute."

"Thanks," Alan said, giving her a tobacco-stained smile.

Edie bounded back upstairs and said to Declan: "Fancy making your paparazzi pics debut?"

"He wants me in it?" Declan said, double-taking. "Why?"

"I think he wants the caught-unawares-on-a-standard-day-being-standard-Peeping-Tom vibe."

"Urgh. Grimy swine," Declan said. "Stalking women for cash. If you want me to, sure."

Edie said: "Very, very grateful."

It was nice having a wingman.

"Wait, won't your being in this make the Jess clique go even madder?" Edie added.

She felt remorse at the fact that blameless, bright Declan had already had her shadow cast over him.

"Oh, fuck that," he said, pulling his duffle coat on. "They've banished me from the kingdom anyway. Imma sexy exile."

Edie guffawed.

Alan waved, camera down, as they passed, and Edie did a thumbs-up in return.

"You're being very nice—I'm not sure I could be," Declan said, pushing his thick, fashionably unkempt hair out of his face after they turned the corner. They paused as a car came hurtling past them over the speed limit, Declan instinctively and unobtrusively holding his arm an inch from Edie's back, before they walked on.

Edie realized the *Jess may have particular regard for him* revelation had been right there to be made the whole time, but Edie was too spoiled by being Miss Elliot Owen to assess anything about other men. Ironic, really: *your target couldn't be in safer hands, Jessica. My hands are full.*

"Elliot's publicist explained to me that if the pictures will be taken either way, you might as well exert any influence you have over them."

"You must really like this guy to put up with all this?" Declan said, then reeled. "Sorry! Fuck. That was so personal . . ."

"No!" Edie said. "Look at what I'm asking you to do right now—it's not. I like that we can talk openly and honestly. A bit more of that in my old Ad Hoc life would've been a good idea. I do really like him, but I'd be lying if I said what comes with it isn't miserable sometimes."

Edie hadn't thought this through before, and she was glad of Declan giving her the chance.

". . . By the time I knew how I felt about him, it was a done deal and the famousness couldn't stop me. That's how it is getting together with anyone you don't meet on a date, I suppose? You start in the middle. If there are difficulties, you simply take them on. You fall in love, then work out what it's going to entail, in that order."

Falling in love is a temporary insanity.

"Very true," Declan said. "You do the crime, then find out the time. I vowed to myself after Aisling . . . you know, my long-term ex . . . I'd not get together with anyone who wanted to live somewhere I didn't. That'll be in my first three questions, now."

"You really don't like Dublin?"

"Ah well, Aisling wanted a rural area, four kids, hens, and an Aga. I was whevsy on staying in Ireland, but it was a whole specific vision within that. I'm not a farm-type lad. Nor am I big city, as you know. I'm a pointless in-between who likes a lot of green but also a decent coffee."

Edie nodded.

On their way back, grasping hot beverages, Alan crouched and snapped.

Declan muttered: "Feels like submitting to a molestation, doesn't it? Poor Mariah Carey."

Edie laughed, hoping she didn't have a double chin.

A horrible illogical stupidity of her situation was knowing she'd be constantly assessed as to whether she was sufficiently attractive enough to be a correct companion for Elliot Owen, despite the fact she was by definition sufficiently attractive to be a correct companion for Elliot Owen, because Elliot Owen found her attractive.

The worst thing was: it didn't make simple evident sense to her, either.

36

The fruits of Alan's labors ran in a tabloid a couple of days later, headlined: *Down-to-Earth Life of Elliot Owen's New Love: Star's Girlfriend Keeps 9–5 Job.* The copy explored the exciting and novel improbability of earning a salary and purchasing Americanos and dating a well-known actor, concurrently, as if contact with his groin prohibited gainful employment.

Edie

For fuck's sake, Elliot, "down-to-earth life"! It makes me sound like I'm a simpleton sat on a hay bale, in stained overalls, hooting vacantly at passersby.

Elliot

Hahahaha. Living La Vida "Local." You look cute in that coat. Who's your friend?

Edie

Declan. Remember, I told you about him? Lovely Irish guy who I'm supposedly line managing but is more line managing me.

Elliot

Ah yeah, of course! Hmm, he's annoyingly tall. So, you've been caught red-handed, sluttishly sharing jokes with other men when I'm abroad? Noted. The sooner I install you pregnant with bodyguards in Graceland, the better.

Edie laughed out loud. Whenever they were handling this, she felt like she could conquer the world. It was a triumphal kind of day—right up until Edie's mobile flashed late afternoon with a call from Meg.

Meg never rang her unannounced, so either she'd dropped her house key down a drain and was about to make it Edie's problem, or it was something cataclysmic. Those were the only two options when it came to reluctant cold-callers in their benighted era: absolute nonsense, or possibly the end of your world as you knew it.

"Edie, it's Dad! He's sick—we're at the hospital! You have to come *now*."

The latter. Edie's heart stopped.

Meg was crying and using her little-sister voice that implored Edie to fix it.

"What? What's happened?"

"He's fallen down the stairs and hurt his leg, and he called me, and he wasn't himself. Edie, you should've heard him. He was gibbering. I think he's had a heart attack or a stroke or something, and that's why he fell."

"Where are you?" Edie said, in a freezing sweat already.

"We've just got to QMC. I called Dad an ambulance and I got a taxi, and we arrived at the same time. Now they've taken him away, and they're seeing him."

"Did you talk to him?"

"Not really. He was on a trolley thing, and he waved hello, but they rushed him away." Meg cough-sobbed.

"Which bit are you in? Of the hospital, I mean?"

"A&E. Edie, please come quickly—I don't want to talk to the doctors without you!"

"I'm on my way to QMC—stay where you are, OK? I'm getting a taxi now. I'll be fifteen minutes."

One thing about a quiet office with two occupants: every word of

Edie's side of the conversation had been heard by Declan, who was already on the phone to a cab company, telling them it was urgent.

He rang off. "Didn't want you relying on an app. What happened?"

"Thank you. My dad's had a fall—my sister thinks he might be . . . critical."

Edie very much wanted to be a pillar at this moment, but changes had taken place during the conversation with Meg and she'd been unaware of her altered state until now. She felt dizzy and realized she was trembling uncontrollably.

"Shit, I can't focus . . ." Edie said. She tried to get up to grab her coat and sat back down heavily again.

"Take a moment." Declan gestured for her to stay put, jumped up, and got her coat.

"You're all right," he said. "It's going to be OK." He kneeled by her seat and held her arm.

"I'm having some sort of turn," Edie gasped, trying to smile, tucking her hair behind her ears.

"You're in shock," Declan said, rubbing her back. "Which is understandable. Try to get your breathing steady—it'll help."

Edie nodded.

"It's what happens when you go from boring day at work to fight or flight in two minutes flat. It keeps us safe from being eaten by bears."

Edie smiled in gratitude.

"Your brain will realize there's no bear chasing you if you give it a minute."

"What if there is a bear?" Edie squeaked out. "A sick dad bear."

"He's in exactly the right place to be sick if he is sick, and you're going to be with your sister, and everything will be OK. It may not feel like it right now, but you can cope, I promise."

He rubbed her back again, and Edie, to her surprise, felt more in control than she had a moment ago.

A horn sounded below, and Declan got up to glance out of the window.

"If you feel you can move, I'm going to put your coat on you and walk you down there, all right? Take it slowly."

Edie nodded in mute gratitude. She pushed herself up from her desk and put her heavy arms into the proffered coat sleeves.

They took the stairs at a pensioner pace, with Declan's arm around her, his other holding her bag.

"Do you want me to come with you?" Declan asked, opening the car door.

"We can't leave the office like that?" Edie said.

"Respectfully, fuck the office."

They smiled at each other, and she said: "I think I'll manage, but thank you so much."

"Call when you can," he said.

The stop-start journey in early rush hour gave Edie a chance to calm down a few degrees. She tried to count blessings. Her dad had been conscious. It was a great hospital, a huge teaching hospital. He'd be fine. He was healthy. He had two kids on hand to help him convalesce.

When she emerged from the taxi, looking up at the concrete edifice of Queen's Medical Centre, she said, "Please let him be OK," aloud, not caring if she looked mad to anyone in earshot. She'd been here with Declan just last month, in very different spirits. Life kept happening.

Edie fumbled her phone out and quickly scrolled to Elliot's number. She'd be strong for Meg and strong for her dad; right now she missed the person who'd hold her up. She knew that with the time difference and his filming, there was no chance he'd pick up.

204

She tried three times anyway, desperate enough to find comfort in a dial tone for a device somewhere near Elliot's person.

Edie pressed the microphone symbol and left a somewhat fraught, vocally wavering voice note, explaining where she was and why, and that she'd hopefully speak to him later.

She did conscious, measured breathing as she walked through the sliding doors into A&E. As she scanned the crowd, Meg came barreling toward her. She was in pajamas with a hoodie over the top and welly boots.

She threw herself into Edie's arms and said, voice muffled: "Good news! It's a fracture and a bad sprain! It's only his metatarsal bones!"

Edie looked at her quizzically. As Meg stepped back, Edie saw that her sister looked authentically exultant.

"Was it? Why was he confused?"

"He fell down the stairs, twisted his ankle, and then dragged himself to his phone, which was on the counter. By the time he got there, he was light-headed because it hurt so much. Dad sounded unusual, and when he said he'd had a fall, I lost it. But he says he didn't even hit his head on the way down! Or have a brain episode that made him fall! He slipped on a Jaffa Cake!"

"Ahhh." Edie's pulse slowed, her adrenaline level began descending, and she gathered that she'd been a victim of Meg's tendency to hyperbole.

Edie wasn't going to make a word of complaint about this.

Firstly, she was awash with too much gratitude. She'd have given anything for this diagnosis mere seconds ago; she wasn't going to insult God by responding with wrath. Secondly, she'd not been a model of proportionate reaction herself. Thirdly, she wanted Meg to feel she could off-load onto her, if she needed to. Sibling duties.

Within half an hour, their father emerged on his crutches, foot swaddled in bandages. Both his daughters ran to him for a hug, awkwardly accommodating walking aids.

BACK AT THE family home, they opened wine and ordered fish (vegan minty pea fritter for Meg) and chips, eating from their cardboard boxes while watching a documentary about Sir Arthur Conan Doyle.

Edie remembered herself and texted Declan:

Massive false alarm, huge relief. It's an ankle injury and nothing else. My sister spiraled a bit ☺ Thank you for being such an absolute rock when I fell apart. xx

Instant reply.

Declan
GREAT NEWS! Ah, Edie, that's put a smile on my face. Love to you all. Tell your sister I'm holding her to the mashed potato promise. Mind you, that was made before I forced her to view my bare buttocks. xx

Edie sniggered. She recalled his summoning a taxi to the hospital before she'd even rung off. He was such a delight of a human being, and she was lucky to have him as a friend. After all the Ad Hoc woe, she'd rolled a six.

Edie
Who knows, maybe that'll have clinched second helps. Will do. xx

Declan liked her reply with a heart. Was Edie flirting? She was too nerve-shredded and two glasses too tipsy to judge. She was mostly glad that if Declan was making light of that incident, he must be recovering from it. She was surprised he'd raised it. It was, as foretold, alchemizing into comedy. A vision of him unclothed swam into her head, and she banished it, because the better she knew him, the odder it felt. And somehow, rather less like comedy.

"How come Sherlock Holmes had so much cocaine?" Meg asked. "Was it allowed in those days? Because life was more boring?"

"Why was life boring?" their dad asked. "No Wetherspoons and Netflix?"

"Yes," said Meg, her usual literalism disarming her father's satire. "They only had pianos and maps and murders."

"They didn't know it did you any harm, I think," Edie said.

"Like sugar now," Meg replied. "In the future, we'll think of Vanilla Coke and Kit Kats like Class As. Injecting a Wispa Gold."

She made a tightening-a-tourniquet mime.

Edie phone-googled and read aloud: "'In the late nineteenth century, cocaine was thought to be totally harmless and was used both as a nerve tonic and for local anesthetic. Cocaine was used in throat lozenges, gargles, and in several alcoholic drinks.'"

"I'd love me a cocaine gargle," Meg said.

Edie continued: "'Holmes took cocaine to help him 'escape from the commonplaces of existence.'"

"Boring! See, Dad?" Meg said.

"Thankfully, you have no need of cocaine, with your Twiglets and *Say Yes to the Dress*," their dad said, dabbing his chin with paper towel.

"What?!" Edie shrieked. "Meg's been watching *Say Yes to the Dress*? Bridal gowns? What happened to Andrea Dworkin and the toxic male gaze on our prostituted bodies?!"

Meg adjusted her topknot of dreadlocks and made a sulky little face. "The patriarchy won't monitor itself."

37

After a draining day, both Meg and her father turned in by ten p.m. Edie left her phone for two minutes to get a glass of water, and when she returned, saw she had racked up three missed calls from Elliot and a WhatsApp.

Elliot
Sweetheart, I am so so SO sorry. I was on set, and I didn't get this until now. Fuck. I'm back. Call whenever you want. xxxx

She carried a blanket into the front room and lay down on the sofa, pulling it up to her chest and putting her mobile to her face. Elliot answered on the second ring.

"How are you? How's your dad? I feel awful I wasn't there when you needed me."

"Don't worry! Everything turned out fine. Dad's in an ortho-pedic boot and chipper as can be. Nothing neurological at all. I was a bit of a mess when I left that voice message . . ." She gulped. "I wish I'd waited. I'm a twat for not waiting."

"*No,*" Elliot said. "Can I say, emphatically, that when I'm this fucking useless to you, you leaving me a message when you're in the turmoil of it allows me to imagine I'm the absolute bare mini-mum of support. Feel free to scream in them if you need to. Leave me ones where you don't speak at all. Anything. I don't mind. Just send them."

"I love you," Edie said, as a hot tear slid down her face. He was the person she most wanted to impress in the world, but he was also the one she could let her guard down with, and it was a powerful combination.

"I love you, too."

They let the phone line hum with a potent shared silence for a second or two.

"The story is that Dad slipped on a biscuit—I never thought I'd miss my sister's strict dietary regimen—missed a few stairs, landed with a bump in the hallway. When he rang Meg, he didn't sound his right self, and she went straight to DEFCON shit. I know it's a little-sister-older-sister thing, but if our situations were reversed, I might've minimized it and kept her calmer for the race to the QMC. But. You understand this so well 'cos of Fraz, I think. We love them so much, and we know the deal."

"Do I ever," Elliot said. "Oldest kid's a certain gig, for sure. I know you'll have been brilliant."

"Actually, I wasn't—after she called, I had a turn. Heart racing, going to faint sort of thing. Like when I almost keeled over on *Gun City*, and you picked me up, remember that?"

"Of course."

"Declan was great about it and helped me to the taxi. I scared myself a bit, Elliot. I just . . . collapsed in on myself, emotionally and physically. I couldn't cope with what might be happening, at all. I didn't expect . . ." Edie felt tears swell and had to pause to get herself under control. "I haven't told anyone this, but I didn't expect to think about my mum so much in those moments."

"You did?"

"Yeah. It felt like pulling on the ropes still tied to a shipwreck," Edie said, being very quiet, as you could never be sure about the acoustics through ceilings and floors, and her dad was right above her. "Down there in the deep. She suddenly, very obviously, *wasn't there* in my life. Like there was a yawning hole where she should be in the world, and my dad was about to disappear through it, too. Sorry, I've had wine, and I'm not making much sense. Anyway. Turns out your long-ago past is always right there. Just round the corner, out of sight."

"I get that . . . You want her support at a time like that. It's a flash point of absence."

"Exactly. It's like I'm thirty-six, cutting about, a responsible adult who has the history labeled, neatly tidied into a box. One frightening phone call from Meg and I'm a little girl again, wanting my mum."

"You're being Meg's mother," Elliot said. "She displaces that role onto you, but you have to be your own mum."

"God, exactly," Edie said quietly.

"It was kind of like that with my father's newspaper story. My own emotions surprised me. I didn't realize how much he could hurt me. I said it was seeing the picture of my mum, and it was, mainly. But the embarrassing part was that I discovered I was upset that my so-called real dad doesn't love me, that the love I somehow expected to exist, despite everything, wasn't there."

"I should've understood that better," Edie said. "And I should've asked you more when the story broke."

"Ah God, no, don't worry. What is there to say? Forever unfinished business," Elliot said.

Edie sensed that Elliot, on another landmass, was in actor-mode Elliot. His tears on her shoulder happened in another country, in more than one sense. She got it: she'd tried to travel light herself.

"Are the stairs a problem—does your dad need to move house?" Elliot said, and Edie understood the implication.

"I'll keep an eye on that," Edie said. "For now, he needs to be tidier."

"Speaking of property, my mum called with some news today. You know my aunt lives in Cornwall? My dad's sister?"

"Yes?"

"She's not in great health, and my parents have announced they're moving down to be with her. Fraz is in London, I'm mostly jetting about as you know, so it's not like they've got tons of ties to Nottingham. They've decided the seaside is their new passion. It's very new. The greatest enthusiasm I've ever seen from them to date is ordering the prawn cocktail starter."

"Right." Edie was surprised by how hard this hit her.

"They've put the house on the market. They want to do a farewell dinner, so I'll let you know."

"Sure."

They chatted *Your Table* trivia and said goodbye with the usual promises and endearments, Edie suddenly keen to end the call so that she was free to cry. She pulled the blanket over her head and sobbed with her whole chest. She'd been through a nerve-racking experience and was too weak to absorb anything sensibly, she reasoned.

But somehow, this totally unexpected departure was quietly devastating. A home city, parents in the same place, was the only thing she and Elliot had ever shared. It was why they had met. Now, that was disappearing.

And while it was in the *well, duh* file, it confirmed that, despite his relationship, their expectation of their eldest son ever relocating back was nonexistent. Actions speaking louder than words.

Was Edie being a gigantic, oblivious fool to even vaguely imagine otherwise, though? Yes, she was.

Edie's phone lit up.

Elliot

Tell me if I'm being hypervigilant to the point of neurotic, but are you sure you're all right? You went very quiet at the end there. But I know it's been a shitty day. xx

Edie

💗 *Your parents selling up got me in the guts, for some reason. It was the one bit of geography we had in common. Stupid, I know. xx*

Elliot

Yeah, I feel the same. I tell you what, I'll buy it off them. Then they still have a base to visit friends here, and we can stop staying in hotels when I'm over. It'd be nice to cook dinner for a change, wouldn't it? Tbh I bet they'll end up moving back. Neither of my parents are suited to fishing villages. They're having a manic episode if you ask me. That solution sound good? xx

Edie

!!!!!??? SOUNDS INSANE. You'd do that?! I'm not sure "thank you" quite matches the moment here . . . xxx

Elliot

Yep. Done. Money is a card trick. I'd rather have been there for you today. X

Edie's tears had turned into heart-warmed, amused disbelief.

Why did his effort feel so good? It wasn't the wealth, the jaw-droppingly grand quick fix, a power available to so few. Edie was good enough at interrogating her own vices and weaknesses to be sure of this. If anything, she found the might of the platinum American Express card overawing and worrisome, another huge gap between them. That was the method he'd used to repair her feelings; it wasn't the meaning.

It was that Elliot had noticed she wasn't all right and done something about it. It was amazing to be in a relationship with someone who noticed, then acted.

Edie

Hey, Elliot Owen, I think you might be, in an absolutely mind-blowing confirmation of your fans' fevered imaginings . . . the perfect boyfriend? xx

Elliot

I think today alone demonstrates I'm really fucking not. But I'm very happy for you—*and my many fans*—to think that. xxxx

38

"Should I still ask Declan to dinner given that I've seen him nude?" Meg asked conversationally, over midweek cannellini, tomato, and kale stew, with sourdough toast.

They were doing a rewatch of the film *Edge of Tomorrow*. (Meg was a fan of the Emily Blunt character. "I am Sergeant Rita Vrataski," she declared. "I'm always training up men who are shit at my job, and then they get all the kudos.")

"I don't think having seen someone nude generally precludes seeing them socially again? Sometimes, it makes it even more likely," Edie said, swapping from fork to spoon. Meg had bought them beanbag lap trays for TV dinners, and Edie loved them, though she'd not be using it around her film star boyfriend.

"Yes, when you're having regular sexual intercourse with them, not when you see their penis by mistake in the middle of making banana-and-Marmite crumpets."

"Continuity: it was almond butter crumpets," Edie said. "Banana and Marmite is a bit of a first-trimester combo—do you have anything to tell me?"

Meg paused. "Have I not lived in the world enough, or was it huge?"

Edie almost spat her stew. "Hahahaha. No, you're right. Huge."

Edie's mind drifted to how you'd feasibly accommodate it, and she shut the thought down fast.

"I think, on balance, I will invite him," Meg said, with impeccable comic timing, and Edie screeched.

"I promised him mashed potatoes! Seriously, when carnivores

try my garlic and black pepper mash with coconut milk, they're converted. And the lacto-ovo vegetarians love it, too—it might persuade them to stop being Nazi collaborators."

Since they began cohabiting, Meg had toned down the politicization of her legume-sludge and started trying to please palates as well as educate diners. It was a work in progress.

"Megan," Edie said, standing up to feed Beryl and Meryl their nightly chef's baby carrot treat, "you can invite him, but *do not* bring it up. He's sensitive about it, as you would be. And don't call anyone a Nazi."

"This Saturday? Would Hannah and Nick like to come? With their girlfriends?"

"Ah, nice thought—I'll ask."

As it turned out, Declan, Hannah, and Nick RSVPed in the hearty affirmative, but without a plus-one in Nick's case.

When the evening arrived, while Meg labored at the stove, Edie made sure wine was uncorked, candles were lit, music was on, and pita corners and dips were plentiful, to make Declan's assimilation smooth.

Nick, Hannah, and Chloe were their easy, chatty selves, and Declan as open and amiable as ever. He was in that category of people you could confidently throw in with anyone and trust that he'd find common ground, but Hannah and Nick's sardonic unpretentiousness was his wavelength. Edie had the pleasure of seeing someone who'd intended to make an effort with a group of unknowns realizing none was required. *A state of flow,* as Elliot had referred to it recently.

After they'd seen off their mushroom bourguignon and the fabled mash, Declan lavish in his praise, Nick announced: "Ros and I are kaput, by the way. I said she was busy on WhatsApp because I didn't want to go into it until I saw you."

"Oh no!" Edie, Hannah, and Chloe chorused.

"If I don't tell you why, those two"—he gestured at Edie and Hannah—"will go on at me about how I didn't give it my all, what with my ex-wife on my case. Ros doesn't care who knows her business. So here it is: I liked her a lot. I welcomed the pet ferret. Schubert had a slight odor, but he was docile. I believe his review of me said much the same. The roller-skating was fine. The crystals woo and reiki healing were tolerable, although I didn't get it. But turns out Ros was very into threesomes, and I wasn't up for that."

There was an astonished pause, during which only Lana Del Rey on the Bluetooth speaker dared contribute.

"Threesomes?" Hannah repeated. "With other men or other women?"

"Yup. Either. I was offered both. I'm too old for shenanigans," Nick said. "When my father was approaching forty, he got into luxury motorhoming. He wasn't worrying about pleasuring strangers' G-spots with vibrating silicone nodules. Doing Clone-A-Willy for a wheeze, or what have you. I'm left cold by satanic gadgetry."

The company held their collective breath and then sank into quiet hysteria as Nick calmly prodded a leftover breadstick into his mash and crunched.

"Clone-A-Willy? Is that a thing you can do?" Meg said, and Nick explained plaster cast molds while Edie studiously avoided meeting Declan's eyes.

"This was a deal-breaker for her?" Chloe asked.

"Yeah, pretty much. Never said in so many words, but it became clear she didn't see long years stretching ahead of her with no 'experimentation.' All I saw was a regular crate dig at Rob's Records and pints. My kink: sonic truffle hunting."

"Making threesomes a basic ask is . . . a lot?" Declan said, and Edie was secretly reassured that someone with Declan's relative youth and options thought it was crazy. "Some of us are glad enough when one person agrees to sleep with us," he added. Modest, too.

"Ros asked: 'Well, what *is* on your sexual bucket list?'" Nick said. "I said: 'Susanna Hoffs,' and apparently that was the wrong answer."

Declan almost slid sideways off his chair, and his and Edie's eyes met in mirth.

"In all seriousness, while I remain terrorized by the sex positivity, Ros is a great person and we're staying friends. I'll always be grateful to her for shaking me out of the drinking phase when I wasn't seeing Max. I feel quite rosy about turning thirty-seven in a fortnight. Please join me in celebrating my two-person-maximum erotic lifestyle, two weeks from today."

"Oh yes," Hannah said. "One request, no venue with a 'living wall' that is in fact plastic rainforest plants, full of pulsing LED lights, or with a brainless phrase in cursive neon. An aesthetic abomination. They've turned neighborhood pubs into kids' soft play areas."

"Our own Nicky Haslam with her things-that-are-'common' list," Nick said. "I was thinking the Mexican place in Hockley. Declan, you're very welcome, too. Edie said you don't know Nottingham? Here's your ticket to its fast lane."

"Grand, that'd be great . . ." Declan said. "A mate's over from Dublin then—I could bring him, if that's all right? Kieran's mostly housebroken."

"Of course," Nick said.

Declan glanced at Edie for reassurance, and she smiled encouragingly.

"You're going to New York this weekend coming?" Hannah said to Edie.

"Yup. Would've been this one, but Elliot's on his brother's stag do in Dubrovnik."

"Are you flying first class?" Nick said. "I've always wanted to know what that's like. Give me the full experience in detail."

"No, I'm splurging on premium economy. Walk-up bar, adjustable headrest, and complimentary prosecco on takeoff," Edie said, doing V for victory fingers.

"You're splurging? Elliot not treating you?" Nick said, with the nosiness rights of a close associate.

"He offered, but I wouldn't let him," Edie said. She felt a gallery of eyes on her and was concerned in case they thought she was covering for him being tight or thoughtless. "Elliot offers to pick up the tab a lot, and it makes me uneasy."

After Elliot had made a failed bid to cover her travel, she dwelled again on why money was disproportionately excruciating. She supposed it was because it was their greatest, forever unfixable disparity. It even bizarrely brought back long-buried memories of hiding how poor they'd become after her dad's breakdown as a schoolkid. She couldn't fathom the connection until she remembered she thought other pupils wouldn't want to be friends with her if they knew their phone sometimes got cut off and that she had a stale piece of cake in her lunchbox.

Obviously, Elliot would never judge or reject her, but every time finances came up, she felt it hung a lantern over how unlikely *they* were as friends. Edie couldn't be his act of charity.

"You're so ethical," Nick said. "I'd be mincing about, dripping in jewels. Or at least the check wool coat I want from Private White."

"I shudder at being a kept woman," Edie said, grinning.

Declan rubbed his shoulder and studied her intently. His eyes had a heaviness, and Edie hoped she'd not misjudged how much of her private self she was parading in front of a colleague. He was a fantastic person, but Edie had made this mistake before.

"May our great feminist forebears strike me down, but so what if Elliot pays for a few things, if you're equal in general? He's rich, so you don't have to be," Hannah said.

"It's that . . ." Edie said, looking at a flickering tea light, "I don't ever want him to resent me or respect me less."

"He knows who you are," Hannah said, and Edie smiled at her in gratitude.

"Anyone want a coffee?" she said, getting to her feet.

39

While she was waiting for the kettle to boil, Edie had an alert that Elliot had posted on Instagram. His presence there remained smoothly professionally anodyne, unlike Fraser's, which was exuberant and unruly, an accurate reflection of their respective taste.

"Fraser's Instagram is set private," Elliot said once, "in the sense that you have to request to follow him. However, given the conditions for acceptance seem to be *sending him a request to follow him*, I don't know why he bothers."

Elliot had shared a ravishing red-gold sunset, seen from the Old Town, which had 7,412 likes. There was also a new post on Fraser's grid.

Ruh roh—English girls hen do in the next villa found out my brother's here 😂

With a stomach plunge, Edie examined a photo of Elliot being flash-mobbed by scores of girls in varieties of miniscule swimwear. They were hanging off him, arms draped round him, taking selfies. She felt the kind of sudden jealousy pang where your stomach contracts and your skin goes cold-hot.

She screen-grabbed it so she could zoom in, squinting at the many stunning bodies on show. Shimmering body cream on tanned limbs, no hair below eyebrows, belly button jewelry. Edie had never felt so pale, underwaxed, soft-fleshed, and unadorned.

(Irrational, given there was no one on earth who'd demonstrated a greater enthusiasm for her body than the man in the middle of that photograph. "My, er, structure is so different to yours," she once said, concerned about being made of yielding wobble instead of taut muscle, and Elliot had replied: "That's how heterosexuality works?")

As soon as the sight of the Austin Powers entourage afflicted her, she surprised herself by almost bursting out laughing. It was intimidating, yes, but above all, it was absurd. The scene only needed some "Yakety Sax," and it wasn't actually anything to worry about. If she lost him, she had a feeling it wouldn't be to a Henrietta from Farnham in a Melissa Odabash triangle bikini.

It'd be to someone else famous, her traitor brain whispered, uninvited. *Your sort is a one-off deal. Your quota is filled. Check cast lists for suspects.*

She sent the image to its subject.

Wow, just wow. Guess that's bye from me, then? Disgusting, Elliot. Like the Costco Hugh Hefner.

Edie ended it with a row of three litter-dropping emojis, to avoid confusion about whether she meant it. She had done this for real not so long ago, and Elliot could be forgiven for being wary.

He replied:

Is making new friends a crime now? SMH.
Edie
If you're "friends," what are you talking about?
Elliot
Martin Amis's short stories.
Edie
Oh, you like his books? Name one.
Elliot
Martin Amis's Collected Short Stories. Got to go—we're playing strip beer pong.

Edie giggled stupidly. She received the "typing" dots and then:

Elliot
(NB: We're not! I don't have the steely nerves for this game with you, Thompson. YOU WIN.)

She beamed. Look at her, living fearlessly, trading the gags. It probably helped she was socializing herself, not trotters up, wearing her period-week nightie and trying to keep track of a Harlan Coben.

An hour later, Elliot sent:

Free to talk? Only brief and non-urgent. Don't want to disturb your evening. xx
Edie
Sure, it's noisy in here, though. I'll nip out into the garden. Give me one minute. xx
Elliot
Got it. Here's your homework! ☹ *X*

Edie refilled glasses and excused herself, as Elliot pinged her a link to a minor item story on the showbiz page of a national.

Things may be heating up with Elliot Owen and his girlfriend, Edie Thompson, who lives in his home city of Nottingham. Our spies hear Owen has bought a house in a leafy suburb as a base to visit the 36-year-old ad exec. It will do nothing to dispel rumors that the *Blood & Gold* sex symbol is planning to break many hearts and make an honest woman of the lucky gal. "Elliot's keen to settle down and says Edie is the woman for him,"

said our expertly placed source. "They've talked about marriage and starting a family and they're on the same page."

Edie closed the back door behind her, iPhone once again weighing like an unpinned grenade in hand. She and Elliot, she noticed, never mentioned the febrile wedding bells element to any write-ups. It'd be awkward if it was true and awkward if it wasn't. This one, however, might need probing.

"Fuck's sake," Edie said, by way of hello.

"Evening, darling! Fuck's sake indeed."

"What's the list of suspects this time?"

"Me, you, Mum and Dad, and my parents told Fraser. End of list. The temporary news blackout plan with my brother isn't working in this respect as I'm not going to tell my parents to keep any more secrets from him . . . The stag do has gone on to a local bar, by the way, and I'm catching them up."

"Only you and the henners in bikinis, eh."

"That reminds me—I let Fraz post that photo. I want to see if it somehow escapes his social media. I don't know why, though, because it couldn't be more obvious that the leak is via Fraser, without his knowledge. I still haven't spoken to him, and I've got to. If he goes ballistic at any Molly imputation, I'm going to say to him: I'm not suggesting I have an explanation; give me your explanation."

"*Imputation!* You're so clever for a pretty boy," Edie said.

"You are riddled with prejudice. Some of us worked in school, instead of truanting with the guy with the smutty DVDs."

Edie grinned. "You know, the timing here is another signpost away from Molly. I doubt she'd have the headspace to be in Palma with her prosecco coven *and* doing this?"

"Smartphones being what they are, I think you can multitask. You know what has been worrying at me and has finally moved from back burner to front brain?"

Elliot's flat vowels in "worrying" was purest East Midlands. Edie liked being reminded of his roots.

"What's that?" She stamped her feet to stay warm: March was spring in name only.

"It's been what, a week since the house decision? If I was selling stories on someone, I'd pick and choose—I'd take rests. I'd try to evade detection. This is relentless. At first, it came off to me as sloppy amateur, but I've realized there's a darker interpretation. What if this is someone who really dislikes me? Properly vindictive: *fuck you, every time you cough, I'm going to the red tops?*"

"You don't have any enemies, though?"

"I didn't think I did . . . maybe Heather, I suppose."

"That description definitely isn't Molly, either," Edie said.

"Honestly, even if she's the leak, I've never thought she's the saleswoman. She's probably telling herself it's an ongoing coincidence that what she's gossiped about is getting out. How're you anyway? Dinner going well?"

Edie cast a look at the low-lit conviviality. "It's really lovely. Declan is getting on like a house on fire with my lot, and my previously rebellious sister is in her element."

"Do you know how much I wish I was there?"

"Is it as much as I wish you were here?" Edie said.

"Is it like a whole-body longing that slides into a supercut of favorite memories? If so, yes."

"Yeah, very much that," she said.

Edie knew they were both simpering, cradling their phones like children with pet hamsters. Nauseating. She cleared her throat.

"You know the part in this story about us discussing . . . a family, and so on? Did you tell anyone about that?"

"God, no," Elliot said. "Not a soul. I didn't think that was any-one's business but ours."

"Me neither."

"They add those claims by rote, I think. Heather and I were constantly off to the Little Wedding Chapel with her Pomeranian dog Snowball as ring bearer or some shit. Safe to ignore it."

"Oh, sure," Edie said, making sure that the fact she was crest-fallen was absent from her tone of voice. *We're not a repeat of you and Heather, and I wanted it to be true.*

Through the window, she saw Declan watching her. He raised his wineglass in acknowledgment at having been caught, and Edie waved back. She'd been unwittingly frowning.

"Everything all right?" Declan said, when Edie came back in. "That looked intense?"

"Oh, no," she said. "A knotty topic being discussed, that's all."

Declan said: "Ah." She could tell he thought he was being fobbed off and that he'd seen a row.

Later, as she banged plates haphazardly into the dishwasher and pressed the *on* button, Edie's phone rang with an unknown London landline number.

Something about the unlikely late hour made Edie answer.

"Hi—is that Edie Thompson?"

"Yes?"

"My name's Simon Brggghhhm from the . . ." Background noise from the appliance obscured the words.

Edie put a finger in her spare ear and said: *"Sorry, what?"*

"We have a story running tomorrow."

Ah, phishing about the Elliot house purchase.

"No comment."

"It's an interview with your ex-boyfriend, Jack Marshall. He's given his side of what happened at his wedding last year."

What? Edie was stunned.

"If I read you his quotes, do you want to make a comment?"

"He's not my ex," Edie said, before comprehending she was simultaneously half-pissed, in shock, and on the record with a journalist—and ending the call.

A text arrived from Declan.

Tommo! Your friends are ACE. As is your sister. I can't thank you enough for how well you've looked after me since I moved up here. A brilliant night, thanks. xx

It was no longer a brilliant night.

40

The bony fingers of her demons prodded her into consciousness at exactly five a.m. Edie lay staring up at her tasseled lampshade. *Your ex-boyfriend has given his side.* Edie felt sure *I digitally bread-crumbed a woman into imagining we had a secret connection*, the only side Jack had, wouldn't be the side he'd provided.

Every so often, Edie listlessly picked up her phone and checked again.

She and Elliot had frantically WhatsApped their mutual alarm the previous night; he'd heard when she did, as Lillian had been approached about it. They agreed to speak today when they knew what they were dealing with. She doubted either of them had had much rest.

The story appeared around seven a.m., and it wasn't a sidebar; it merited the site proper, with a large photo of Jack and an inset one of Edie, holding a cocktail, head on one side, smiling winningly into the lens.

She clicked and scrolled. The quantity of words and pictures felt huge. It *was* huge. This was a novella, a macabre pulp romance with Edie as involuntary protagonist. Her own face grinned back up at her in a variety of snapshots torn from half-forgotten evenings out of recent years. Party dresses, bright lipstick, flicky eyeliner, and face pulling.

"I Fell for Edie and It Destroyed My Wedding Day . . . And My Life"
EXCLUSIVE: Elliot Owen's girlfriend's ex warns him: "You don't know who you're dealing with"

Jack Marshall was in a blazer, manspreading on a Chester-field sofa, giving a dynamic look to the camera. His hands were clasped between his legs. It was as if you were midmeeting with him, and he'd decided to order a couple of single malts, drop the company spiel, and give the offer to you straight.

The pictures included one of Jack in wedding attire with Char-lotte's face obscured, and a couple of Edie and Elliot at Fraser's party, including the one kissing, then the one of the fight with Elliot in the street, Edie flipping the V-sign at the amateur lookie-loo paparazzo.

Wait, there she was with Declan?! The caption said: *Thompson pictured with a colleague last month. There is no suggestion they are involved.* Nice legal fireproofing, except your entire editorial direction suggests otherwise.

Oh, and they'd dug up an image she'd never seen before, ob-viously supplied by Jack, where she and he were at either end of a sofa at an office party, their faces accusingly circled. As luck would have it, Edie was chatting to another male colleague in it: a picture editor's dream.

It was like true crime. Edie identified as the murderer of a marriage.

When actor Elliot Owen was snapped cuddling up to copywriter Edie Thompson last month, all eyes were on the loved-up duo. How had a 36-year-old from Not-tingham, a total unknown, landed one of the most eligible bachelors in the world, the British heartthrob now a rising star in Hollywood?

After all, the 32-year-old wasn't single at the time. When he and Thompson met, Owen was with model-actress Heather Lily. She publicly pleaded in vain for

Owen to return to her side. When it became clear his interests were engaged elsewhere, she made her sense of betrayal clear.

Yet some onlookers were less surprised that Thompson's job ghostwriting the *Blood & Gold* star's autobiography turned into such an unexpected romantic coup.

Jack Marshall, 38, an advertising executive from Herne Hill, knows to his cost that Edie Thompson's charms can be distracting.

"When I saw the photos of her and the actor entwined together, I thought, here we go again," Jack says, speaking to us about his own involvement with Thompson for the first time. "Edie makes men feel protective. But Edie doesn't need protecting—it's the other way around."

Jack lost his new wife, his job, and his good name when he and Thompson were caught—by his bride—passionately kissing in the hotel grounds on his wedding day in Yorkshire last summer. Thompson was then a colleague of both the bride and groom at London-based advertising agency Ad Hoc.

WEDDING DAY CLINCH

"I'm not proud of what occurred and take my share of the blame," Jack says, admitting that he finds reliving the episode very painful. "I had been with my then girlfriend, now ex-wife, for two years when I joined Ad Hoc. Edie made it pretty clear she was interested in me from day one. She always knew I was in a committed relationship. We bantered and would message and so on. She was obviously a fragile person, quite lonely even. My heart went out to her. I feared she was becoming attached and I stupidly thought I was looking after her by being her friend. With hindsight, I can see I was encouraging something that I shouldn't have."

The couple were both close enough with Thompson to invite her to their £35k bash in June last year at the Old Swan Hotel in Harrogate, where the bride's family lived.

Marshall has to take a deep breath before describing the chaos that ensued.

"I'd gone out for some time alone in the garden after the speeches. Obviously, wedding days are fabulous but intense, and I wanted to take a moment to reflect. Edie must have seen me leave and followed me out."

Marshall shakes his head. "I'd had a few drinks—I was already emotional. Edie decided that was the moment to tell me she was in love with me, that she was devastated I'd promised to spend my life with someone else. Then, to my shock, she kissed me."

Jack blinks back tears.

"In my mind, it was like the moment Keira Knightley kisses Andrew Lincoln in *Love Actually*, except I was Keira. Acknowledging someone's declaration—allowing just one tiny lapse of indiscretion, for their sake, before you both put it to one side, forever."

Unfortunately, it was less like a rom-com and more a horror film—as Jack's new bride stumbled upon them. The day ended in hysterical upset and explosive recriminations. The newlyweds separated for good six weeks later.

"I suppose it's natural to think the woman was preyed upon by a rogue, but in reality, it was six of one, half

a dozen of another—two guilty parties," Jack says rue-
fully. Yet he refuses to blame Thompson for what happened: "At the end of the day, I should have stopped
her. I was the one wearing the wedding ring, and it was
my responsibility."

Jack was sacked for the indiscretion, and his former
bride has also since left the Ad Hoc agency by mutual
agreement. Thompson mysteriously won a reprieve.
She remains employed by the company at an office in
Nottingham—a post created for her.

Another colleague from Thompson's workplace, who
wished to stay anonymous, said: "After the wedding,
a lot of staff wanted her to leave and even signed a
petition asking her to have the decency to go, but she
ignored it. It felt very unfair that others lost their jobs
over it, and she didn't. But Edie has a way of making
the friends that matter. Elliot Owen is just the latest
example."

Sources close to Owen have described him as "head
over heels," and sources close to the star predict he will
soon pop the question.

"Good luck to him," is all Jack will say about this,
grim-faced, a man still picking up the pieces from an
event he says he will "never live down." "He'll need it."

Lucie Maguire, 35, property agent from Dulwich, is
more direct about the prospect of Thompson's reward
in snagging a *People* magazine winner of "Sexiest Man
Alive." She was chief bridesmaid on the fateful wedding
day. Lucie says the former bride, her best friend, still
cannot bear Thompson's name spoken in her presence.

"Edie caused absolute mayhem for my beloved friend.

Her selfishness obliterated what was supposed to be the happiest day of her life. She moved on to Elliot Owen without an apology or backward glance," Lucie says.

"My advice to Elliot is to run as fast as he can, in the opposite direction," Lucie says. "I'm sure he's bought into the idea that Edie is a wronged angel, but seducing a man into that behavior on his wedding day? Make no mistake—she is a truly cold vixen."

If there are wedding bells in her and Owen's future, Thompson must hope her own guests understand the phrase is "you may kiss the bride" . . . but not necessarily the groom.

Edie Thompson and reps for Elliot Owen declined to comment when contacted by our reporters.

As usual, that paragraph resounded with: RENDERED MUTE BY GUILT.

A dazed Edie sent the link—still without comment as she was incapable of formulating one—to Nick and Hannah.

Five minutes later, her phone buzzed with the WhatsApp group notification.

Hannah
Fuck me, I will fucking murder the lying cunt. How is this not libel?
Nick
I say we come back at this hot, sassy, and strong. I'm getting a T-shirt made with COLD VIXEN for your next pap shots. In fact, I think there's legs in a whole COLD VIXEN line of merch. xxx (I hope you're laughing Edie, cos that's all it deserves)

Edie wasn't laughing; she was crying.

41

When Elliot rang her, it was one of those rare occasions where Edie had so much to say, she was temporarily rendered near-speechless.

She'd been forever enshrined as a homewrecking, Machiavellian, and desperate sexual mutineer, in SEO eternity, with Jack Marshall. It was almost as awful as the original aftermath.

Worse, they'd now drawn a direct line between him and Elliot. The barely concealed thrust of the entire piece was: this nondescript woman is such a devious harlot, she addles men's minds. *How had a 36-year-old from Nottingham, a total unknown . . .* Why not caption it simply: *Seriously—her?!*

"Edie. I'll be honest with you, you weren't my first call," Elliot said, into the back-and-forth of aghast monosyllables and deep breaths. "I didn't want you to deal with me at that point. I did my ranting and raving to Lillian first, got it out of the way. I don't want you to think I'm not raging, because I am. I thought I'd be more support to you if I'd done the swearing already." Elliot paused. "Er . . . with some understatement—how are you?"

Edie said brokenly: "I can't believe he did it. I know he's a bastard. But to do this?"

"Oh, Edie," Elliot said, down the slight echo of a phone in Croatia, "it's so fucking despicable and out of order, and I'm so, so sorry. I actually can't believe how nasty it is, and it's not like I'm easily shocked at this point."

"And Lucie, *again*. A woman who started a sock puppet account to abuse and harass me and said my dead mother must've killed herself through the shame of having me." Edie gathered herself. "She's certainly not a sufferer of excess shame, eh."

Elliot was obviously making an effort to stay calm. "They're venomously amoral. It's like dwelling in the Upside Down."

"Should I have stopped Jack? By answering his message?" Edie said. "He contacted me recently through Facebook, trying to get me to bite, and I left him on *seen*."

"He did? Did he tell you he was going to do this?"

"No, it was mainly trying to get me to go for a drink, saying he missed me. Kind of contradicts this version in print. Then a weird aside about how he had something 'in his inbox' that I should know about. I thought it was a try-on. I mean with Jack, it had to be. But what if I missed my chance to prevent this?"

"In order for it to be worth it for him to look a completely greasy shitbag in the nationals, to have this story live in Google searches by prospective employers and Tinder dates forever? I'd have thought he got a high six figures for this, easy."

"Fuck. Of course. That much . . . ?" Edie said. How had she not realized this was a hard cash transaction? She'd been too blindsided to examine motive. She had thought he wouldn't want to disgrace himself in order to disgrace her and forgot filthy lucre could change that.

"Oh yeah. They have the resources to make it appealing to him, and they weren't dealing with someone of firm principle— that goes without saying. I guarantee you, if he was going to say anything to you beforehand, it was only to give you an opportunity to outbid their offer—with money or some promise of sex. It's fair to say, I don't think we'd have gone for either? I'm not being blackmailed by anyone but certainly not by someone who dresses like a young Tory."

Edie gave a weak laugh. God, the shame of having kissed him. She was lucky Elliot wasn't repelled.

"Hope I've not dragged you from the stag do brunch . . ." Edie said.

"Hah, no," Elliot said. "They're all still comatose. I'm off to flip duvets in a minute and check for hen do girls."

Edie tried for a laugh, but her rib cage was still made of lead. Yet another insight into Being Elliot Owen: he had to stay alert and sober to handle PR crises from a holiday villa.

Edie would tell Meg when she emerged and downplay it as much as she could. Should she tell her dad? She decided she wouldn't: it was assigning Jack importance he didn't deserve.

"Lillian's going to talk to you in a minute, is that OK?" Elliot asked.

"Yes, sure," Edie said in a thin voice.

"*Edie*," Elliot said. "You are a spectacularly great person, and he is spectacularly not, and one crappy pile of exploitative coattail riding lies in a tabloid on a boring Sunday won't convince anyone otherwise."

"Thanks . . . it's just hard knowing it'll be on my record now," Edie said. "It was one thing to have the wedding day reported last time we dated. At least it was light on detail. Now there's Jack's false Mills & Boon version, complete with invented dialogue from me. I feel unclean. I feel like by shoving words in my mouth, he's assaulted me."

"Unless . . ." Elliot said, and uncharacteristically hesitated, as if his suggestion might be too much. "Unless we bump it right down the searches with better and more positive stories? More . . . newsworthy ones?"

Edie held her breath. *Sources close to the star predict . . .*

"You think we could?"

"Yep . . . We're going to have to get a lot of coffees and get off with each other at a lot of parties," Elliot concluded.

Edie breathed out.

They add those claims by rote.

After they hung up, Lillian rang within minutes, brisk as always. She wasn't someone who Edie wanted to be vulnerable with, yet she had no choice. She'd been stripped of her outer layer of skin, left a quivering mass of nerve endings, begging for help.

"How is it possible to print so many lies and get away with it? It's absolute bullshit!" Edie said. "Jack chased me for months. He followed me into the garden in Harrogate. *He* kissed *me*. Lillian, I want to sue."

"I hear that," Lillian said. "I do. It's galling. But you kissed him back on his wedding day, right? His bride left him? He got the sack?"

"Yeah," Edie whimpered. "Because he was the perp, and our boss knew it. Jack's done it before, too. I still have an email from a woman from his past who said so. She got in touch after the last story about it."

Edie remembered with gratitude the testimony from another Jack victim, Martha Hughes. *He's led one woman on, while seeing another. It's his "thing."*

". . . I have bags of receipts. I have texts from Jack. I have a message from him from weeks ago asking me to go for a drink with him, saying he misses me!"

Lillian let a short silence elapse—a *get your shit together* subtext silence.

"Even if those messages somehow definitively prove what you want them to prove—which is a high bar to clear—you're smearing more dirt on someone who is already in a ditch, in a dirt-rolling contest with you. The public won't see any difference."

Edie took a shaky breath. "Right."

"It's not libel if the facts are true. That's called justification. I agree with you that their quotes are stretching the definition of fair comment—even I was surprised they went this hard. I'm afraid it's linked to Elliot's value. He's gone from upper B- to lower A-list now, and they will come for you as a result."

Lillian drew breath. "But they've built this on uncontested facts. The rest is he said, she said. If you sue them, you will lose, cost yourself millions, and Streisand effect the motherfucker through the roof."

"Streisand effect?"

"When trying to make something go away, all you do is make the information more widely known."

"So that's it? He gets away with it."

"At Elliot's level, there's often nothing better than saying nothing. This is a *say nothing, rise above* situation. Kiss-and-tells are for lesser people on the other side of the red rope, not the ones at the Golden Globes."

"Mmm," Edie said, thinking the obvious point she wouldn't make was that the only person being invited to the Golden Globes was Elliot. Edie was the one who might be heckled in Greggs. She was collateral.

"You know when I first spoke to you, you asked was he going to be a problem, and I said no?" Edie wasn't sure if the masochism of this line of inquiry was wise, but she couldn't help herself. "If I'd said yes and foreseen it, could we have avoided this?"

"Honestly, I should tell you yes for my professional efficacy and as your best advice going forward. Off the record, with checkbook journalism, it's gonna happen. If only we could un-fuck people, right?"

"I didn't sleep with him," Edie said.

"Oh. Apologies! Yes."

She had underscored something else Edie had avoided: that plenty would assume that she and Jack had a full-blown affair, and privacy laws and gentlemanly discretion—*hahaha*—must've forbade Jack from saying so.

"Something to be grateful for," Lillian offered.

"I'll write it in my gratitude journal," Edie said.

"You know what, Edie?" Lillian said contemplatively. Edie was both gratified to finally win softness from Lillian, while concerned at how bad things needed to be for this to be the case. "I've been doing this job twenty-five years. Something I've found, without fail, is the truth gets out eventually. Sit by the river and wait for this jerk's body to float past. It will."

Edie thanked Lillian, while thinking that was a long wait for which she'd need many packs of cigarettes, a fully charged Kindle, and a gun.

42

The sense of game, set, and match to Jack was hard for Edie to accept. The final coup was her looking up his abandoned shot-across-the-bows message to her. She started to type responses, practicing varying degrees of eloquent contempt and seething derision, demanding to know why he'd lied.

However, she knew why: to make money and clear his own name. Plus, he was far too canny to make useful concessions to Edie in a screenshottable format.

Therefore, what would letting him know he'd got to her achieve? Nothing but more mendacious, enraging bullshit would flow from Marshall, and he'd no doubt derive satisfaction from forcing Edie into making contact. If he lacked the moral inhibitions that would stop him doing that story, nothing she said was going to hurt. Edie wasn't sure he had "shame" in his repertoire.

Elliot had said: "I'd gladly serve him a cease and desist from frightening Hollywood lawyers or organize a manure delivery on his driveway or whatever. But he'll only use it to show off that he's rattled us."

Edie glumly concurred.

And in the not-her-fault-and-yet-very-much-her-fault file, Edie had to make extensive apologies to Declan for his featuring in Jack's takedown. He assured Edie he couldn't care less—whether this was true, Edie didn't know. Declan was skillfully gracious and could hide it well if he did mind.

On Monday morning, Edie endured a meeting with vegan frozen yogurt makers, full of boggling looks and an undue sense of fascination with her remarks on live cultures that told her they'd googled her.

Even with his high opinion of her and their Nottingham venture running well, Edie wondered how long Richard could withstand his agency being embroiled in this.

When she got to the doorway of the office, Declan was audibly still in a Teams meeting with Jessica. He'd given Edie prior warning, but she had hoped it would be over by now.

". . . I told you she'd suck you into her bullshit. At least I hope she's only sucking you *in* . . ."

Hearing her speak reminded Edie of Jessica in person, someone she'd wanted to like her—and yet.

"Edie's not here right now, thanks for checking," Declan said.

Edie waited at the threshold. This time it wasn't eavesdropping; it was reasonable self-preservation when trapped. She couldn't be sure where Declan had positioned his laptop and Edie wasn't walking across the range of the camera and giving Jess safe-distance bullying thrills. Not today, Other Satan.

"She's playing hooky? Surprise."

". . . Out at a meeting, actually."

"Oh good, you can enjoy this morning's project—we've done her a song. It's to the tune of 'Sexy Sadie' by The Beatles. *Seedy Edie / You made a tit of everyone . . .*" she crooned. "*Seeeeedy Edie.*"

"This is cruel, Jess. It's shit behavior. This isn't who you are."

"No, the shit behavior was telling a man you're in love with him and jumping him on his wedding day—happy to help."

"You bought that story? The guy is clearly a streak of lying piss who cheated on his wife."

"Doesn't make Edie honest."

"I dunno—I think I might have let a twenty-second snog go by now. Why the fixation?"

"Do you really think that's all they'd ever done? *Lol*. If you're getting off with someone at their wedding, then very obviously you've been at it like rabbits for months. Amelia saw them coming out of the Betsey Trotwood late, hand in hand, bold as brass, weeks before the wedding."

Edie started. *What the . . . ?* If you were clandestinely involved, why would you take that sort of risk? Edie had forgotten that subset of people involved in a scandal who were prepared to mint their own coinage.

"Yeah, yeah, and I saw them bumming on Alton Towers's Nemesis. I think you need a new hobby," Declan said.

"Honestly, Dec, I thought you were too clued up to fancy her," Jess said. "And *Elliot Owen*—how on earth? She must have a magical vagina or something. Let us know when you get there."

Edie's face flared red.

"I don't fancy her. Is there anything relating to the meeting left to discuss, or can I leave the cast of *Mean Girls* due to creative differences?"

There were stilted goodbyes and the electronic dinging sounds of screens closing.

Edie wasn't able to hide the fact she was stood where she was and, consequently, that she'd overheard.

She walked in, and Declan turned around, startled. Fair to say, despite her unpopularity, she didn't expect her private parts to be mocked. *Seedy Edie.* In front of a male friend and colleague, it was so invasive and mortifying.

There Edie had been, thinking HarrogateGate was behind her.

It was if she'd had her stitches from a wound picked open and her innards pulled out, under surgical lamps.

"Edie . . . I wasn't going along with any of that . . ." Declan said, discomposed, ruffling his pre-ruffled hair.

Edie nodded. "I know. I didn't sleep with Jack or go on any pub dates. He was with someone—I wouldn't do that. I didn't tell him I was in love with him, either. It's a free-for-all, because no one trusts me. It's like *The Purge*, when crime is legal, except it's lying about me, and it won't stop after twenty-four hours."

"It's deranged," Declan said. "Also, some people do trust you."

Edie intended to thank him, walk to her seat, put her things down, and start work. Instead, she found herself breaking down. She put a palm over her eyes as her chest heaved.

"Hey, come on, Tommo! You are a wonder and a triumph of a person," Declan said. He leaped up to put his arms around her as Edie shook. She had to bury her face in his shirt for the ugly sobbing, face-collapse phase where she couldn't bear to be observed.

"Sorry, sorry," Edie said when she could risk looking up blearily. "To think when Richard told me I'd have a desk mate up here, I was determined we'd set standards for professionalism."

"I think I ruined that first," Declan said, with a grin.

Edie wasn't a public weeper or even a liberated weeper full stop, in the normal order of things. As she pulled herself together, she was worried that it looked like she'd done a damsel-in-distress routine at him on purpose, forcibly assigning herself victimhood by appealing to manly instincts. In either sex, Hannah called it the *help me, I'm tiny* move. Declan hugged her tighter, before letting her go again. It felt like a little too much, but Edie had compelled it.

"This is a reason, not an excuse," Declan said, as they sat down, "but this may have less to do with you than you might think. I'm told Jess's husband, Wes, left her for someone at the college where he's lecturing. Not many dots to join there. Like I said, though, no excuse."

"God, really? I'm Patron Saint of the Other Woman to her," Edie said.

"Something like that."

Edie pondered if it was unsisterly to say the next thing and concluded that she didn't owe Jess much. "Is it also possible she feels . . . especially possessive of you?"

"It's possible," Declan said, and Edie liked his straightforwardness. His face fell. "There's nothing going on! She's married. Or she was."

Edie smiled. "Too late, Seedy Edie is sitting in judgment."

"Urgh. Jess is going to have one awful shame hangover from this."

Edie doubted that. You needed to sober up to have a hangover. From what she could tell, the court of public opinion had cleared Jack and convicted Edie, with no right of appeal.

"In other news, I'm now the proud owner of a mangy long-haired cat," Declan said. "I found him licking a crab stick he'd nosed out of the bin. I'm calling him King Prawn. I've taken him to the vet to check if he had an ID chip, and he's registered as mine. It's official: I'm a father."

Edie managed to laugh. "Why not call him Crab Stick?"

"I don't want to make him a figure of fun. Ah look. We've got an email from the boss," Declan said.

"Oh shit," Edie said. If Richard was scheduling his royal visit, that timing didn't bode at all well. *Perhaps, all things considered, freelancing would be a better fit . . .*

Declan scanned it. "I don't think you'll hate it . . ."

Mouth dry, Edie opened it.

You two! The Pepsi proposal is rather, if not very, impressive. They're taking the meeting and suggest the details below. Knock them dead. I'll take you for lunch afterward.

Well done. Much more of this and I'll have to assume you're doing some actual work up there.

R

PS Thompson: I hope you are observing correct procedure when it comes to a certain former colleague and treating him with the shattering indifference he deserves. Apart from anything else, bloody dreadful jacket.

God, Edie loved Richard.

43

Edie had an unhelpful superstition that any day of travel that began badly would continue the theme. It would be start to finish "tomfuckery," to borrow a Nick word. ("Like tomfoolery, but darker. The way Pennywise the clown in the sewer is not a children's entertainer. You do not enjoy tomfuckery.")

After a fidgety, sleepless night, her American trip started with her taxi rolling up forty-five minutes late. Every traffic jam they encountered en route saw Edie nervously recalculating her chances of making the departure, instead of enjoying her podcast.

She fielded a nerve-jangling rant at Heathrow from a fuming client who'd been stood up after their mis-diary of a meeting, initially refusing to accept it was their error. Then a child cannoned into her leg in the queue for the gate. The small boy deposited a strawberry milkshake down her leg, with the frankly self-absorbed expression of regret, given she was in Wolford tights, "Oh no, I've frowed my eat."

Edie knew LHR to JFK today was pure tomfuckery territory.

By the time Edie was seated next to a fractious family of five who had apparently not encountered a social taboo they recognized—arguing, clothing removal, personal information repeated in public zone, breaking wind, sodcasting entire Micky Flanagan routines, egg-mayo sandwiches in their carry-on—she limply accepted it as her due.

"They're from Braintree," said the bespectacled man next to her, by way of full and entire explanation.

By the time she was passing immigration, Edie was utterly

spent. She had the very specific, shop-soiled clamminess of long-haul travel, complete with bone-tiredness, shadowed eyes, and furry mouth. She feared she had the aroma of a vet's thermometer and absolutely wasn't fit for presentation, let alone a whirlwind evening out on the tiles in the city that never sleeps.

As the car that Elliot sent to collect her approached the glittering iconic cityscape, Edie knew she should feel euphoric. As it was, among other woes, she was annoyed at herself for not feeling euphoric—what sort of privileged jerk turned this experience into a negative?

But not only did Edie feel like a used dishrag, she was having a very ill-timed prolapse of confidence. How much her physical and mental state were feeding off each other, she couldn't tell. She was overawed. Her partner was so successful that he was famous *here*, too; it fair blew the mind after she'd sat on a jumbo jet for eight hours. Edie even wondered if she'd delayed visiting him in the States so that she could cosplay Elliot being a boy next door, keeping him carefully out of context.

The disorientation continued as she was deposited outside a forbidding security-fortress apartment block, her driver getting out to jab the relevant buzzer.

Edie shouldered her bag and dragged her case into a private elevator that took her to the second floor, where she found the relevant door. Oh God, were those multiple voices she could hear on the other side? Oh, fuck this forever.

It was flung open by Elliot, who was in a white T-shirt and, naturally, looking as fresh as a springtime crocus. The room beyond was Manhattan loft as it existed in the mind's eye: a cavernous box shape, broken up by curved red sofas, freestanding lamps, and splashes of modern art. High windows ran down the left-hand side.

"You found it! This is my girlfriend! Edie, this is Jim and Dulcie.

They're in the apartment across the hall," Elliot said. Two unfeasibly tall, toothy, and Ralph Lauren–clad Americans stared down at her. Edie smiled an overcompensatory smile that could induce jaw ache, muttering effusive greetings.

As soon as small talk resumed, she mumbled *justgoingtodropmythings* and Elliot pointed her to a doorway. "Bathroom there, bedroom the one after."

Edie dashed off with her trolley case, trying a handle and finding herself in a subway-tiled bathroom the size of the ground floor of her entire house, where she locked the door with its heavy key.

Actually, maybe Jim and Dulcie (was that really a name you could have?) were a blessing in disguise. They'd afforded Edie valuable time at this double basin to improve on the rock bottom she was at: toothbrushing, makeup repair, greasy hair thrown up into ponytail, more perfume. She looked longingly at a walk-in shower that could fit the entire Braintree family in at once and at the freestanding slipper bath. Actually, she could do a clothes change. Edie hurriedly shed her begrimed travel apparel for a creased alternative. She wasn't exactly fresh, but she was improved.

"Find everything all right?" Elliot said, as she emerged.

"Yep. Have they gone?" she whispered.

"Yes, argh," Elliot whispered back. "Not ones to take a hint."

Elliot moved to kiss her, and Edie stepped backward.

"Are you OK? Getting here not too arduous?" he said.

She'd intended to power through, and yet her chest suddenly concaved.

"I'm so sorry—I'm knackered. My flight was awful, and I feel like absolute death. You deserve better. You're also not helping, looking like this much of a contrast."

Elliot laughed. "Did you go business or first?"

"Premium economy," Edie said.

"Oh, you principled chump," Elliot said, grinning, pushing

a wisp from her ponytail back over her ear. "When you do this often, do it right. Want me to cancel the dinner reservation and get takeout instead?"

"Could we?" Edie said. "Would that be OK?" She felt the best she had all day. "I'm sorry to be such a let-down," she said. "When I think of all the times you've come out with me straight from this journey like you've hopped off a bus. I'm resembling a rattly pensioner . . ."

"*Edie Thompson*," Elliot said. "It's not a performance review. You're here. That's all that matters. Have a wine and stop worrying. It took me years to get used to the transatlantic twatting about. Give me that . . ."

He indicated her luggage, taking the handle and rolling it into a bedroom glimpsed beyond. There was a low divan the size of a boxing ring, and Edie wasn't ready to contemplate it.

"It's not you who needs to grovel, it's me," Elliot said, once they were arranged on the couch, the DoorDash app on Elliot's phone blipping with imminent Thai food.

"Oh?" Edie sipped. He was right about the remedy. Two inches of Malbec and Edie felt remarkably more in sync with her surroundings. *Woohoo, New York, baby.*

"Believe it or not, Fraser's here. Planned the trip ages ago, with Iggy. He wasn't even seeing Molly at the time. However, Molly's third-wheeling anyway to select bridesmaids' necklaces from Tiffany's, or something. Is it a massive intrusion if we meet them for dinner tomorrow night?"

"Hahaha—what? Are they following us around the world?"

"I'm starting to feel claustrophobic, to be honest, which is no mean feat given the geography involved."

"Think of it as homely!"

"Aye, *right*. There's the lurking worry that this tracking of my movements is connected to story-selling. I forced myself to be rational: Fraser booked this when drunk, six months back. There's no grand plan . . . except . . ."

Edie got there: ". . . Except Molly is a late addition?"

"Yes."

They exchanged a look. Neither of them said anything more. It was increasingly unpleasant to harbor these doubts and increasingly impossible not to.

"You've not talked to him about the leaks?"

"No, unsurprisingly the stag didn't afford any opportunities. Tomorrow night isn't the time—I'm going to have to call him once he's back in the UK, I think. I would've preferred face-to-face, but it's not practical. Sure you don't mind? I have no qualms about saying no if needs be," Elliot said.

"I like the idea! It'd be good to meet Molly properly before the wedding. And it's comforting seeing familiar faces so far from home."

"How are you so sweet and forbearing? I need to be more like that."

"I'm not sure I am really—it's within certain limits. If you'd said sorry, they're squeezing in at mine, it's airbeds, and we're all in one room, I might lose my Elliot-sharing chill."

"Oh, I see. All you want me for is sex. There's something else I wanted to say to you, actually," Elliot said.

Edie looked alarmed, hoping experimentation wasn't about to be tabled. "Unrelated, I hope?"

"Hahaha. I've got this airbed . . . No, unrelated—regarding the horrible Sunday papers bullshit last week. I know this isn't the way you think, whatsoever, but for my own honor, I have to say— that story wouldn't have run if we weren't seeing each other. It's indirectly my fault. If you wanted to stop seeing me to stop stories like that, I'd understand. I'd hate it, and it'd break my heart, but I wouldn't blame you, either. I can give you a lot, but I can't give you a peaceful life. I get a lot of perks in return for that shit, and you only get me."

"The greatest perk of all," Edie said.

"I mean it."

"I know you do, and I love you for it," Edie said. "Firstly, it's nowhere near enough to put me off—it didn't even occur to me it was an Elliot drug side effect. Secondly, if you think I'm putting Jack fucking Marshall down as cause of death on our death certificate, you're high."

Elliot laughed. Edie wound herself round him, head on his T-shirt, and listened to his heart beating. It was probably the most generous heart she'd ever known.

Generosity she depended upon when she drank three wines, ate a pile of larb, and passed out like she'd been put under general anesthetic at quarter past ten Eastern Standard Time.

44

"New York is different to London," Elliot said, as they got ready to head out for brunch, Edie pulling fingerless wool gloves on.

"Wow, really? Thanks, Bill Bryson," Edie said, to amusement. One decent night's sleep and some caffeine and she was certainly resembling herself.

"Oh, for fu—! I'm talking about the nature of the hassle. People are more open and shout at you here, but keep moving quickly and we should be fine. There's not usually any paps on this street, and I'm going to avoid their usual haunts. Also, I can't really take you to any tourist sights—is that OK?"

"That's fine—I did it all when I came here about seven years ago. The Empire State can't have changed much."

"Ah. Who with? Friends?"

"My ex, Matt."

"Oh, right," Elliot said, then paused. "Slag."

Edie hooted with laughter.

"How long were you with him?"

"Three years. Twenty-six to twenty-nine."

"Gross," Elliot said, and the air crackled with the frisson of comic jealousy and real jealousy.

"He's dead actually."

"Shit, really?"

"No. Engaged with a baby called Lila, according to what he posts on Facebook," Edie said.

"Hmm, liked him better when deader," Elliot said.

In the elevator on the way to street level, Elliot pulled his hat disguise on. "What a life this is. Do I look like a *Home Alone* robber?"

"Hahaha. I never think of you as famous anymore, except when I have to," Edie said.

"I don't think of myself as famous, either."

"Don't you?"

"Not really. It's so separate to me. It feels like a prank that's got out of hand. Like I did something silly, and I can't take it back yet. In my head, I live fifteen minutes from you at home, and I'm still exactly like you, but I'm on this mad adventure, for the time being."

Edie surveyed him thoughtfully. "I think I get that. I really do."

"Nothing imaginary about the amazing table I'm getting us tonight, though," Elliot said. "Loser Matt could *never.*"

They held hands and strode with purpose once outside, Edie's chin buried in the neck of her coat, relishing being with someone who knew where they were going. No start-stopping and bovine Google Maps staring.

Elliot took her to an unshowy diner, and they sequestered themselves in a far corner booth. Edie could tell they were following tried and tested paths that Elliot had designed for himself in this environment, offering lower chance of occurrences, mishaps.

"It's tons of pressure but totally different to *Void* pressure," Elliot said, twiddling his fork in his huevos rancheros, after Edie asked about work. "There, the responsibility was business. This one is heart, not head. I want to do it justice. The pressure is coming from me, not a boardroom."

"I understand why," Edie said, sucking on the paper straw in a large beaker of ice water. ". . . From only the scrap I read, it's special." (Speaking of special, this was the best mushroom omelet she'd ever had.)

252

"That's it, exactly! It's special. You know, the whole pitch of *Your Table* is Matteo's coming back to the city and running the restaurant his late father owned, his father who was an industry legend. Awful parent, sensational at his job. People don't think Matteo can do it. It's all about him proving himself and striving for paternal love he'll never win. Feels, uh, thematically deeply meaningful to me," Elliot said, smiling. He paused. "Could you get a better demonstration of why my life is nonsensical? I'm explaining why I have to be in America for the sake of someone who doesn't exist."

Edie smiled and squirmed. This was too much clarity for comfort. That *Your Table* meant he wasn't coming back to the UK for a long while was obvious, but she didn't want to dwell on it. And although Elliot wasn't pitting his love for her against the dramatic needs of a fictional legacy restaurateur, he was.

"I think of it very much as an ensemble, but Matteo is the premise and the linchpin. The thought of letting the other cast and crew down by screwing it up is unbearable. Which means I'm truly committed."

"Plus, if you're too modest to say it, I will—you're the star, you're the draw," Edie said. "Matteo is a main character, but in the real world, so are you. Heavy is the head that wears the crown, and so on. Why doesn't England adopt *home fries*?"

"Good?" Elliot said. "I hoped you'd like it here."

"It's great."

"I suppose that's true about being the lead, but I try not to think about it as it's a group effort and there are people in it far more talented than me. Ines has hit it out of the park. She won't be given decorative roles after this. Or she will, but she won't have to take them."

Edie squirmed some more. "Great," she said. She could tell

Elliot had that home-from-school-trip unbridled enthusiasm where he wasn't gauging her reaction. Was Edie going to be her higher self, and say nothing snippy? No, she decided. "Does Ines manage not to straddle you in your cigarette breaks?"

"Er . . . oh. Haha. Yeah. Calmed down entirely," Elliot said, the beat where he figured out what Edie was referring to making it obvious that, until now, the Padrona outrages had been entirely forgot. "She's just a very touchy-feely, affectionate person. Too nice and trusting for this industry altogether, I fear. I worry."

"Do you?"

"No! Not like that at all. Like a sister. I know you didn't have the best introduction to her, but I think you're going to love Ines in the show."

Edie nodded and said nothing, because she no doubt would, and that wouldn't be easy, either.

"Hey, I saw this dress I think you'd like . . ." Elliot said, fishing his phone out and showing her a website.

Edie looked at the Vampire's Wife shimmering chiffon, with a four-figure price tag.

"Can I get it for you? For Fraz's wedding maybe?"

"Ehm . . . are things I own already not going to be good enough for that?" Edie said, wondering if this was a subtle inter-vention. Even imagining a coded maternal conversation: *Darling, you're going to look after Edie, aren't you . . . ? What's she planning for her outfit?*

"*Wow,*" Elliot said. "That was uncalled-for. 'Can I buy you a present?' 'So you think I look like crap?' Jeez, Edie."

"I didn't mean that!" Edie said. "I don't want you to think I'm a gold digger, that's all. I'm sorry I was spiky—that's really kind, and I would love that dress, thank you. You've got my taste exactly right."

There was a strained silence, during which a waiter refilled their coffee.

"You don't want me to think you're a gold digger?" Elliot repeated, and Edie fretted that she'd really hurt his feelings and spoiled the day.

"Yes. I know it says more about me and nothing about you . . ."

"Amazing. You'd be the worst gold digger ever known. Truly the most ineffectual, unsuccessful, embarrassment to the profession of gold-digging. You've told me to kindly piss off literally every time I've tried to buy you anything more than a pint. 'Edie, have I taken that hint right, you like diamonds?' 'Shove your solitaire up your arse, creepy Bluebeard.'"

Edie put her hand over her mouth as she laughed, and Elliot shook his head. Thank God for the glue of a shared sense of humor.

As they left, hand in hand, not only was she glad they hadn't fallen out but she registered that he'd casually and possibly intentionally implied that what he'd have bought her was an engagement ring. Another zero on the great check of expectations that existed only in Edie's head.

It's not any promise that you'll feel the same in a year's time.

45

"The place we're going in the West Village tonight, I think you'll really like it," Elliot said. "It's a bar with food and pretty much functions like a restaurant, except you keep your table all night and the meal never really ends. They keep bringing small plates. Someone famous usually ends up playing the piano. No photos get taken. A friend calls it the 'anecdote generator machine.'"

Edie hoped "friend" wasn't generic cover for "Ines."

"Is it members only?" Edie said.

"Kind of. You couldn't call up and book a table if they didn't know you."

There was a question about how they could get to know customers if they didn't recognize cold-calling new ones, and Edie decided to leave it be. Let it dwell in the heavy mists of being an illustrious personage, like disappearing through a doorway full of dry ice.

Elliot was right; she did like the venue: the wood paneling, round leather banquettes, gilt mirrors, red-fabric dining lamps on every table: a very midcentury infidelity-and-martinis aesthetic.

The Fraser group was there on their arrival. He'd WhatsApped Edie fifteen minutes before with:

v glad you're here to cheer the bastard up FYI! He was glum as hell on the stag. Could only get him to have two lap dances. (Joke) xxx

Edie was troubled that the brothers were on a collision course, if Fraser couldn't anticipate the way Elliot was thinking. She said nothing to Elliot.

Iggy up close was a striking-looking individual: red hair like copper wire in curls, a chili-powder color Edie had never seen other than in youthful experiments with box dyes. He had a half-dozen freckles that looked penciled on, like a *Bash Street* kid, and a laugh like that wheezing cartoon dog in flying goggles. It was like Roald Dahl had thought him up and Quentin Blake had drawn him.

("Is his name really Iggy?" Edie had asked Elliot in the cab on the way there.

"Oh, no. He's called Eric, after his dad. Iggy was some school nickname that stuck. 'Iggy Stardust,' as I first remember it— dunno why, though. Don't ask. With Fraz and Iggy, it's always better to leave a mystery unsolved.")

Miniscule Molly's conker-brown hair had been ironed into a geometrically perfect, poker-straight parting, a coral manicure on show as she clasped a jeweled clutch bag.

"Can I sit next to you, given we've had no time to talk before?" Edie said, choosing Molly's end of the upholstered seating horseshoe.

"Oh yes! That'd be so nice, thank you," Molly said, bumping her backside along several inches, as Fraser beamed.

The waitress sold them on a "chilled red wine," which sounded like a descent into the inferno and tasted like heaven.

Molly was fluttery with her, and Edie very quickly ascertained, to her surprise, that she wasn't the most nervous about making a good impression. All Edie had to do was demonstrate she wasn't either stuck-up or pulling rank in any way, and Molly was enchanted.

Edie told her about her flight, and Molly gurgle-laughed. Elliot shot Edie a very pure adoring look for her effort and its evident reward. Edie liked it, while thinking she didn't really deserve it; Molly wasn't difficult.

Edie saw the problem with Elliot's perception of Fraser's fiancée within half an hour: they had a personality clash. Molly was extremely apprehensive around her brother-in-law-to-be— Edie guessed it wasn't so much his fame as his sharply confident Elliot manner. She might well have been intimidated by him without his IMDb credits.

The more edgy Molly got, the quieter she got, punctuated by bouts of skittish giggling—which in turn made Elliot surer she was a bit of an airhead.

Whenever Edie gently sent Elliot up or disagreed with him, Molly looked at her in astonishment, like she'd snout-slapped a crocodile.

Food kept arriving—Elliot had ordered the whole menu, it seemed. Edie would try an arancini ball or a tiny crostini, and it was somehow the best example of the genre she'd ever had.

"I have a call I need to take . . ." Elliot said, when things had degenerated to a liveliness where no one was going to notice much.

Edie was surprised to see a message arrive from Elliot, seconds later.

I don't have a call—Lillian sent me this, and I have reached my hard limit and had to walk out. Literally, only you and Fraz knew about it. Fuck this, I have to talk to him. I'm absolutely fucking incandescent now.

Edie opened the link he'd added.

EXCLUSIVE: ACTOR'S HEARTBREAK
INSPIRED TEARJERKING HIT

Blood & Gold star Elliot Owen's turbulent love life is the real inspiration behind platinum-selling Cameron McAllister's new song "Last Time."

The lyrics describe a heartbroken man returning to ask a woman to rekindle their affair—not knowing if this is the "last time" he has a chance or if he's missed the opportunity to win her back.

The song was written after the actor had a late-night heart-to-heart with the 34-year-old Scottish singer, a close friend of Owen's since they were both struggling artists. McAllister was encouraging him to patch things up with his former girlfriend, copywriter Edie Thompson, while she was still single. The couple split late last year but have recently got things back on track, suggesting McAllister's advice when playing Cupid worked.

"Edie ended things with Elliot because of their incompatible lifestyles, but he couldn't get her out of his system," said a source close to both. "Cameron persuaded him to tell her how he felt before it was too late, and it looks like it paid off . . . and spawned another monster hit for Cam."

Edie stopped reading, palms in a light sweat. She felt the embarrassment and exposure for both of them. She didn't want the ins and outs of their relationship picked over like this, didn't want this emotionally intimate detail about their reconciliation cast up for Ad Hoc to ridicule. She didn't want them pointing at her when "Last Time" came on at the Christmas party disco.

Edie looked over at Fraser, arm around Molly, loquacious and genial as always. It was impossible he was knowingly betraying his brother's confidences. His concern was wholly genuine, as was his loyalty. It seemed barely less impossible that Molly was.

Stay where you are. I'm coming to talk to you. x

Edie slipped out and found Elliot in the lobby, leaning against the wall, arms folded, wearing the unmistakable air of someone revving themselves up for a confrontation.

"Couldn't it have been Cameron? It's great publicity for the song," Edie said. She felt Elliot on the brink of doing things that would not be easily undone.

"Cam is utterly Masonic about the inspiration for his songs and everyone who works with him knows that. He'd not have told anyone, either, to make sure. This is the same person who's been leaking about me throughout, and I'm absolutely done with it. It's affected my girlfriend, my family, now my closest friends. Whatever privacy I had is now gone, like there's a silent breather on my phone line. I want to crawl out of my own skin, Edie."

"Totally empathize, but . . . is it a good idea to raise it tonight?" she said. "Especially after we've all been drinking . . ."

"Probably not, but everyone's got a plan until they're punched in the face," Elliot said. "Sorry. I will try my best to keep it civil and brief. But Fraser has to help me find the answer here."

"Don't directly accuse Molly, will you? I don't think she's capable of this, not at all," Edie said, while knowing events, and Elliot's resolve, had overtaken her. It reminded her of a piece of Richard wisdom: *if there's "never the right moment," the wrong one will find you instead.*

"I know she's nice," Elliot said. "But so much of this information has been known only to me, you, and Fraser, and by extension, her. The *only* person he'd tell about our being the background to that love song is her. I know that for sure. Enough's enough. Can you tell Fraser I want to have a word?"

46

Edie said to Fraser apologetically: "Elliot wants to talk to you. He's in the lobby," and Fraser—not unreasonably—looked confused.

"What's he out there for?"

"He wants a word alone, I think," Edie said, and Fraser frowned.

"Always something going on with the troubled diva." He grinned, set his drink and his phone down on the tablecloth, and made his way out.

"What's up?" Iggy said.

"Oh, family politics." Edie shrugged.

"Everyone's all right, aren't they? Their parents are OK?" Molly asked, stricken. "It's not the wedding seating plans, because we can change those? And I did tell Fraser the hot sauce table favors were asking for trouble."

"That was my idea!" Iggy said.

"It's not funny if my gran gets one of the Mad Dog Ghost Pepper ones."

"If it says Mad Dog on the label you've been forewarned."

"She might not have her readers on and think it says . . . *Glad Dog!*"

Iggy spluttered with delight.

Edie reassured Molly, while thinking her natural assumption was the product of a non-guilty mind.

Molly excused herself to the ladies, and Iggy merrily sloshed out more wine, while Edie decided she needed a soft drink. She wanted to face the fallout better hydrated.

Unable to locate their waitress, Edie stood at the bar and opened her phone. The WhatsApp from Fraser was still on the screen.

She clicked away from it, and as she did so, spotted a tiny detail that snagged her attention. She couldn't make sense of it. *How was he . . . ?* She clicked back into WhatsApp and stared. On impulse, she typed a reply and hit *send*, to see if it would get blue ticks. Grey ticks: delivered, but unread. She looked toward the double doors at the end of the room, the ones that first Elliot, then Fraser, had departed through, and scanned the room.

She carried her Diet Coke back to her seat, turning over a puzzle in her mind. She did a mental inventory of the detritus on their table.

"Tastes better from a bottle, right?" Iggy said, and she smiled absently.

Molly returned from the toilets.

Within minutes, both Owen brothers were back, expressions similarly stormy. Edie had never seen Fraser's sunny countenance contorted like this before, and it made her heart pound.

"Mol, get your things. We're off," he said.

Edie's hopes that they'd find a way to unite over this were immediately dashed. She could tell it had gone exactly the way she'd hoped it wouldn't.

"Why?" Molly said. "I've got a tuna tartare on the way—I don't want to go."

"I'll explain later. Come on."

"Elliot?" Molly said. "What's going on?"

"Don't ask him," Fraser snapped, and Edie winced.

She doubted Elliot had held back and, if Fraser had done nothing wrong, how it would've been received, and after this concern for him. She could see both sides. This was a fight that could turn into a feud and a rift. Edie looked at Molly, who was deeply disconcerted and obediently gathering her coat.

Edie had to speak up. She'd intended to talk to Elliot about her hunch, but they were out of time.

This might be the only moment where it would help.

"Iggy, don't do this," Edie said, looking at him.

Everyone stared at her in confusion.

"Do what?" Iggy said.

"Don't let them fall out over this, if it's you who's responsible."

"Responsible for what?"

"Selling stories on Elliot."

"Why would I be selling stories on Elliot?"

"I don't know why," Edie said. "But I think you look at Fraser's phone behind Fraser's back, so I bet you have the material."

She nodded toward Fraser's phone, case side up, lying on the table.

"What? Do you?" Fraser said to Iggy.

"No, I don't! Why would you make something like that up?" Iggy said indignantly. "Bit bloody rude."

If she was wrong, not only had Edie slandered Iggy, but she might well be doing serious, lasting damage to her popularity in Owen world. It was a testament to the strength of her bond with Elliot that she'd risk it, based on so little. And it was little; it was virtually nothing.

Edie swallowed. No turning back now.

"Why d'you think he does?" Fraser said to Edie.

"When you and Elliot were talking, and Molly was in the loo, I looked at my phone when I was stood at the bar. It said you were Online on WhatsApp, even though you weren't with your phone—you left it here. I sent a message to you and as it landed, Iggy looked up, right at me. I think you were checking his messages—" She addressed Iggy. "You must've seen it arrive. My guess is you leave those ones in preview, and then Fraser opens them and thinks he's seeing it first? Obviously, any messages he's already seen, you can scroll."

Edie, having unburdened herself, stood feeling foolish. She was no expert on iPhones and hoped to hell there wasn't a simple explanation for the anomaly, that she hadn't taken a shit situation and made it even worse, while making an absolute imbecile of herself and traducing Iggy.

Edie waited for someone to quietly correct her understanding of the vagaries of messaging formats owned by tech conglomerates.

"All right, Jessica Fletcher! I have no idea what you're on about," Iggy said. "Jesus Christ, how weird . . ." Iggy's nose was wrinkled in disdain, but his cotton-cloth-white skin, curiously, had turned Heinz tomato.

"Is this true?" Fraser said to Iggy.

"No, of course not! Don't listen to Princess Nut Nuts there," Iggy said.

"Oi, watch your mouth," Elliot said. "Don't insult my girl-friend."

"You know my passcode," Fraser said, thoughts ticking on, clearly willing to at least entertain this possibility.

Edie's body flooded with a fresh wave of adrenaline. Could she really be right?

"You've had it since we saw the Chemical Brothers last year?" Fraser said.

"Seriously, you gave *him* full access to your phone?" Elliot said to Fraser.

"Only to book an Uber!"

"Did you change your passcode afterward?" Elliot said.

"No, but he was only using it once to book an Uber!"

Elliot pinched the bridge of his nose.

Eyes moved to a hunted Iggy, whose demeanor suggested he might just have done more than book an Uber.

"When was this gig?" Elliot asked Fraser.

"Uh . . . December? Yeah, definitely—mid-December."

"Right before the leaks started, around Christmas," Elliot said, looking back at Iggy.

"Whatever, my dude," Iggy said, raising his palms. "I have literally no idea what this is about. I've only looked at my own phone."

He put his handset, in shockproof case, on the table.

"If we looked at your WhatsApps, we'd not find any journalists in them? No tips for them about me? *My dude,*" Elliot said.

"No," said Iggy, though he was still scarlet. "I'm not showing you my WhatsApps. None of you would want everyone browsing yours, either."

"Let's try this another way: Fraz, have all these stories been things you've referred to in your messages? Like Cameron's song?" Elliot said.

"Ehm . . . I'm not sure? There's been a few. As you made *abundantly clear,*" Fraser said, row still fresh and stinging.

"Cameron's song? Do you mean 'Last Time'?" Molly said, in a small voice.

"Yes," Elliot said. "The one about . . ." He looked over at Edie. The most recent invasion still hurt, too. ". . . us."

"You did discuss that with me on WhatsApp?" Molly said to Fraser. "I sent you a link because I wasn't sure which song it was?"

"Oh, OK. There we go," Fraser said, looking back at Iggy.

"How about if we check your photos from their engagement party?" Elliot said to Iggy. "Any shots of me and Edie on that we might recognize?"

"If it was him, he'd have deleted them?" Fraser said. "He's not stupid."

Elliot smiled broadly. "Yes, absolutely. Only a reckless dickhead, a dickhead who hadn't taken them in the first place, of course, would forget to delete the evidence. With that firmly in mind, Iggy, can we have a quick look at your camera roll from that night? Put our minds at rest, clear your name."

"No, you can't! It's my private data! I'm not letting the Bottom Inspectors here browse my Tinder photos. I've got spice for the ladies on it. And in return."

"You don't put sensitive stuff in your Hidden album?" Elliot said. "You risk your mum getting an eyeful of pubes when she's looking at your new kitchen?"

Iggy shrugged. "I mean, sometimes, not always. I'm not sure enough to let you into it."

"Hmm. All right, how about I check your contacts against the bylines on the stories about me?"

"Again, who's going to be stupid enough to put journalists in under their own names?" Fraser said.

"Who indeed?" Elliot said, extending his hand. "Quick look, please? Surely you're not going to say your phone book is violently private?"

Iggy's eyes moved from side to side, hand resting protectively over his mobile.

Edie hadn't fully trusted her own intuition until now. Iggy's furtive manner said maybe she should have.

"Is that a no, you won't show us?" Elliot said.

"I don't get it, if there's nothing on your phone then let Elliot check . . . ?" Fraser started.

"He'll get into it for one thing and start looking at all sorts!" Iggy said.

"I won't let him," Fraser said. "Only your phone book. I'm on your side, Ig. There's no way you talk to journa—"

"I'M SORRY!" Iggy wailed, shocking them all into stillness. "I'm so fucked—they're going to take the flat! I hate myself! I'm sorry, Elliot."

He put his head down on the table.

It was like a police drama when the suspect finally breaks under interrogation and admits they were the killer, detectives holding their breath while the tape spools forward to record the confession.

47

"Hey, guys, I don't want to interrupt, but are y'all good for drinks?" said a waitress, blissfully unaware of what she'd stumbled into, twirling a round tray like a cheerleader with a baton.

"Can we have another bottle of this?" Elliot raised the red wine. "And five fresh glasses, please?"

Fraser and Edie both looked at him with total surprise.

They sat in a taut, loaded silence as the waitress returned and poured the wine out for each of them.

Fraser sniffed his glass, after she'd left. "Big 'Last Supper' bouquet. But we already know who's betraying us."

Iggy looked genuinely haunted, and as if he might burst into tears. His wine sat untouched.

"Should I go?"

"*No,*" Elliot said. "Definitely not. You can stay and explain yourself. Do you have even a small percentage grasp of how it's felt to be on the receiving end of this? I know empathy and . . . *ethics in general* aren't your strong suits, but this is lurid even for you?"

"I'm garbage!" Iggy said. "A garbage person. I was so scared, I needed money fast . . ."

"At what price—selling Elliot out? Someone I shared a school playground with," Elliot said. "I thought this must be the work of some implacable enemy I'd unwittingly created. Someone who hated me with a burning ferocity."

"I don't hate you! I'm not your enemy!" Iggy cried.

"I know! You're a dickhead without a difference!" Elliot snapped back, at the same pitch.

Iggy wiped tears from his face. Elliot heavily sighed. Fraser looked at Iggy in disbelief.

"Fuck, I might've known it'd be the sodding Hamburglar," Elliot said, sipping his wine. "He even looks like the Hamburglar." Elliot looked at Fraser. "He's been behind every stupid plan you've had since you were six years old."

"I'm really sorry." Iggy sniffled, as Fraser reiterated his total stupefaction. "Are you sure I shouldn't go?"

"Do more groveling," Fraser said. "I trusted you, you twat! What made you think you could do this?"

"I got back into the online gambling," Iggy said. "I'm about 150K in the hole, Fraz. I'm so fucked. I've got this evil debt collection agency after me, and I needed money really fast."

"Not Leprechaun's Luck again?" Fraser said. "It's not even a good game."

"And the rest. When I got dumped by Nadia, I started staying up until two or three every morning on payday weekend, and it went from there."

"Ah, fuck. You should've told me."

"I was going to stop, and it got out of hand . . . When you lent me your phone that night, you got a message from Elliot about how he hated that superhero film." He looked shamefacedly at Elliot. "The one where you can disappear."

"I think I know the one," Elliot said, with a rueful look at Edie, and she smiled back, feeling a rush of relief.

"I had this *bingo* that I could pinch the odd bit of gossip and flog it, and no one would care or notice. I didn't think the people I contacted would like what I gave them so much, push me to get more. Like the gambling, it got totally out of hand," Iggy said.

When Elliot and Edie had mused that the leaker's prolific work rate indicated they were either inept or spiteful, they'd missed the third option: desperate.

"I'd have lent you money to help you out," Fraser said. "Why not ask me? We'll get the paperwork out once we're home—we'll make sure you don't lose the flat. Then we'll get you counseling. There's rehab you can go to for addiction."

"Thank you," Iggy said. "I felt like such an idiot, such a worthless turd." A tear slid down his cheek. "You guys are so *good* at life, you know? You always have been. Look at you. The numbers on the letters got worse, and they got more threatening. I was like a rat in a trap, gnawing his own leg off to escape."

Elliot cleared his throat. "Pretty sure that was my leg you were gnawing."

"Yeah. Sorry."

"I can see you've got yourself into a mess, and I do have some compassion for that, having got into one or two myself," Elliot said. "Aside from what we officially call reputational damage and I'll call having my underpants drawer humiliatingly turned out for the public to poke through . . ."

Iggy hung his head.

". . . As you can see, me and Fraz were on the brink of falling out over this, in a serious way. If he and I had stopped talking to each other, right before he got married, what would you have done then? That's the part I find harder to forgive than tattle in the press."

"Yeah. You had us all at each other's throats," Fraser said.

Iggy looked at the tablecloth. "I didn't think you'd suspect Fraz, 'cos you're so close. I thought maybe Elliot told, like, a dozen people this stuff. I thought I'd have paid off my debt before you worked it out."

Edie felt a sort of incredulous pity toward Iggy.

"With anyone else, I'd call bullshit," Elliot said, "but given I've never known you to foresee an obvious consequence in your life, it might be true. Can you apologize to Edie and Molly, please?

Edie for calling her 'Princess Nut Nuts,' and both Edie and Molly
for putting them under suspicion, as our confidantes?"

Molly had yet to process any of this, and Edie thought this
was a deft way of Elliot accounting for Fraser's indignance and
devaluing it to her, at the same time. If the same question mark
had hovered over Edie, it couldn't be as offensive. And thanks to
Lillian, it had.

Neither Elliot nor Fraser were anything like as furious with
Iggy as they might've been, it seemed. As far as Edie could tell, it
was a product of their kind natures, the length of the association,
and because, on a practical level, Iggy as the culprit was, in the
end, a least-worst and manageable outcome.

It exonerated Molly and short-circuited the brothers falling
out. Fraser could hardly continue with his golden flounce now
that Elliot was being so forgiving about Fraser's passcode cock-up
and Fraser's best friend's subterfuge. And Iggy had been frightening as an omnipotent, unknown quantity, a shadowy agent of
chaos—but he was merely a daft boy. They'd had a nightmare
and now the big light had been turned on.

"I'm very sorry, ladies," Iggy said. He looked at Edie. "I
thought if I admitted it, none of you would ever speak to me
again. My mates are all I have left."

Elliot made a skeptical face. "You've got your job, your home,
your family . . ."

"Yeah, but they're not as good as my mates," Iggy said, and
against all odds, Edie could see Elliot stifling laughter.

"Wait," Molly said, large blue eyes like saucers in horror,
"Fraser's got nudes of me on that phone!"

"I didn't see any?!" Iggy said, palms up. "On my mother's life,
I promise I didn't. I will swear on the Bible. You know I'm telling
the truth because if I knew they were there, I'd definitely have
looked at them."

"Impeccable logic matched only by impeccable morals," Elliot said. "Thank God someone knows how to use the Hidden album . . . Speaking of which, at the risk of you saying I'm insulting your intelligence, Fraz . . ."

"As if you would ever do that," Fraser said.

". . . can you change your passcode, please? Now? Tonight? As a matter of urgency? Before a leprechaun tries their luck again?"

"A big fat amen to that," Molly said to Elliot, and Edie was pleased to witness a moment of bonding between them.

ELLIOT GRASPED FOR Edie's hand once they were alone and two nightcaps had been requested with the bill.

"Oh, Edie. What a fucking evening. Thank you—you're a genius. In case you don't know, you saved Fraser's wedding, if not the fraternal relationship for some years to come."

"I did?!"

"I'd been stood down as best man."

Edie's face fell. "Shit! It really went that badly?"

"Oh yeah. I was in a state, as you know. I said if it wasn't him who'd briefed the Cam story, it was someone he was talking to. He puffed his chest out and said: 'Well, I only told Molly about that.' Dared me to accuse her. You can imagine the amount of furious brinkmanship that then went on. Fraser went into defensive mode that it couldn't be Mol and that I've never approved of her, etc. It got worse and worse. I can't really blame him. As I said, he'd have got even shorter shrift from me if he was accusing you. He was no more protective than he should be."

"You've been incredibly understanding. I'm glad you didn't lose it with Iggy, but he'd have deserved it."

"I was too relieved to have an answer, to be honest. I didn't know what else to do other than show mercy. They've been friends since they were in junior school—he's like the third brother. Fraz had told me Iggy's got addiction problems. I should've thought of him earlier, given he absolutely fit the profile of someone capable of it, but I was so stuck on this idea that because the crime was new, it couldn't be an old friend."

"Plus, you didn't know he could read Fraser's messages."

"Right? Who thinks affording Iggy snooping rights temptation is going to go well?! Those two, honestly. The lovable fuckwit and the maladaptive live wire. The buddy cop comedy we didn't want."

Outside, when they didn't immediately succeed in hailing a cab, Elliot slid his arms round Edie and kissed her neck.

"You're not going to pass out tonight again, are you?" he said. "I want to show you the view from my apartment."

"The *view* outside your apartment . . ." Edie repeated.

"Maybe the view inside it, too."

He went for a pretty full-on kiss given they were in public. Edie had never seen him this drunk before, and she liked it.

"I think there's photographers across the street," Edie hissed.

"Can I say, with some vehemence, I don't care?"

48

"Back to life, back to reality, as great philosophers once said," Declan said, setting down a large Americano on Edie's desk by way of greeting on Monday. "How is it being sentenced to a cell with me, after swagging round the world's greatest city with a top-level actor hunk?"

The enlivening workspace was bathed in spring sunshine, and Edie was actually quite elated by the return to comforting familiarity—if a little hollowed out by fatigue and short on funds for the rest of the month.

"Horrifying, if I may be frank. I know now how defendants feel when the court copy says they 'remained impassive as the guilty sentences were read.'" Edie pulled a morose face and toasted him with her drink. "Cheers, however."

"Shouts of 'premium economy wanker!' from the gallery as the judge called for order." Declan laughed. He had a sharp memory.

He fished a paper packet out of his coat packet. "Well, ta. Regret getting you a Pret pastel de nata now."

"You hero!" Edie accepted it. "Not only did you go to a second venue—you remembered I like these? Thank you!"

"Thought you'd need reasons to be cheerful. Nice time?" he said, putting on Talk Talk's "Spirit of Eden." He'd made them playlists appropriate for every day of the week: Monday's was an easing in.

"I'd call it tumultuous," Edie said, a variety of vivid imagery flashing through her mind. Turned out the shower *was* roomy.

Declan gave her a questioning look, and she remembered he thought she and Elliot fought.

"But rewarding," she added quickly.

It was a little saddening, but the illustrative tale of Iggy the mole wasn't fit for Declan consumption. Even though she trusted him implicitly regarding not conveying it back to Ad Hoc, Edie had just had a protracted lesson in the value of discretion.

"Seeing each other again soon?"

"Elliot's passing through for one night on the way down to London this weekend—as luck would have it, on Nick's birthday evening. I get to introduce you."

"Oh, sound! God, I best warn my friend Kieran not to ask for autographs and selfies. He was well into *Blood & Gold*."

"Elliot's very easygoing about that, so don't worry if he does once he's had a few. Don't ask if there was anything under the wolf pelt, though—he gets that all the time. It was a kind of warrior's nappy, I believe. Sight of which might lose him a few girl fans."

Declan guffawed.

They worked in a companionable hush until Edie saw Declan checking his phone and darting uncertain looks at her. He seemed like he was working up the courage to raise something.

"Er . . . Did you know someone at Ad Hoc called Louis? A friend of yours?" he said eventually.

"Yes?" Edie said. "Not a friend anymore. Of course."

"He's posted on Instagram about the Jack Marshall interview."

"Oh God." Edie sagged. "When will these bastards stop getting me down? Who's funding Louis? Arms manufacturers? Lockheed Martin?"

"It's actually really . . . good?" Declan said. "He properly goes for Jack. I wasn't going to tell you before I read it myself. My sister Cara sent it to me with 'game changer,' and she doesn't appear alone in that view."

Edie hid the fact she was disconcerted that Declan's sister in Ireland closely followed this soggy soap opera.

"*Louis?* Goes for *Jack*?" Edie repeated, disbelieving. She remembered Louis's former role as shape-shifting courtier in the palace of Jack and Charlotte. "It's probably some innovative long-game fuckery."

"I wouldn't mention it if it was more of the same—see what you think. Want the link?"

Edie nodded. It was pointless to imagine she had the willpower not to look.

She opened Louis's profile, an account she'd long ago unfollowed, and saw stark black text on a pink background, set across six installments on his Story.

Hello, everyone. Not like me to do PSAs, but I'm going to address @jackmarshall00's newspaper exclusive about how Edie Thompson tore down his life.
First up: almost everything he said was a lie. You want to know who did that, Jack—get a mirror, love.

Edie didn't chase Jack. He chased her, in the kind of covert op you can run on smartphones. His having a girlfriend was a perfect cover. We've all met DM Slide Guy, right? He was a DM Slide Guy posing as a Wife Guy. Edie was the resident pretty, forever-singleton, nice to everyone. She was fit and smart but shy about her love life, and we all kinda wondered behind her back why she didn't have a boyfriend. Jack's ears pricked up, obviously. A prick's prick pricked up.

On the wedding day, she went into the garden, and he followed her. I know because I was watching. Edie was so quiet that day that I finally started to work out there was something between her and Jack. I was ALIVE for the gossip, NGL. My guess is Jack knew she couldn't ask anything of him once he was a husband, so that's when he went for his little reward for all the minor-key mindfucking.

Edie shouldn't have gone along with it, but have we not all been idiots for someone who's crawled under our skin? For longer than a minute usually, too, in my case 😄

Afterward, Charlotte was sent so deranged by the idea her shiny new husband could do such a thing that it was easier to say Edie had led him astray than attack him as common enemy. There was a LOT of ugly online dogpiling, and the mood was that we should destroy her. I remember Lucie, Jack's sidekick in that article, saying we wouldn't have succeeded if Edie didn't leave the country.

I went along with it, because there was one of Edie and many of them, and I thought Edie was leaving Ad Hoc anyway. Plus, I've been on a bit of a journey in my personal development since then, but that's for another time.

We all got the sack because Richard—the boss—figured out who was bullying and who was the victim, nothing more than that. Oh, and he sussed Jack was a massively untrustworthy twat. 5/5.

Now Edie has broken her dry spell with men in SPECTACULAR fashion. (Edie, if you ever read this, respect due—I would ride him like a stolen quad bike.)

It couldn't be more obvious they failed to break her or turn her into a pariah. So off they go again, pointing the finger in the wrong direction. The one person other than me who could confirm it was all driven by Jack, not Edie, is Charlotte, and obvs she's not inclined to do Edie any favors. I'd point out she dumped his Winklevoss-twin-looking arse, though, so make of that what you will.

Gotta ask—much did you get PAID to blame the worst thing you did on a woman instead, @jackmarshall00? The same day YOU broke your wife's heart and blew up your wedding? It's called DARVO: deny, attack, and reverse victim and offender. I have the number for my therapist, babe. I really suggest you consider it.

Finally, don't come at me with any accusations of running Edie's PR. If you've been paying attention, you'll work out why we aren't friends anymore. She told me I was fake, shallow, and duplicitous, and guess what, loves, I realized she was right.

Plus, I'm gay, so you can stop with any "clungestruck" insinuations 😂 *(FYI @luciemaggy is it 1955? You need to reconsider the devil-whore misogyny. And that's me saying that—A MAN.)*

Edie doesn't know I'm posting this, and I don't even know if she'd want me to, given we parted on bad terms. I'm not Team Edie. I'm a fan of the truth. Which might be the same thing here?

HAVE A BLESSED DAY

xxx

Edie concluded reading with a huge whoosh of emotion and thought: *well, well, fucking well.*

"That's . . . quite something," Edie said, tears springing to her eyes. "I never thought anyone would see it clearly. And Louis! Of all people."

"Innit? I hope you don't mind, but I rejoined the work Whats-App to send them this. The entire conversation has switched to how Jack's a fetid male archetype abuser. Jess is reading every message and saying nothing."

"Thank you. Sod it—I'm sharing it, too."

"Do it!"

She stubbed a metaphorical cigarette out on Jack's corpse, screenshotting every frame of Louis's post. She set her Instagram public again, shared it to on her stories, fired her metaphorical gun.

It might Streisand effect it—good: this vindication was too meaningful to pass up. Let the gossips repeat this as much as they wanted. She tagged it:

This is the first and last time I'll discuss this. A lot of lies have been told, and it can be a struggle to be believed. Thank you for your accuracy, and your honesty, @princesslouis. x

People could disappoint you, and they could surprise you, too. The papers ran with it within twenty-four hours:

Elliot Owen's GF Hits Back at "Homewrecker" Allegations on her Social Media

Interview requests from women's magazines and news sites crowded her inbox, different in tenor from previous approaches: now, she was sympathetic. She deleted them all, thinking *last time I'll discuss this* covered her position.

Edie came home the next day to a huge bunch of flowers from Elliot on her doorstep, but best of all, somehow, was a message from the fearsome Lillian:

The current washed up his skinny ass even faster than I thought it would.

49

"Hi, I'm staying for one night. Double room."

To date Elliot Owen was to have a luggage case handle near-permanently welded to one hand.

"What name, please?"

This time, she'd asked Elliot to clarify that. Edie felt ridiculous repeating it, more so in her city than a foreign metropolis. This was the land of the Brian Clough legend, green buses, and a university boating lake, not pseudonymous hotel check-ins. She felt like she was part of a sunglasses-indoors, tranquilizers-and-champagne-era Fleetwood Mac.

"Uhm, it's under Roger Thornhill."

They still wanted to see Edie's ID, so she was glad she'd not called herself Ada Minge.

("Why the phony name? No one our age is called Roger—they'll think I'm on the blow job payroll of a sugar daddy!" Edie had said, additionally irked that the aliases were an old wheeze of Elliot and Heather's.

"Why do you think?" Elliot had said. "Cuts down attention, and cutting down attention cuts down hassle."

"Would anyone honestly notice?" Edie said, a little waspishly, and Elliot replied: "That's what we're not bothering to find out, Mrs. Danvers.")

"Ah, you're in the suite," said the man on reception, jabbing at a keyboard. *Of course.*

Elliot's parents had yet to vacate their house, and Edie was glad. When that day came, she'd have to take in the fact that

Elliot had bought a house for her. Yes, you could rationalize it as an investment, a favor to his parents, a base for him.

The fact remained it was, truthfully, for her.

The plan was drinks then dinner, but Elliot was running late, so Edie ended up meeting the group on her own. She felt more antsy than usual, she supposed because there were people present who didn't know Elliot. She'd learned you could never anticipate exactly how people would react to a famous face.

Edie
We'll be at this restaurant from half 7! Will you be all right making your way straight there, if I go on ahead? xx

Elliot
I have Maps on my phone, I used to live here, and I'm a grown human man, so I think so, yes 😊 *xx*

"Happy birthday Nick!" Edie said.

Hannah, looking especially beautiful and like a young Sissy Spacek in a high-necked blouse, ceremoniously produced Nick's gift, jointly acquired between herself, Edie, and Chloe. It was a limited-edition test pressing of Bob Dylan's *Blood on the Tracks* and had cost a hefty sum on eBay. Edie insisted only Hannah was responsible enough to take care of it. Edie could imagine Meg using it as a plate coaster. She'd not been able to attend tonight due to her shift pattern, but Edie had been touched this had been communicated directly with Nick by Meg, with promise of a drink another time. She and her sister shared friends now. They'd come a long way, baby.

"You've made this vinyl collector Peter Pan very happy," Nick said, wiping away a tear.

Edie tried not to hawk-watch the door and was gurgling like a fool at a Declan witticism when Elliot was suddenly in front of her, shrugging off a navy jacket with a crimson lining that she'd not seen before: a man of many coats.

"Elliot . . . !" Edie said. "Declan, Kieran, this is my boyfriend, Elliot." She was pointedly defining him by their relationship, not his career.

There was some brisk hand shaking, and Elliot waved hello at Nick, Hannah, and Chloe.

Elliot said: "Ah, I recognize you from your pap pics," to Declan, and Edie thought it was funny, but Declan only looked bemused and unexpectedly starstruck. Kieran had been no doubt told not to stare; he still did.

Elliot didn't notice, in a very-well-practiced-at-not-noticing kind of way, accepting a bottle of Modelo. Being famous meant you didn't get to do standard hellos and introductions; you changed air pressure instead.

They fell naturally into three groups, conversationally: the Nick trio, Declan and Kieran catching up with each other, leaving Edie and Elliot to confidentially couple chat.

"Next time I see you is the wedding, then," Elliot said. "I'll send a car to take you there on the morning. My parents are going down the night before for lots of rigmarole with the Molly clan."

Edie, deciding not to argue the convenience and wisdom of the car, said thank you.

"I'm flying overnight to make it in time. I'm going to take an Ambien and wash it down with a G&T to get some rest. I'll look like Beetlejuice," Elliot said.

"They don't give you time off for close family members' weddings?"

"They have done—they've bumped a few days filming, but may I remind you that this involved very little notice. I'm popular with my workmates for it at least—Ines is thinking of doing a UK trip."

"Hopefully not to Suffolk," Edie said.

"Hah. The last thing any of us wants to do is spend time with each other on our days off, I assure you."

Edie was emboldened sufficiently to add: "Note that I've not asked when you're filming *that scene* because I am such a Cool Girl."

"Oh, it's done."

"*What?*" Edie whispered, alcohol curdling in her gut. "Really? I thought you were shooting chronologically?"

"We are, but Ines asked to get it out of the way. I don't blame her."

"Why didn't you tell me?"

"You said you didn't want to know!"

He had her bang to rights there. And meanwhile, he'd right banged Ines. She should drop it at once, in company, and of course, she couldn't.

". . . What was it like?"

"It wasn't too bad," Elliot said, and Edie flinched because her nerves needed something like *ugh, it's given me PTSD*. "It was a strange way to spend an afternoon, but we got it in a respectable number of takes. You're trying to simulate the throes of passion while remembering where you were told to put your hand. It's like following complicated dance steps while trying to story-tell a tango. It's absolutely nothing like the, er, real thing, I promise."

"Right," Edie said flatly.

"Sorry to interrupt," Declan said. "Edie, I was telling Kieran about your incredible story about the pissed-up wine merchant from a few years back?"

"Ah . . . Olly?"

"That's the one!"

Declan encouraged Edie into reciting funny tales of Ad Hoc past. The seating arrangements dictated the limits of the socializing: Declan and Kieran were breakwaters between the rest of the company.

Elliot was quieter than usual, Kieran knew no one, and Edie tried to compensate by leaning on her ease with Declan. Edie felt the beer, then mezcal, acting as bonding agent.

"Have you seen Meg's got a new weapon in her culinary armory?" Declan said, at one point, showing Edie a photo of a utensil. "Corncob peeler. Apparently vegan creamed corn is the next frontier."

"He's got Meg's number?" Elliot said, under his breath, perplexed.

"Oh, there's a backstory involving a potato masher," Edie said.

Conversation moved to Declan's single status. He'd not dated anyone since Aisling, and once Kieran was merry, that became a reason to berate his best friend.

"Why not try the apps?" Kieran said. "You've got loads going for you. Hasn't he, Edie?"

"Sure," Edie said. "Height. Girls love height."

"Do they?" Declan said.

"Oh yeah, isn't that a whole thing? Setting minimum height preferences?"

Kieran put a hand up to cup his mouth, the gesture for *imparting a secret*. "Also, length. Dec is rumored to be hung like a horse." He put his hands down. "Hahaha—wait, you can actually tell us if that's true, Edie? You've unfortunately had eyes on the prize, I hear?"

Oh no no . . . NO. He'd told Kieran about his sleepwalking?

Edie had said it would alchemize into a pub yarn—little could she have known it would in fact become radioactive matter.

50

She and Declan exchanged a look of mute alarm, witnessed by Elliot.

"Oh boy, that's enough from you. Help me get the next round in," Declan said, propelling Kieran up and off to the bar. Unfortunately, the swift intervention only increased the impression that she and Declan had done something wrong.

"Why would you know that?" Elliot said to Edie.

She steeled herself. "When Declan cycled into work on the first morning, he got hit by a car. He was concussed, so he had to stay over at my house as he couldn't be left alone for twenty-four hours afterward. The nurse asked me to look after him."

"OK," Elliot said. "Why would you know anything about the size of his wang? Did you give him a bath?"

Edie cringed. Some part of her had intended this to be amusing, if ever retold, and it was very much not that. "He went sleepwalking."

"Without his clothes?"

"Yup." Edie gritted her teeth, but Elliot wasn't reacting. "Poor sod."

"Where to?"

"Er, the kitchen. Was confronted by Meg with a bread knife."

"Also by you?" Elliot said, and Edie had an unease in her stomach she pretended wasn't there.

"Yes. Meg screamed, and I came running. I worked out Declan was catatonic and woke him up."

"How did you do that?"

"He was about to piss in the bin, and I yelled."

"Right," Elliot said, swigging from his beer bottle. "And is he?"

"What?"

"Hung like a horse?"

Elliot wasn't sparing her. What was she meant to say? *Comparison is the thief of joy?* Edie knew there was no version of this going well.

"I guess so—it wasn't the pressing issue at the time."

Elliot shot her a look that said "I guess so" was three words of agreement too many.

There wouldn't have been a good way for Elliot to learn about this, but Edie reckoned this might be one of the worst. Declan and Kieran returned with more drinks, but things never recovered, and they soon called it a night.

On arriving back at the hotel, Edie's phone buzzed with a WhatsApp from Declan. Elliot saw her see it arrive. She palmed her phone swiftly back into her bag. Declan no doubt meant well, but pissed alerts when he knew she was with her boyfriend were hardly likely to help.

"You can read it," Elliot said.

"It'll keep," Edie said.

"If you don't want to open it in front of me, I'm not going to feel great about that," Elliot said.

"I've not got anything to hide!" Edie said.

"Then read it."

Edie pulled her phone out with her heart racing, and Elliot's point was being made. She felt sure it'd be nothing and at the same time, worried as hell.

Edie opened it.

Tommo, I'm so SO fucking sorry, and I have absolutely blasted Kieran for that tactless remark, totally inappropriate. He was drunk (obviously). I will always be grateful for the way you rescued me from jumping off a cliff over that escapade. I really hope it didn't cause you any trouble. Elliot seems a lovely bloke. Night. X

"Tommo?" Elliot said, taking his jacket off and throwing it over the back of a chair.

"Thompson."

"Yes, thanks, I got that far—I didn't know you were at the stage of special nicknames. Or him messaging with your sister. How did you rescue him?" Elliot said. He was maintaining his threatening calm.

"I talked about how I knew what crippling shame felt like after the wedding incident. That it passes, and it doesn't stay that acute forever."

"He didn't do anything wrong on purpose, did he?"

"No! He was a victim of a couple of misadventures. I feel really sorry for him. Do any of us want to be naked in front of someone we just started working with? Apart from, y'know, Ines Herrera."

A cheap shot that tumbled from Edie's mouth before she'd scene-checked it, a clumsy and obvious attempt to level up.

She threw her coat over Elliot's, as the temperature became even more frigid.

"That scene was intimacy coordinated and its precise detail haggled by our representatives to every last gesture—there was no room for it turning into anything spontaneous," Elliot said. "Also, I don't know that Ines wanted to do it, exactly. She was prepared to do it, which isn't the same thing. It's much worse for actresses with all that stuff."

"All right, I was only joking. I've not been impressed by her *boundaries* in the past."

She had twinged at him white knighting his exquisite coworker, though she knew it was only his innate decency speaking. Edie had got what she'd deserved, using it against him like that.

"I don't get why she's being dragged in at all," Elliot said, again with a hint of protectiveness that sent Edie secretly spiraling.

". . . Nothing spontaneous was going to happen with Declan, either. Except maybe Meg removing his ability to have kids."

"His genitals have probably taken up enough of our evening now," Elliot said. "I'm going to have a shower. Oh, your dress is on the bed."

Edie didn't know what he meant. She found a black-gold designer bag and recalled the conversation in New York. She unpicked the tissue paper and shook it out. It was perfect—the timing of receiving it, distinctly off.

She couldn't fathom or combat Elliot's tactic of determined equanimity when he was obviously annoyed. She got into pajamas, then bed, and waited it out, sat hugging her knees and listening to the water running in the en suite.

He returned, unsmiling and in jogging bottoms, rubbing wet hair with a towel. It was a sure sign of passive-aggressive fighting when you avoided getting undressed around each other.

"The dress is beautiful, thank you," she said.

"Welcome. Glad you like it."

"Look, Elliot . . ." Edie said, in a diplomatic tone.

He cut her off: "It's six a.m. my body clock time on a day that's lasted thirty hours. Would it be all right if we saved conversation for the morning? I'm fit for nothing."

Edie said: "Sure," and it turned out that he really meant nothing, rolling away from her so she couldn't see if he was awake, chest rising and falling steadily.

The exhaustion was one-third true, two-thirds convenient alibi—of that she was sure.

Edie lay in the dark, trying to work out why it felt like Elliot was disappointed in her, somehow.

51

Edie woke before Elliot in the morning and decided on a long shower herself to scour away the night before. Also, if there was going to be more sullen bickering, she'd rather do it looking presentable.

When she emerged from the noise and the steam, Elliot was sat up in bed, scrolling on his phone.

He put it to one side. "Come back to bed."

Edie lay down next to him, pushing wet hair out of her face.

"I meant without the towel."

"Oh, did you?" she said, insouciant, with concealed relief.

Elliot gently tugged at the fabric's edge above her knees, failing to make any progress. "My God, you're not so much mummy wrapped in this—it's like a sarcophagus," Elliot said, making her squeal as he wrestled with the bath sheet.

Edie was grateful at humor returning, and other things, too. They were fixing the distance that had developed in a way that therapists probably didn't recommend but appeared to have worked.

"Are we not going to talk about last night?" Edie said, lying in his arms afterward.

The incendiary device was safe for defusal and disposal now, and it was safest not to leave it there.

"What about it?"

"About you going Jeremy Paxman when questioning me about Declan crashing at mine."

"I didn't?" Elliot said. "I asked questions that I think any boyfriend would ask. You explained. Subject ended."

"When we talked about Ines climbing you like a monkey on a car at a safari park, you said neither of us needed to know about anything completely insignificant that might be unsettling."

"Yes?"

"Then why do I feel like Declan staying at mine and me not mentioning it was a fail?"

"I haven't complained about it?"

"No, but you've been very . . . quiet. Like a hit man when he unpacks the gun from the bag and screws the pieces together."

Elliot shifted away from her a little and picked at embroidery on the duvet. "I think I feel something akin to what you did about the Ines story. I didn't like finding out about it through his mate, like that. I didn't like the way it felt like a secret you and him were sharing. I caught all the *oh no, not in front of her fella* flapping, which didn't make it seem innocent. Obviously, I don't like that you have intimate knowledge of him. But you can acknowledge nothing out of order's gone on while still not feeling great about it." He paused. "I should probably admit I'm not a Cool Boy, capital C, capital B."

"Fair," Edie said. His eloquence meant she understood him perfectly, if slightly painfully. She added: "I'm more sorry if it's any obstacle to you and Declan being friends, because I think you'd really get on."

"I don't think that's very likely anyway, Edie."

"Why not?"

"He's in love with you," Elliot said, looking up at her.

A crystalline moment of dread-silence followed.

". . . Or something on the way to love. I don't pretend to be able to mind-read him to that extent, and thank God I can't, frankly," Elliot said. "I'd probably have to *Blood & Gold* disembowel him for the pornographic thoughts he's had about you."

"*Declan? Me?* No!" Edie said, stunned. "Absolutely not, no . . . I've literally overheard him telling people he doesn't fancy me!"

"In what context?"

"A colleague accusing him."

"Call it confirmation bias, but I'm going to say the colleague accusing him of it is more significant than him denying it, because of course he fucking did."

"This is insane . . ."

"Edie, I'd picked it up by the time the guacamole arrived. You haven't, in how long? Why is that." He phrased it not as a question, but as if there was a probable answer.

"You're not accusing Declan . . . me of . . . ?"

"I'm not suggesting either of you have done anything."

There was an intimidating edge to the way Elliot said this. *Either of you.* He was already grouping them together.

"How can you know this for sure about Declan? You knew this at the *start* of the evening?"

"I noticed it at the start and was absolutely sure by the end. I don't think he was trying that hard to hide it from me, which is another lovesickness symptom. Pushing your luck."

"How?!"

Edie scoured her memory and could only come up with excitable, innocent chatter, gregarious Declan being himself, and trying to rein Kieran in. No improper wooing.

"Where do you want me to start? His ardor was swirling around us like fog and practically making me cough."

Elliot's articulacy was extremely uncomfortable when deployed against you.

"I'm going to need specifics."

Edie's assertive tone belied her thumping heart rate. Apart from anything else, it was upsetting to suggest she'd unwittingly subjected Elliot to this display.

"The way he looks at you. Like there's no one else in the room, or possibly the world. The way he brings every conversation back round to you. The moment when the strap of your dress slipped down your shoulder, and he stared at your bare skin like it had a narcotic effect on him. Then he twitched to put the strap back, before remembering himself and meeting my eyes. The way he couldn't look at me directly at all for the first hour, and then once he'd had a few, was giving me these sidelong glances all the time."

"You're a famous person who people don't look at in a normal way," Edie said, in a tight voice that she was effortfully trying to normalize.

"I am, but as a result, I am well used to those looks and know the difference—not least because he wasn't interested in me. He was interested in what I could tell him about you."

"He was looking at you, but you could tell he was thinking about me? This does feel a bit clairvoyant."

Edie was walking a fine line: not wanting to mock Elliot when he was upset, while firmly dissuading him this idea had any merit. However, it was obvious he'd made up his mind.

"When you're madly into someone who isn't single, their partner becomes a ton of clues about the object of your desire. Then after the assessment, it's competitive, what you're up against. They're covertly figuring out your strengths and weaknesses, running sums, sussing where they have advantages. Whether they could take you in a fight. Metaphorically speaking."

"Declan's not at all aggro or macho. He's a goofy adopter of stray cats who's probably never exchanged blows in his life."

"I said metaphorically, but you rushing to defend him isn't really likely to improve things here, is it?" Elliot snapped, with a sudden flash of temper.

She understood now: he'd not broached it because he didn't trust himself.

52

"I think you might've added two plus two and got thirty-four, that's all," Edie said carefully.

"I wish I had."

Elliot's jaw clenched, and Edie had never seen this mood before. She knew right now that she wasn't able to reach him by any usual route.

"I haven't detected Declan has any special feelings, and I'm still not remotely convinced he does."

"You've never sensed an attraction?" Elliot said, with evident disbelief.

"No, we're mates. I'm the only person he knows here—he's probably clung on to me a bit. Plus, I don't go around thinking, *oh no, I hope this man working with me isn't into me.* I'm not a femme fatale. I wear a coat with Pret tomato soup stains on it."

"The fact you need to get your coat dry-cleaned doesn't change the fact you're very easy to fall in love with. I may know what I'm talking about."

Edie thought, more likely, Elliot Owen had picked her, and her stock value had shot up. Declan's introduction to Edie Thompson, as a concept before a person, involved two stories involving highly newsworthy amounts of male attention. It wasn't a fair test; he didn't meet her cold, in her thoroughly overlooked era. If there was too much *noticing* going on, it might ironically be more to do with Elliot than Edie.

"Could it be your natural protectiveness, making you—" she began, instead.

293

"Oh, *don't you dare*, Edie," Elliot said, with another flash of temper. "Don't use how much I care about you to pretend it makes me unable to tell the difference between a nuisance and a threat. You once accused me of gaslighting—well, that's gaslighting."

"He's not a threat! Can I remind you I have to be OK with you playact boning total goddesses?"

"That is shit beyond belief for you, but this is different."

"Why?"

"It's real."

Elliot kept dropping these certainties at Edie's feet like bombs.

"Except it isn't—you're speculating about Declan's feelings while mine don't exist."

Elliot said nothing. Edie wasn't sure why she felt so culpable: she'd done nothing wrong, unless "immediate rapport" was a crime.

Yet, as she thought it, she realized immediate rapport between straight members of the two sexes could be deemed something else entirely. Had she really made a huge category error, then custard-pied it into Elliot's face? It was never comfortable to do a high-speed recalculation of whether you were in fact in the wrong, mid-argument.

". . . The fact remains, if anyone was sizing you up, strengths and weaknesses, they'd give up instantly. That's got to be a comfort."

"Of course he has a huge advantage over me, Edie. Time with you. The boring days and the funny anecdotes and being there when you get a bad phone call. Proximity."

She'd had whispers of it from their earliest acquaintance, but Edie finally confronted just how lonely Elliot's life could be. He was, for all the stardust and riches, a glorified contractor for hire, of no fixed address. The earthbound gravity of *pint after work?* didn't exist for him and likely never would again. He was Doctor

Who, with British Airways business lounge as his TARDIS. For the first time, she could see he'd won huge and missed out.

"It's not going to make any difference to how I feel about you."

Elliot looked downcast. "The fact you've done this emotional super-injunction on yourself about him—it worries me."

Edie swallowed hard. Had she? "I don't know how to defend myself against this charge. I've seen nothing and done nothing, and that means I have, what, feelings I've hidden from myself? What do I do with that?"

Edie grasped this low-key wrangle might be quite serious and felt sick.

"I don't know what to do with it, either. I spent a whole evening with ringside seat for your spark with the man you'd have gone out with if I'd not come back. A role he's still auditioning for. My understudy, hoping I break my leg. I'm sure he's a nice enough person, but no one's really nice in this scenario. His attitude to me can be summed up as: *tick-tock, motherfucker*."

"How do you know I'd have gone out with Declan?!"

As Edie said this, a series of moments flashed through her mind. Jolts at physical closeness, eyes meeting in laughter, the ways he'd looked out for her. The way he'd held her. Here was a tall, winning Irishman with a physique that could grace a Calvin Klein ad, who was Tim to her Dawn in *The Office*. This representation of Declan was a shock to her; it wasn't, in fact, a reach.

"You're telling me Declan wouldn't have been the next person? The 'Last Time' person, if I'd left it another six months?" Elliot said. "You don't know yourself very well if you're denying that."

His words hung in the air as evident, unassailable truth. Elliot's incisiveness was considerable. Edie had never asked herself this, and now she did, and he was right.

"I've never thought about it for a moment," Edie said, glad that much was true. "I'm with you. I'm very much with you, which-ever country you happen to be in. What do the What Ifs matter? Or the Who Elses? Those people don't stop existing—they stop mattering."

Edie was quite relieved she had produced this, under duress.

"If you're adamant I have nothing to worry about with Dec-lan, then I accept that. I trust you. Also, I desperately want it to be true." Elliot smiled an unhappy smile.

"You have nothing to worry about. Whatever you need me to do for you to believe that, I'll do it."

As she said it, Edie realized that she'd resist any demand to stop working with Declan. That'd be a great email. *Hi Richard, I need to request a transfer for Declan: he allegedly looked too covetously at my clavicle area.*

"OK, then I do have a request," Elliot said. "The day soon when he comes to you and tells you he knows he's completely out of order as you have a boyfriend and blah blah, but that he has to tell you that he wakes up thinking about you, goes to sleep thinking about you, and he only exists now to make you laugh, that if there was the smallest chance you felt any of this, too, blah blah—I want you to tell me he's done it. He doesn't get to keep secrets with you. Promise?"

"Promise, but what the hell . . . ?!" Edie trying to joke Elliot out of it was obviously futile. "All we did is go for birthday tacos, and now I'm in some . . . scripted fiction love triangle?"

Elliot spoke of trusting her; it certainly didn't feel like the whole story.

"How do you know he'll do this?" Edie said, concealing that she was thoroughly rattled by the diatribe.

Elliot leaned back against the headboard. "It's what I'd do if I was him."

"I don't think you would. You'd not go after someone in a relationship?"

"As I said, nobody's nice in this scenario."

"What scenario?"

"The one where you can't bear to let someone go."

53

"Look at the two of us, being corporate swish," Declan said, in a long coat over a suit, as Edie met him on the train station concourse, her lace-up heeled boots clip-clopping on the concrete. "Like Harrison Ford and Melanie Griffith in *Working Girl*."

"Pepsi is our Trask merger?"

"Well remembered! I've had to see it loads thanks to Cara and Sinead. I must warn you, I have a 'bod for sin,' and the sin is a Sausage & Egg McMuffin." He brandished a paper bag. "Got a spare in case you want to partake."

Edie laughed heartily, while wishing he wouldn't refer to his body. Every time he did, she had to work out what facial expression best conveyed: *I have definitely forgotten what you look like naked.*

Before Elliot's outburst, Edie would've overlooked the fact Declan had referenced a film where two people fall in love at the office. She'd been pushed into greater awareness, no doubt as Elliot wanted. *This super-injunction, it worries me.*

Edie squelched such concerns; today was business. They were about to do their best two-hander act for the Pepsi meeting in London. They spent the journey down with their notes in front of them, mock-interrogating the other to find the weaknesses.

"What if I said you're devaluing a beverage with over one hundred and thirty years of history for cheap laughs from the extremely online peanut gallery?" Edie said, as they passed Kettering. ". . . Diarmuid."

298

"Why am I Diarmuid?"

"I'm wrong-footing you by forgetting your name and thus hazing you about how insignificant you are."

"Fuck's sake. I'm pitching to make funny clips on TikTok, not joining the Marines, *Edna*."

"Swearing and petulance. You've lost the account."

Declan grinned at her. He looked good in T.M.Lewin, slightly unexpectedly, given his usual look was more unironed free spirit.

"Whatever happens, this is fun," he said, indicating the pair of them. "It's been fun putting it together, too. Let's go after more big fish. What is there to be scared of in trying, even if we fail? The only thing to be scared of is boredom."

Edie nodded, while thinking that this might be precisely the sort of moment she'd previously missed. On the surface, all Declan was doing was being boosterish about their work. Underneath that, he was emphasizing their connection, their value to each other.

Couldn't that be him being nice, though? she interrogated herself. It was still a leap that it indicated a desire to peel her Fair Isle cashmere cardigan off. Elliot's being vigilant and articulate didn't make him infallible.

Once they arrived at Chancery Lane and nerves were jangling, Edie was nothing but grateful for their effortless mutual support. They agreed afterward, cautiously, that the presentation had gone well. They knew their case back to front, and when questioned, had a sixth sense about when to cede the floor to the other. Both of them liked a win; neither of them was cutthroat about it, and nor were they fans of pretending to be someone they weren't or laying it on thick.

Whether Pepsi liked their ideas or not, Edie decided, was the luck of whether the meeting room members were their way inclined. Like selecting a jury: whether you got people who were sympathetic to your worldview or not was entirely a matter of chance. At least they'd acquitted themselves respectably.

Afterward, they met Richard for a late lunch at the Midland Grand. He arrived looking typically and impossibly sharp in a three-piece brown wool suit and claret tie. He was in entirely in tune with the opulent Grade I listed dining room.

"Worth it for this alone," Edie whispered, looking up at the gilt plasterwork ceiling. "Like being in an Agatha Christie. I hope we *have* made it worth it."

"A bottle of champagne to start, please," Richard said, snapping the wine list closed and handing it back.

"I hope that doesn't jinx us," Declan said.

"Unlikely, given Pepsi have already called me. The digital contract is ours for the next eighteen months—conditional on the two of you being the ones who run it. Neither of you has plans to leg it to one of my rivals anytime soon, I hope?"

Both Edie and Declan whooped. Edie found herself grateful they were seated and couldn't hug, however. Had guilt infected her, or was this telling her something?

"Oh my God! Already!" Edie said, dumbfounded. She wasn't used to overachieving.

"We were lucky it was the right idea at the right time," Declan said.

"Luck is simply when opportunity meets readiness," Richard replied.

Once a waiter had ceremoniously filled flutes, they clinked, and Edie momentarily basked. She'd finally repaid Richard for his faith in her. He'd been life coach and friend at a time when Edie badly needed allies. She'd never forget it.

When Declan dipped out to take a call, Richard turned to her. "I hope you won't find it too paternalistic if I say I'm very pleased you're doing so well. In your professional and private life."

"Thank you," Edie said. "It does feel like I've found . . . equilibrium."

"Declan pushed this particular project forward, I know, but the ideas and spark come from you. All you lack sometimes is self-belief. No one else sees why you should doubt yourself."

"Hah. A *lot* of people see why, I'm afraid," Edie said. "Hence why I'm bloody grateful not to go into the HQ today . . ."

"Ah, Edie . . ." Richard said, shaking his head. "You were an object of scorn, and now you're an object of envy. Treat those two imposters just the same. Notice instead that when you persevere, good things happen."

"Is that it—the secret? Stop caring about what people think of you? Move forward regardless?"

"I'm not sure about *secret*—I'm not pretending to be any guru," Richard said, topping up the superb red wine that had made Edie's earlobes grow warm. "But how much was your life—I mean the one before the Harrogate contretemps—dictated by what people thought of you? And would you want to go back there? Your former status quo, not the Yorkshire spa town."

Edie did a double take. "Do you know, I'd never considered that. All this time I've spent yearning to go unnoticed again." She paused. "I suppose I spent a lot of time trying not to make mistakes or stand out or be talked about. To be liked was everything. I rated myself by the negatives that hadn't happened, not by the good things that . . . hadn't happened, either."

"There you go," Richard said.

"How did you become so wise?" Edie said.

"I made lots of mistakes, of course," Richard said, smiling broadly.

He looked from Declan to Edie as he left, saying: "Congratulating myself on my professional matchmaking here. Have a drink in the bar next door and charge it to expenses."

Edie, inhibitions loosened, leaped forward and kissed Richard on the cheek. "Thank you! For everything, not just my sirloin steak."

"Water on the train, perhaps," Richard said, but he looked rather touched.

They took Richard at his word and finished strong with a couple of whisky sours.

By the time she and Declan piled back on the train at St. Pancras, they were somewhat the worse for wear. Edie was glad of a grainy coffee in a cardboard cup to help straighten her out.

They spent a rewarding hour picking over the presentation, safe in knowledge of the result.

Declan toasted her with his builder's tea. "To many more days like this."

Edie said: "Here's to you for suggesting it."

"Here's to . . . you," Declan said. "If that sounds like less praise, it's the exact opposite."

"Thanks for being such a mensch over the Jack Marshall wedding bollocks," Edie said.

"No thanks required," Declan replied.

The journey flew by fast, thanks to prior alcohol and no shortage of topics.

"Ah, looks like the bog is finally free!" Declan whispered to Edie, leaping from his aisle seat as they passed East Midlands Parkway. She banished the mental image of having seen him almost going to the loo. Her brain was juvenile.

Declan's phone on the table next to her lit up with a message. It was a WhatsApp group, "Dunne Roaming Charges," indicating family.

Cara
Gutted EO is boring brat. Must be with him for shagging & clout & view. Don't blame . . .

Edie was startled at recognizing the subject. EO. She tried to barter with herself that it wasn't him, it was a coincidence, yet the rest of the content made that a ludicrous hope. Her mind raced with a radical and upsetting realignment of who Declan Dunne was and how much he was to be trusted.

Once he returned, she saw Declan see his phone. She kept her eyes carefully trained on the window but in the reflection, she caught the *shit, did Edie read that?* thought rolling across his face. It somewhat confirmed his treachery.

Edie was mature enough to know people told white lies, cut their cloth. It wasn't that Declan disliked Elliot, though obviously, it hurt. It was the discovery of another false friend. *Elliot seems a lovely bloke.* She didn't pressure Declan to lie. If he'd come to that withering conclusion about her boyfriend, the proper thing to do was omit an opinion entirely. Presumably he was going to agree with Cara's analysis of why she'd be with a "boring brat," too— why else would you be? *No, she's just got really poor taste.*

Edie examined her tattered feelings and realized she'd have rather lost the Pepsi work and kept Declan as a friend, than this way round.

"Looks like there's enough cabs for both of us," Edie said blankly, once they left the station and were in sight of the rank.

"I like a walk when I've taken the drink. I'll catch one at the other end of town," Declan said. He was avoiding her, and she wasn't going to argue.

"Night, then," Edie said. "Brilliant effort today—well done."

"Night," he said. "Helluva day for the Notts branch."

She gave a miserable fake smile and raised her hand in farewell. *Don't try to make friends at work,* Edie thought bitterly. Or friends full stop. Nick and Hannah were a fluke; clearly, Edie had no judgment whatsoever.

She adjusted her bag on her shoulder and faced into the cold.

The first hackney with its light on peeled off, and she quickened her step to get the next one.

"Edie."

She turned to see Declan looking windswept, out of breath, having run back to catch up with her.

"That reply from Cara. I want to explain . . ."

"Really, no need," she said. There was no point in pretending not to know.

"There is a need, because I have a choice now. I either let you go on thinking I'm another one of the arseholes, or I tell you the truth. I said what I said because my sisters had me sussed. The amount I talk about you, the way I talk about you. They were right on the brink of finding out, and the only way I could stop them was raising an objection."

He drew breath, and Edie quaked.

". . . I had to invent one. Apologies to your fella, but I went with him. He's a nice guy, self-effacing, not a brat at all. Sharp and annoyingly witty. It's not his fault I wish he didn't exist. It's not his fault I was praying for him to be a boring brat, someone you might need saving from."

Declan shrugged, and Edie's skin was hot under her coat.

"What I didn't want my sisters to know is: I fucking adore you, Edie Thompson. Gives-me-stomach-pain type of adore you. I know there's no hope, no chance—I'm never going to mention it again. I know you're madly in love with someone else. I'm settling for colleagues and friends. I'm grateful for that, and I don't want to ruin it. But I didn't want you to think I'm a two-faced shit. I'm only two-faced insofar as I don't want anyone to know this. Including you, but—I forgot to turn off lock screen previews, and here we are."

"Understood," Edie said.

She did understand. Not only that, but somehow, she discovered she had understood this all along. Elliot was right. She'd chosen not to know, which wasn't the same thing as not knowing.

"You and I haven't done 'drama free' from the word *go*, have we?" she said, after a pause, surprised not to find this at all awkward. Somehow, there was no awkward left. "We've packed in about ten years of getting to know each other into a few weeks."

"Hahaha, right enough," Declan said, with a look that blended love and humor and sadness and gratitude, all at once.

They needed a reset.

"Thank you for being honest, and I'm glad I've got to know you, Declan," she said.

"Thank you. So am I. We're good?"

"Good," Edie said, extending her hand for him to shake. "You know, I'm starting to think smartphones are like keeping a pet rattlesnake."

54

Much as Fraser and Molly's wedding being precipitous had been a talking point from the start, Edie still couldn't quite believe how fast it arrived. There was getting on with it—then there was this.

"Nice day for it," said Edie's driver, as he punched the postcode into the satnav. Edie had gamely resisted the Elliot Owen trappings, but she'd started to get used to the chauffeuring.

Inevitably, the hotel was the variety to have wrought iron gates and an "approach." Inside, everything was soft carpets, thickly lined curtains, and framed prints of noteworthy historic animals. It was sufficiently large that Edie encountered no others from the wedding party as she checked in—or not ones she recognized.

She made at herself at home in the room, getting ready in leisurely fashion, and wondered at the practicality of roll-top baths in front of uncovered windows—especially if strangers were keen to take photographs of you.

"Fuuuuuck, the traffic was a bastard," Elliot said, crashing in at midday, pulling headphones from his neck. "Hi, you OK? I can't stop, I need to get in that shower . . ." He stopped. "Wow. You look amazing."

"I don't look like I'm going to a funeral?" Edie said. She had teamed the Vampire's Wife with a birdcage mesh veil, attached to a thin band, which covered her eyes.

"If so, even if it was my wife in the coffin, I'd be all over you at the wake," Elliot said. "My clothes arrived?"

Edie pointed at the suit bag on the wardrobe.

"Magic. Right, sorry for neglecting you, but—hygiene . . ."

He disappeared into the bathroom to the sounds of running water and emerged shortly afterward, clad only in boxers, looking like he should be filmed in sepia and scored by a retro torch song. Edie was a girlfriend and not a common or garden voyeur fan, yet sometimes she felt like both.

She'd never divulged that when she was particularly missing Elliot, she looked up a famous, PG-13 scene on YouTube in *Blood & Gold*. His weeping servant wench love, Malleflead, tenderly sponged his battle-brutalized body by candlelight, then matters developed. It was Prince Wulfroarer's heavy burden to still inflame ladies' loins when requiring first aid.

(Meg walked in once and said: "Eww, and why's she clambering on top of him if he's that fucked up?"

"Why do you think?"

"If I was Elliot I'd shout, 'Get off me, you mad bitch.' Maybe he saves that for you, hahaha."

Edie turned it off and said: "Wank ruined," to screaming from her sister.)

"Oh God, I feel like I've been kicked from the back of a Bedford van at sixty miles an hour. I'll wait for the adrenaline proper to gush through my veins and put me back in the room. Probably better that than alcohol," Elliot said.

His suit was narrow black pinstripe, with pale pink tie, white shirt, brown-and-white dress shoes.

"Not sure about it, are you?" he whispered, holding it up against his chest. "Am I trying to run 1920s Chicago with an iron fist?"

"You look good in anything," Edie said, rolling her eyes.

"Even with my Beetlejuice complexion?"

"Even as a dead miscreant jester."

Elliot sat down to pull the trousers on, then shrugged the shirt on and buttoned it. "Wait, where's my flower thingy?"

"Over there." Edie indicated a writing desk in the bay window. "With your tie and cuff links."

"Oh, thanks."

He carried on scurrying around, piecing immaculate best man together, while Edie investigated the cable channels on a television in a wooden box. It was a pleasant gender reversal to have the man finicking over his appearance and Edie ready and at a loose end.

"The Pepsi account, by the way," Elliot called from the bathroom. "Any news?"

"Oh my God! I meant to tell you! We got it!"

"Edie, amazing!"

He put his face round the door so he could exchange a smile with her: "When you talked me through it, I felt sure you would. Brilliant."

"Thank you."

Edie wiggled her heels in satisfaction on the quilt: satin black Mary Jane courts with a glitzy buckle. They gave her a pleasing undulation when she walked, an extra inch and a half in height, and despite the gel insoles, would no doubt cripple her later.

Hard not to think of the last time she was dolled for an occasion like this. Thank God she was so far away from it, in so many ways.

When Elliot emerged, mid-toothbrushing, Edie was supine, feeling self-congratulatory.

"By the way, did Declan say anything amorous, on your trip to London?"

"Er. Sort of," Edie said as an empty, embarrassed reflex.

Thinking about how to broach what had gone on there with Elliot—and whether to broach it at all—was an ongoing internal debate. Declan appearing to insult her to deflect others from realizing he had feelings for her was something Elliot had done, once. This echo made her even more sympathetic toward Declan's predicament, yet that similarity was likely to make it worse from Elliot's point of view.

But she knew she couldn't lie to Elliot now he'd asked and amend it later. It would break fundamental things between them if she did.

"Something *was* said? What happened to promising to tell me?"

"I wasn't sure if it qualified."

"Did he say he had feelings?"

". . . Yes."

"Then why wouldn't it qualify?"

"He didn't mean to tell me. I saw a message from his sister that I wasn't meant to."

Elliot looked quite shell-shocked. "In other words, you were respecting his confidence instead of keeping your promise to me. There's that adrenaline I ordered."

"No! It wasn't that at all . . ." Edie started.

She berated herself for not foreseeing it could come out like this. She didn't think in the melee of Fraser and Molly tying the knot, Elliot would spend a second on it. She'd not considered the way this issue uniquely troubled him.

"He didn't intend me to see anything . . ."

"Sounds familiar. Hang on . . ." Elliot ran off to rinse and spit and returned without the toothbrush.

Edie sat up straighter.

"Yes?" Elliot said, arms folded.

". . . I accidentally saw a message from his sister that made it look like he'd been misspeaking me." Edie edited out misspeaking Elliot, as it would add nothing other than even higher blood pressure. "I saw his phone on the train . . . He was forced into correcting it by admitting he likes me."

"'Forced'? I refer you to my point: not trying hard enough to hide it."

"Well, he stressed he'd never do anything about it. He was mortified."

Elliot stood, staring, as he took this in. "I need the actual wording for 'likes me.'"

"He said he adored me."

There were several beats of silence before Elliot spoke. "You weren't going to tell me, were you?"

"Yes, I was. Just not today," Edie said, with conviction. "I promised you I would. I was finding the right time, and I didn't think this was it. Well done for being entirely correct about it all," Edie continued. "Safe to say, I feel a right twat."

"It's not a victorious feeling. I'm now worrying how much I was right about. I don't want to be right twice."

"What do you mean? You don't trust me?" Edie said.

"I do trust you. I know when the day comes that you have to speak to me, you won't have done anything, and you'll still hate yourself."

"Have to speak to you about what?"

Elliot picked up his tie and started putting it on. He stopped and said: "It's not working, is it? One of us has to say so."

"What isn't working?"

"Us."

"It *is* working?" Edie said, shocked. She could already hear her voice sounding unnatural.

"Whenever we're alone, it works. It couldn't be better. Then we go back to daily life, and the rolling shit show resumes. This is the latest episode. I don't know what to do about someone competing with me when I'm not there most of the time."

"You don't have to do anything?" Edie said. "I sorted it."

"I don't ever want you to stay with me in order to keep your word," Elliot said.

"I'm not!"

"Nor do I want you to feel you have the responsibility of saving me from the life I chose."

"Why are you saying these ominous things?!"

An inner voice piped up: *wakey wakey, sounds like you are being dumped*, and she could not begin to comprehend it.

"Not passing that on about Declan has forced me to confront this."

"I was waiting to discuss it with you face-to-face!"

"Now we're face-to-face, and I had to drag it out of you."

"It's an hour before your brother's wedding!" Edie whisper-hissed.

If Elliot needed a gesture of commitment to get past this crisis of faith, it was definitely time.

"If you think this isn't working as things stand, I could move to New York," Edie said.

There was an ugly, strained pause before Elliot replied: "I don't want you to."

Time stopped. They were words Edie realized she'd spent their whole time together fearing she'd hear.

"You don't?" she said. It was like he'd kicked her in the stomach.

"I don't want to take you away from your dad, your sister, Nick and Hannah. A job you enjoy and that you're great at. A life that's right for you and makes you happy. For what—to sit alone in an apartment, waiting for me to get back late from a very long day? Me keeping you like some kind of pedigreed house cat through my own entitled inability to recognize or accept what's best for you, not best for me? The guilt would kill me. And probably kill us."

311

They were doing this again, with roles reversed? Now that she was all in: heart, body, and soul? Edie was light-headed.

Elliot couching it in concern for her made it deadeningly real—like management going into HR-friendly speak about what a great effort you'd made in your time at the company, and they'd truly appreciated it, because the decision had been taken and the ink was dry.

"You're now saying that this is impossible?" Edie asked. "The distance? That you knew about on Christmas Day?"

"It's not only distance, it's context. I didn't know *Your Table* was the highlight of my career, and how it would feel that so many people's jobs would depend on me keeping it. I didn't fully appreciate how much I was asking you to give up in England until I spent time with you there. All I could think about was how much I wanted you back. It was selfish."

"Loving someone that much isn't selfish," Edie said.

"Actually, I've found out it can be."

"I wasn't a princess in a tower and you a knight climbing up to rescue me, you know," Edie said. "If you don't think what we have is worth the trouble anymore, then you have to say as much. Don't do this patronizing *what's best for you* stuff, because I know what's best for me, and it's you."

There was a perilous dead quiet where Edie feared he would take her up on this. She was bluffing; his thinking was clearly somewhere else.

From the first time they separated, Edie had been anticipating and avoiding this very showdown. He'd awakened from the desire stupor, the thrill expired, and he'd thought: *God this is a lot of work.*

Don't try to outrun your destiny: it would come and find you after you'd peeled the price stickers off new shoes in a country house hotel in Suffolk.

Soon, they'd need to have their happiest faces ready for hours on end. They shouldn't be doing this now, but unfortunately, they were.

"I'm not patronizing you. I'm admitting that I'm trying to be somebody to you that I can't be," Elliot said. "I'm trying to have something with you that I can't have."

"You can only have—what, a geographically mobile, rich, famous girlfriend? Would've been better for me if you'd worked that preference out a lot faster. Even the newspapers have been telling you I was the wrong fit for you."

"Fuck's sake, Edie, that's low. That's not what I mean, and don't pretend to think it's what I mean, given it's a character assassination."

"If this isn't working, who *can* you have, then?"

Edie wasn't at all sure this was her wisest or most logical line of attack—how will Elliot Owen ever find another suitable female companion?—but she was panicking and floundering.

Had he and Ines got closer still? Enough to make him daydream about something different? It was so painful that Edie couldn't even contemplate it.

"What's the other conclusion from you saying my being normal and your lifestyle don't mix?" Edie said.

"*Normal?*" Elliot said, and there was the handbrake release sensation of a proper, no holds barred fight breaking out. "You know what, I have never, not once, raised my job up at you as if it means I automatically deserve you or as if I have the upper hand. Yet you've thrown it at me endlessly—it always comes back to how I hold all the cards, how I can't possibly find anything as hard as you do."

"I'm trying to work out how we got from *a man I work with hit on me* to *let's not bother with this ruinously important love affair I persuaded you into, after all*? Am I being punished for something somebody else did? Do you know how much Buddhist calm I've had to find about a costar you've very literally made out with?"

"It's not a competition."

"What is this, then? Tell me."

Elliot simply glowered.

There were many connections to be made, but Edie had no time to make them. She'd been careless in her management of this situation with Declan and was confronting the terrifying possibility she had awoken to its damage too late.

Unless, even worse: Declan was the excuse, not the reason.

55

"Listen, we'll talk later," Elliot said. "This isn't the time."

"That's what I said, and it made me a liar!" Edie was too upset to keep her voice quite quiet enough, underscoring Elliot's point. "Then you went and nuclear dropped 'we're not working'!"

"Sorry. I shouldn't have."

"Because you want to take it back, or because you don't?"

"Edie," Elliot said, shaking his head, and she knew.

She was about to go through this wedding waiting for her verbal dismissal to be formalized and confirmed as such. Edie was therefore in too great a state of distress to simply stop.

"Are the cold feet connected to your belief that falling in love is a temporary insanity and that I'd never offer to move to be with you"—yes, *have that*—"and that the intensity of the initial frenzy is no promise of anything lasting? That it's a flood of drugs in your body designed to make you want to make more humans?"

Elliot frowned. "What are you talking about?"

"I heard you with Fraser, when he came to the hotel in Nottingham to discuss his stag do. He said you didn't think we'd last. You were explaining why we weren't . . . ever likely to do what they were."

"You're using things against me that you got from listening in to a private conversation I had with my brother?"

Edie hated him thinking less of her, and she could see that he did.

"I didn't mean to hear it. Fraser arrived really late, so it clashed with when I got back to the hotel, and you were talking about

Anto. Then my name came up, and it was difficult to tune out. I didn't know I'd end up being the focus."

"What you heard was Fraser's take on us, not mine."

"He was quoting you."

Elliot stared at her before he spoke. "The problem with something you're not meant to have heard is that you're not meant to have heard it. The purpose of that talk was to dissuade Fraser from being an impetuous idiot. Of course I was going to be a hard-ass about new love being a brain fog. I was trying to do a job. I'm hardly going to say: *I'm more mature than you and a better judge of character, do as I say not as I'd do.* How far would that have got me? Not that I got very far anyway." He gestured down at his attire.

"I see . . ." Edie said, thinking that admittedly made sense, and Elliot didn't seem wrong-footed. And unfortunately, he was too bright not to join the dots that Edie had indulged her own crisis of faith in him as a result.

"Given I've told you many times I wasn't being casual about us, you thought—what, that I was telling you what I thought you'd want to hear?" Elliot said. "Do you not think the fact you doubt me all the time might be significant? That you might need me to give you an out?"

"It's not that I'm hunting for problems. It's being highly strung."

"Fact remains, you had a choice between *Elliot is being pragmatic* and *Elliot is a bullshitter*, and you chose the latter."

"I didn't! I wasn't sure what to think. You're not someone who says things he doesn't mean."

There was a knocking at the door that made Edie jump, and Elliot hang his head.

"Are you decent?!" Fraz called. "I've got *marrying* to be doing very soon, you know?"

"Nearly there. Right with you!" Elliot said, with the necessary jollity. "Five minutes."

"*Nearly there?* Nearly where?! Oh no. Edie, you're not in a harness, are you?" Fraz said.

His humor had never been more misapplied. Edie replied: "Yes, but I'm pretty sure I know how to undo it."

Having to perform this way was entirely necessary and utterly wretched. *In fact, Fraser, your brother is ending things, and the only thing I am in is pieces.*

"See you in the lobby in five, then," Fraser said. "I'm shaking like a shitting dog here, Lell—I need you to give me some of your awards speech tips. Also, I need a nip of whatever Iggy's got in that hip flask."

"You do NOT need whatever Iggy's put in his flask—it's probably toad venom. We'll get you a whisky at the bar. Wait for me, OK?" Elliot said.

"Come on, then! Five minutes! Let Edie go—she'll let you molest her at the end of the night," Fraser implored, incorrectly.

"Five minutes!" Elliot said, Edie alone able to hear the note of desperation.

"Downstairs!" Fraser replied, and it seemed, retreated.

They breathed out.

Edie looked over at Elliot to share a moment, whatever moment that was, but he'd purposely stalked back to the bathroom to avoid such a thing.

56

It was a tribute to what an effortlessly joyful wedding it was that at times Edie found herself carried away by it, even in her invisible purgatory.

Fraser looked, in turn, absolutely petrified and then quite overcome when Molly arrived on her father's arm; the official photographer's job was a cinch. (And he was the only one: either the long-lens brigade had missed the wedding banns or they couldn't get a good enough vantage point).

Molly hadn't opted for the Cinderella ball gown that Fraser feared but for something beaded, sinuous, and halterneck, with an open back.

They held hands and whispered when she reached him, then stumbled and giggled like teenagers through the vows.

Edie had never much craved this event for herself; being happy with someone was enough. Yet she had an envious, inward sigh at the dazzling, upmarket vision of having found The One—the envy sharpened like a knife by the fact she was about to lose hers. She noticed that whenever Elliot scanned the first few rows, he was careful not to meet her eyes. Meeting her eyes could now be taken as hope, and he wasn't dispensing that if it was false. Edie was all lipsticked smiles, clapping, and dread. It seemed fitting she was watching it through a mourning veil.

In the applause as they were declared husband and wife, Fraser and Molly appeared to be near-levitating, their faces suffused with wonder that life could be this good.

If it was a *marry in haste, repent at leisure* mistake, Edie thought, both the haste and the leisure looked damn appealing. If this was getting it wrong, why bother to be right? There were certainly worse ways to spend whatever it cost, as Iggy had shown.

With Elliot detained on post-ceremony duties, Edie traveled with his parents in a cream beribboned Rolls Royce from the church to the vast marquee in the garden of Molly's sprawling family home—or rather, the grounds. You could go as far as rolling parkland. The pink-bricked, white-gabled house itself was dripping with wisteria, the size of a hotel.

"Goodness me," their father, Bob, said, as the tires crunched onto gravel. "They must think Molly's married into peasant stock, haha."

If the well-to-do Owens with their multimillionaire prodigal son were peasants by this measure, what were the Thompsons? Rodents in their sacks of grain. Edie decided not to voice the notion she had been nibbling on their sack.

The reception was a sea of white-clothed round tables adorned with white-and-pink floral arrangements and very tall brass candlesticks, the roof crisscrossed with strings of Edison-bulb festoon lights. As the light outside faded, it went from charming to magical.

Elliot being best man was sadly functionally useful in separating them. He was constantly occupied and not even in his seat next to her much at the meal, what with a blizzard of introductions and the relentless *discreet word* admin.

And in the normal way of things, Elliot's parents would be mostly by Edie's side; however, the fast-forwarded Fraser courtship meant they'd met Molly's parents once and no one else, so they were busy with a thousand hellos with the relatives, too.

Molly, train over arm and bearing a flute of fizz, barreled up to Edie: "*EEEEEDIE!* Oh my God, you look gorgeous! I love the Gothic Winona Energy!"

Even though she had mere seconds available, Molly still managed with no free hands to give her a tight hug drenched in Tom

Ford White Patchouli and ascertain that Edie had liked her beef tenderloin and was definitely having a good time.

Molly's nature had been unfairly conflated with her parents, who were socially ambitious on their kids' behalf, Edie reckoned. Molly was a born enthusiast, like her groom—an observation Edie would quite likely never get to make to Elliot now.

Molly's parents were youthful and yet royal-looking in bearing and clothing—clearly éminences grises of the parish. Her father was in full morning suit, her mother in pistachio-green headgear with ostrich feathers so large, it was like a play on perspective.

("It looks like Boy George hat," Fraser whispered to Edie, making her clap a hand over her mouth before she spat champagne. Champagne, not prosecco, which apparently Molly's mother considered déclassé piss. Fraser reported her saying: "What next, a Colin the Caterpillar for the wedding cake?")

When Edie was put in front of them, she merited a minute of explicit, narrow-eyed assessment and interrogation. When they found out she worked a desk job and had no discernible stature beyond dating Molly's brother-in-law, Edie was hastily dropped in favor of someone more worth bellowing at.

Thanks to her connection with Elliot fracturing, she already felt like an imposter.

"Girlfriend? For how long? What happened to 'no ring, no bring'?" she even heard an arsehole uncle of Molly's saying in supposed jocularity in her hearing to Elliot, who replied: "Social progress and basic manners?"

Maybe arsehole uncle had inadvertently helped her cause as, minutes later, Elliot finally appeared by her side, sliding his hand into hers, squeezing, and muttering: "Hey up. You all right?"

"Sort of," Edie said, a complete lie, gathering that it wasn't a real *you all right*, it was a: *Bearing up? I am not letting this descend into hostility.* "You? Confident about your speech?"

"Actually, I'm very nervous, which I didn't expect. Turns out the fuss about weddings isn't entirely a myth—you do feel the hand of history on you and all that."

"You'll be great," Edie said. "Pretend we're all naked."

She immediately wished she'd not said that.

"Picturing Iggy naked has never helped anyone's psychic state."

He fiddled with his tie, and Edie said: "Here," and reached up to adjust it, forcing him to face her.

Their eyes met fully as she dropped her hands, and Edie couldn't resist the liberty of kissing him on the cheek. "Good luck."

Elliot kissed her back hard and quick on the mouth, muttering: "You're not my gran," before turning away to deal with the latest applicant for his time.

Edie was left reverberating from it, disconcerted. On the one hand, it was a voluntary kiss; on the other, it might be the last kiss.

Fifteen minutes later, his two-hander speech with Iggy was a riot. No one had lived lives more suited to best man stories than Fraser and Iggy. Even Edie was left helpless by the story of their suffering norovirus in a Las Vegas hot tub, color provided by Iggy, punch lines supplied by Elliot.

Elliot brought it to a close with sincere words about how he'd never met anyone more openhearted and goodwilled than his brother and that Molly and he were ideally matched in this regard.

He even admitted he'd worried about their rushing into matrimony and concluded: "Looking at you both today, I'm going to have to break and say the words I most hate saying in this world. *Fraser, you were right.*"

There was thunderous applause as Fraser leaped out of his seat to hug Elliot and Edie cried warm tears that she had to carefully ration, so they didn't turn into a flood.

If this was their final evening together, it was nothing short of sadistic. She looked at the brothers talking animatedly, thought how Elliot forgave Iggy, protected Fraser, saved that friendship. How he lived his big life, as Hannah called it, yet never lost sight of what mattered. Or who.

It was inconvenient, to say the least, to have complete and total perspective on the size of a human being who'd come into your life, right at the point you were losing them.

Edie was so proud of him, and he no longer had a use for her pride.

57

The table plans dissolved into mingling, the music got louder, and somehow, in the blur of it, she and Elliot had still barely interacted. Every so often, he'd have to beckon her over, Edie having been identified as his plus-one, or place his palm on the small of her back as he chatted to someone.

Edie was soothed by these public displays of affection, but only for a second. What else was he going to do?

Oh, hi, Aunty Susan, yeah, this is technically my girlfriend, but I called it off before the ceremony and will be officially agreeing it's curtains when I'm removing my cuff links later. In short, don't get too attached, yeah.

Also, Elliot wasn't vindictive and wouldn't exclude her. They were on show, on his brother's big day. Her presence couldn't be undone, though Edie saw a future where his loved ones tactfully selected portraits without her for display. It was difficult amid the joie de vivre to accept what had happened. It was tempting to huff down another Moët, clutch at him, and pretend it hadn't. But, as she said, Elliot wasn't someone who said things he didn't mean.

Edie was in a secret follow spot of sadness, her face carefully composed into a beatific expression at all times, blankly checking her phone. Gothic Winona Energy veil set aside, lipstick reapplied.

She kept internally replaying: *I don't want you to.* Those were five words you didn't utter without serious intent and the fifth was probably surplus.

In the time she was unexpectedly gifted in her own head, Edie thought hard about why she'd not seen Declan's declaration coming

323

and how her blithe dismissal of their attachment must've felt to Elliot.

Jack had got closer to her than he should have done because he was a sly charlatan. Declan had got too close because he wasn't one, but it didn't mean he was harmless to her.

She imagined it reversed: visiting Elliot, some gal pal Girl Friday appearing, a fast friend and coconspirator. Their cackling away together. Edie sussing that woman was hankering after him and would be scheming. Edie would've worried, she could see now, that if Elliot politely rubbished her concerns and refused to address it face on, she'd be fearful of what he'd find when he did.

She saw that her mindset that she was Just Another Girl and He Was Him hadn't helped. She'd thought it was humility, but it had been used as a pass. It was other people's right to treat Elliot as a superhero with the ability to turn himself into a spatial vortex, not hers.

He'd made it plain that Declan made him anxious, and if she was really, truly truthful: she'd never taken it entirely seriously.

There was in fact a frighteningly simple question she needed to ask him.

Had the Declan incident alarmed Elliot enough to bail on them entirely—in which case, she might be able to rescue it—or was it a catalyst for doubts he was having anyway? In which case, they were done.

Don't let it, whatever it is, trigger the ongoing fear that, somehow, someone you love that much will leave.

Was this it? Had Elliot been, as his mother put it, appearing to cope when he wasn't coping?

Trouble is, Deborah, Edie thought, *how do I tell the difference between abandonment tremors and his genuinely wanting to abandon this?*

She wasn't going to be allowed to stay blissfully ignorant about who replaced her. Before she could stop herself, she imagined the first informal shots of Elliot and Ines surfacing, their hands clasped again over an outdoor table or arms linked on a sidewalk, their ease and casual clothes declaring not date, but *breakfast out after night spent together*. Edie would feel differently about her entire time with Elliot, knowing she was an aberration before common sense returned, and that common sense was waiting in the wings the whole time, Edie to become a historical footnote.

The DJ announced the first dance, and guests flocked to see Fraser and Molly waltzing on the black-and-white vinyl tiled dance floor, bookended by potted palms.

After a few bars of Arctic Monkeys' "I Wanna Be Yours," Fraser was gesticulating at Elliot over Molly's shoulder and then at other key personnel, indicating, *don't leave us out here.*

Elliot put his drink down, made his way over. Edie was perturbed to notice a failed attempt to intercept him by a pretty cousin of Molly's. She looked in puzzlement at Edie, and obviously hadn't realized Elliot was here with anyone. They had been orbiting satellites enough tonight to present as single.

"Will you dance with me?" Elliot said, polite but unsmiling, extending a hand.

If it hadn't been for the sake of others, all things considered, Edie would've said no. *Not because you* have *to ask me.* She let herself be led onto the floor and swung into his embrace, his arm round her waist, holding hands.

It should've felt good to Edie, despite everything. In fact, it was terrible: their carefully avoiding eye contact again, the tension in his body, like he was enduring it, counting down to being released from the charade.

The refrain *I wanna be yours / I wanna be youuuuurs* swirled heavily around them, a plea and a taunt, a whirlpool sucking Edie down into the ground below, like the film score credits roll for their relationship.

Despite knowing it was a very bad idea, Edie leaned up and said, into his ear: "Is there someone else?"

"What?" Elliot said, pulling back to look at her, possibly as much in surprise at her timing as the question itself. "Of course not. Like who?"

Edie shrugged. "Ines?" she whispered. "I don't know."

"Er, no. I don't cheat."

"Neither do I."

"Don't do this now," Elliot said, speaking into her ear, his head right by hers, looking as if it were a sweet nothing. "Stop. Please."

He wouldn't meet her eye again. Edie had succeeded in putting an end to one worry and swapping it for comprehensively toxifying this moment, alienating him further.

As the song finished and she had to let him go, possibly forever, something in Edie snapped. She wasn't going to let this to happen; she wasn't going to simply wait.

Edie put her hand into Elliot's and grasped it firmly, saying: "I need to talk to you."

If he objected, she'd decided she'd make it clear that, in that case, she'd do it right here, but he let her lead him through the crowd. She moved at a clip that implied they were heading somewhere in particular and didn't want interrupting. If someone tried, she might snarl. She craned her neck to locate a gap of purple-blue night sky in the wall of the tent, an escape hatch.

They emerged, suddenly alone, which felt more alone than Edie expected. She trailed him across the darkened lawn, stopping by a large oak tree with a whimsical wooden swing dangling from its branches.

Edie looked back, making sure there was enough distance from the light and hubbub of the marquee that they'd see anyone approaching.

She faced him. Elliot was slightly party worn, hair tousled, skin in a light sweat and dark eyes sparkling with drink. His expression wasn't intrigued or even friendly: it was somewhere between skeptical and reluctant. He'd never looked better, and it wasn't helpful.

"I need you to be totally straight with me, even if it's crushing," Edie said, knowing that whatever the outcome, she'd remember this conversation for the rest of her life.

58

". . . No matter how upsetting it is, say it. It'll still be better than trying to decode each other, because I feel like we were speaking in different languages earlier," Edie said.

It was a starless, blowy night and was cold away from the patio heaters. Something about the vast canopy of sky in the country-side made Edie feel the size of the moment more acutely. What a strange set of unlikely chances had thrown her and Elliot together. What a strangely fitting way for it to finish. She was fated to have tonally inappropriate conversations in gardens at weddings.

"'I don't want you to move in with me' feels like a terminal statement. If you're saying we're over, say so now. I'll go back in there, hold a smile, and leave early tomorrow, no scenes. I owe Fraser, Molly, and your parents that. I can't spend any longer wondering if that's how tonight ends. At a celebration of love, it's like being tortured before execution."

There was a heavy silence, and Edie knew a *no, don't be silly, we had a spat, it's not over* would've come immediately. *Don't cry.* There would be time for that later. She had the rest of her life available.

Elliot cleared his throat. "You offered to move because I'd found out about Declan's advances. Even if I could see a way it'd work, I'm hardly going to say yes in those circumstances." He glanced back, to confirm for himself that they couldn't be heard. "I said I didn't want to be right twice. My second prediction is that you're falling in love with him."

Edie's eyes widened, and her mouth flew open.

Elliot shook his head. "I know, I know, you deny it. But I know you really well, Edie. We understand each other like nobody else does; it's why we've . . ." He had to pause as he choked up a bit. ". . . meant so much to each other."

"Don't talk about us in the past tense," Edie said, distraught, having to gasp the words out fast. Her eyes filled up anyway, and then Elliot's did, too.

"This is why this conversation should've waited . . ." Elliot said, looking away while he got himself under control. "You don't think you are, but I couldn't figure out why you'd brought him into the center of your life with such speed. Then I realized: I did know why, but I didn't want to face it. You and Declan are more than a friendship, and it's not unrequited love on his part, either. It's you suppressing something that's happening, whether you consciously choose it or not. When I say I trust you, I trust your actions, not your feelings. From my perspective, I can't prevent it, and even if I could, I don't think I should. He can give you a life that I can't—one where the tabloids aren't ripping you apart every month and the paparazzi outside your office go away. So . . ." Elliot had to make an effort to look her in the eye. "Yes, I think we should probably call it a day now rather than later. I'm no less devastated by that than you are."

"What happened to our belonging with each other?" Edie said. She was tarnishing the memory of the most romantic thing ever said to her, but there was a much bigger tarnishing in progress. She needed answers.

There was a lot of silent swallowing and gulping on both their parts before Elliot was able to reply.

"That's why it hurts like nothing else."

"OK," Edie said, shaky, but exercising self-control in a dire emergency. "I want to explain. I've thought about this, at last, and I'm going to give you complete and total honesty. After that, you can decide if you still think that's where we stand."

She folded her arms and took a deep breath. Her heels did hurt.

"Not to be a stuck record, but it starts with that wedding again. When I got trashed by everyone after Harrogate, I found out what it feels like to be loathed. I became this distorted version of myself I didn't recognize. I even wondered: have I actually been this person my whole life and not known? Is this the real me? You know exactly what I mean: when your identity gets created and pulled apart by other people."

Edie took another breath. "I lost the ability to make friends, and it had been a core part of my identity, my survival mechanism. I'd always been good at that. School, university, moving to London. I wasn't the best at the courting-via-apps horrors, but being *well liked*, being a girl who got invited to things and got on with everyone—I could accomplish that. *Fitting in*. Then obviously I became someone who couldn't even adapt herself into not being hated.

"When Declan turned up, he didn't treat me that way, and it wasn't because he was ignorant of what went on. It wasn't due to meeting some Reboot Edie who'd airbrushed it out. He was from the same place as my enemies, knew about Harrogate, and didn't care. For the first time, I thought maybe I could get past it, that some people might take my side. I could be the old me again. And I instinctively knew that if there was sexual attraction involved, that changed it, and it ruined it. It invalidated his approval, because it turned it into yet more grubby misconduct, exactly what everyone accused me of. But if I never noticed anything like that from him, didn't participate, it didn't exist."

Elliot still said nothing.

"That's how I got here. I was desperate for it to be clean and good and redeeming, to not to be dirtied up by any of that. I went into denial, and ironically that's made you think my wishes were the exact opposite. I'm so sincerely sorry if any of my eagerness and relief at being liked again appeared to you as anything else. You're right that I was complacent, because in my mind, you couldn't be threatened. Not treating you as a mere mortal, too—it's a weird type of inequality, and it's not fair. You told me you disliked it numerous times, and I of all people should've listened."

Elliot remained inscrutable.

"You often talk about not being there for me. The day my dad had the fall, I knew there was only one person I wanted to speak to, only one person whose support I needed. Your instincts don't lie in those moments, Elliot. Not when I thought I might be facing something I wasn't actually sure I could face. Then when we spoke, you did help, the way no one else can. It felt like my breathing only got steady and my heart rate only fell once I heard your voice. That's when home is another person. Wherever you are, you're home to me."

Edie's voice had grown thick, and she had no idea if any of this had convinced him, but she carried on. If soul-baring didn't work, she had nothing else.

"Part of me always knew this is how it'd be if we were serious. I finally know exactly why I didn't dare try the first time. I had a sense you weren't going to let me down. I feared you were exactly who you told me you were, that you loved me as much as you said you did. So, it was too big a responsibility to take on. How do you get over losing that? I didn't want to add to my tally of unimaginable losses."

Elliot was staring at her intently, brow furrowed, and Edie had no idea what he was thinking. None whatsoever.

With some difficulty, she gathered herself for a finale that prioritized dignity and parting on amicable terms. In truth, she wanted to grab his lapels.

". . . If this arrangement we've got isn't right for you anymore, fair enough. We said we'd try, and we said it might be a

331

heartbreaking catastrophe. All I can say is: being with you has transformed me. You've changed what I expect from a relation- ship, from life—expect from myself, even. And if you leave, it can't be for a misunderstanding. What we've got is too important for that, Elliot. Tell me we're over because the wanting has been outweighed by other things. That's brutal to accept, but at least I'll know there's nothing I could've said. Don't do it because you think you're losing me or doing me a favor, because you aren't, and you're not."

59

They stared into each other's eyes for a few long seconds. This hadn't been real for Edie, not yet. His next words would be definitive, and she'd abandon hope. Edie expected he'd repeat it was agony for him, too. She was on the edge of a cliff, grey sea far below.

"What do you want to happen with us? Say in a year's time? If we're being completely cards-on-the-table honest," Elliot said, in a gentler register than before. "I know New York right now isn't it, though I appreciate you offering it."

Completely honest? Edie glanced at the marquee, from which the sound of "Maneater" and excitable shrieks were now emanating. There wasn't any benefit in Cool Girling this. She knew what she wanted; she'd known since the roses on the doorstep. She didn't want anything less than everything.

"Honestly?" She pointed at the reception. "I want that."

"Hall & Oates?" Elliot said. "Or you want to marry me?"

". . . I want to marry you. Not sure 'Maneater' is a smart choice for me."

"Really?" Elliot said, taken aback. "A big white wedding like this? That's your thing?"

If they were flaming out, Edie was certainly doing it in style. "Yes, definitely, if it's with you."

Elliot frowned. "Even the mobile churros cart?"

". . . What?" Edie said.

"It's got *You Make Me Melt* written on the side."

Elliot's face was completely straight, and Edie didn't dare let herself believe. Was he . . . ? Were they . . . going to be all right? *Oh my God . . .*

"What do you want?" she said, heart in throat.

Elliot put his hands in his pockets. "Although I didn't know it until a minute ago, I wanted to hear every last thing you said." He paused. "Thank you."

The night was starless and blowy, but no longer cold away from the patio heaters.

"Including your proposal."

"I proposed?" Edie said, feeling weightless. "Fuck, I suppose I did?"

"I'm afraid so, and even worse, I accept it. My answer is yes."

Elliot was looking at her from under his brow, smiling, and Edie thought she was smiling—she wasn't sure.

"*Where the hell is Elliot? Has anyone seen my other best man? I'm downgrading him to Merely Adequate Man,*" came Fraser's voice, from the din in the tent.

"We better go back," Elliot said, reaching forward and putting his hand in hers.

"Sure," Edie said.

They walked a few steps.

"*Edie.*"

He stopped her, spun her round, and kissed her. Edie threw her arms around his neck. Since their first kiss, none had meant quite as much as this one. Elliot had this way of expressing so much in the way that—

"UNBELIEVABLE!" came a male voice.

They broke apart to see Fraser right by them.

"I've met some filthy shits in my time, but you two are a class apart. You couldn't last my *reception*? Seek medical help."

"We've been *talking*, Fraz," Elliot said, faux wearily. "Grown-ups were talking."

"Yeah, it looked like it," Fraser said. He looked from Edie's rapturous expression to Elliot's guarded one. "You were talking? Really? About what? Something's gone on here. Edie's pregnant, isn't she?"

"I'm not pregnant!" Edie said. "I've been drinking like a sailor on shore leave."

"Well, something's up," Fraser said. "Elliot's got his Mr. Important Decision Maker face on. There's a feverish mood, like I threw water over mating cats."

"OK, look. We got engaged," Elliot said, under his breath, looking at Edie for her approval. She'd thought it was more of a private pact between them about the intended direction of travel, rather than an official decision. Elliot really meant it? Enough to tell his family? Her heart might burst.

"DO NOT tell anyone tonight, *no one*, promise? When everyone's pissed, it'll spread like wildfire, and you'll give our parents' nervous system dysregulation after your antics," Elliot said.

"At our wedding?! OH MY GOD, THIS IS THE COOLEST THING TO . . ."

Molly appeared at Fraser's side, white dress making her a moth in the late twilight. "What's happened?" she said, agog.

Fraser looked panicked by the pressure to dissemble. "Erm . . . they shagged on the swing."

Elliot made a disapproving exhalation. "We did not shag on the swing!"

"I used to play on that as a child," Molly said, dismayed.

"Fraz, really!" Elliot said.

Molly looked appraisingly at Edie. "That dress Edie's in wouldn't go above her knees. You'd have to unzip it and take it off entirely—I call bullshit, Fraser."

"Thank you, exactly!" Edie said, appreciating Molly being a "fashion buyer" at last. She sensed she could derail further inquiry if she moved fast enough.

335

"Molly, can I say, in all sincerity, this is the best wedding I've ever been to. Not top five, top one. Best day of your life, but for others, too."

She squeezed Elliot's hand, and he squeezed back.

"Really?! For real?" Molly said.

"Swear," Edie said. "The standard that all weddings will have to meet for me, from now on."

"You next!" Molly cried, and Elliot saw the moment to smile indulgently and herd them all back into the party.

Inside the tent, it was a sensory overload, with the tumult already inside Edie. The music had returned to something Bon Iver romantic, and Edie saw a chance to be sort-of alone.

"Can I have this dance?" she said, leading Elliot back onto the dance floor. "I feel we could improve on the last one."

"That's a low bar," Elliot said, as they resumed a dance hold. *"Are you knobbing someone else? I wanna be your Ford Cortina and run you down."*

Edie laughed until she shook. "I was collapsing, playing out hideous scenarios in my mind. Tormenting myself with corrupted imagery."

"I know the exact feeling," Elliot said. "Shall we draw a line under all that?"

"Let's," Edie said.

"There's no way Fraz doesn't tell Molly our news later, by the way," Elliot said quietly. "In light of that, do you mind if I break it to my parents in the morning? We don't need to rush into doing any marrying. They have to see so much secondhand blather about me in the papers—I couldn't stand them hearing about this from some in-law of Fraser's and saying, *Elliot, what on earth?"*

"You could tell them we shagged on the swing and constructed the engagement as a cover?"

Elliot grinned. "It's an option . . ."

They tightened and relaxed their hold on each other; Edie laid her head on his chest. They spent a minute appreciating the moment they'd arrived at.

"We've come a long way since I was hired to write your life story, haven't we?" Edie said.

"Fair to say, you understood the assignment," Elliot said. "You haven't stopped writing it since."

"When I think about how many things needed to happen for us to end up here, it gives me vertigo," Edie said. "The chances we would ever even meet were so incredibly low."

"You don't believe in 'meant to be'?" Elliot said.

"I don't think we were meant to be," Edie said. "That suggests we could simply wait. I didn't wait for you, Elliot Owen. I was busy finding myself—at the same time, I found you. Then you chose me, and I chose you."

"A division of labor that's worked. We can bear that in mind for the future? We'll keep choosing each other. Maybe the trick is to spot if it's your turn."

"That must be what they mean in golden wedding anniversary write-ups when the couple say it's about 'give and take,'" Edie said.

"We're trying for golden?" Elliot said. "Ambitious."

"We are. I'm going to try. I think that *trying* is the lesson I've had to learn. I thought I feared failing, but actually I was used to that. I was scared of trying." She leaned up to kiss him, in a crowded room. "But not anymore."

Epilogue

One year later

"Will the microphone people ask me things, too?" Edie said, as the streets of Hell's Kitchen flashed past, through tinted windows.

"Yeah, but it won't be hardballs. *What do you think of the show?*, that sort of thing," Elliot said.

"I liked the script so much I made him do the sex scene?" Edie said.

"I mean, you can say that, but it has an instant headline quality, so on your head be it."

They grinned at each other.

Edie twisted her mother's rose-gold diamond engagement ring on her left hand. She hadn't known her dad had such an item until she broke her big news. There were cathartic tears after he fished it out of a Ziploc bag in a hiking sock. They agreed her mum would've been very pleased with Edie's choice of fiancé. "Not because of who he is," her father said, "but because of who he is."

(He also solicitously asked Meg if she minded Edie having the ring.

"I'm never getting shackled to anyone in this putrid system, let alone a member of the penis-having male oppressor class. I like Elliot, though; he's my friend. It's not his fault he is one of them."

"Perhaps keep Meg away from the speeches," her dad said.)

"If they ask if we've set a date, I say no?" Edie said.

"Yeah. I'm sure they'll turn up on the day anyway—we don't need to tip them off to go looking. They'd probably figure out we're doing it near home." Elliot shifted in his seat. "Ugh, I hate tuxedos. Do I look like I'm going to wheel you the dessert trolley?"

Edie laughed. "Yes, but I would definitely ask for your trifle."

"Maybe later," Elliot said. "You look utterly amazing."

"Thank you! I feel like a different person."

Edie had been seized upon by a bunch of practitioners of the glossy arts, who declared themselves a Glam Squad.

She'd been handed putty-colored corsetry, buttoned into a loaned dress that was as heavy as chain mail. Tufts of false eyelashes had been applied with tweezers; a camp man with a hypnotic wrist movement had dried her hair over a round brush.

"You don't look like a different person, just a very high-definition Edie. An F. Scott Fitzgerald party Edie. If I forget to say it later: I appreciate you being here so much."

"My pleasure," Edie said. "My pleasure, and my abject terror, as a red carpet first-timer."

"Hold on to me. You'll be fine."

Edie slid her hand into his. "This has never been proved untrue."

"Ready?" Elliot asked, as the car stopped and the clamor beyond was audible. So many people, so many cameras.

Edie looked at the throng, then looked back at him.

"Ready," she said.

Acknowledgments

First things first, thank you to my expert reader and friend Kay Miles and her affectionate exasperation with Edie's decision at the end of *Who's That Girl?* ("She could definitely ask Richard about remote working?!"). It prompted me to explain my character's thinking, which gradually made me realize I didn't just have an answer for Kay, I had a sequel. Cheers to you and your love of books, support for authors, and thoughtful analysis.

I owe thanks also to my agent, Doug Kean, my editor, Lynne Drew, and assistant editor, Olivia Robertshaw, who, when informed of my surprise novel pregnancy, scrubbed up and delivered it with completely unruffled confidence, good humor, and enthusiasm. (Is that an awful analogy? Look, the book part's over now, it doesn't count.) I'm so happy with some of my favorite characters getting a second life and the HarperCollins team has done them proud.

Much gratitude to my expert advisor in the field of advertising, Michael Gray-Buchanan, for his valuable insights. Any errors, bad taste, or irreverence toward Pepsi is strictly mine.

Thank you, Tara and Katie de Cozar, and Kristy Berry, my ever-reliable litmus test audience for first drafts and getting romance stories right in general. Apologies to Tara, given she always wants more filth, though. May your ice planet be always full of Barbarians.

Cheers to the prog wizard of Whitley Bay, Sid Smith, for the phrase "sonic truffle hunting."

And thank you to the people who read my books, who give me their time, who invest their feelings, who sometimes get in touch: it's the greatest privilege. This is, in part, a tribute to those who screamed "McFarlane, you sadist!" at the end of *Who's That Girl?* and told me how much they'd like more Edie and Elliot, which made me realize it wasn't only me who missed them.

Despite what my GCSE Humanities teacher said, I am listening.

ABOUT THE AUTHOR

Sunday Times bestselling author Mhairi McFarlane was born in Scotland, and her unnecessarily confusing name is pronounced Vah-Ree. After some efforts at journalism, she started writing fiction and her first book, *You Had Me at Hello,* was an instant success. She's now written ten novels, and she lives in Nottingham with a man and a cat.

READ MORE BY INTERNATIONAL BESTSELLER
MHAIRI McFARLANE

BETWEEN US

International bestseller Mhairi McFarlane delivers a witty, clever, emotional new novel about a woman whose life unravels spectacularly after her screenwriter boyfriend uses their relationship as inspiration for his new television show.

DON'T YOU FORGET ABOUT ME

A funny, romantic novel about a young woman who, after getting fired and dumped on the same night, takes the first job available without realizing the one that got away is her new boss—and he doesn't recognize her.

IF I NEVER MET YOU

A heartfelt romantic comedy about two colleagues who agree to a mutually beneficial fake relationship that gets a little too real...

JUST LAST NIGHT

In the aftermath of a tragedy, a woman uncovers juicy secrets about her lifelong friends and finds love in the last place she ever expected.

MAD ABOUT YOU

A sharp, emotional novel about a woman who calls off her engagement to "the perfect man" and moves in with a charming stranger who makes her question everything about her life, her past, and the secrets she's kept for far too long...